**This book is the second half of
"The Tirrell Gang".**

The Lykens Legacy

**Author:
Mildred E. Lykens**

The Lykens Legacy

Printed in the United States of America
by Lulu Publishing Company

Resources and acknowledgements:
Verbal and documented history from living relatives.
Verbal history from learned friends.
Shared research with Tina Tirrell
Edited by: Myrle Neville Olson
Palo Pinto County Texas Courthouse
Morehead, Kentucky. Newspaper
Mineral Wells, Texas. Index Newspaper
U.S. Dept of Census Records 1900, 1910, 1920, 1930
Terrell Society of North Carolina

Websites:
Mineral Wells, TX
Morehead, KY
Bisbee, AZ.
Wikipedia

ID # 4700804
ISBN # 9780615262116

Dedication:

I wish to dedicate this book to those that rode the trail, dug up the bones, and found the pieces of the puzzle with me.

Chapter 1...The Lykens Legacy.

The dusk of the rising sun gave little light as Hasten and Lillie made their escape. They had left Will lying in the bushes near the Brazos River, bleeding from a head wound he received from Lillie's cast iron skillet. They knew that he was alive when they left, much like her husband Samuel Briles back at the ranch, but also knew there was no guarantee that either one would survive.

Each of the men had tried to stop the couple from running away. Samuel blocked Lillie's path with his body and was run over by one of the wheels of her cargo-laden hack.

Will Hall was Hasten's brother-in-law and during their confrontation had tried to persuade Hasten into giving up five-year-old Edward, then sleeping under the wagon. Will had promised his sister Mary that he would bring the boy back to her.

They were unaware that young Edward had witnessed both confrontations; which left him puzzled as to why his father and Lillie would be doing these mean things to the people he loved. After the episode with Uncle Will, they had looked his way but he had feigned sleep and Hasten had gently pulled his sleeping pallet out from under the wagon and placed him back among the cargo where he had ridden during the run from the ranch.

Now, Hasten on his horse, a roan stallion named Rascal and Lillie driving her mule Maudie were on the run from those they left behind: *her* husband, *his* wife and the entire Tirrell family which included not only his parents, but two sisters and two brothers. And there was no cellar dugout, under the barn floor, waiting to hide them.

Out running posses had become common to Hasten, but that was when he had a place to run *to*.

For years Lillie had hidden him and his young Tirrell Gang out at her ranch until the posses gave up. This happened after each of their "camp outs" which were in actuality hold ups, carried out miles away from their homes.

It was spring of 1917 when Pa and Ma Tirrell had come with the best of intentions, to shield their grandsons from the constant fighting and bickering between their son Hasten, and his wife, Mary. The feuding couple was told that the boys would be returned only when they could 'stop their bickering', and provide the boys a stable home. The incident happened so fast that it left the young couple speechless until they were standing alone in their cabin, unsure of what had just happened.

The argument that then ensued between them had made it impossible to continue the marriage and left Hasten no alternative than to take the boys any way he could. He was able to grab Edward the next morning from his parent's front yard, and then trick Mary into thinking he would leave the boys with her and give her the divorce she wanted. But instead, he had taken Edward when she entered the home of her two brothers, Will and Arch Hall, to ask them, in private, if she and the boys could move "home".

This gave Hasten enough time to swing Edward up behind him on the saddle, and run to the one person he linked with safety, Lillie.

Leaving Edward with her, he went after two year old Alva, but Pa was waiting and ended the confrontation with the blast of his shotgun. When the barrel of Pa's shotgun rose to his level, pure instinct urged Hasten to jump behind the huge porch pillar that absorbed the brunt of the buckshot and spared his life. But the column wasn't wide enough to absorb all the blast and some of the pellets found their target.

5

Hasten got to the frightened roan and mounted on the run. He had no other choice but to leave and put as much distance as he could between himself and the second barrel load of buckshot. He swore he would never forgive his father, and the only regret was that of leaving Alva and the rest of his family behind.

When he found Lillie near the river she took one look at the bloody shirt and quickly retrieved her medical bag from the cargo. Absorbed in her chore she was unaware that Edward watched as she dug buckshot out of his father's back, neck and side by the light of the campfire.

Pain had made sleep impossible so it was still dark when Hasten urged Lillie to harness Maudie and follow him over ground that showed no previous traffic. The moonlight did little to help, but she relied on Maudie's eyesight to follow Rascal, just as Hasten trusted the roan. They rode in silence as night surrendered its darkness to the morning light.

Rascal had found an easier route on a wider path so Hasten reined him in and allowed Maudie to pass. Riding along side Lillie's wagon he spoke quietly in order to not wake the boy. "Lillie, we're gonna haffta change our names and make up a story that Edward will accept about what happened ta Mary and Alva. We can use his middle name 'Francis' and once in awhile 'Buster'. I called him that once and he seemed ta like it. I've been thinkin that it'll mainly be our last names they'll be lookin for, if they come lookin."

"Of course they will come looking," Lillie responded barely above a whisper, "Or send the law, or both. Mary will not take the loss of a son without a fight. I'm pretty sure that Will and Samuel will survive but we can't be positive." She paused for a moment before adding, "Would you object to my taking your last name?"

"No, it'd be best if we went as husband and wife, but I can't use Tirrell anymore. I think I'll use Ma's maiden name of Likens, only change the spelling. That oughta throw people off. An I'll go by 'Hacey' like Lewis calls me."

"Why don't you go by 'Acey'?" she asked.

"Hhmm, you know I like the sounds of that; Acey Lykens. Yes, that's what my name'll be. Are ya goin ta change yer first name?" he asked

"No. I think 'Lillie Lykens' has a nice ring to it." She smiled in the glow of the morning sun as its rays produced long narrow shadows of the sage and white oak that lined the small path Rascal had chosen.

In his desperation, Hasten's first thought was to head north, to Robber's Cave, but sad memories reminded him that those he had shared it with, years ago, were now dead. He had spent time in the hideout, near McAlester Oklahoma, with three older brothers while running from various posses beginning as far back as Morehead, Kentucky. Because of their escapades the boys had been chased across many county and state lines, in search of a place to settle down.

But as he rode he realized that Robber's Cave was no place for a woman and a child, recalling the incident that drove him and his brothers from the sanctuary.

A large outlaw, all full of himself, was itching to prove to others his handiness with the pistol he wore holstered and tied low on his hip. The boys had known that their age and experience was no match for the man and was given the opportunity to leave, with their egos in tact, by the outlaw's companion.

A crippled Indian had eased his way to their campfire and told them about a town that held 'healing waters'. He had overheard two of the boys speak of ailing parents while waiting for their older brothers return. The Indian's directions led the gang to Mineral Wells, Texas, where they were assured that the special water there could cure all forms of illness and disease. The boys had then sent for Ma and Pa and the siblings they had been forced to leave behind.

Hasten let Rascal set the pace as his mind retreated back and into a time some eight years ago when a "camp out" had gone wrong. Each year the boys had carried out a camp out which took them many miles from home and into unfamiliar areas. They would find an area and beat the sage and scrub oak, gathering cattle strayed from nearby ranches or cattle drives and had later given birth to young that were unbranded.

The boys pushed the herd to tanning houses where proprietors held fewer scruples and were usually located on the out skirts of large cattle towns. There they would sell the branded mothers and herd the unmarked calves back home to be divided between the two neighboring families.

It had been coming on dusk, near Stephenville, Texas, when the herd had been spotted. Without seeing the whole gang the rancher's men were unsure of how many they were chasing, but had come riding in hard, shooting from the saddle.

The young Tirrell Gang, consisting of six Tirrell and two Turner boys, were cornered, but the leader had split the gang and urged Hasten to take the younger boys and head up and over the steep rocky hill that blocked their fast get away. The three that held ground were twenty-two year old Grant, twenty

8

year old Charley and nineteen year old Jimmie. They were the eldest of the Tirrell boys and Hasten adored them.

Grant thought he might be able to bluff their way out of the situation with a forged bill of sale or perhaps elude the rancher with fewer of the gang to worry about. But mostly he wanted to insure the safety of the younger boys before the men closed in.

That was the night Hasten had found Lillie. She had hidden him and the younger boys in a fruit cellar dugout under her barn floor. She then doctored and nursed Jake Turner, after removing a bullet he had taken that night. The next morning Hasten found the older brothers. The rancher and his men had left their bodies hanging from a tree where they had split up.

After cutting his brothers down Hasten realized that he was now the eldest, at sixteen years old, and as leader of the gang he had immediately changed their camp outs from rustling to robbery. First because he did not want to cut down another brother, and second out of retaliation to the town closest to the hanging. He had left the bodies of his beloved brothers, as well as the injured Jake Turner, in Lillie's care as he led the rest of the boys, aged from fifteen to eleven, back into Stephenville the next day.

His plan of two simultaneous hold ups had gone off without a hitch, mostly due to the surprise the storeowners had of young boys brandishing pistols and demanding adults to comply to their wishes. At first it was thought to be a joke or a prank, but as the seriousness of the situation had flooded over the victims, the demands had been obeyed, sparing everyone bodily harm.

Chapter 2... Lillie Also Reminisces.

Married, and perhaps ten years his senior, Lillie first saw Hasten down the barrel of her rifle. But she soon felt a long forgotten stirring in her soul. Before the night had ended she knew that she would follow this young man and eventually somehow, someway share his life; all she had to do was wait.

The wait had been long. Years with her watching ever close, but still just an observer as he matured. She withheld her emotions as he met and married Mary, who bore him two sons. Each time when she thought she could take no more, she had summoned inner strength and held on, reminding herself that a life with Hasten was a destiny worth waiting for.

Now that time had come, and he was riding only a few yards ahead of her and the feeling of relief was like an engulfing soft warm feather mattress, with one of Mother's homemade quilts as a cover. Her highly strained but undying patience had finally been rewarded.

Her feelings were flooding through her now as she looked across the rump of her mule Maudie, to Hasten's long lean figure molded to his saddle and riding as if he were born to it. A checking glance over her shoulder told her that Edward was still sleeping safely on the pile of bedding between the boxes near the front of the wagon. She knew that what they were doing was breaking her best friend's heart, but to balance the friendship with Mary ...to her love of Hasten, the sleeping boy and the chance of having a family of her own ...held no equal in her mind or in her heart. The waiting had been too long to give up what she knew would bring her a life of satisfaction and fulfillment. Her desire for a family had ended when she found out that she would never have children of her own.

Her father Amos had been a drunkard and physically abusive to her, her brother Luke and mother Mae. Those beatings caused Luke to run away and later her mother's death.

Her father had run the night her mother died and as far as she knew, had never paid for the killing. She hadn't seen him or Luke since. As Lillie was left alone at the age of nine, the townspeople had decided she would be better off in an orphanage somewhere because the bank was foreclosing on the house and property for back taxes. She had quickly packed what she needed and had left Oklahoma Territory, and the fine citizens that would have put her away like a caged animal.

Lillie had helped support the family by taking in laundry before the death of her mother and carried that career with her into Texas. That business continued until after her first marriage, a few months past her thirteenth birthday, to a young man that showed his true colors on their wedding night. During their reception he had shared the jug that was passed around with long slurping gulps, then took her to his family ranch instead of the hotel they had planned.

When she refused his advances because there was just a blanket wall between them and the rest of his family, he beat her unconscious and forcibly claimed his husband rights.

Knowing what her mother had endured for years, and that it eventually caused her death, Lillie knew what she had to do. She left him the very next day under a pretense of work, and with the help of a young doctor friend she filed for divorce immediately.

Dr. Dan Bradley had been one of her customers when she decided to make Stephenville her new home. There she had set up a small business of taking in laundry when she was but ten years old. He had been kind to her from the day they met and had secretly hired the local schoolteacher to tutor the girl. He wanted to fill the gaps of her education and instill in her self-confidence, which would eventually give her a better life.

He found Lillie irresistible and wanted to ease the heavy load she took upon herself at such a young age. She took in laundry not only from the hotel and its residents, but some of the townspeople as well. He himself had hired her not only to add to her financial support, but also because of her superior work. He didn't expect to fall in love, but after years of friendship and taking her secretly under his wing, he realized he desperately wanted her to share his life.

After two bad experiences with men she thought she could trust, she refused marriage but instead begged his indulgence in allowing her to move into his home, with a room of her own, as his housekeeper and assistant around the hospital.

Much as a wild animal must learn to trust and come to a human, while the patience of the human is sometimes strained beyond endurance, it succeeded in establishing the complete and trusting bond that grew between them.

And so it was for years, with Doctor Dan's kind and gentle personality treating her with patient tolerance that she was able to accept his quiet yearnings and without hesitation one night she stepped into his waiting arms.

Under his guidance and support Lillie grew and matured into a proper genteel lady, learning not only etiquette to rival the higher elite, but also nursing skills of which students twice her age could not grasp. Her life with him became invaluable, not only as his hospital assistant, hostess to traveling colleagues, but a soul mate as well and she finally learned the true meaning of trust, contentment and love.

Life with Dr. Dan was the happiest Lillie had ever known. From fulfilling her mind's insatiable appetite, to accepting the warm embrace of his ever-open arms, there seemed to be no boundaries.

He was her mentor, her lover, and her friend, and on the fateful day that tragedy struck and snatched him away, she felt she could not cope without him. There were so many questions that would never be answered. *How could life be so cruel? How could she finally find someone to love, and who truly loved her, only to lose him when the horse carriage slipped off the road and into the swollen river? Why did that lady have to go into labor on that rainy winter night? Why didn't they wait until the rain eased up before starting home? Why did she fall asleep and not see what was happening? Could she have prevented the mishap? Why did the river pull her away to live but twist him in the blanket that became tangled in an uprooted tree to drown?*

Lillie shook her head to clear the painful thoughts and realized Hasten's voice had intruded in her reverie.

"What's wrong? Why are you crying?" came his voice again.

She didn't realize she had slipped so far into her memories that tears were streaming down her face. Quickly she grabbed her handkerchief from her apron pocket and wiped her eyes and cheeks. "Oh, silly me. I was just thinking how long I've waited for this moment. We are going to be happy Hasten... Acey. We *will* be a happy family."

He smiled and shook his head. *I wish I'd known her feelings years ago. It would have saved a lot of hardship and heartache for all of us. But she was married when I met her and I thought I had no chance. Women are a hard lot to figure out, and I have no hopes of doing so in the near future.*

Chapter 3... Samuel Briles

Jake Turner stood at the bedroom door as the doctor finished checking Samuel. "Is he going to be alright, Doc?

Dr. Corthell removed first his stethoscope and placed it in his leather bag, then his wire rimmed spectacles, as he pulled a handkerchief from his breast pocket to clean them. As he walked toward Jake shaking his head in concentration, "Well, it looks to me that he is pretty bunged up. He has at least two broken ribs and a broken collarbone on the left side. It's a miracle that the wheel missed his head or there would be no need for me to be here. I'm going to have to wrap those ribs up real tight and make a sling for the collarbone. He's going to be in need of looking after for a few weeks and I'm leaving a bottle of laudanum just to ease the pain. I couldn't hear any puncture to the lungs and we'll watch close for signs of internal bleeding, but his size and strength have kept it from being far worse. I think he'll be ok."

"I'll see if one of the Tirrell girls can come and help him until he can do for himself. Knowing Samuel, it won't be long." Jake added, "He's stubborn and will refuse help and try to do more than he should."

Doc shook his head again and chuckled, "Well, I remember quite clearly how stubborn his wife Lillie can be. Years ago she came to me when Samuel's mother Nancy was ailing. And I have to admit that she was right. You say that she ran off with the oldest Tirrell boy? What about his wife, Mary isn't it? You wouldn't want to fill me in on exactly what brought all this to pass, now would you?"

"Uh, I'm not sure," Jake lied. "All I know is that Hasten came to me and told me to come here and check on Samuel, so I know he didn't mean no harm to come to him. I'll have to check with Mary for her side of the story. If she feels it's anybody's business I guess she'll let me know and I can get back to you."

Nodding his head as he put the spectacles back on and the handkerchief away, doc added the rest of his supplies to his bag and snapped it shut. "Well, he doesn't need the bouncing that the buckboard would do to those broken bones so I will be back in the morning with the bandages. The laudanum will keep him sedated for the rest of the night."

"I'll stop by the Tirrell ranch tonight and see if Mr. Tirrell will allow Sarah to watch over him. If not one of us Turner boys will, but Sarah has a way with people that makes them feel that they are doing her a favor by waiting on them. You'll see one of us tomorrow when you come back," Jake assured him as they parted outside, with the doc climbing into his carriage and reining the horse back towards town.

Thoughts ran through Jake's mind as he mounted his horse and urged it towards the Tirrell ranch. *Yeah, there is a lot riding on what Mary will feel is anyone else's business. If she goes to the law we'll all be on the run or be in jail for a long time.*

The Tirrells, Turners, and Briles had made up the Tirrell Gang and had operated for many years. A lot depended on what Mary had to say and to whom. Who knows what a woman will do to get her child back, even though everyone knew that the couple had been fighting almost since their marriage. This last fight had caused Hasten to blurt out the outlaw activities that she had known nothing about. Her Godly nature could never allow forgiveness for his lies nor the lawlessness to continue and have her boys placed in harms way. She held everyone's future on the tip of her tongue.

Chapter 4... Will Hall

Will awakened with overwhelming pain, unsure of its source until he tried to move. Then it centered in his head and behind his eyes, a deep overall pain that seemed to grow with each heartbeat. Something was telling him that he had to move but the pain was in command and kept him prone. *Why all this pain? What happened? Where am I?* He lay still trying to give his brain time to remember. He knew he was cold and that he was laying face down on the ground. He opened the eye opposite the ground and saw nothing. He panicked and opened both, still nothing. He pushed his chest up with both arms, forcing his body to overcome the almost intolerable pain. He rose to all fours and could still see nothing. *Blind! I'm blind!,* raced through his thoughts *Why? What happened?* As he straightened further and sat back on his heels he was flooded with relief to see the reflection of stars twinkling on the lake's surface. He reached toward the pain and brought his right hand away wet and sticky. *Blood I reckon, but how? When? I can't remember what happened?*

He heard a soft whine to his right and turned his eyes to see a shadow of something close to his own size just a few feet away. He sat very still except for the slow movement of his hands searching for anything he could use as a weapon. *A rock or big stick would come in real handy right about now.* He found nothing and the shadow moved toward him. He knew he couldn't stand, let alone run, so he eased back further on his heels until he had to reach behind to stable himself from falling. That's when the shadow advanced until they were face to face. With one large swipe of her tongue the dog licked him across his nose.

Will almost fainted with relief. "Mollie, what are you doing here? Where's Lillie?" *Lillie... Hasten... Something about Hasten... Oh yes, I remember now. Hasten and Lillie kidnapped Edward and are running away. I was trying to stop them, trying to reason with Hasten to give me the boy to take back to Mary. Lillie must have hit me over the head with something very hard.*

Mollie gave him another lick. "What are you doing out here Mollie? I'll bet you've followed Lillie's scent and found me. You are a good girl for not leaving me and running off after them. Yes, you like your ears scratched don't you! Well, it's best I try to get up and head back to Mary. Oh, Mollie, I've really made a mess of things. I promised Mary that I would bring Edward back to her. She's never going to forgive me for failing her. Can you help me get up old girl? Yes, there, I can use you to steady me for a minute until I get solid footing." *I have a horse around here somewhere unless Hasten took it or it strayed away in the bushes.* As he gained his footing and straightened his aching body he saw the horse. Its reins had been secured to a large bush at the water's edge. He spoke aloud, "I thank you, Hasten. I know you did this. You're not a bad man. You've just taken the wrong path and are being lead away from God by the archangel right now. I pray that you will see the error of your ways and bring the boy back to his rightful mother." In the stillness of the night the two animals heard his voice just as the Heavenly Father received his prayer.

As he led the horse over to a large rock to mount, he saw Mollie put her nose down and without a backward look she was off. Will knew she was following Lillie's scent, but she was getting old and if they were too far ahead it would be days before she

18

would catch up to them. He knew too that he should follow her, but in the shape he was in, he would be useless if he managed to catch up. The lump on his head and the blood soaked shirt was proof of that. He would just have to go back to Mary empty handed and find another way to hunt them down.

Chapter 5... Mary

"Where is Will? Something terrible has happened, I just know it." Mary was wringing her hands as she paced back and forth in her brother's small living room. "Arch, what can we do? Where can he be?"

"Mary, relax," Arch answered, "Will will find them and bring little Edward home. We don't know where all he had to go to locate them. You're going to make yourself sick if you don't sit down and try to stay calm. At this point all we can do is wait."

"But what if something horrible has happened to Will? What if he is lying injured somewhere? He's not the best rider and he had no saddle. He could have been thrown from the horse or perhaps a limb from a tree..." She babbled out her worries, refusing to sit. "We don't know what Hasten is capable of, now that I've learned of his outlaw ways. I should go to the sheriff and tell him everything. Who would have known? Am I truly that naïve?" She asked aloud, not really expecting an answer.

Arch reached out and touched her shoulder as she passed by for the hundredth time, stopping her long enough for their eyes to meet and exchange the helplessness they both felt. "We don't know who knows about them and who doesn't, but as far as going to the law Mary, I would think heavy on that. The Tirrells can't all be involved. The girls and young Lewis, they are innocent for sure, and Mrs. Tirrell; she's too ill to be a part of it."

"Oh, I'm not so sure." Mary argued, "She has a sound mind, even with the disease eating at her face, she's certainly capable of knowing what her sons are up to, and perhaps even help them plan their lawless ways. The money from those holdups had to be accounted for and she's not stupid. From what Hasten told me all three families, the Tirrells, Turners and Briles were all partners, dividing what they took between them. Our Good Lord only knows how long they have been doing this."

"But still, Sis, those young ones. If you bring in the law you will be setting their fate to an orphanage somewhere, if they charge all the adults with the holdups the children will have no one to turn to. Perhaps if the law decided Sarah and Mattie were someway involved they would be put in reform schools, leaving just Lewis alone. What if the law decided that *you* were involved? They would ask you how you could be married to a man for over five years and not know that he was an outlaw. They could question you about the money and perhaps even Will and me? There is a lot to think about Mary, and you must take some time to see the law's side of it. If you were the Sheriff, what would you believe? Are you ready to face jail and lose the boys anyway? They would go to an orphanage if we were all taken away. You must think this through for the good of all, the guilty as well as the innocent. There are many lives to consider."

"Oh, Arch, I never thought about that. Of course the sheriff wouldn't believe that I didn't know about their holdups all these years. You're right. I can't go to the law, but I must find out what is going on right now. I want my babies back!" Mary wilted into the rocking chair and buried her face in her already wet kerchief.

Arch knelt down before her and putting a hand on her knee, he spoke reassuringly, "We'll get the boys back, Mary. Will is out there now and he will bring them back to you. Keep your faith strong and talk to the Lord. If Will isn't back when it's daylight enough to see, I'll go in search of him. We will get to

21

the bottom of this. If the boys are at the Tirrell ranch and the Tirrells won't give them up, *then* we will threaten to go to the law. That will give us some leverage to make them accept our terms.

Mary just nodded as she continued to weep.

Chapter 6... Arch goes for Alva.

Will staggered into the house and slumped into the old rocker. Through his pain he tried to explain what happened. "Hasten has not only taken Edward, but Lillie as well. I don't understand a bit of this. I should have kept an eye on her I reckon, cause she had to have been the one that knocked me out. I saw Edward, but I didn't see Alva, so it might be that Hasten didn't get him yet." He leaned forward with his head in his hands and his elbows on his knees. He couldn't look Mary in the eye. "I'll go see the Tirrells and see what has happened to Alva. He has to still be there. I know that Lillie went willingly because she had her hack loaded with her belongings. I don't understand all of this," he repeated," I truly don't." His voice trailed off as he leaned his head back and let his eyes close.

"No, I'm afraid you're in no condition to go anywhere big brother," Arch stated. "It's my turn to find out what's happening."

As Mary set to cleaning Will's wound, Arch set out for the Tirrell ranch. Heat of the morning sun caused the dew on the foliage to create wisps of fog. *Much like the fog we are all in these days, with all that's happened in such a short time*, Arch thought.

Mattie met him as she was returning to the house with her aprons full of eggs. Their greeting was reserved because even though she had known him for years, he was a quiet man and quite reserved by nature.

"Good morning, Miss Tirrell", he started.

"Good morning, Mr. Hall," she answered.

"Do you think I could speak to one of your parents?" he asked.

"I'll get Ma, or you can see Pa, he's milking down at the barn," said Mattie.

23

"Uh, well, uh thank you, but I'd prefer to see your mother, that is, uh, if she's willing to speak to me," he stammered. He did not want to face the hard man he had heard so much about.

As he dismounted and tied the reins to the post at the gate, he turned and came face to face with Ma. "Hello, Mrs. Tirrell. How are you today?" he asked as he quickly removed his hat.

"I'm sure you are not here seeking the condition of my health, Mr. Hall. What can I do for you?" she spoke curtly.

Arch turned his hat clockwise by its brim as he answered. "I'm not here to cause any trouble. I just want to know if you know the where abouts of Alva? Will caught up with Hasten last night but before he could talk any sense into him someone hit him over the head and knocked him unconscious."

Ma eluded his question with a question of her own, "Where did he find them?"

Trying desperately to stay on her good side, he stated, "Down by the river where they used to go on picnics, Will saw Edward but not Alva and he thought that perhaps Hasten had not come after Alva yet and we wanted to warn you."

"Well, your warning came too late, Mr. Hall," a voice boomed from behind him. The force of it made Arch visibly jump and cringe inside.

"Oh, Mr. Tirrell. I uh, didn't hear you coming. I'm glad you're here though, so we can all talk." Arch shifted his weight from one foot to another as he turned so he could face all of them. He continued, "So Hasten got both boys then?"

"Jake Turner came by and told us that Lillie left Samuel and when he tried to stop her she ran over him with her wagon," offered Lewis. He was standing in front of Mattie who had continued up the porch steps to the doorway.

"Hush your mouth, Lewis!" Pa growled. "Get back in the house and leave the adults to talk. Mattie, see to it!"

"Who's here?" asked Sarah as she came to the door with Alva in her arms.

"Get back in the house, all of you. Mr. Hall here is about to leave." Pa growled, as his cold hard eyes met Arch's questioning ones.

Seeing Alva, Arch became bolder, "You must know that Mary is distraught with grief over this whole mess. She has every right to have her son with her. She is the boy's mother for crying out loud. What is wrong with you people?"

"What the hell do you mean by *you people*?" bellowed Pa. "You get your scrawny ass out of here and don't come back. Alva is staying *here* where he will have a decent home."

Arch was scared but he stood his ground. "You have no legal right to the boy. He belongs with his mother and rightfully so. We will go to the law about everything Hasten told Mary if you do not turn him over to me right now." He watched to see if his bluff would work and saw a glimmer of fear strike their faces as he looked from one to another. This gave him courage to press harder. "Is that what you want for the boy? Who among you will be around to take care of him when you are all in jail? You women folk are just as guilty and the law will not go lightly on those who profited by your lawlessness."

"Pa, he may have a point there," came a voice behind Arch once again. This time it was Sam.

Arch was quivering inside but put up a heroic effort to remain calm as he scolded himself, *That's twice they could have had the drop on you. You didn't learn from Will's mistake of not paying close attention to your surroundings.*

Ma spoke then. "Mr. Hall, I don't believe you would call the law, but I think we should all be a little more understanding of each other's feelings. I agree with you that the boy should be with his mother..."

"NO by God," interrupted Pa.

"Hear me out, Francis! The boy belongs with his mother." Then turning a questioning eye toward Arch, she continued, "But perhaps Mary would agree to let us see Alva once in awhile, for short visits?"

Seeing an opening, Arch made his move. "Of course she would allow visits. After all you are his family too and he loves you very much. She would like to keep her connection with the family too, if you would allow it. The argument with Hasten does not have to alter the relationship between the two families." He knew he was stretching the truth a bit, but he knew that Mary really did care about the Tirrell children.

"I don't like being blackmailed boy! And if it were up to me I'd see this thing through, but if Martha has her mind set, and I see that she has, I will not fight you. Mattie, bring the boy here, Sarah, you go get his belongings," ordered Pa.

"Mr. Hall, I would appreciate your letting Mary know that we hold no hard feelings against her and we would surely consider it an honor if she would see her way clear to letting us see the boy now and again." Ma declared.

Almost beside himself for his good fortune, Arch held his ground and nodded to each of them, not trusting his voice because of the lump in his throat. *I can't let them see a weakness now, not now!* Arch thought as he waited with a slightly stiffer back and planted feet.

26

"Would you prefer I take him by wagon to Mary, beings you'll have quite a load there?" asked Sarah as she came through the door with Alva's clothes tied in an old flour sack.

"No, that will be quite alright. I can handle everything by tying the bag to my belt and having Alva sit here in front of me on it. We'll do just fine, thank you," Arch bluffed again. He had no idea how he would be able to manage everything with his lack of experience in riding. All he knew was he had to get Alva out of there before they changed their minds. "Yes, We'll do just fine. Just let me mount up and you can hand me the sack and then Alva."

He was finally able to breathe easy after he had everything under control and was headed home.

Upon arriving there, Arch relayed the events to Will and Mary. Will was particularly pleased that Arch had been so clever to have tricked the Tirrells into turning over Alva. He smiled up at him while still holding the compress Mary had made for the bump on his head.

"I'd give you a pat on the back little brother, but I don't rightly know if I want to face another wave of pain from this old noggin of mine," Will praised him.

Mary just kept holding Alva tight against her. And as she rocked she repeated over and over, "Thank you, Lord. Thank you Arch. Thank you Heavenly Father," as the tears of gratitude flowed.

For the next few weeks, not a day went by that one of Mary's brothers didn't find her crying. Not the gut wrenching wails that had escaped her that fateful night, but the silent tears of a woman that had given up all hope of seeing her first born again.

The two brothers quietly took over the care of Alva, while she went about her everyday chores or sat

27

quietly in the rocker in front of the fireplace. She never looked up nor spoke unless pressed for an answer to a question. The boys felt helpless as they witnessed their beloved sister withdraw deeper and deeper inside herself.

Will gave Mary her space and time to grieve, but when he felt the time had long since past he went to her. "Dear sister, you have to snap out of this and move on. You have to pull yourself together, if not for yourself, then for Alva. He doesn't understand what has happened, only that you are not the mother he used to have. Children live by what they experience and see and by repetition of these things. He is only seeing sadness and mourning. He doesn't deserve this kind of life. You must understand that you are not the only one hurting here. Don't you know that Arch and I are hurting too? We love Edward very much too, and Alva doesn't even know why his world has changed. It's time you took control of your life and move forward, no matter how bad your hurt is, Alva deserves a mother."

Mary looked up into Will's eyes. She saw the love and hurt that he now expressed. "I'm sorry, Will. I guess I've been wallowing in my own hurt so much that I didn't think of anyone else. Of course, you're right. You boys have taken on quite a load haven't you? And Alva *does* need a mother. I'll try very hard to not let Hasten ruin anymore lives than he has already," she proclaimed.

So she slowly began to look forward instead of dwelling in the past, and while shopping in Mineral Wells one day she stopped by a lawyer's office and asked for help in procuring a divorce from Hasten.

The lawyer advised her, "Since your husband is not present, you will have to place an advertisement in the newspaper for a few weeks stating your intention." He continued, "if he doesn't show up to contest it, you can then file, but it will have to be done at the county seat." She immediately went to the Mineral Wells Index and placed the required ad.

In September of 1918, and in the same week that "Acey" was inducted into the army, miles to the north, Mary had Will take her to the courthouse in Palo Pinto, a few miles west of Mineral Wells, where she filed for and received her divorce.

Holding no grudges against the Tirrell children and realizing young Alva's need for companionship with children his age, Mary kept Arch's word and allowed the visits to the Tirrell family so he could play with Sarah's children.

Chapter 7... On the Run.

The new Lykens family headed in a north east direction and skirted the small towns where they may attract the attention of a bored lawman itching to put his hands on a "wanted" couple, if indeed Sam or Will had succumbed to their wounds.   Camping at the edge of larger towns made it easier to merge with the residents and not be as conspicuous. In this way they traveled, crossing the Red River into the ten-year-old state of Oklahoma.

Their northward trek criss-crossed trails that each had used years earlier, and under similar circumstances. They had both been on the run from the law in their separate lives, now they ran together.

Lillie was beside herself. Her dreams of being with Hasten were at hand as she had always hoped. She had her very own family now and they needed her. There was a need in her so deep that she did not know the extent of it, nor to what length she would go, in order to keep it. Her mind followed each link in her chain of thoughts, which occupied her mind as the miles rolled by under the wagon wheels. *I guess that situation has played out now and I know what I'm capable of doing to keep them. It's been a long time coming and I won't give them up! I just wish we could have gotten Alva, he would never even remember having another mother. Edward does and he will be asking questions. Hasten is...ACEY is right. We will have to come up with a believable story that he will accept.*

Acey's thoughts were running the same gauntlet. *What am I going to tell Edward about where Mary and Alva are?   Lillie was stern when she said that he would be terribly confused if we forced him to call her mother because he knew she wasn't and in order to make it easier on him, he could call her what he has always called her... Lillie. We will just have to find another way to justify his loss.*

The warmth of the sunrise was releasing wisps of light fog from the tall grasses that surrounded the campsite when they heard something approaching.

Facing the sound Hasten reached for his .22 and brought the rifle to his shoulder. Lillie realized too late that her pistol was under the seat of the hack. Edward sat tense but quiet, sensing the seriousness of the situation. The noise became louder until it was unmistakably that of an animal. Old memories flooded back to Lillie when coyotes had approached her camp because of the cooking odors. She had promised herself that never again would she let herself be that vulnerable. Now she had endangered not only herself, but Acey and little Edward too. Just as Acey wedged the rifle against his shoulder, a hound's head broke through the tall grass. It took a few seconds for everyone to grasp the situation and realize that this was Mollie! With one swipe she covered Edward's face with her tongue, causing him to fall over backwards, laughing.

"My gracious where did you come from girl?" Lillie shrieked as she jumped to her feet and greeted her beloved and very tired hound. "Look at your paws, they are worn to bleeding. And you're nothing but skin and bone. Come here girl and let me hug your neck. Oh. Acey, look at her. She has followed us all this way and for all these past weeks. Now I wonder where Josey is!"

"And there could be someone followin *her* as far as we know," he warned. She fell silent again and tried to quiet the boy as he wrestled with the hound. "Shhh, Edward. Let's be still for a minute," she whispered. "Someone might be out there and we need to hear them."

31

Edward obeyed and fell silent as the dog continued to stand over him and lavish his face with one lick after the other.

As the minutes passed and no one appeared, Acey decided to break camp and move on, just to be certain that the dog was not being used to track them.

A day or two passed before nerves were back to normal and they resumed their northerly trek.

One night Acey came to Lillie acting as if he wanted to say something but wouldn't. She waited but finally grew impatient and asked, "Is there something you need to get off your chest, Acey?"

Startled at her observance he admitted, "Yes, I got a favor ta ask ya." She nodded and waited. He finally got his courage up and asked, "Could ya teach me ta talk better? Mary said I talked like an uneducated baffoon and I don't want Edward followin in my footsteps. At times I've heard ya speak like the teachers I had when I was able to go to school or what Sarah taught me afterwards and I'd like ta be able ta do that. I wanna get a decent job somewheres and if'n I haffta deal with people I want ta sound educated."

Lillie smiled and replied, "I grew up speaking poorly too and was educated by a teacher and friend in a boarding house down where we met in Stephenville. I was told that I became 'quite refined' and I felt very good about my self, but I've let some of that slip away over the years, so I understand your desire to want to better yourself. I'm proud of you for that and that you came to me for my help. We will start by my correcting your speech as you speak and help you to understand what you find difficult. English is not as hard as one might think, and the proper use

32

of it can make or break a person in the eyes of others."

He smiled, "I knew I could count on ya, Lillie. When da we start?"

"By saying 'to' instead of 'ta', and "you" instead of "ya" as you did just now. It takes a little effort but with repetition you will learn it quickly," she promised.

"Well, I been thinkin that it was way too hard fer me ta start at my age." He stated.

"Think..*ing*, with an i-n-g sound. You have many words that you mispronounce. Let's start with three. Words ending in ing, 'you' and 'to'. We'll work on those to start with and others as I hear them. This way I can review and correct myself as well and we'll both be speaking better." She answered.

Meals were out of the back of the light hack from supplies either bought in towns, traded for work at farms along the way or shot by Acey. Many a night found a jack rabbit stew over the campfire, along with Lillie's homemade biscuits. Although hunger was a constant threat, Lillie would not let more than a day go by that Edward did not get milk, and Acey a lesson in English. She found him a fast learner and realized that it wasn't long before he was correcting her at times. When this happened she would pretend her hand to be a pistol, point it at him and make a "click, click" sound with her tongue. At those times he knew he had scored a point with her.

When they were near broke, she and Acey devised a plan. After Edward fell asleep, Acey and Lillie left him in Mollie's care and would enter a town after dark, she dressed in her finest. Men seated alone would be singled out, at the nicer eating establishments. She would enter and sit alone, attracting the attention of one of these men, discretely flirting with him. When it was time for her to pay her ticket, she would act horrified and embarrassed that she was unable to find her coin purse. "Oh, I'm so embarrassed. I know I put it in my purse....unless I left it on my bureau at the hotel. Would it be possible for me to go and fetch the money and bring it back?" she would ask the owner. The chosen gentleman would come to her rescue by stating that he would pay the ladies ticket. At which time Lillie would exclaim, "Oh..but..I really couldn't... allow a total stranger...."

To which he would offer, "It's nothing. I insist!" Lillie would then suggest, "Please, if you would be so kind as to escort me back to the hotel, I can retrieve my money and repay your kindness."

By this time his thoughts conjured up a more rewarding payment and he would pay for both their meals and escort her toward the hotel. As they crossed a designated alley Lillie would pull him into it, nudging his ribs with her .38 special.

Acey would stand in the shadows to prevent a physical confrontation as she took his wallet and asked him to turn around. She would then strike him soundly over the head with the butt of her pistol. Upon awakening, if any of the men overcame their embarrassment for their stupidity, and reported the incident, she seemed to have disappeared.

"Lillie, where's my momma?" asked Edward for the umpteenth time.

Lillie had always put him off with questions to distract him such as, "Did you see that pretty bluebird, Edward? Its been flying ahead of us all day. Do you think it's showing us the way?" Or, "Look, Edward, look at the beautiful sunset. God made that just for you to enjoy as we have our last bit of supper." These usually did the trick but eventually he would get back

34

to the subject and she knew it was time to tell him something. After consulting with Acey, it was decided that the time had come to answer his concerns.

Acey waited until almost bedtime, "Edward, you are a big boy and I think you are grown up enough to know that your mother and brother got very sick and have both gone up to heaven to be with Jesus."

The five-year-old had witnessed death in farm animals and realized that once gone, always gone. He began to cry and Lillie took him in her arms and held his shaking body until he cried himself to sleep. She crooned to him as her tears silently dropped on the boy's nightshirt.

Each day found them further north. When the span of time and miles brought confidence that they were finally safe, they chose a spot to settle.

His first employment was working on a farm much like the one he remembered back in Kentucky, where he was born. His Grandpa Charles P. Tirrell, had been a prominent man, working his way up the ladder from Jailer, to Deputy Sheriff, to Sheriff, then to Rowan County Clerk before his death a couple of years earlier. The familiarity of ranching gave Acey comfort in tending stock each day and mending fences when and where needed.

He was working there on September 12, 1918, when he received his induction notice to the U.S. Army. What a shock this was. The fear of being caught ran through his soul as he filled out government papers and signed documents proclaiming to be Acey Lykens. This was something that neither Acey nor Lillie had even considered. Yet here he was, dressed in a uniform the U.S. Army had issued, standing on the train depot platform of Antlers,

Oklahoma, beside a train that would take him away from the two people that needed him most.

"Oh, Acey, we are going to miss you so much. We just became a family and now this. Life is so cruel sometimes," wept Lillie.

Hasten tipped her chin until their eyes met. "In the words of a fair maiden, "Tomorrow is tomorrow, not to be worried about today."

She dropped her head knowing that he only echoed the saying that she had used many times in her lifetime. She was uncertain when or how many times he had heard her use those words. They somehow didn't bring the comfort that they usually did.

Seeing that Lillie was upset, Edward began to sidle up to her and take a handful of her dress. He was almost seven and thought, *Dad is very handsome in his new clothes, but if it makes Lillie cry, then something must be wrong.* The train blew its whistle, which vibrated clear through his body. Scared almost to tears, he stepped closer to Lillie, but he felt excited too. *I wish I was taking a ride on that big black train that makes all that nasty smoke.* He watched closely as Lillie and his father embraced, then Acey picked him up and hugged him harder than he ever had before. *Dad almost squeezed all my breath away! Wow, this must really be important. I hope he don't get mad if I cry.*

Acey's military career was short because soon after he began to fulfill his duties, a military doctor diagnosed him with the early stages of Rheumatoid Arthritis, and signed discharge papers.

With no time frame in a child's head, Edward felt that his father had just left on one train and returned on the next, leaving little time to experience missing his father, as it is with most children, he accepted the event with only the few short anxieties.

The medical examination Acey had undergone found some concerns and regarded him as "unqualified to serve". That was all he would tell Lillie, and she was too happy having him back to question.

Upon his return, he feared the government might somehow connect him to his past and he decided it was time to move on. The family packed up and moved further north, near McAlester, Oklahoma, where he took a job in a remote logging camp.

Lillie took on the single men's laundry, while he put in his day on one end of a two man cross cut saw. It was hard and dangerous work and the first few days he was in agony with his hands and back. But he ignored the pain when he could and soaked his body in hot bath water when he couldn't. As the days melted into weeks he added strong muscle to his lean frame and aching bones.

The heat of the long summer found them picnicking down by a wide creek, near the log camp. The smell of fir, pine and juniper merged to secrete a clean and luscious fragrance to Lillie, loving the trees as she did. She sat crossed-legged most of the time, but today she chose to lean against the embankment and watch the "men" in her life paddle around in the camp's small rowboat.

Edward's stature was frail and slim, and his lack of confidence worried Acey. Perhaps that is why, as they reached the middle of the creek, Acey picked him up and, to Lillie's horror, threw the boy overboard.

Edward fought his way to the surface to find his father rowing away from him!

"Swim or drown, Son. It's up to you," challenged Acey.

Lillie leapt to her feet and ran into the water's edge. "What are you doing? For God's sake, Acey, you can't leave the boy. He'll drown!" she screamed.

"Don't you dare go after him, Lillie. He has to learn to swim sometime, and it might as well be now," Acey yelled back.

Edward fought the water, kicking and clawing at the surface, searching for something to grasp to save himself. He fought his way, inch by inch, coughing out the water that entered his mouth with every breath. He was afraid to cry out for fear of gulping in more. He could see through the water running over his face, each time he fought his way back to the surface, that his father was getting farther and farther away, and Lillie was wading out to him, cussing Acey up one side and down the other. Edward knew that she couldn't swim and feared deep water. Panic drove him to fight harder. *I have to get to her.*

Lillie waded out up to her chest. As she reached toward Edward she felt her footing begin to slip. *Oh, God help me, don't let me drown too! I've got to reach him. He's counting on me.*

Why did dad do this? Is he trying to kill me? What did I do wrong? I try to be good, but it's hard sometimes. Doesn't he love me anymore? He continued to kick and claw at the water, with each inch bringing him closer to Lillie. His human instinct for self-preservation took control.

He was near exhaustion when he felt her hand grab his wrist and pull him into her arms. He clung to her then, never wanting to let go, as she turned and made her way back to the bank.

'You are a sorry son-of-a-bitch!" she yelled at Acey.

He just laughed and said, "Let him grow up, Lillie. Don't you realize that he now knows how to swim in case one of us are not around to pull him out?"

Realizing later that he *had* learned to swim, sort of, Edward forgave his father, but later he sometimes wondered, if only to himself, if that had been his father's true intention.

Lillie washed clothes down by the mess hall of the logging camp. There was more room for the wash tubs and the camp cook was there for an extra hand.

Having no playmates except for Mollie. Edward helped at times, but would quickly become bored and would explore the woods around the area, knowing that he could rely on Mollie's nose to get them back home if they got lost. Sometimes he would just lay in a clearing with Mollie by his side and watch the clouds float by. And other times he wondered about his mother and Alva, but knowing they were up in those clouds with Jesus, helped ease the loneliness.

One day he came home a little after his parents and peeked through a crack in their bedroom door as they dumped the contents of one of their traveling satchels on their bed. It was a pile of money. He thought nothing of it, for as far back as he could remember they always had money, so he turned and walked away.

Early one morning, as he was sitting on the porch of their cabin, one of the logging crew drew his buckboard to a stop in front of him. "Hey, young feller, I'm headin inta town and wondered if thar might be anythang thet yer family needs that I can brang back. I gots my list here and I'd be right happy ta bring ya whatever ya might have a hankerin fer. Wanta go fetch yer Ma?"

"Lillie's not here. She's doing laundry at the main house down below," answered Edward.

"Well, kin ya thank of anythin y'all might need? We don't get ta town often an I wouldn't want ta disappoint no body," the driver added.

"I sure would like to have some candy," stated Edward.

"Any special kind?" The driver asked

With a shake of Edward's head the driver nodded, "Wall, candy it be then. I'll put er on the list an brang it by onest I get back." He licked the end of his pencil and scrawled on his note then replaced it in the bib pocket of his overalls, picked up the reins and turned the two-horse team toward town.

After dinner that night the man came to the cabin and gave the candy and the bill to Acey. Acey paid and thanked the man, but when he was sure the man was gone he called Edward to him.

"Why did you tell the man that we needed candy?" he demanded.

"The man said if I wanted something I should tell him, and I wanted candy." Edward answered.

"We cannot afford candy and you have to be taught that you cannot go around ordering things that I have to pay for. Go get the strap." Acey demanded.

"Acey, No. The boy didn't know any better," defended Lillie.

Acey shook his head, "Lillie you stay out of this. The boy has to learn the value of money."

"He's learned his lesson, let it go at that," she pleaded.

"I said the boy has to learn. Edward, get the strap!" He raised his voice as he got to his feet, pointing in the direction of his razor strap hanging on a nail near the back door.

Edward took his licking with cold indignation and gritted his teeth in defiance. He knew he would get even for this undeserved spanking.

His chance came the very next day when he was again left alone at the cabin. Retrieving the satchel from the closet, he dumped its contents in the middle of the bare wooden living room floor. *If I can't spend any of this here money, then they can't either* was his only thought as he struck a wooden match to flame, slid it under the pile of money, then sat back and watched it burn.

Only Acey and Lillie knew how much money was in that pile, and the spanking he got the night before came no where near the spanking he got *that* night. But he held on through the pain by knowing that he had gotten even; *If I can't use any of that money for what I want, then they aren't going to spend it for what they want!*

Chapter 8...The Tirrells.

"I'll not hear his name mentioned in this house ever again!" burst from Pa as he overheard the girls wondering about Hasten's where-abouts. Both girls jumped and Sarah almost dropped the plate that she was drying. "I forbid all of you to bring up his name, now and forever."

Ma came to see what the ruckus was all about and hearing his last statement she straightened to her full four foot eleven inches. "You listen to me, Francis Oliver, I WILL speak his name and that of the baby if I've a mind to. He is my son, a part of me that has been ripped from my soul and I pray each night that I will see them again before I die."

Pa's eyes dropped for a second and then stubborn pride took control and he countered, "Well, maybe you want to see him again, but I sure as hell don't. He is a disgrace to this family with his running away with that... that *woman*."

She took a step closer and looked up into his face. "Well, *that woman* took care of our three boys when they needed burial tending and did a fine job of it, according to your own words. She has a loving heart and I'm glad she is with him to take care of our first born grandson. Don't badmouth her, she's done right by this family for years, hidin' them out and tending their wounds. No Frances, you leave Lillie out of it."

Ma had never stood up to him as she was right now and it brought a hush over the household. Sam, now eighteen, came to stand close in case a hand was raised against her. The girls stood frozen in shock as they secretly admired her strength. Lewis was the youngest, now ten and he too knew his father's wrath.

Pa's chin came up slightly and he clenched his fists. *What in tarnation set the woman off like that? Right in front of the youngun's and all.* "I'll honor your motherhood, but you and you alone can mention his name in this house. I'll not tolerate anyone else!" As he looked around at his wide-eyed offspring he demanded, "YOU HEAR ME? NO ONE else will speak his name." With that he stomped out the back door, almost tripping over Hasten's hound, Duke. "Get the hell out of the way you mangy mutt. Worthless as your owner, you are!" he yelled as he went down the steps two at a time and headed for the grove of trees, behind the barn, where everyone knew he would open a jug and sit for hours.

"Ma, it's time we tried to find Hasten and Edward. I talked to the sheriff and he said there was nothing he could do, because Edward is his son and he has a right to him, but if I wanted to find him I could possibly hire a private detective. Since I've been working at Ulrich's Mercantile, I have saved most of what I've earned. I will pay for the man myself if it will mean finding Hasten and getting him to come back and make up with Pa. Everyone knows that Pa is just being stubborn, and that he wants Hasten back too," offered Mattie.

"Maybe we can all chip in and help pay," came from Sam. "We all miss him and Edward." His eyes swept from the floor up to Ma's. "And Lillie too, Ma. She was always there for us boys, and we couldn't have pulled off a camp out without her. Since I started at the cedar camp cutting posts with Pa, I've saved some."

"What about Mary?" asked Mattie, "Maybe she and her brothers would like to pitch in too. I know she's having a real hard time coping with the loss of Edward and she mopes around all the time. Never a smile on her lips since that day. She hardly speaks to anyone anymore, let alone us Tirrells. She allows Alva to visit and play with Betty, Fannie and Oliver, but I see her in town once in awhile and she keeps her head down and speaks to no one. I think she blames us for the whole thing."

Ma's head shot up. "Well, if that little gal hadn't enjoyed her hen peckin Hasey all the time, your Pa and I wouldn't have had to go and take those boys. It was for their own good. We tried to make them stop that infernal bickerin and fightin in front of the young'uns."

Glancing toward the door, and in a hushed voice, Sarah interrupted, "It's no use hashing all this over again. It's been too long without a word, nor has anyone seen hide nor hair of them anywhere. We need professional help, and I'm going to town tomorrow to find someone."

The name on the door was "George Eckstein, P.I.," in gold scroll lettering. *Very impressive* Sarah thought. *I hope the man is capable of living up to the handiwork of his name.*

He stood, straightening to his full five foot six inch frame and was buttoning his coat as she entered the small office. "Mrs. Fulfer, I presume?" he asked, and with a slight bow from the waist he added, "George Eckstein at your service." His arm swung down and across to point to a high back leather chair in front of his large mahogany desk.

Sarah always held her judgment of people but the thought did cross her mind that this man was pretty impressed with himself, and now she would have to listen to his questions and answers to decide if she had chosen the right man for the job.

44

She was not expecting to have to answer so many questions, such as why were the husband and wife of the runaways not there, sending the sister instead? Had the runaways absconded with any money or goods from their spouses? Were there any legal charges against the two? After what seemed like hours of story telling and skipping around the truth here and there, Sarah admitted that the woman had only taken her own possessions, and other than the child, her brother had only had time to take very little clothing. The detective scratched his short beard in thought. Then using his thumb and forefinger of his right hand to seperate and smooth his full mustache, he asked, "You say they stole nothing but the boy? And your brother is the boy's father?"

"Yes, that's true, but he left behind another son and his wife, who had to move in with her brothers in order to survive. Well, uh, she could have lived on the ranch, in the house she had shared with my brother, but uh, she chose to accept her brothers offer to live with them." She felt embarrassed by her stammering explanations and started to rise.

Motioning her back in her seat Mr. Eckstein questioned, "Well, is finding your brother and nephew the main objective? I won't be a part of stealing the boy to bring him back to his mother because that would be kidnapping on my part and in my kind of business I cannot afford to break the law. And speaking of affording, do you understand that I charge a fee whether I find the man or not?

At the sight of Sarah's eyebrow suddenly arching, he quickly added, "For traveling expenses and that sort of thing." You'll find that my prices are reasonable, even less that some, but you know the old saying, "You get what you pay for."

Sarah scooted to the edge of the chair and said, "I'll pay you $50.00 now, and $50.00 IF you find him. No more, no less. You see we have to pay the grocer, the feed and grain, the doctor bills, and *that sort of thing*," mocking his previous statement. Then added, "That is what we can afford and that is all we are going to pay."

Seeing his fee about to take wing, he hurriedly agreed that the financial arrangement was adequate, and that he would be by the house the next day for any photographs. When Sarah mentioned that there was a very good likeness of Hasten, but it was a large oval portrait that her mother would not part with, he told her not to worry that he would have a camera to take a photo of the painting and use that.

He then stated, "I will need a photo of each of the runaways if you have one. If not, a detailed description of not only their physical make up, such as their height, weight, coloring, scars, tattoos, as well as their mannerisms, likes and dislikes. Do they have any weaknesses, such as drinking, gambling, fancy clothes, that sort of ... such things as that."

Sarah agreed and paid him the first $50.00. After collecting the receipt she stood, and with a nod to each other she left his office with a feeling that Mr. George Eckstein might not be as competent as she would have liked.

Chapter 9...Another Move.

Realizing the money Edward had burned had to be replaced, Hasten and Lillie knew what had to be done. After his payday at the mill and her collecting from her laundry clients, they decided to move on.

They again chose north, and traveled up to Oklahoma City where they knew the population was greater, making it easier to replace the lost money. As the days passed into weeks Lillie had used the same techniques as before. After making sure she had hooked her mark in a plush restaurant, she would feign leaving her money in her hotel room. The plan was a good one and had served them well. So far to their knowledge none of these men had ever contacted the law.

As their funds became substantial they decided to make one more score and move on.

The men Lillie chose were always smaller than herself, with an apparent meek and mild appearance. She believed they were more apt to be flattered by her attention and less likely to fight if it came down to it. This night was no different, and she set her soft blue eyes on a man that appeared to be well mannered and elegantly groomed.

Everything went as planned until she pulled the man into the alley. As soon as he felt the gun in his ribs he side stepped and grabbed for it. His hand encircled her wrist and he twisted. Lillie cried out in pain as he wrenched the gun from her grasp. He swung her around and slammed her back against the side of the building.

"Think I was born yesterday, little lady?" he sputtered between clenched teeth. "I'm not the fool you take me for!" Still holding her left wrist he jerked her toward him, twisting her arm down and behind her back and pulling her body up against his. "*You* are the one who will lose this time. I'm going to get my money's worth out of you before I take you to the sheriff."

"Sorry to disappoint you, fella," came an icy voice from the shadows behind him.

The man kept his grip as he spun around to encounter a large fist that gave a smashing blow across his left cheek.

With the gun still in the man's left hand, Lillie reached with her right and grabbed it. Realizing his plight, he swung her around between himself and his attacker, using her as a shield. She came to a sudden stop with her back against his chest as the second blow swished past her right ear and landed solid against the man's nose. He was going down, still clinging to Lillie, with blood gushing from the broken nose and split cheek. She smelled the blood and felt the warmth of it on her shoulder. As he dragged her down with him the odor released an old memory which came flooding across her mind. It was that of removing a bullet from a young outlaw years ago.

She felt arms around her, stopping her descent, which would have landed her on top of the now prone man. His grip finally released as he lost consciousness.

Acey pulled her to him. "You all right, Lillie?" He whispered in panic.

"Yes I think so. Get his wallet and let's get out of here." Her voice barely audible, and rubbing the wrist he had twisted, she inched over to the edge of the building and checked, "Hurry, we haven't got much time before he wakes up. I think this one *will* go to the sheriff."

Acey's eyes were more accustomed to the dark being's he'd been waiting there for the past hour, so he searched the man's pockets and found a thick heavy wallet, some important looking documents and a ivory handled .38 pistol.

Gathering everything he shoved the papers into his tucked in shirt, the pistol in one pocket and wallet in another. Then taking Lillie's arm they strolled out of the shadows as if nothing had happened and made their way along the board sidewalk that led them out of town and back to their campsite.

Chapter 10…Carnival Comes to Town

A carnival was setting up near Mineral Wells and Will and Arch decided it was time for Alva to experience the fun and excitement of the "Big Top". Although truth be known, the excitement was felt more by those who had already seen and anticipations were high in the older folk.

Mary even seemed to perk up a bit, after finally being coaxed by her brothers into joining them. She fought back the thoughts of how much fun it would have also been for Edward.

When they arrived at the carnival Arch swung Alva up to his thin shoulders. Mary chose to walk between her brothers.

A loud bell attracted their attention and brought them to a large crowd standing around an apparatus with a bell mounted on the top of a ten-foot pole. Looking much like a giant thermometer, it had a type of lever on the base that when struck with a large mallet would propel a metal object up the post toward a bell at the top.

"Step right up there young man, test your strength. You look like a strong strapping fellow. Ring the bell and win a prize!" Came from the barker standing near by.

When the young man bought a ticket and stepped up and took hold of the mallet, he knew he was in trouble with the weight of it alone. But with the crowd cheering him on, he was able to hoist it first up to his shoulder and then with a mighty heave he swung the hammer up, around and down hitting the lever with a glancing blow. The propelled metal left the ground and went about two feet up the pole.

Sounds of disappointment went up from the crowd as the barker feigned sympathy and coaxed, "Oh, too bad young man, but try again. You got a bad hit that time, next time you will hit it dead on...and win a prize!"

The lad seemed to know that he had barely been able to lift the hammer the first time, and didn't want to waste his money with a second try, besides face another humiliation. He shook his head, tucked his hands in the pockets of his overalls and backed away from the center of attention.

Arch took this chance to tease his big brother, "Come on, Will, let's see what you can do! I know you can do better than that kid."

Will just shook his head and said, "Not this time Arch. My head still starts to throb when I exert myself. Lillie really did a number on this old skull." Immediately he hated himself for his words. Mary dropped her eyes and lost her smile. The quiet, which followed, was finally interrupted by Alva's squeal. He was pointing and jabbering his childish language that only a mother can decipher.

They turned in unison to see a very tall man with very long legs. He towered over the crowd and was smiling as he tipped his top hat to everyone. He was dressed like Abraham Lincoln and was leading people to the entrance of a large tent at the end of the row. The signs outside the tent claimed that it housed "World Wonders" such as a two-headed goat, the smallest man and a bearded woman.

As the boys discussed whether they should take Alva, Mary answered, "I think not. He does not need to be subjected to others less fortunate right yet. I'll take him with me and we'll wander around and perhaps get him a glass of milk."

Arch let him down from his shoulders and gingerly straightened his back. The tow-headed boy was big for his three and a half years and heavier than he looked.

She strolled the aisles between the barker's tents of games enticing people to "Have a go at winning a prize." and "Knock all the bottles over with one ball and win."

The aromas were tantalizing her taste buds and guided her to a horse drawn concession wagon. Her hunger was sudden and she glanced up at the sun. It was nearly straight overhead and she realized Alva had not eaten since breakfast almost six hours earlier. After checking the menu on the wall of the cart, she checked her draw string purse and decided to get a bite to eat. It advertised a "Hamburger sandwich made famous at the 1904 St. Louis World's Fair", for a nickel.

As she stepped forward to give her order a gentleman arose from his chair near the back of the cart. She noticed that he had dark hair and dark eyes that sparkled as he flashed a warm smile.

"Well hello, young man. What would you like to order for your pretty sister?" he asked.

Mary dropped her chin and felt heat rush from her chest to her cheeks. No one had commented on her beauty since Hasten, and that seemed like a lifetime ago. "I'm afraid I'm his mother." She corrected him.

"No, you can't be, why you're much too young to be a mother, and why be afraid? Is he a fearful child? He looks pretty harmless to me," he teased.

"No, of course not." She stammered, searching the crowd for her brothers. *What is taking those boys so long? I should not have wandered off without them!*

The man seemed to enjoy her frustration. As he removed a pouch of "Bull Durham Tobacco" from his left front pocket and began to roll a cigarette he asked, "Is his father going to be joining you?"

"No, no he has no father. I, I mean we're divorced," her words tumbled out, as she became even more embarrassed, realizing she had divulged to this total stranger some of her most private affairs.

"Now look at me jabbering away. I haven't even let you place your order yet. What would you like? Have you checked my menu on the side of the wagon?" He was surprised at his own awkwardness. *She's like a tiny bird ready to take flight. What would a pretty thing like this have to fear? She should have the world on a string. No husband, hmmm. Careful now, Nevy ol' boy, she's already got you all discombooberated.*

Regaining her composure she answered, "Yes. Yes I have and I would like one of those famous hamburger sandwiches, and two glasses of milk, please."

The man then smiled and turned to begin his task, first by extinguishing his cigarette. As he cooked the patty he decided to make small talk to keep her close, "Are you having a good time at the carnival?"

Relieved that the conversation had turned less personal, she answered quickly. "Oh, yes I suppose. I'm not comfortable around a lot of people. It makes me feel uneasy."

Pure innocence, that is the picture she portrays; naïve and innocent. Not in the marriage sense, for she held the hand that showed proof of that, but in worldly ways. Why should I have this overwhelming urge to protect her from what life can dish out?

"Well, carnival crowds can be pretty pushy at times, and it is a good idea not to ignore those feelings. There are pick pockets and con artists everywhere, ready to separate the unwary from their wallets or purses. So hold yours close and don't lay it down anywhere. Just paying attention to those around you, will keep you safe most times," he warned.

As he wrapped the sandwich and slid it towards her, she reminded him, "The two milks?"

"Oh, of course. Where's my mind? Coming right up." He turned to the icebox near by and brought out a bottle of milk, which he used to fill two glasses. "There you go pretty lady. Mack Neville Lacey at your service," he offered.

Mary smiled as she pushed a dime toward him. "Well, thank you, Mr. Lacey."

He rolled and lit another cigarette, drawing smoke into his lungs at close intervals. "Am I to go on living without knowing the name of the prettiest woman at the carnival? You wouldn't be that cruel would you?" He asked with a teasing grin.

She again began to stammer, "Mary, Mary Tirrell, uh I mean Dikes."

"Now which is it?" he queried.

"Tirrell was my married name, the divorce was recent and I sometimes forget." she explained, again not knowing why she felt at ease with this man, much less obligated to answer him.

She took a seat on a bench nearby and Alva climbed up beside her. As she watched the people come and go from Mr. Lacey's food wagon, she broke off pieces of the sandwich and offered them to Alva.

When she returned the empty glasses the adults both said, "Thank you" at the same time, then laughed when they countered with "You're welcome" again at the same time.

Their laughter was interrupted with the appearance of Will and Arch, who stooped and each grasped a hand of the boy and began to swing him between them.

Taken slightly aback at the forwardness of these men to his new friend's child, and her seemingly acceptance of their familiarity with him, he fell silent.

Both boys swung the child while staring questioningly at their demure sister holding a conversation with a total stranger. Seeing their bewilderment, she made introductions, "Will, Arch, I wish to introduce Mr. Lacey. Mr. Lacey I wish to introduce you to my brothers, William and James Hall."

"Oh, brothers, of course. Hall? Not Dikes?" he asked.

Seeing the boy's exchange glances she quickly added, "In conversation I explained I was Alva's mother and why we had different last names."

"Oh," said Arch.

"I see," said Will.

"Well, you see he thought that I was Alva's sister and I was trying to explain…"

"Oh, I see perfectly, sister dear," Will interrupted, "Perhaps Arch and I should have a talk with Mr. Lacey ourselves and explain things even better. Arch, does she look like Alva's sister to you? I think I've heard that line before, haven't you?"

"Might have even used it a time or two myself", said Arch.

"Boys, you stop that!" Mary spoke through clenched teeth and barely above a whisper. "Don't you go embarrassing me in front of everyone. He was a perfect gentleman and he stayed inside his wagon the whole time. We were just making conversation."

Will and Arch exchanged unnoticed winks, then Arch began, "No, I think we ought to find out what intentions this man has with our sister."

Will nodded and started rolling up his sleeves, "Yep, me too, little brother. Think you had better come down out of there Mr. Lacey, for we aim to defend our sister's honor."

Lacey looked at both men in disbelief. "What in the world are you talking about? This fine lady and I were carrying on an innocent conversation."

"Well, I can believe the "carrying on" bit, but as far as "innocent" goes, I'm not so sure *yours* were," accused Will.

"Step down from there, sir, so we can have our own conversation," prodded Arch.

Seeing a crowd begin to gather, there was nothing left to do but step forth and see if he could reason with these men. He removed his apron, snuffed his cigarette, walked out the back door of the wagon and around to where they stood.

As Arch stepped forward he stated, "All I have to say to you, Sir is…any friend of Mary's is a friend of ours!"

Arch and Will started laughing and slapping Mr. Lacey on the back as they rocked on their heels, laughing at their own joke.

Mary was furious. "How could you embarrass me like this? Am I to remain in my house forever to keep you two from torturing me?"

Nevy smiled with relief as he shook their hands and absorbed the good-natured slaps on the back. "It's alright, Mary, they meant no harm. They're just doing what brothers are supposed to do, checking the character of a stranger that becomes familiar toward their sister."

Exasperated, and with her voice barely audible, Mary stated, "Maybe in medieval times, but not in this day and age and I'm never going to forgive them for this." She took Alva's hand and with a determined step she marched through the crowd back toward home.

Arch watched her back as he raised his hands and shoulders in a shrug, "I'll never understand women. Here we were, defending her honor and she goes and gets mad about it. Got any root beer in that there wagon, Mr. Lacey?"

"Sure do, Mr. Hall, and call me Nevy." Lacey offered.

"Only if you call us Arch and Will," came the reply in unison.

Chapter 11… The Detective.

The man reached for his jaw, afraid to move it without support. He cupped his hand around the chin and gingerly moved it back and forth. *Jaws ok, but I'm soaked in blood and I can't touch my nose without excruciating pain. How did she get that arm loose and hit that hard?* As he pulled himself up to lean against the building his memory recalled the other voice just before the two smashing blows that had rendered him unconscious. *How could I have been so stupid? Come to think of it her description matches that woman, Lillie! And Mr. Tirrell could have been waiting here. If so they are up to mugging now. They must be desperate to try something so dangerous. I could have used my gun…my gun, oh no! They got my gun! My badge, my wallet, and my gun. I have to go to the local sheriff. No, can't do that…and be made a fool of! A laughing stock! Falling for a trick like that. They may even wonder what I had in mind escorting her back to her room…No, I'd just better get back on the trail and find them quickly. I don't want anyone to know about this. My reputation is at stake.*

Retrieving his bowler beside him, and checking for the hidden cash inside his sweatband, he thought, *I'm glad I stashed this in case of an emergency, because this definitely is an emergency.* He replaced it on his head and straightened his tie before stepping out of the alley. *I'm glad it's still too dark for anyone to see the mess they made of me!*

He scurried past the hotel clerk and made it to his room without being questioned about his bloody appearance. It took several pitchers of water to cleanse himself and what he could of his clothes. He retrieved the clean water and emptied the bloody water down the hall in a room labeled "Water Closet"

Upon waking the next morning the image in the mirror reflected a man who could barely see out of his swollen right eye, dark circles under both eyes, as well as a slightly crooked nose too tender to touch. *He broke my nose! He'll pay for this, mark my words they'll both pay. I'll get those two, come hell or high water. They will woe the day they messed with George Eckstein !*

With a set jaw and hat pulled low, he first paid for a telegram and then for his laundry. *That Lillie was a smooth one, and darn right pretty too, but she has a tad bit of larceny in her blood and she seems to be a natural at getting what she goes after. But even the best of them slip up eventually and I want to be there when they do. I want to be the one that puts those two away. I don't think that young Tirrell man knows what he's got himself in for, but I think she's been on the wrong side of the law before.*

His masculine pride would not allow himself to believe she was anything but a professional, because an amateur could never fool him. He couldn't have known the facts; that the Hasten Tirrell he was chasing had been on the wrong side of the law many more years than she had.

Chapter 12... Back on the run.

"It says here that he's a private detective Lillie! They hired a private detective to hunt us down!" Acey held the wallet and badge in one hand and papers and pistol in the other as he whispered hoarsely, "Can ya believe it? Look at these here papers. He even has a picture of me and a description of you and Edward to go by. He had ta have gotten them from my family cause this picture hung in Pa and Ma's living room."

Mollie still kept her guard near the sleeping Edward and thumped her tail on the hotel room floor as Lillie glanced in her direction. Lillie put her finger to her lips and the well-trained hound stopped the tail and laid her chin between her outstretched front legs, keeping a constant eye on her beloved mistress. She only raised an eyebrow now and again as the conversation continued.

Lillie too whispered, "It doesn't surprise me about the detective. If Edward was taken from me I would do everything in my power to get him back, and I'm not even his real mother." She undressed and put the bloody part of her dress in a bowl of water and began to scrub first herself then the stained garment.

Placing the items on the bed, he sat beside them and began rubbing his hands. She realized that he had been doing that a lot lately but had considered it to be just nerves. She decided to ask, "Did you hurt your hand? Let me take a look."

"Naw, they've been hurtin a lot lately, and sometimes even get kinda hot around the knuckles," he answered.

Looking closely at his hands she noticed that the knuckles on his right hand were swollen, but only a little more than his left. "How long has this been going on?" she asked.

"It's nothin. It's been comin and goin for a while, but lately it's been more often. It's worst in the mornin until I get'em flexed a bit, then they're better."

"It's the arthritis. I'll read up on it as soon as we get somewhere where I can drag out Dan's books. They'll tell me what can be done for it," she said as she studied each of them closely.

Pulling his hands away he said, "Well, don't worry about it now, I'll be fine. We havta get goin' fast. Somewheres far enough to where he'll give up and go home." Acey's voice rose as he fell back into his backward speech. "What if he has more ah these here papers with my picture on 'em and takes 'em to the sheriff? My God, it's just like a wanted poster without a reward. We gotta get going, *now*"

"Keep your voice down. And I know you're excited but remember what I've been teaching you about your vocabulary! Speaking different is just as much a disguise as looking different. You *have* to concentrate even when we are alone, so you won't slip up when we are in public." Lillie softly corrected. "We can't get our hack until the livery opens in the morning. That detective could be watching the streets right now. We don't know if he's gone to the sheriff and that will mean a posse. We can't outrun a posse with a hack let alone having Edward with us. Just start packing and first streak of daylight we'll be on the road. We have enough money now to start a small business somewhere, but we have to get away from here."

"What if he's gone to the sheriff and they have someone watchin…watching" he corrected himself, "the livery in the morning? He can recognize you and he's been carry'n…carrying this here picture of me for Lord knows how long." Acey sputtered.

Lillie decided to let the "here" in the sentence go uncorrected because he was trying so hard, "I'll lay out a set of clothes for each of us for tomorrow and we can pack the rest. Don't worry, I'll think of something." She assured him.

As they packed she spotted the garment she had purchased months ago when she had formulated a plan, for just this reason. She had not discussed it with Acey for fear he would object, but as she saw it right now they had no alternative. She was pretty sure it would work if she could get cooperation from both Acey and Edward. She knew a man's ego was as fragile as a pullet's egg and would take a lot of convincing.

"I have a plan, Acey, and I need you to hear me out before you argue with me. First I want you to go down and settle our livery bill through tonight and tell them that we will be leaving very early in the morning. It's dark enough that you can keep in the shadows outside on the streets, just in case he sees you and remembers your description. Then I want you to shave very close tomorrow and we will exchange clothes. We are close to the same height." She held her palm toward him to hold back argument, and explained quickly before he could interrupt, "I did this when I was a young girl running from people determined to put me in an orphanage. Remember I told you about it? Well, I traveled in my brother's clothes from Oklahoma to Texas. My hair is short enough to be combed back under your hat and you will wear one of my bonnets with the brim forward. If you keep your head down no one will be able to see your face. I will bind my chest. We will look entirely different." She looked up to see the shocked look on his face.

"I don't think that would work at all. How are we going to get Edward to keep quiet through all this? And besides, I can't wear your shoes." he argued.

"You can wear your own boots, the dress will cover them. We will just tell Edward that we are playing "dress up" and "pretend". He will be happy to have a game to play," she insisted. "It will work, Hasten! It has to. I will go after the hack and harness the team as if I was a man. You be ready to come down stairs and straight out to the wagon when I pull up. We paid the hotel bill for the full week, so there's no problem there. It's the only way, Hast....Acey."

She realized that she too was overly nervous and decided they both needed to sit down and relax for a bit to gather their nerves. "Do you have a bottle of something to settle our nerves?" she asked, knowing that he usually carried one with him.

He pulled the bottle out of his saddlebag and handed it to her. The look on his face told her that he was mulling over the plan in his mind and making decisions. "I guess it's worth a try. It sounds like it just might work. Do you think he knows about Mollie?"

Lillie hadn't thought about the hound, but as she took a swig from the bottle her eyes came to rest on her shoes sitting where she had removed them. "Did you think to pack any shoe polish?"

"We don't have time to worry about how shiny our shoes are, Lillie!" Acey sputtered in disbelief.

"Would you just listen for a minute? Do you, or do you not, have any black shoe polish?" She demanded in a whisper.

"Yes, but...." he started to answer.

"Then get it," she insisted. "We can make Mollie's brown spots black or blacken her whole body. If he has a description of her then she will get by him."

63

Acey saw her reasoning and went for the polish. "We can do this just before we leave because we have to get some sleep before morning. It will be a very serious play we will all be acting in."

"Yes, and one that will cost us dearly if we fail to make people believe in the characters we'll be portraying," she warned.

Chapter 13... Carnival leaves town.

After the Hall brothers had finished their root beer floats and shared one of the famous hamburgers that Nevy Lacey had generously made for them, they each felt that they had made a good friend. The Halls decided to invite Nevy to breakfast the next morning as his evening hours were consumed with the carnival.

The carnival usually only stayed for one day in each town, but this had fallen on a weekend, making it a two-day event. Nevy jumped at the chance to see Mary again before he had to leave. She had stirred his curiosity and he wanted desperately to find out more about her. He had tried to be discreet with his questions, but the boys recognized his interest in her and as they saw it, there would be no harm in her receiving a bit of attention for they knew that she sorely needed some kind of distraction.

The next morning the boys were up bright and early and Mary could hear them whispering and chuckling to themselves as she dressed Alva and made breakfast. She wondered what had got into them. They were acting a 'might peculiar', as her father used to say.

Just as she was about to set the table and call them in for breakfast she heard a third voice in their conversation, muffled and indiscernible, but evidently welcomed by the brothers.

Could be one of the Tirrell boys or the Turners, she thought, as she set Alva up to the table and went to call the boys. When she reached for the door it opened and in walked Nevy Lacey with the brothers close behind.

She jumped back with both feet, her eyes wide and both hands went to the sides of her face. Then one went in search of any loose strands of hair that may have escaped her quickly made bun, while the other quickly untied her apron.

"Look who's here to share our morning meal? Arch and I thought he might like a home cooked meal instead of his own cooking from that wagon of his. We invited him yesterday after you left," offered Will.

She saw everything in slow motion as she faced three smiling faces. All the while she was backing out of the kitchen and heading to her bedroom. Stammering a welcome and for them to start breakfast without her.

"Nonsense, Mary, we'll wait for you. We're not in any hurry, or are you, Nevy?" Arch quipped. The boys were absolutely ecstatic as they saw the influence Nevy had over Mary's desire to make herself presentable. It had been a long time since she took that much interest in her appearance.

It only took a moment and she was back. Every strand of hair was in place and she had changed clothes. The change did not go unnoticed by anyone, especially Nevy who smiled as he commented on her pretty dress. She was so flushed that she needed no rouge to color her cheeks.

Mary managed a whispered, "Thank You".

Will offered, "She made it herself. She's quite a seamstress you know. Makes lots of peoples clothes around here. Made these here curtains and…"

"Will, I'm sure Mr. Lacey did not come here to hear about my sewing. And besides they are just simple things that anyone could make, nothing special," she scolded.

"Oh, that's right. He did come for another reason. Nevy, have a seat here. Mary is also a great cook. You'll have to go some to find better biscuits and gravy anywhere."

"WILL, *Please*. Just sit down and eat! Mr. Lacey, forgive my brothers. They relish in embarrassing me every chance they get. And as for my cooking, they have had very little to compare it to. We are pretty much a stay-at-home family." Mary stated as she glared at Will and turned to Alva, "Come sit on Momma's lap and eat your breakfast. And Arch, you can lead us in the breakfast blessing."

After the platters were empty, Mary began to clear the table. Nevy reached over and touched her forearm. "No. You sit there and we will do the dishes. And I have to agree with Will. You *are* an exceptional cook. That was the best meal I've had in a long while."

"WE? Who's this WE are you referring to?" teased Arch.

"No", Mary argued, "Don't be silly. I'll do them later. Just leave them."

"Oh, I guess us men can handle a little dish washing once in awhile. As long as you don't go getting used to it," Arch chimed in as he patted her shoulder. "You can sit there and supervise. Every job needs a supervisor, don't it?"

"Now just wait a minute, little brother. I ain't puttin on no frilly apron, and besides, that dish washing may soften my hands too much for my wood working. Gotta have my calluses you know. They help sand the wood," countered Will. But he was already stacking the plates as Arch was stoking up the wood stove to heat more water.

Mary decided to just sit back and enjoy the moment as the three men stumbled around the kitchen and took twice as long as she would have to get the job done. All the time they were bantering back and forth about how next she would be having them sweep the floors and beat the rugs out on the line.

She realized it had been a long time since she saw the boys enjoying someone's company as much as they did Mr. Lacey's and wondered how they had all felt so much at ease with him. As if they had known him a long while and not just since the day before.

When it was time for Nevy to leave he asked Mary to accompany him while he saddled his horse. "There's something I'd like to ask you. I hope you won't be offended," he said while he swung the saddle onto the horses back.

"What is it?" She asked.

"Could I write you? Would you care to exchange letters?" He asked, "I'm not real sure when I will be back this way, but I sure would like to keep in contact with you…and your brothers of course."

"I think I would like that very much, Mr. Lacey," she answered.

"And one more favor. Would you call me Nevy? I don't remember how long ago I was called Mr. Lacey and it seems unfamiliar. I'm just plain Nevy. I'd like it very much if you would call me that." he explained.

"Well, I'm not sure how proper that would sound to others, but I will use Nevy when I write you," she answered.

"Well, that's a start anyhow. And I'm already looking forward to receiving your first letter. Do you receive mail addressed General Delivery here in Mineral Wells?" He asked.

"Yes, but if you are moving from one city to another every day or so, how will I know where to mail your letters?" She asked.

"Hmmm, that's a good question," he answered. He thought for a moment as he tightened the girth strap, "I know. I will send you the rest of this year's itinerary and you can send your letters a few days ahead of where I'm going to be and they will be waiting for me. The schedule will tell you where and when our performances will be and I will write you when we close for the winter. I always winter in San Angelo, Texas. I have family there." He seemed quite pleased with his strategy and smiled broadly when she agreed to the plan.

Chapter 14...The Tirrell Gang regroups.

The leaves on the oak and birch trees were showing the signs of autumn when Pa motioned for Lewis to join him out at the barn. "I want you to send for Sam. It's time for a campout, I want ya to round up the boys and get things started."

"But Pa, you sent Sam away and besides, without Hast..." started Lewis

"Don't ya say it! Don't ya mention his name!" Pa interrupted in a deep growl, "and don't 'but' me, boy. Sam'll come, and be the leader now. He's near to eighteen, older than...*he* was when he took over"

"I know Pa, but we're down to five now, iffen Sam and Mr. Briles is up to it. He may not be healed proper, or may not care to go no more. That'd leave just four. If Sam says no, I can't see how it could be pulled off with only three. Besides, I ain't seen Jake nur Nate in some time. They may want to steer clear, beings we came so close to getting caught when Mary threatened to tell."

"I said don't 'but' me! Either Sam or you WILL lead the boys. Tomorrow I want you to ride over to Briles ranch and then to the Turner's. The family's counting on ya."

Dawn was breaking as Lewis saddled up his young mare, Queen. He thought of the beautiful horse Sam had in Raven. It never ceased to amaze him how black the stallion was. *After a good brushing the shine gave a luster of navy blue. Sam and the stallion had made a good team over the years and were bonded in more ways than the love and trust between animal and owner.* Lewis smiled as he remembered how well they seemed to fit together, *as if they were two jigsaw puzzle pieces snapped in place.*

He sent a telegram to Sam stating, "Pa says time for campout. Come. Need you."

Then faced Samuel and explained his problem.

"I'm not sure I have the heart for it anymore Lewis," Samuel Briles began. "With Lillie gone it just isn't the same. Don't get me wrong, though. You all can still hide out in the cellar, and I'll do as I did before in covering your tracks, but I don't feel like a whole man anymore. Not even sure I wasn't doing it all for Lillie anyway. She loved skirting the law, and had no qualms about stating her contempt for it."

"Well, would you give it some thought. Pa's decided that Sam is to pick up where Hasten left off and I'm not so sure he can handle it with just the four of us," explained Lewis.

"Let me think on it some and I'll get back to you," Samuel said, "I know you need an answer soon, so I'll think it over and let you know."

Turning Queen towards the Turner ranch he shouted back, "Thanks, Mr. Briles."

A warm reception was waiting as he entered the Turner home.

"I was wonderin' iffin' ya was goin ta let Hasten and Lillie runnin' off stop our camp outs," said Jake.

"Not a chance as far as Pa is concerned. But no one's to use Hasten's name in his presence. He gets madder'n a wet hen if he hears," warned Lewis.

"Well, as far as we're concerned that's yer family business, nobody else's, so you can rest easy there," said Nate.

"If Sam and Mr. Briles decides to continue we'll have five. If not, just us three. I'm thinking that we should have more, but Pa says we can handle it," Lewis stated, "I can't see trusting anyone else."

Isabel, the Turner boys ma came from the kitchen, still drying a dish. "I'm sure Mary'll keep her mouth shut cause it could turn against her and her brothers as well. And she ain't gonna say anything in fear of losing that last boy of hers. Right, Joseph?"

"You have the female savvy, not I," Mr. Turner answered. "But it makes sense that she'd be scared to open her mouth after all these years."

Upon returning to the ranch, Lewis reined Queen into the barn, leaning low across the saddle horn for clearance. Seeing his father he shattered Pa's sanctity of silence with, "The Turner boys are in, but Mr. Briles said he'd have to think on it."

Pa was so intent on his milking that his nerves exploded and began racing along the outer edges of each appendage, from the scalp to the tips of his fingers and toes, raising the hair in its wake. Finding no escape, they rerouted themselves inward, all meeting at the pit of his stomach. The convulsing body seemed to have a mind of it's own, sending Pa's brain into a "flight or fight" mode. Without conscience thought it chose "fight" and Pa shot to his feet and turned swinging. The blow of his right hand landed squarely on Queen's left shoulder. Like a frightened cat she arched her body and sought safer ground skyward. Lewis saw the rafters up close and the thought ran through his mind that he was relieved that they weren't in the stalls where the hayloft created a solid roof above.

In a matter of split seconds three minds were racing for answers. Pa's as to *who*, Lewis' as to *what*, and Queen's as to *why*?

With ears back, eyes wide and stance spread Queen waited. The men's confusion began to evaporate as recognition first set in to Pa and his mind registered *who* it was and Lewis' as to *what* happened. Of course the mare's *why* would go unanswered, but a soothing rub down and soft voice calmed her nerves.

"Confound it boy, don't be sneakin up on a man like that! I don't know why a body can't even do their chores in peace around here. '*Your brother*' sent me into a tail spin a few years back that cost the family a dear amount of milk," Pa bellowed.

"Sorry, Pa. I thought ya heard me comin. I'll whistle next time," Lewis apologized.

Francis went back to milking and as Lewis rubbed Queen down he began, "Well see that ya do. Now back to the campout. I been thinkin while milkin and if Sam or Mr. Briles don't join up, Oliver is old enough to join you boys. He's going on six and that's old enough. Ya put him where ya think he'll do best, I'm sure you'll figure it out."

Staring, unbelieving Lewis asked, "Has Ma agreed to lettin Oliver go?"

"Don't make no difference what Ma says. I'm the one that decides. She knows we need the money not only for the food and clothes but for her medicine," he answered gruffly. "Pick a place yet?"

"I'm still not sure about Mr. Briles. He said he'd let me know soon, so we can make plans. He might know of places we don't, bein' he's so much older," Lewis felt walls closing in on him.

"Age ain't got nuthin to do with it. But I suppose he's traveled a bit more than some. Talk ta the Turner boys. Ya'll hash out the plannin together," Pa stated as he left the barn with the pail of milk.

Lewis was relieved when Sam sent a note stating that he would make up a story to his wife and be down. Samuel also agreed and that meant they no longer needed Oliver.

They met at the Briles Ranch. After going over the maps, spread over the dining room table, Sam asked, " Well, what do you think? Last time we went

73

north, up where you got that wild boar, Samuel. Guess we better choose a different direction this time to keep to the overall plan. I'm not as keen on this plannin as Hasten was, so I'm goin ta ask all of ya for yer input. We haffta plan it together."

"Don't ya worry, Sam. We'll all give ya our two cents worth and we can smooth out the rough edges as we go along. With all our heads together we'll do fine," encouraged Jake, "We all know what our part is, except maybe Samuel here. This time he should be part of the holdup itself, and not lolly gag around a campfire where it's safe and cozy, like last time."

"Lolly gag my backside, young man. It was hard work holding down the fort and bringing in the game and cooking it. I had a devil of a time fighting off all those wild animals. It takes skill to hunt them varmints, not to mention the killin, cleanin and cookin each one," Samuel defended.

"Awe come on now, ya done told us that there boar came wandering into camp. I'll bet all the others did too. Ya probably didn't even have ta leave the campfire. They just all probably strolled in, one at a time, to commit suicide", Nate joined in the bantering.

"Well, all I can say is however he got'em they was mighty tasty, especially that boar. That ham was right delicious, Samuel, and my family was truly grateful," Lewis stated.

With a nod of acceptance Samuel turned to the others, "You older boys could take a lesson from our new recruit here. He knows who to appreciate."

"Awe, he's just glad something was there to fill his belly. As fast as he's growing he'll be as tall as me in no time, and that takes a lot of vittles, don't it Lewis!" Sam added, "Now let's get down to business. I can see why Hasten would be worrisome during the campouts."

"Yer right, Sam, let's see where we want to go next and settle on a plan," Jake agreed, "This is Lewis' maiden run and we have to get ever thing real clear so we don't have any mishaps."

"Well, we've been in all four directions haven't we?" asked Nate. "I think maybe being's we have two new ones this year we'd better hav'em split up and go with one that's done it. They can be the backup in case somthin' goes wrong. Besides we never know what's gonna happen each time."

Sam took the lead, "That's good thinkin, Nate. I agree. Samuel, you were in on the plans of the last one and heard all this before, but you were our backup with the campsite. Lewis, listen up. "The basics are that we ride in by twos, from different directions, and look over the town. We locate their mercantile and feed store and the safest route for escape. Then we find a way to cause a commotion just outside of town, which will draw the attention away from the businesses, and we strike at the same time. Each pair will make no contact with the other. It has to be fast and clean. We have never had to use our guns other than for show, and I don't want to start now. So make sure the storeowners know we mean business. Surprise is on our side, so you can't look suspicious beforehand, nor dally around afterwards. In and out, that's how our plan has always worked. I want you to team with Jake"

"How do you know which team hits which business?" asked Lewis.

"Good question, little brother," Sam answered. "We decide beforehand and keep to ourselves. This way the town has no idea how many we are. We were all younger before and that caused confusion as to whether we were pulling a prank or if we were serious. We've all gotten older, so it's going to be a bit different. They'll take us serious instantly. Lewis, you hang back in the shadows and act casual. You will learn by watching Jake."

"That's what I was thinking. I know we can pull this off," Lewis stated with mock confidence, "All we have to do is keep a level head and stay calm but convincing."

"Another thing, Lewis, we try to hit county seat towns. They usually have many routes going in and out and a railroad running through it," offered Sam. "I've been looking at the map and I see that if we go southeast there's a town called Hillsboro. It lies between Dallas and Waco. Lot's of escape routes and a train station, so it fits what we want. What do you think?"

They all bent over the map murmuring their consents. Samuel asked, "Should we go south to Stephenville and then east? Or as the crow flies?"

"I think we should stick as close to our original plan as we can. That would mean not drawing attention to ourselves, going or coming home," answered Nate.

"So do I," agreed Sam. "We want ta stick with what we're all used ta. It's been good ta us so far. So we'll go as a group "huntin'", pair up at the destination, then get back together fer the ride home. Anyone got any questions?"

"I do" chirped Lewis, "what if we don't bring down any game? And in case ya haven't noticed, there are five of us now, not four like you have planned. What is the fifth person goin' to be doin?"

"Well, we won't have trouble bringin' down enough game ta cover our plan, but ya do have a point bout the odd man. Gimme some ideas boys, I'm open fer suggestions. Do we leave Lewis back makin

76

camp like we did Samuel last time? Or do we have him holding the horses?" asked Sam.

"That *would* look suspicious," offered Nate. "if he's just sittin' on his horse, holdin' reins of two more, besides, he would only be able ta help one team."

"It'd look just as bad if we left Lewis ta tend camp, he's too young ta be out camping all by hisself. Might get people to wonderin'," added Jake.

"What if we have the fifth man hanging loose in town during and after the hold ups to see what happens. If possible, he could station himself to watch both stores and see how much of a head start we'd have. He can meet up with us at some place and let us know if we should back track or split up like you did coming from Stephenville. As a curious bystander, he could hear everything the towns people had to say, whether they give a good description, or which direction they send the posse. It would give us ideas for the next one, which would come in handy," offered Samuel.

"Good, Good idea. That would be helpful," Sam agreed. "Who wants to volunteer to hang back and watch what happens?"

With no reply, Sam folded the map, put it back in the leather pouch, and replaced it in his saddlebag. When he finished he looked up and no one would make eye contact. "Well, it's something to ponder. I'll make the decision later after I've mulled it all over some. Every stranger will be suspect, so whoever hangs back could possibly be accused of being part of the hold ups and pay dearly. It wouldn't be a very easy job."

Looks like I'm going to have to appoint someone, and when I do feelings are going to get hurt. I could choose Lewis, but he has no experience out in strange towns and a boy his age, traveling

77

alone, would draw a second look. It would make more sense if it were Samuel. He's older and no one would think twice at him traveling alone. He'll be disappointed, but will accept my decision far easier than the younger guys. And after all it was his idea.

When Sam explained the details, Samuel agreed, "I'll be there to cover if I see anyone in trouble, otherwise stay in the shadows. If all goes well, we'll be wiser for it."

Sam called the boys together a few more times before they set out, just to familiarize each of them with maps, routes, and meeting places.

Chapter 15...Sarah

Sarah was due to deliver her second child and her two-year-old was playing at her feet. "Henry, would you get Betty Lee ready for bed? I don't feel like I can handle her tonight."

"Sure, Sallie," he answered.

She smiled at his pet name for her. He was a loving and quiet man, proud of his Indian heritage. She was proud of his handsome features.

Her thoughts reflected back to when she had married Henry Howard Fulfer on June 13th 1914. The family was happy then, or so it seemed. She and Mary had each brought a child into the world in 1915. Betty came in February and Alva in April.

It had now been years since Pa and Hasten's fight and Hasten had run off with Edward and Lillie. Sarah thought to herself, *What would I do if Henry were to run off with Betty and another woman?* She could only guess how Mary must have felt.

She shrugged the thought off and went about her nightly chores. "I wish I would get over this back ache that I've had all day," she said aloud.

"Well, why don't you just lie down on the sofa for a while and get off your feet?" Henry asked.

"Oh sure, and leave all this work for who to do?" She laughed.

"Well, I think I can handle some of it and what I can't, can wait. Why don't I go see if Mattie wants to come over and visit? She always seems to cheer you up." He offered.

"No, it's late and I don't want to get her in trouble with Pa. He probably wouldn't let her anyway. Being she's the only girl home now, he treats her like a slave. The day will come when she'll get married too. Then who will he get to take care of Ma?"

"Oh, he'll find someone. Remember when Sam married that Elkins girl and…It's funny how he went for another Sarah…anyway…your Pa thought he could bully her like he does everyone? That sure backfired in his face." Said Henry

"Well for one thing, Sam calls her Sadie, and you call me Sallie, and Pa didn't think Sam would stand up to him like he did…this backache is getting worse. I'm beginning to think it just might be my time," she muttered.

"Time for what?" he asked.

"My TIME. You know. Time for this baby to see what the outside world looks like," laughed Sarah.

"OH, Well. Uh, what do you want me to do? Want me to go get Mattie? Your Pa can't argue about your needing her for the birthing," he offered.

"No, not yet. It'll be hours before anyone will be needed. Might as well let someone get some sleep because I don't think I'm going to," she moaned.

Pa's wrath was lathered on Henry after he heard of their elopement. He couldn't accept Henry's Indian blood and muttered more than once, "There's no place for that heathen in the Tirrell lineage and I won't tolerate it."

Ma was not fond of the situation either but was a little more discreet in her remarks to her son-in-law; keeping them just out of her daughter's hearing.

Sarah believed they would change their minds once they got to know him, but their constant pestering caused him to give up trying to prove himself worthy in their eyes.

Little did she know then, that years later, after the birth of this child, Fannie Maude, and a son that Henry graciously allowed to be named Oliver Francis, she *would* come to know some of what Mary felt. One day Henry simply mounted his horse and rode away.

Left behind with the three children, Sarah was forced to move back to the Tirrell ranch, answering her own question of who Pa would get to take care of Ma.

Even with the pain of Henry's leaving and her role as Ma's caretaker, she couldn't help but smile as she remembered the scene when Sam announced his intentions of marrying Sarah Elkins, and met the same resistance. *What makes Pa and Ma think they are so superior to others? When Sam stood his ground Pa was mad as a wet hen, and tried his bullying ways on Sam, telling him that he forbid the marriage. That drove Sam to retaliate and threaten to move closer to the Elkins family in Oklahoma.*

Pa had stepped closer and lowered his voice. "How da ya think yer goin to carry out the camp outs from that far away?"

"I was coming to talk to you about that too. After this next one I'm quitting that business. We've pushed our luck and we've done well. But it's time to break loose and live our own lives now. Sadie wouldn't abide by it and I won't lie to her like Hasten did Mary."

"Ya know better than ta use that name again. And since when da Tirrell men answer ta their women? Ya can't leave yer Ma and me and the younguns to starve. How will we afford her medicine and mine? You owe us boy! We've done gave ya a good home, put food in your belly and clothes on yer back..."

"I owe you?" Sam interrupted, "Who was it that brought the money in to pay for the food on the table and the clothes on our backs? Don't try to lay guilt on me because I've done what I've been told my whole

life and since HASTEN has been gone I've tried to fill his shoes. Well it's time to stop now, Pa. Before the rest of us are strung up like Grant, Charley and Jimmy. It's time for YOU to support the family."

"Ya know damn well that I'm too sick ta work and yer Ma has her affliction. How can ya be so heartless as ta turn yer back on yer own Pa and Ma?"

Pa's face turned red and the cords of his neck enlarged, pulling his head closer to his shoulders as Sam continued, "You're not that sick Pa. You can do anything you set your mind to, we've all seen it. You and Ma have meddled in Hasten's and Sarah's families and lost them their marriages. You are NOT going to do that to Sadie and me. And don't even think about hiring anyone to come looking for me."

With fists doubled at the end of his bowed arms and back straighter than it had been for some time Pa growled deep, "Well, don't ya worry none, boy, I'm wiping my hands of ya right now. Get yer things and get out!"

Later Sam had whispered "Sarah, I'll keep in touch either by friends or with letter writing." he knew that Pa couldn't read.

Samuel Briles welcomed him as a roomer, until just before the wedding when he did move up to Woodward and married Sarah on 19th of March 1919.

We didn't even get to go to his wedding but at least he was smart enough to keep his family away from Pa and Ma's clutches. Henry and I should have too.

Some day, I will run just like Sam and Hasten. I'll bet they're happy being free of Pa's controlling ways. Someday, someday…

I wonder if it's right to keep hunting for Hasten? Yes, I think so. I'm a mother and I know how

82

it would have hurt if Henry had taken one of the children. Then nodding to herself, *Yes, it's right.*

As once again Sarah tended to Ma she wondered, *Maybe I should hire someone to find Henry. He was such a loving husband, and adored each of our children. Why couldn't Pa and Ma leave him alone? Why do they have to interfere in everyone's life?* She resented them both for what they did. *They were the ones that drove him away.*

In her parent's minds Henry's leaving justified their actions, believing that one-day Sarah would realize their good judgment and find a more suitable man. Until then these well-intentioned grandparents had three more children under their roof and that suited them just fine.

Chapter 16...A Close Call

Lillie pulled the hat brim down to her eyebrows and kept her chin close to her chest as she made her way to the livery, remembering to walk with a bit wider stride and as manly as she could.

As she was harnessing Maudie to the hack and saddling Rascal, Acey was explaining to Edward that they were going to play a game. "It will be like dress up, but we will pretend to be girls."

"Why?" asked Edward.

"Just for the fun of it. Just for a little while. Until we get a ways out of town," insisted Acey. "You can do it, can't you Son? Help me trick all these people?"

"Like play pretend?" Edward asked.

"Yes, Son, like play pretend. Lillie is doing it too. She's dressed up like me and I'm dressed up like her and she bought you this dress and bonnet just for the play. Don't you think it will be fun? "

With a frown, Edward cocked his head and pooched out his bottom lip, "I'd rather be a sheriff or a cowboy," as he stepped back away from the dress.

Acey was beside himself, "Edward, please. Just do this for me. You can be a sheriff next time. This time we already have the outfit and we can't afford all the stuff the sheriff needs, you know the badge and leather vest. Next time though, I promise, but this time let's do it for Lillie. She has this all planned out. Look at me... I have to dress up like Lillie, don't you think I'd like to be the sheriff too?"

Edward looked up at his father and just shook his head. Hesitating only a moment before he said, "Well, if it's what Lillie wants, then I guess I'll do it this time but just for a little while, right?"

"Right. And look at Mollie I've even got her all different too. All her brown spots are black and I would have made her all black but I ran out of shoe

84

polish. Look, she doesn't care, she's ready to play the game too," coaxed Acey.

Edward turned to the hound and saw a different animal. "Wow, she really does look different! OK, Dad, lets do it!"

As quickly as his stiff hands allowed and before the boy could change his mind, Acey dressed Edward and himself, and made one last check around the room to make sure they weren't leaving anything. "Let's go, Son...I mean uh, What should I call you? What girl's name do you want me to call you?" Acey asked, knowing the boy would be drawn more into the "game" if he were given choices in his role.

"My momma's name was Mary, right?" Edward asked.

"Yes, Son, that's what her name was," Acey stated quietly.

"Then I want that name. I'll be Mary. And do I call you Lillie?"

"No, Son, you call me Mother," Acey answered.

"No, Dad, you can't call me 'son' now. I'm Mary," Edward insisted.

Acey chuckled and said, "And you can't call me 'Dad' either, I'm 'Mother'," then Edward laughed too.

Even though Lillie had chosen her largest dress, Acey found it to be a little snug in the shoulders. The lipstick made him very uncomfortable. Glancing out of the corner of his eye, as he began to apply it, he saw the boy start to laugh. He turned and threatened Edward with it but the boy backed away with his hands over his mouth and shook his head, giggling uncontrollably.

Acey and Edward took turns looking in the mirror and repeated to each other, "It's only going to be for a little while."

They were dressed and heading down the stairs of the hotel, followed closely by Mollie, when Edward whispered, "What are we going to call Mollie?"

Acey was proud of how the boy was really getting into the 'play pretend' and whispered back, "We'll just wait and see if we have to call her for any reason, ok? And I won't be able to talk because my voice would give me away. We just have to get loaded into the wagon and be off. The sooner we get out of here the sooner we get out of these clothes."

"That's good…Mother…because I don't think we are very pretty girls." Edward huskily stated.

Lillie reined Maudie up to the front of the hotel with Rascal tied on the back.

Acey's gloved hand was holding Edward's as they came out the hotel's front door and face to face with Detective Eckstein!

Acey recognized the man he had knocked unconscious the night before, and dropped his chin to his chest just before their eyes met. Pulling Edward closer to him, he stooped his shoulders a bit, trying to lower his height.

"Oh, excuse me, ma'am," offered Eckstein, as they each tried to side step the other, stepping in unison in the same direction and staying face to face.

The brim of Acey's bonnet was deep and he tried to pull his head clear to the back of it. He gave a slight nod as they successfully maneuvered clear of each other. In Acey's panic he had shuffled Edward back and forth with his grip on the boy's hand getting tighter and tighter.

"Ouch, let go, my hand, you're hurting me" whined Edward.

Easing his grip, Acey squeaked out, "Come along Mary, off we go now." All the while keeping his face turned away from the one man who could destroy his freedom.

With the painful pressure removed, Edward fell into his role and squeaked back, "Alright, Mother dear". But could not refrain from giggling. Acey's grip tightened again, encouraging Edward to silence.

Lillie was just a few yards away, taking in the whole scene and forcing herself to stay put and let it all play out. She descended slowly as the detective's back was turned and motioned Edward to come to her.

Edward saw her and started to laugh and point when Acey's grip on his hand became so tight that he automatically cried out. He jerked his hand loose and ran to Lillie.

With the brims of their hats almost touching she sternly whispered, "Play pretend, Edward."

He dropped his chin and nodded, not resisting as she placed him up on the wagon seat.

The incident did not go unnoticed by Eckstein and as he turned to see where the "little girl" was running to, he almost tripped over Mollie. One knee plunged into her side as his other foot came down on her back paw.

Mollie yelped and jumped sideways. A low growl came from deep as she faced the man who had caused her pain.

Eckstein reached for the dog saying, "Easy girl, easy. Didn't mean to hurt ya none."

Acey leaned down and grabbed her collar and pulled her out of his reach, diffusing the incident.

He led the hound to the back of the wagon and motioned for her to jump in and settle among the cargo. In his confusion, Acey started to untie Rascal's reins and prepared to mount.

In one quick move Lillie was beside him and patted his gloved hand much like a husband would thank his wife for getting his horse. She led Acey by the hand over to the wagon seat before he realized his near mistake. She steadied him as he stumbled over the dress hem in his climb up to the seat. Lillie then turned keeping her back to where she had last seen the detective, and mounted Rascal.

It had felt, to all the 'pretenders', that this scene had taken hours, but in reality only a few minutes had elapsed.

As they distanced themselves from the town Acey started to relax, easing his shoulders and leaning back against the seat. That's when he noticed the smudge of black shoe polish on his gloved hand.

Eckstein removed the bowler and scratched his balding head. As he watched the family leave town he thought, *Sure got odd folks around these parts. And what I could see of that woman, they come pretty homely too.*

Chapter 17... Eckstein

The detective had continued his search for Acey and Lillie in Oklahoma City but the town was big and he had to wait for the money and picture of the man he knew as Hasten to be replaced. He had nearly used up the fifty dollars Sarah had fronted him, but his need for personal appearance would not allow his clothes to show anything but what his opinion of a man of his proper stature should reflect.

He had found a smudge on his slacks, near his knee, that he couldn't determine and needed them dry-cleaned. He wore an older suit to the local laundry and presented the clerk behind the counter with his problem.

The little man unconsciously smoothed his mustache as he waited. The proprietor examined the stain and explained the situation. "Sir, it seems that your pant leg has encountered a highly polished shoe somewhere in your travels."

Receiving a blank stare from the detective he then asked, "Or perhaps you packed your suit without first separating your shoes and suit in a proper manner?"

This brought a frown to the blank expression and Eckstein stepped back a foot and straightened to his full height, which still made him look up to meet the man's gaze. "I'll have you know I am an experienced traveler and am not lack-a-daisical in my packing. I always separate shoes from garments."

"Perhaps you received a swift kick from someone with less than an amiable attitude?" the proprietor offered.

"No, nothing or the sort happened. I've no idea how I could have received a smudge like that from someone's shoe." Eckstein defended himself. "I would have remembered."

"Possibly a careless shoe shine boy caused it while you were otherwise entertained..."

Frustrated, the small man interrupted, "Well it makes no difference *how* it got there, it has to be cleaned. Can you or can you *not* remove the stain?"

"Yes, yes of course. But it is an intricate procedure and will require extra labor and therefore a bit more costly," explained the proprietor.

"How much more?" asked the investigator.

"Well, depending on how many times the spot has to be processed....."

"How much will it cost, for crying out loud?" demanded Eckstein.

"Oh, I'd say somewhere in the range of ...say...one dollar," tested the proprietor.

"What? How could it possibly cost that much? That's outrageous and you know it," sputtered Eckstein.

"You are more than welcome to take it to another establishment, sir. There is another across town on Second Street," offered the owner.

"I should. I really should, but I don't have time to haggle any longer. I have a job to do and I'm losing time standing here. Just do it and I'll be back this afternoon to pick it up."

"Oh, sir, I'm sorry, but we won't be able to get to this today, and tomorrow is Sunday, so I won't be able to have it ready for you until Monday," explained the owner, now with a slight smile spreading across his face.

Eckstein deciphered the statement as coming from one who had gained the upper hand and had full knowledge of it.

Acknowledging defeat Eckstein crammed his bowler down so hard that he knew it would take a hard tug to remove it. "Just give me the damn ticket and I'll be here early Monday for them. I must continue my business elsewhere." *If I find the source of this stain someone is going to reimburse my costs...they sure as hell will.*

"We open at 10 A.M. on Mondays," reached the little man's ears as he made his exit.

Chapter 18... The letters

The only spark the Hall brothers saw in Mary's eyes was when she received a letter from Nevy.

"You sure been getting a lot of letters from that Nevy fellow," Arch teased her.

She continued to read in silence.

Will joined in, "Being's you get all the mail, you can go to the post office from now on."

Still no response.

She had found Nevy's letter near the top of the stack and she had immediately opened it, ignoring the others in her lap. She finally looked up, "I told you that Nevy winters near San Angelo, where he has family." Then added, "Isn't it strange that we both have family there? It's where Virginia lives. It sure would be nice to visit Ginny," she thought out loud.

Arch sprang to life, "Oh, so it's *Ginny* that you all of a sudden desire to visit eh? Hear that Will? Our sister wants to go visit *Ginny*."

"Well, now that would be one long trip, just for a short visit," chimed in Will. "Isn't one of those letters from her anyway?"

Looking down at her lap she picked up the other envelopes and answered. "Why, yes, there is a letter from her, how nice."

When they didn't get their desired response the boys ceased their teasing and went about their outdoor chores. They seldom received mail and only collected it when there was a reason to go to town. They were just as glad for it, because if a person received mail the person sending that mail expected the person receiving that mail to answer, and they were not fond of letter writing.

A knock on the door brought Mary out of Ginny's letter. It was a man in uniform, holding a telegram addressed to her.

As the boys returned a short time later they heard a gasp and then a sob. They first looked at one another then rushed to Mary's side.

Arch pelted Mary with questions, "What is it? What's wrong? What's upset you?"

Mary couldn't take a breath without sobbing and shaking her head in denial of some news that her mind would not accept. In shock she had neatly folded the telegram and replaced it in its envelope, which she now offered to Will.

Will took the envelope and first read aloud the return address. "Austin, Texas." Frowning he looked at Arch.

"That's where mother is! What does it say?" Arch demanded, then thought, *Who can be sending her a telegram and why?*

"Oh God, Arch, Mother has died. This is from the Director of the Sanitarium where she lived. It says here that she died of "Pellagra", however you say it."

"When?" asked Arch in disbelief.

"It says here December 28th. That was day before yesterday," Will stated, then added, "I can't believe this".

"What? What else?" Arch asked.

"They are burying her today! We won't even get to say goodbye or have a funeral," added Will.

Suddenly all went quiet. Carlantha's children faced their personal loss, whether it was guilt for not trying harder to take care of her at home, or in not visiting more often, or just withdrew inward to recall personal memories of their beloved mother.

Will and Arch knew there was no use traveling that far just to look at her gravesite, so December 31st midnight of 1919 found no one at the Hall residence in a festive mood nor eager to welcome in the new year.

Chapter 19.... Hillsboro holdup.

They split up before entering town with Sam and Nate on Main Street while Jake and Lewis took a back street. Samuel was making camp along the Brazos River, not far from town, as he had before. While Lewis and Nate covered the mercantile, Sam and Nate were in charge of the feed and grain store. The first day in town was just to look things over and make their separate plan of action. They regrouped back at camp and finished the overall plan.

The next day found them ready as they had already tied off their scarves above their noses and then pulled them down to rest in place until needed. All but Lewis felt confident as they rode back into town and dismounted in alleys either behind or beside their targets.

"You alright?" Jake asked.

"Yeah, sure, why?" Lewis responded with a tremor in his voice.

"Well, you're lookin and soundin mighty nervous and ya can't let it show. I know how ya feel. We've all been there. So just relax and keep it in your head what we are to do and how we're goin to do it," encouraged Jake.

"What if something goes wrong?" Lewis dropped his eyes to the ground.

Jake patted his horse's neck and spoke low, "Ain't nothin goin ta go wrong. Get it outta yer head. Now take a deep breath and do as we planned. Be ready for the signal from Sam."

Sam and Nate found an empty wine keg in the alley behind a tavern, a few blocks from the feed and grain store. Dropping dry grass into it, and counting on the alcohol soaked slats to ignite easily, they positioned it against the tavern and tossed in a match.

They were strolling along Main Street toward their destination when the smoke became evident and residents began to shout, "FIRE, FIRE at the tavern!"

When the confusion was at its utmost they entered the store. Customers were rushing out, either to help or to see the source of the excitement.

As the last customer left the store, Nate stepped forward and blocked the proprietor's path. "All you have to worry about, Sir, is your life and how much it's worth to you."

The middle-aged man had a rotund belly and as he stepped back he looked down the barrel of Nate's pistol, positioned inches away from his nose. He almost lost his balance as he stumbled backward. His eyes showed the fear he felt and traveled from the gun to the man behind it, where he found the scarf-covered face of a man in his early twenties.

"Is this some joke?" the man sputtered.

"Do you see me laughing?" asked Nate coldly.

"No, sir, I do not," answered the man.

"Well, then we're back to the first question. Do you value your life more than the money in that register? I certainly hope not because I'm not in the mood to take a life today," Nate was tall for his age and the older man continued to look first to the gun and then up to Nate's cold stare.

"You can have the money. Just don't shoot," pleaded the man.

"That's what I wanted to hear. Now lay down behind the counter, on your belly and put your hands behind your back," Nate demanded.

The man responded quickly, "Alright, alright. Just don't shoot."

Nate had him hog tied with a rope he wore around his waste for this purpose, gagged with the man's own hanky and the money from the register tucked inside his shirt in a matter of minutes. The storeowner had not even seen Sam, hanging back in the shadows.

One block over and a few doors down, Jake and Lewis had entered the mercantile. The cry of "FIRE" spread to their area and was met with the same response, customers hurrying to satisfy their curiosity or as concerned citizens on their way to be of assistance.

The proprietor was one of the latter and left his store in the care of a young employee. "Lester, mind the store until I return," yelled the man as he hastily removed his apron and threw it over a display of flannel shirts on his way out the door.

The young man's apron, tied around his waist almost touched the floor. It showed dirt from days of cleaning. His attention was drawn to the commotion and what he could see as he craned his neck between and around the people running past.

As the store became empty, Jake's voice filled the room. "Now, Lester, let's not make any hasty moves and cause this itchy finger of mine to squeeze this trigger."

The lad turned slowly toward the voice and saw a person, face hidden behind a triangle tied kerchief, in possession of a gun pointed directly at him. As his mind registered what was taking place his facial expression went from fear to a slow smile spreading across his face. "By all means we don't want that finger to get nervous. Y'all take whatever ya want. Hell, I'll even wrap it for ya!"

His response took Jake and Lewis by surprise. "Don't try no funny stuff. Nothin's worth anyone getting hurt here," warned Jake again.

"Hey, I told ya, This ain't my place and that old man treats me like dirt. You'll get no trouble from me.

Here let me help," He rolled out a length of paper across the counter, ripped it off, emptied the till, piled the money in the middle, folded the corners inward and rolled it closed. He grabbed the end of a spool of twine and deftly tied it off. "Now you won't lose any."

Jake stared at him in utter confusion.

"Well, ya better get goin afore he or someone else comes back," shooed the boy.

Finally realizing the boy was for real and was indeed helping them rob the store; Jake grabbed the money and thanked him.

"Before you leave do ya think ya should maybe hit me or knock me out or somethin?" asked the lad.

"Oh. Well, I usually tie the person up and gag 'em," explained Jake.

"Yeah. That'd be great! Come on. Hurry up. He ain't gonna be gone all day," the boy gleefully offered his hands in front of him.

"No, It has to be behind, so you can't get up. You'll have to lie on your belly and I'll gag you with your apron." Jake said, now laughing with the boy.

"Where do ya want me? Here? Ok, hurry up. Ya can have whatever else ya can carry. I don't care. Makes no never mind ta me." Lester said pointing around the store. Then he positioned himself on his belly and offered his hands behind his back but asked them to not use his apron. "It's filthy and would taste somethin' awful. How about a pair of clean socks from that shelf there?"

Jake complied and as he and Lewis left the store they could hear the boys muffled giggling.

Once outside the teams gathered their horses and moved into the flow of people still gathering to watch or fight the fire that had consumed the barrel and part of the back wall of the tavern it stood against.

Each team joined the crowd at different intervals and eased their way to the outer edge and retraced their way out of town, unnoticed by the citizens intent on stopping the fire threatening to consume not only the tavern but the nearby businesses as well.

This was one campout that was going to be remembered for years to come. Jake was still shaking his head at the chain of events that had placed the well-wrapped package now resting inside his tucked in shirt. He was certainly going to have fun telling about the help he got in robbing the store around the campfire tonight.

Chapter 20... A New Business

After the close call with the detective, they turned their faces southwest and traveled until settling in a small town and purchasing their first business. The "Lykens" family, became the proud owners of a steam laundry in Snyder, Oklahoma.

It had been an obvious decision with Lillie's life long experience when they saw the small "For Sale" sign in the window. The price had consumed most of their ill-gotten gains, but in no time they were running a very successful business; or so it seemed.

Acey was having a hard time adjusting to doing what, in his mind, was "woman's work". He kept it to himself and it festered inside, gnawing at him to the point that he felt men customers questioned his manhood. He tried to fight it off and let it go, but he envisioned men laughing at him behind his back, and women whispering. He read, what his mind felt, in every look and every statement a customer made.

Being in her comfort zone, Lillie did not notice the change in Acey immediately and was unprepared when things began to surface. It had been small things at first, graduating to the point that could no longer be ignored.

As long as he was doing what he had taken upon himself to do, such as the heavy lifting and chopping the wood to keep her fires burning, he was satisfied that he was an asset to the business. But it was when she needed him to mind the counter and deal with the customers that the problems began to surface.

She first noticed with his shortness to a woman customer when the lady commended Acey on how white he was able to keep her banker husband's white shirts.

"Thank you ma'am, but it certainly is not *me* that does the laundry. But I will certainly pass on your compliment to my wife. I help her with the heavy loads and the tubs of water that has to be emptied and changed periodically." Acey's tone was brisk and did not go unnoticed by either the customer or Lillie.

This incident caused Lillie to reflect back to her knowledge of the male ego. *Why can't they just relax and enjoy life and not worry about what others think? I wish he would realize that we are safe here and adjust his attitude.*

The next incident was a verbal confrontation with a gentleman customer. Upon examining his soiled garment, the man innocently stated, "I was eating at the restaurant down the street and my steak flew off my plate and right into my lap. Will you be able to get this grease stain out of my slacks?"

"That's a question you'll haffta ask my wife. I don't do the laundry 'round here. I help with the heavy liftin, not scrubbin other people's clothes," Acey spoke hoarsely.

Both Lillie and the man's heads shot up and they made eye contact as Acey marched out the back door. She hurriedly untied her wet apron and approached the counter. "Let me take a look at that for you." Her smile was apologetic.

He quickly became absorbed in their conversation and the incident was forgotten, on his part.

After dinner that evening, and when she felt that he was in a receptive mood, she confronted him by asking softly, "Acey, do you realize that today you fell back into your old talk? When you were with the customer with the grease on his slacks, you completely lost everything we've both tried to put behind us. It was all there, blurted out and making you

100

sound totally uneducated. We can't slide backward honey, what is bothering you?"

He finally opened up, "I'm real tired of people thinking that I'm doing the laundry around here. I don't like it, not one bit. I see how the men look at me, as if I was not able to hold down a man's job. I hear the women whispering and looking at me. You can't deny it, Lillie. You can't say you don't see it too."

Lillie took a deep breath, "Oh, Acey, IF the men are looking at you in a strange way, it is because they admire someone that can do something that they can not. And as for the women whispering...Yes, Dear, they probably are. All about how good looking you are and what a great body you have. And 'how did such a dowdy woman as *her* ever catch such a handsome devil as him'."

His smile assured her that she had soothed his ego for the time being, but she knew him too well to believe the problem was settled, as she thought *"Tomorrow is tomorrow not to be worried about today"*, and braced herself for another move.

It was quick in coming, for just days later Acey overheard a discussion while getting Rascal shod.

Owners of a livery were expected to do many jobs, such as repairing modes of transportation that ranged from the horse, to wagons of all sorts, to creating branding irons for the ranchers, and were called by various names, depending on the job. Most common was Blacksmith, Smithy or Smith, if building or repairing vehicles, and Farrier if shoeing a horse.

In most towns there was usually a conversation to be found either at the barbershop or the livery and Acey found a very interesting one being shared with a lively group of elderly gentlemen who reminded him of his father's group of old cronies back in Mineral Wells.

101

The circle of men was gathered there with one approaching the blacksmith's fire, sticking one end of a thin piece of kindling into the amber coals. He tamped a pinch of the tobacco into the bowl of his corn cob pipe with his little finger and said, "Up north in Clinton, I hear they've decided to pave their streets and they're looking for some strong backs."

He made his way over to a pile of neatly stacked firewood and took a seat. Then he touched the burning end of the stick to the tobacco and took a long draw on the pipe. His suction on the pipe's stem pulled the fire down to the tobacco until it's leaves ignited and forced smoke up the stem and into his mouth. After another drag to make sure it was lit, he held the burning stick out to the man on his left and continued, "Trouble is, the job won't be permanent. After all, once they get them streets all paved the job will be done. But I hear the pay is pretty good."

The others had found seating on a few old chairs or equipment left for repair and were each busy with his own tobacco "makin's".

One man was concentrating on rolling his cigarette with the string of the tobacco pouch still gripped between his teeth. Another was just a bit ahead of him and was licking the long side of the tissue and in one motion he formed the cigarette with the ease of a veteran smoker. Another had the ends of his cigarette pinched closed and was reaching for the offered fire the story teller had just used to light his pipe.

Each man had his own way of rolling his cigarette, but the custom was to cradle the index finger tip inside a tissue thin paper that was held by the thumb and middle finger. This curve of the paper formed the gutter for the tobacco to be sprinkled into from the pouch using the free hand. The string that opened or closed the pouch usually was closed by a tug between the teeth. After licking the length of one side of the paper the dry side was rolled under and the wet side over to seal the tobacco in. Now some men could do that with one hand, while most used both. Then the ends were pinched, trapping the tobacco in the center.

The scene had made Acey reflect back on happier days of his older brothers and the days when the gang had been on "camp outs" and how they had sat around the campfire after dinnertime and shared stories they had heard here and there.

Hasten sized the men up to be perhaps the elders that occupied most of their time swapping tales and trying to "one up" the other with each tale told.

"Well, if that don't beat all," said a scrawny little man with a shining bald head, "That's up near Weatherford, ain't it? Gettin pretty high and mighty aren't they, just like them easterners."

Nodding and pointing with his freshly lit pipe, the storyteller added, "Yep, some day you'll look out across the way there and you'll see nothin but paved roads criss-crossing the country side."

Shaking his head, one old timer combed his beard with his fingers. "I'm hearing more and more people are sellin their teams and buyin them horseless carriages. Fools they are. That contraption will be just another fad that comes and goes only for the rich. I have no use for one on my ranch."

To his right sat a round man whose belly forbid the fastening of the top button of his overalls, "I beg to differ with you, old friend. You mark my words, the 'automobile' will be the star of the century. It will improve all makes of life from the farmer to the lawyer to the doctor on his rounds, it saves time and does not have to be fed unless it is used. The day is coming when every family will have one."

"Nonsense!" the bearded man argued, "You don't know no more about those machines than I do, and what's more I don't care to know. My team has seen me through many years on the ranch and I don't see a future in a machine that needs oil and gasoline every mile it goes."

Acey turned his mind and attention to the smithy as he bent to work on Rascal.

Standing close, the man always let the horse know he was there. After a pat or two he ran his hand down the leg he wished to work on, then standing sideways and facing backwards, he pulled a hoof up and clenched it between and just above his knees.

Using the old shoe he matched it as closely as he could to those he had in stock and set three of them aside and one into the hot coals then cleaned in and around the inner hoof. With each hoof being different, each shoe had to be forged to fit accordingly.

He gently trimmed and filed the callused frog, a growth protruding from the center of the hoof, to determine the depth of it from the quick, which established how much of the hoof to trim and still allow the shoe to be nailed in place. He knew if he misjudged the depth that he could cripple the animal and he prided himself in knowing that no horse ever suffered from his care. He was quick at his task, switching from trimmer to rasp, cutting and filing, all the time shaping the hoof to a perfect balance. Hunks of curved trimmings fell at his feet and the dust from the rasp rose up into the man's nostrils generating the odor of burning hair.

It was backbreaking work because he not only had to support his own bent weight, but that of the horse who would invariably shift its weight and lean heavily upon him.

As Acey observed the man at work he began to understand many things about the smithy's appearance, as well as his shop.

Long handled fire tongs were used to move the glowing red shoe from fire to anvil, and the sparks that flew from each contact of hammer to metal bounced harmlessly off his heavy leather gloves and apron. But the scars on his bare arms and face were proof that some of those glowing cinders had contacted flesh before landing on the clean dirt floor.

Acey thought to himself, *Those sure could cause a mighty hurt or catch the whole place on fire if landing on skin or loose straw.* He unconsciously backed a few feet away.

With Rascal shod and Acey's payment in hand the blacksmith was free to either join the conversation with the old cronies or continue with his work. He enjoyed their camaraderie but right now he had a room full of items, which needed repairing, and he could not allow himself the luxury of sitting and swapping lies.

The smithy knew that the horseless carriage or automobile, as it was being called, either could be his downfall or his salvation. He could either change with the times, and learn what repairs these machines would need as they passed his way, or find his present line of business dwindle away. He knew that change was inevitable and could see progress was the way of the future, so he had best learn all he could to keep up with the times.

Between the puffing sound of the billows, stoking the fire, the deafening blows of the hammer and the hiss of metal being plunged into the water filled trough, the men's banter could still be heard.

The sounds faded as Acey rode Rascal away with four shiny new shoes and a plan forming to persuade Lillie into moving to this town called Clinton, where he could get a real job and support his family, as was proper.

Chapter 21... Clinton, Oklahoma.

Upon their arrival in Clinton, and after securing a hotel room, Lillie received the landlord's permission to take up her laundry business in its backyard.

She first had to remove the workman's stains with kerosene, and then double wash each garment to remove the ignitable residue and smell. She was hard at work when "Can I have a bicycle, Lillie?" came from behind her.

She jumped like she was shot, "Edward, son, for crying out loud you near scared the daylights out of me!"

Quickly, before he could be told 'no', he added, "I could run errands and such on it. Just like some of the other boys around here. Did you know that one of the boys in my class even has a paper route and makes his own money delivering papers just around town? I could help pay for groceries and things."

"We don't need your money to get by. Your dad and I are working and I don't want you out where only God knows where you are. You can get seriously hurt and how would I explain to your dad when he asks me why I wasn't watching you?" Lillie explained.

Knowing he had a better chance with Lillie than with his father he pressed on. "But I could run errands for you and dad. And I'm getting big enough to take care of myself. He can't say anything when he knows you're working and can't keep an eye on me anyway. Sides, all the other boys have one."

"It is *be*sides, Buster, and if all the other boys had a boil on their butt would you want one too?"

Edward smiled at the nickname, but dropped his chin to his chest and turned away. He knew that Lillie would help him now that she knew he really wanted one. He would just have to wait and see.

Paving streets was not as easy as Acey thought. It was back breaking, hot, sweaty work and the smell that rose from the melted tar of the asphalt was nauseating. He hadn't worked this hard since he split fence posts with his father back in Mineral Wells.

Once in awhile he would find his mind drifting back to the days when he was not constantly on the run, looking over his shoulder or searching a crowd for lawmen, the detective, or anyone familiar.

He knew he could never go back. His pride wouldn't let him. But he realized when he found himself drifting back that a sadness was attached to the memory much like this filthy tar as it stuck to the tools it touched. He knew that it would take the latter part of his shift to clean the shovel and rake that was assigned to him. He found that in the cleaning of the sticky residue that it also cleared his mind of the family he had left behind.

It's not that I'm unhappy with Lillie. She has been a Godsend, but I wonder if Samuel and Will are alive after all that mess on our leaving. I wish I knew how Ma is doing, and how is Sam providing for the family now that I'm gone. I wonder how much Mattie and Lewis have grown, and if Sarah and Henry have had any more children. I sure don't miss Pa. Why did he have to shoot at me? His own flesh and blood and he tried to kill me! Don't make no sense, that's for sure. I wonder how and where Mary and Alva are.

"Lykens! Watch what you're doing there fella! You have to work faster or your area will set too thick in one place and too thin in another, and cause dips in the road, it will!" shouted the foreman from the side of the road.

Acey snapped out of his reverie and quickly smoothed the thickness as even as possible. The embarrassment of being shouted at in front of his

108

coworkers angered him to the depth of his ego and he decided right then that this was not an occupation that he would pursue. *I would like to shove his face into this stinking mess and see him holler then!* He thought. *I'm through with this. I'm telling Lillie tonight to pack and we'll move on. There has to be something better than this.*

Lillie was thrilled at the news. It had been such a burden on her to clean these men's clothes of the awful grime and filth. She breathed a sigh of relief, "You don't know how happy you've made me Acey. I've hated this place ever since we got here. The way you come home each night, completely worn out and the smell has penetrated every fiber of my being. No matter how many baths I take I can't get rid of it. I roll over at night and can smell this stench in my hair and it seems to be seeping out your pores. I can be packed in an hour."

Acey laughed, "Let's not get too hasty. Let's wait until after payday. Where is Edward?"

"He took that BB gun that you bought him and is off seeing what mischief he can do with it no doubt," she answered.

"Now, Lil, you know that I bowed to your wishes when buying it for him. If it were up to me it would have been a .22 rifle. A boy has got to learn to hunt. But you were afraid he'd get hurt so I got him the BB gun instead. He'll be alright," he assured her.

She was near the window and automatically looked down on the street below looking for him. "Oh, he's probably hanging around down at that livery on the corner. I know he's got his eye on one of the bicycles there, but we can't afford one yet." Lillie told Acey about her and Edward's conversation earlier and then added, "You know I called him 'Buster' today and like you said, he seemed to like it. He's so good

Acey; he's had to work twice as hard on all the schooling he misses with us moving so often, but he's smart and he really wants to learn. I've taught him between schools, but it isn't the same as proper schooling. We should reward him some how. He'll be coming on to nine years old soon. Let's think of something nice for his birthday."

"Is that all that's going on in that pretty little head of yours?" Acey asked; already relaxed just in the knowing that they were getting out of this dreadful place.

Smiling from the hidden compliment, Lillie directed the bicycle conversation so that it would become Acey's idea, "Oh, I'm just not sure about it. I know he wants a bike, but how would we pack it with our every move? And we never know where or how we are going to be going next."

"Maybe he could ride it along side the wagon, or if we are traveling too long we can figure out a way of attaching it to the outside. It could come in handy and give him more exercise than just sitting around. It would be near worthless in the high country or the desert in most places, but in and around towns I guess he could get a use out of one, besides, who says we have to wait until his birthday?" Acey agreed.

Changing the subject she added, "And I might say that I'm pretty proud of you and the way you've been using better English. You don't sound like the boy I met over ten years ago."

"Well, you're right about one thing. You *are* pretty, and I'm *not* the boy you met ten years ago. He smiled as he came up behind her, allowing his fingers to trace along her apron ties until they met in front. He closed the distance between them with a gentle tug.

She responded by leaning back against him, and with a flirty scolding, "In the middle of the day? What if Edward should..."

He interrupted with a soft whisper in her ear, "Just lock the door. That'll give us time to get straightened up if he does. The longer you argue the less time we'll have."

She wasted no more as she crossed the room and turned the key.

The next day Lillie was at her chores in the back yard of the hotel when her suspicions were confirmed. She looked up from her wash tub to see the local sheriff with Edward in one hand and the BB gun in the other.

"Is this your boy?" he asked huskily.

"Yes, Edward come here, Son," she answered, reaching out a wet hand for him.

"Not so fast, ma'am, this here boy has had himself a good old time shooting out glass insulators on several of our town's telephone poles," he said as he restrained Edward from leaving his side.

Drying her hands on the already wet apron she lowered her head and mumbled, "Well, Sir... Officer... Sheriff, I...I'm sure he meant no harm. Uh... he doesn't realize the seriousness of his actions, but I...I assure you that he will be severely punished," She kept a hand to her face, rubbing her forehead, in hopes of hiding her features. Then added, "My...my husband and I will be more than happy to pay for the...the replacements of each one he destroyed," she stumbled through her words with her heart in her throat. *I hope he doesn't have our descriptions on file and recognizes us.*

She reached out again and this time was rewarded as the sheriff relinquished his hold so she could pull Edward to her.

"Well, you see that he gets a fit punishment and I won't file charges. And after you pay you can have this gun back. I could keep it! I could, you know." He threatened. "I'll be back with a total of what you owe the city. What room is your residence?" He asked as he turned to leave.

"It's upstairs, room 308, sheriff," she pointed upward.

He nodded his head and grunted, "Good day, ma'am."

Holding his upper arm she bent down and demanded, "EDWARD. What were you thinking? You know better than that! Now your father and I are going to have to pay for each one you shot. How many were there?"

"I didn't shoot all of them. My friend, Mary Humphrey was with me and she shot some too," he whimpered, "Are you gonna tell dad?"

"Don't you think he should know what you've done? As for now you go to our room and you stay there. I can see the stairs, so don't try sneaking out," she warned.

Edward obeyed and went to their room. He was mighty worried about the whooping he was going to get when his dad found out. After he reached the room his thoughts became fears and he decided to run away. He found some rope in the closet where Acey kept his saddle. He tied one end around the bedpost and a large knot in the other. When he was satisfied that the rope would hold he went over the windowsill and down the side of the hotel. He eased himself downward until he came to the knot. Then to his dismay he found that he was still at least fifteen or twenty feet from reaching the ground! He knew at that height he would injure himself and he tried desperately to climb back up. After only a few feet he realized that he wasn't going to make it. His fear turned into panic and he cried out, "LILLIE, LILLIE, HELP. HELP ME LILLIE." Over and over he screamed her name, holding desperately to the knot.

From the backyard Lillie heard his cries but was unsure of which way to go. She ran to the bedroom as her mind raced to understand. She then followed her eyes and ears to the windowsill. Seeing Edward dangling on the end of that rope, half way between herself and the hard ground below, she panicked.

Edward felt a sudden tug on the rope that nearly torn it from his grasp. He looked up to see Lillie's head and shoulders hanging out the window as she pulled him up, hand over hand until she was able to grasp his wrist and pull him into her shaking arms.

"What in tarnation were you thinking?" she half scolded as she smothered his face with kisses. "You could have fallen and been killed!"

Edward clung to her, still too scared to let go. "I didn't want a whooping from dad. I was running away," he answered.

Trying to control her shaking, she said, "Well, I'll make a deal with you. If you promise to NEVER shoot at things that you're not suppose to, I'll take care of paying the sheriff and we won't have to tell your dad. Will you promise me?"

"Yes, Lillie, I won't shoot out no more glass things," he promised. They each kept their word.

Chapter 22...Time goes by.

"Alva, you stay close to mama now. Don't you go wandering off while I'm shopping. I have just a few more things to get and we'll head back home." Mary called to the boy who was in search of more interesting things than "girl stuff".

"Okay, Mama." He answered as he ventured toward a colorful bird sitting on a high perch, near the back of the store. It's feathers were a bright red with hues of blue and green, One couldn't tell where one color stopped and the other began. It was alive and rocking back and forth from one foot to the other, as if walking in place. It made noises he had never heard before and he wanted a better look.

"Aarrkk" came from the bird. "Aarrkk" echoed Alva. The bird turned his head and focused one eye on the boy who was mimicking him.

"Hellow" greeted the bird.

"Hellow" mimicked Alva, with a smile almost too big for his cheeks, and eyes sparkling with wonder.

"That's a parrot, Alva, I believe the man said it was called a macaw," said Mr. Ulrich. "He came from across the world on a big boat."

Alva stood transfixed, and just nodded without removing his eyes from the colorful bird. A full minute went by without bird or boy saying or doing anything but standing and staring at each other.

"Want to feed him? He likes crackers and slices of apples," offered Mr. Ulrich as he peeled and sliced an apple from a barrel near by. He bent and whispered in Alva's ear, "Say, 'Polly want a cracker'? And he'll answer you."

Alva still not taking his eyes from the bird spoke the words, "Polly want a cracker?"

"Polly wanna cracker?" mimicked the parrot. Alva squealed with glee. "Mama, Mama, come see! Come see the pretty bird. It came on a big boat from....way far away" he shouted to Mary.

"What is all this commotion about, Alva? Mr. Ulrich?" Mary questioned as she came toward the two. Following Alva's gaze she continued, "What bird are...oh my, what a pretty bird."

"Pretty Bird, Pretty Bird" mimicked the parrot.

"Purty bird, Purty bird" repeated Alva, who had accepted the slice of apple from Mr. Ulrich and was offering it to the bird. He stood on his tiptoes but his reach was too short, as the perch was high over head. Mr. Ulrich stooped and lifted Alva to his shoulder to enable the boy.

The parrot sidled over to the end of the perch closing the gap between them.

"Are you sure he won't bite?" Mary asked worriedly.

"Hasn't yet, Mary, doubt if he starts now. I think he has taken a shine to your son here," he answered as he lowered the boy back to the floor, "Look, Alva, how he rocks back and forth and bobs his head up and down. He wants to be your friend."

Seeing the delight on Alva's face Mary quietly asked, "How much is it?"

"Oh, I'm sorry, Mary," he whispered, "He's very expensive. I traded for him or I couldn't have afforded him myself. If I put a price on him it would be around fifty dollars. I didn't mean for the boy to desire to own it, I just thought he would enjoy talking to it."

"That's very thoughtful of you Mr. Ulrich, and you are right, it is way out of our price range. It is a wonder how Alva has taken to it though. I've never seen the like."

"It'd be a shame not ta let the boy have thet bird, with'em taking ta each other as they have," came a voice from behind them.

Turning Mary was suddenly frightened to see the all too familiar bulk of George Snider standing so close she could smell not only the liquor on his breath, but his unkempt, sweaty body. The smile left her face and she started backing away, almost walking over the top of Alva.

Mr. Ulrich grabbed the boy and pulled him to safety behind him, then stepped between the two adults, sandwiching Alva between himself and Mary. He knew the history of these two and felt a masculine need to protect her.

"What can I do for you, Mr. Snider?" Mr. Ulrich asked coldly.

Although he blocked their escape he ordered, "One thang ya kin do is get outta my way. I was talkin ta the little lady here. She may not be the blossomin flower she was years ago, but she's still jest as purty," George slurred his answer, then looking past the storeowner he wobbled, balanced himself and continued, "Well, what say purty lady? Want me to buy that purty bird for that youngun of yers? I got me an ider how ya can pay me back."

Mr. Ulrich started backing up with Alva between himself and Mary. Mary retrieved Alva, relieving her defender of one obstacle. Glancing around quickly she saw that they were pretty much cornered.

"George, that is no way to talk to a lady and you are not welcome here when you've been drinking. You know that. The sheriff's already told you after the last time you came in here causing trouble. I'm asking you to leave. NOW," Mr. Ulrich straightened all five foot seven inches of his slight frame and only came to the drunkard's chest. Exhibiting calm authority he did not feel, he hoped to bluff his way out of this dilemma. His time came with the next demand.

"Get outta my way, I said." As George staggered closer to his prey he began to smile. Tobacco juice ran out the corner of his mouth, down his chin and onto his shirt. "None of them Tirrells is here ta stop me this time. Got any music old man? I'm goin ta get that dance I didn't get bafor."

"Why, yes. George. I do have some music. Let me wind up my Victrola. It has great sound. Would you like a waltz?" offered Mr. Ulrich.

Mary could not believe her ears. *What in the world is he thinking? To allow this monster to even touch me is beyond comprehension. And here he was first my defender, and now a coward.* Her hopes were dashed as she heard George agree.

"Yeah, thar ya go ol man. A waltz ta start off with." He stumbled a bit but caught himself on a blanket display. Mr. Ulrich dashed past, before the man straightened himself.

I can't believe this. What on earth has come over Mr. Ulrich? I've never known him to be such a coward. Oh, if only Will or Arch had come to town with me. Mary looked around desperately for a weapon, a place to hide Alva, a way out. *God, help me. Help us.*

Just then a series of events took place. First George took a step backward and reached for his forehead. His hand brought back a glob of gray-white parrot excrement that was slowly sliding down the side of his face.

In rage he made a lunge for the bird that squawked and raced to the opposite end of his perch. George grabbed a blanket and wiped his face, smearing it into the stubble of his beard. As he turned and cursed the feathered bomber, he came face to face with someone very near his own size.

"Well, looky who we got here. Mr. Briles ain't it? Ya wanna dance too? I get er first, then ya can have er," slurred George.

"I don't think so, Mr. Snider. I think the lady answered you a number of years ago and I doubt if she's changed her mind since then. I think you had better leave." Samuel's words came barely above a whisper as he fought the urge to do more bodily harm to this man than Hasten had after the previous altercation.

"Get outta my way, ol man. I'll break ya in half. Everybody knows how yer old lady and her old man done run off together. You "dancing" with *her* now?" George taunted.

"That's enough!" Came a voice from behind Samuel. "You get out of my store and don't ever darken my door way again. Your whole family can go hungry as far as I'm concerned and you can be the one to tell them why. You are a disgrace to this whole community, George Snider."

As both men turned toward the voice, Mr. Ulrich was standing with a double barrel shotgun. Samuel backed down the narrow aisle until he squeezed by Mr. Ulrich, who then aimed both barrels at the drunk man's chest.

George could see the angle of the barrel and knew that the load would take his head clear off his body. "I'm leavin. Didn't mean no harm. Just wanted to dance with the little lady," he claimed.

"We've heard that song before mister. No one believed you then and I sure as hell don't believe you now," growled Mr. Ulrich.

As George made his wobbly way to the door, he was once again bombed by the beautiful bird.

118

After the incident Mary became even more withdrawn and quiet. She refused to go to town and used any excuse to relieve her of the duty.

Letters from Nevy were all she had that kept her looking toward the future instead of the past. She tried to ease the pain of losing Edward by burying herself in her chores. It was hard to put the thoughts of Hasten and Edward out of her mind completely because Alva was the spitting image of his father.

He was growing much faster than Edward had, and his features mirrored his father more each day. He spent his days at play with anyone that had the time. Mary was still allowing him to visit with his cousins out at Tirrell Ranch.

He was in his glory there, with everyone showering him with attention. Family photographs were taken; some with his cousins at the ranch and once Sarah took him to the main photographer in Mineral Wells, where he posed alone by the same chair his mother had sat in for her portrait many years previous. Sarah used the excuse that it was for gifts for everyone, but she kept one tucked away, just in case Hasten came back for the son he had to leave behind. She was taking no chances of Alva being kidnapped like his brother Edward.

Will and Arch did all they could to keep him occupied and in doing so helped him learn his "manly" ways.

The brothers knew that Mary's brooding had left Alva feeling abandoned again. There were days when they would find him standing beside her chair trying to get her attention.

"Mama, Mama, Mama," he persisted, but Mary was so far into her thoughts that she could not hear him. At those times they directed his attention elsewhere. They knew that they could not fill the void of a father, but now that he was without one, they were willing to do their best to bridge the gap.

"Mama, Mama, Mama...." Alva started again.

This time Will broke through Mary's reverie with a sharp tone, "MARY, Alva wants your attention."

Her eyes snapped wider as she straightened in her chair, "What? What did you say, Will? I'm sorry, I wasn't paying attention," she answered.

"I know. You haven't been for a long time. The boy needs you. Arch and I can fill in a few gaps here and there, but we can't do it all. You have to pull yourself back out of your sorrows and pay attention to Alva. He needs you, now more than ever." Will scolded.

"What? What do you mean?" she asked defensively.

Will's voice softened, "Can't you hear the boy calling for you? Over and over he calls out your name. He *needs* your attention."

Realizing that she *had* heard the small voice but it had been so far away that she couldn't connect it to her conscious thought. "Oh dear, I'm sorry Will, I didn't mean to ignore him."

"No need to apologize, dear sister, just tend to the boy you have and not the one you don't. I'm not trying to be cruel, but you have to move on with your life. We've had this talk before, this time I think you need to get away from here and go somewhere where you won't have so many reminders," he offered.

Arch was leaning against the doorway to the kitchen and added, "Maybe go see your half sister Virginia. Didn't you say she lives in San Angelo?"

"How would I go? I have no money to squander on a trip," Mary argued.

Ignoring her comment, Arch added, "And pack a little extra in case she allows you to stay a bit,"

120

"But you boys need a woman around here. Who will cook and clean and mend your clothes?" she asked.

Arch was ready to counter the argument that he knew was coming, "Same person who did when you were married." He regretted sounding so cold, but continued, "We are not helpless. And besides, if the house gets too dirty we may just up and move down there closer to you. How's that sound?"

"But....", she started.

"No buts about it", interrupted Will. Arch and I have a wee bit of money set aside, enough for you and Alva to ride the train. You need to get away for his sake, if not yours. He needs a whole mother with no distractions for awhile."

"And he's getting so big that he can help carry some of your luggage. Your big trunk would probably fit nicely on his back," teased Arch.

His statement ejected a burst of laughter from each of them and for the first time since Nevy left they saw a small spark of hope come alive in her eyes.

"I'll have to write to Ginny and ask her if it would be alright," she thought out loud.

"No you don't. She's asked you to come with every letter she's sent, so go! You know she would love to see you," argued Will. "Why don't you just surprise her. And if after a few days she doesn't beg you to stay, you can write and we'll send you the money to come home," offered Arch.

"Alright. Alright, I will," she answered. Then turning her attention to the boy, she asked, "Alva, would you like to go for a long ride on a train?"

A smile spread slowly across his face, then he blurted out, "Can we? Can we go now?"

Still laughing, Mary answered, "No, Son, but soon... soon."

Chapter 23...The train ride.

Acey had been mulling over a plan and thought he had worked it out before he presented it to Lillie. She was usually game for his plans, but she always made him spell it out so they both knew it to be flawless. This time there were a few unsure segments that he had to work out, and he knew she had a clever mind when it came to polishing a plan.

They had been following the Canadian River just west of Oklahoma City, and were camped on its banks. After the evening meal Lillie was mending a pair of Edward's overalls and with him playing out of ear shot, Acey decided to explain his idea and get Lillie's reaction..

He spoke softly, "Lillie, I've been thinking."

"And?" Still concentrating on her mending, she waited.

"I want to try something new and different," he added.

"In what way?" Her hands became still and she gave him her full attention.

"Well, uh, I'm not sure what you will think." he continued.

"And you won't until you spit it out. What is it for crying out loud?" She wasn't usually short on patience, but tonight when he didn't get to the point she got a bit edgy.

He hesitated, "It's something we've never tried, and it's been awhile since anyone has. Not much since the James Gang, anyway."

"Rob banks?" she questioned aloud. Then, glancing at Edward, she whispered, "Are you out of your mind? Look what happened to them up in Northfield. And then that little pipsqueak shot him in the back. I swear I don't know where you get these ideas..."

"No," he interrupted whispering, "Slow down and let me finish. What I was wondering was, do you think we could rob a train? Just the two of us? You know, just rob the passengers, not the train itself."

She put the mending away and turned toward him. "Let's hear what you've come up with so far," she replied. "But remember there's three of us."

"That's the part I'm having trouble with. What we can do with Edward while we pull it off, but this is what I've thought. You could board the train and ride between two stops, checking out the passengers to see which you believe would be carrying the most money. I could board the train in between stops..."

"How?" she interrupted.

"I can ride Rascal along side the train, catch hold and pull myself aboard." He explained.

"And then what would Rascal do? How fast is the train compared to Rascal? How close could you get to the train while Rascal is dealing with the bedrock beneath the railroad ties? How are you going to escape? Why can't we both board the train together?" She bombarded him with questions.

He took a deep breath and let it out slowly, "Well, I don't know. I don't want them knowing we're together. I'd pretend to rob you too, then they would be looking for a single man, and we could meet up after you get off at the next stop. I didn't think about all that other. Do you think we should bring a third party into the plan?"

"Who? Edward? Absolutely not! He's too young and I'll not have him put in harms way. Some stranger we don't even know? No. We are not going to trust anyone but ourselves. That's why gangs usually get caught, because there are too many people and one that will eventually turn against the others," she shook her head, repeating "No. We will just have to put more thought into this. And the best place to start is at the next town's train depot. Give me more time to think it through, then we'll see."

He knew that as the leader of his young Tirrell Gang he had planned well and they had always made it safely to Lillie's ranch from their "camp outs", but that did not include this new element of a train.

With Edward wandering back toward them, Lillie retrieved her mending and Hasten took out his pocketknife and began to sharpen it. He would give her the time she needed and then they would continue the discussion.

They made camp in the shadow of the recently closed Fort Reno, near the small town of El Reno, where they went separately to the train depot.

With Edward at her side, Lillie made her inquiries, while Acey nonchalantly checked the distance from a train's handrail to the outside edge of its bedrock, and even walked Rascal alongside a parked train that was taking on water.

Next she found the town's library and under the ruse of moving there, asked about the school, church, businesses and the more prominent families that might be in need of a laundress. The librarian was very helpful and provided her with much needed information, as well as maps of the vicinity.

Meanwhile Acey was visiting the assayer's office in search of property for sale and asked if the agent knew of any work that might be available.

All said and done each found his answers and met back at camp. After picking the small town of Yukon, they spent most of the next day aboard the train. Taking window seats on opposite sides of the train they were able to study the terrain to find the best location to fulfill the plan.

Just as the train slowed to climb a slight grade, Lillie spotted a likely site, pulled her hanky and coughed into it. Acey acknowledged the signal and rose from his seat, walking up and down the aisle as if to relieve a leg cramp, he saw the grove of trees to the south and returning to his seat he gave a slight nod. With the location chosen their plan was underway.

That night, after Edward was fast asleep Lillie motioned for Acey to walk with her out of hearing range but within eyesight of the sleeping boy.

"I think I've got it all worked out, so let's go over it step by step. We've already established, in the minds of a few, that we are planning a move here. One main problem was 'what to do with Edward', right?" she hesitated to insure she had his attention, then went on, "I will enroll him in school and leave him there where he will be safe all day. You ride Rascal and I'll follow with Maudie and the hack to that thicket. You can leave Rascal there and we'll take the hack to the depot and purchase our tickets separately, board the train and sit as strangers..."

"What if someone sees us together in the hack?" he interrupted.

"Oh, right. Well, let's see." She pondered a moment before continuing, "I know, I'll throw some bedding in the back and you can hide under one of the blankets until I give a signal that it's clear for you to hop out. When you do, go straight in and get your ticket." she offered.

"Okay, where are you going to park the hack?" he asked.

"At the livery behind the depot. That way Maudie won't be harnessed to the cart for long. I'll tell the proprietor that I'm going shopping in Yukon and will return later in the day." She answered, then added, "At the designated place you will pull your handkerchief over your face, remove the pillowcase from inside your shirt and start demanding people to put their wallets and purses in it."

Visualizing the scenario as she described it Acey suddenly asked, "How can I hold the pillowcase open and threaten them with my gun?"

Lillie realized his point. Lines creased her brow as she thought, then suddenly exclaimed, "I know. You will make *me* hold the pillowcase and threaten to shoot me if anything goes wrong. I will act frightened and plead with the people to spare my life. And you can order them all to face forward and not look at you as I move down the aisle to each person."

"Yes, that's good. I like that." Acey smiled, nodding as he added, "You've always been able to think things out. I'm glad you're on my side."

She accepted the compliment and continued, "When it's done, you can back your way to the exit, still threatening people to keep looking forward. When we get to that incline it should be slow enough for you to jump off safely. And in case someone ignores the threat and looks back, head north on foot. As soon as the train is out of sight, double back and run like crazy to Rascal. When you get to him, change your clothes and dispose of the ones you took off before you get to our camp. I'll do what I have to and return on the next train."

"Where do we meet afterwards?" Acey asked.

"According to the train schedule I will be home in time to get the rig and pick up Edward, but in case something happens and I'm not on that train, you'll need to pick him up. Get a room at the hotel that looks out onto the depot's platform. You'll see me get off and I'll go straight to the livery."

126

"But how can I go and pick up Edward when we are not suppose to know each other?" he asked.

"Good point," she was pleased that he was on his toes and covering all angles. "Hmmmm, I know no one has seen us together yet. But they don't know that we weren't married and just running errands separately. But we won't use that unless we have to. I think we had better do it as if we're traveling alone."

"I agree. I don't know about you, but I'm about all *thinked* out." He sighed. "It's funny how just the planning can tire a body out."

She nodded in agreement. *Tomorrow is tomorrow not to be worried about today,* she thought to herself. *Now just believe it!*

When Edward entered the school, Mollie followed Lillie's command to "stay", and found a comfortable spot nearby to wait. Lillie then picked up Acey at the designated spot.

He decided to hobble Rascal and loosened the girth, for comfort. Then he removed the bridle and emptied a small bag of grain beside the creek running through the thicket.

The plan continued to run smoothly as they reached the depot. With the train already in the station and a small group gathered on the platform, she approached the ticket window and inquired quietly, "How much for a round trip ticket to Yukon?"

The depot clerk checked his schedule and told her the price. She made the payment and with ticket in hand she found an empty bench on which to wait. Her eyes swept the platform and spotted Acey leaning against the corner of the building with hands in his pockets and hat down low. He wore his oldest clothes and looked totally opposite of herself in her finest dress and carrying a laced edged parasol.

Their eyes barely made contact as they kept a close eye on the group of waiting passengers. She noticed those inside the waiting train that had declined the offer of stretching their legs during the short stop at El Reno.

Lillie was taken back in time as she watched two Negro porters leave the depot, loaded down with luggage. They placed the baggage on the platform near the train steps as one continued to climb aboard. The first porter handed each piece up to the second who checked the labels to determine which stateroom he was to deliver them.

i wonder if Zeke is still at the Hexagon Hotel back in Mineral Wells? He was such a helpful and dear person. It was hard for her to place people in categories of race or occupation being of a lesser status than another. Each job had to be fulfilled by someone, and the lesser of those jobs should not be left to what some people felt was a lesser class of people. *No matter the color or the job everything should be treated equally. Why was there hate for people because their skin was a different color? All the righteous people that I know have a different color of white skin.* But this memory also included Samuel and she shook her head to clear it of another dear person she had left behind.

"ALL ABOARD. THE ROCK ISLAND LINE TO YUKON AND OKLAHOMA CITY," shouted the conductor.

With another quick glance at each other, they mingled with the group and boarded the train, sitting at opposite sides in the back row seats.

The train had progressed about halfway to the thicket when Lillie saw a motion out of the corner of her eye. After Acey had her attention he slowly nodded and looked at something forward. She eased over to the aisle seat and looked to where his eyes directed. She saw the bowler hat and glanced back to Acey. He was ever so slightly shaking his head. She knew that he could see more of the gentleman under it than she could and realized he had recognized the detective that hounded their trail! Knowing that he too could recognize both of them, she felt fear rise from the pit of her stomach and into her throat.

As she was struggling to clear her mind and think of a way out of their situation she saw the bowler rise followed by the man under it. Acey pulled his hat over his face and feigned sleep.

Eckstein turned and began scanning the faces of the passengers. Before his gaze could reach Lillie, she retrieved her hanky from her sleeve, rumpled it and covered as much of her face as she could.

Sliding back to her original seat, she allowed her body to lean into her hand and pretended to cry softly to herself. She needed very little acting to tremble with emotion.

Slowly he made his way down the aisle, his hands touching the top of each seat that he passed. She turned closer to the window.

"Ma'am, is there something I can do for you? You seem to be quite upset about something, I am a security agent for the Rock Island Line Railroad and if something has happened to upset you I would like to know so I can relieve your stress," he inquired.

She shook her head and with her voice muffled by the hanky she whimpered, "No. Thank You, it's personal. I'm sorry to have disturbed anyone." With her free hand she waved him away. "I'll be alright."

"Perhaps I could get you a drink of water? I carry a canteen on these long rides," he offered.

Nodding she answered, "Perhaps the water may help. Thank you."

"Well, that's better, I'll be right back," he said.

Knowing that he was going to recognize them at the next stop she motioned Acey to leave the train.

As Eckstein offered her the tin cup, he claimed the empty seat beside her.

Her heart was pounding so hard she thought he must surely hear it. *If you don't be careful girl you will really faint and then it will be all over. Get hold of yourself and think.* She reached for the cup and purposely let it slide out of her trembling hand.

The cup first landed in his lap before continuing to the floor, splattering its contents all down his front.

"Oh, how clumsy of me, please maybe it's best you just leave me. You see, I've just got word that my mother has passed away and I have to make all the arrangements," still hiding behind her hanky.

Frustrated now, at the clumsy woman for messing up his uniform and spoiling his neat and tidy appearance, he retrieved the cup and stated, "If you're sure there's nothing I can do, then I'll leave you to your grief. If you change your mind, I'm right up front here." As he tipped his hat he added, "George Eckstein at your service." With that he turned back toward his seat.

When Lillie quickly glanced in Acey's direction she found his seat empty. She was relieved to know that her deception had given him the opportunity to get safely off the train. Now all she had to do was find a way of dodging the detective at the Yukon station.

Fear can do many things to a person's body, and it played havoc on Lillie's. She realized that it was giving her the out she was looking for.

As they began to disembark at the Yukon station, she took the back door and hopped down to the platform and asked one of the porters the location of the nearest privy. He pointed to the outhouse on the hill behind the ticket office and with a sweeping glance she located the bowler hat in the midst of the passengers as they mingled near the front of the car.

Hurriedly she picked her way across the baggage filled platform and rushed to the outhouse, locking herself in. *All I have to do is remain here until the train continues on to Oklahoma City.*

The wait had been a bit longer than she anticipated and she was forced to send uncomfortable passengers in search of other privies near by.

As each person turned away she peeked through a knothole to see if the train had left yet and while waiting she thought to herself, *Well, its pretty near true. Between that close call and the stench in here, my stomach is threatening to eliminate, and I'm not sure which end it will choose.*

Finally she heard, "ALL ABOARD THE ROCK ISLAND LINE FOR OKLAHOMA CITY AND POINTS EAST!" and watched through the knothole as her fellow passengers and the bowler hat boarded the train. When it was out of sight she felt safe enough to leave her sanctuary and board the next westbound train.

Chapter 24... Letters from Nevy.

Spring of 1920 found few changes in the lives of the families left behind, but life goes on and one day Will brought news home to the Hall residence.

"Sis, I got the mail, and it seems you have a letter from Nevy, probably asking why you didn't make that trip we spoke of. Or did you even tell him that we offered?

Mary was at his side before he could retrieve the bundle from inside his tucked in flannel shirt. "Yes I told him, and he understood when he found out Alva had come down with the measles. I was just as disappointed as anyone, but it was God's will and we just have to accept it. There will be another chance to make the trip one of these days."

Still holding on to the stack he changed the subject, "I spoke to Sam Tirrell at the store today and it seems that Sarah's having a birthday party for one of her little ones and wanted us to know that Alva was invited."

"Oh, I don't know," she answered," He was just out there last week and every time he comes home he doesn't want to mind me."

She tugged at the mail but Will held on, with a smile spreading across his face. "You know he loves to play with his cousins, and even if the Tirrells spoil him a bit, he settles down after a day or so. You know he'd love to go to a party."

She tugged again, giving him a threatening look. "Well then you're just going to have to find out which one of the children the party is for and I will have to find them a gift. Would you let go?"

"Of course I'd let him go." He teased her, knowing what she meant.

"You know darn well what I mean, William, and I will think better about it *after* you release your hold on this mail!" With a furrowed brow her eyes were locked on to his.

When he saw that her neck was bowed and her spine was stiff in a stance as if readying for battle, he smiled and relinquished the letters so quickly that she had to take a step backwards to steady herself.

Mary was used to the brotherly teasing after all these years, but it sometimes could get aggravating. Especially when she recognized the handwriting of Nevy. She just wanted her hands on the letter and to be left alone so she could absorb his written word.

He saw the smile begin to spread as she turned her back and hurried to her bedroom for privacy.

Will's words followed her as she swept across the living room, "Be sure to tell us everything he has to say now. I'm sure he is writing to Arch and me too."

At the dinner table she divulged that Nevy *had* mentioned their names, and asked about their health. He also mentioned that the carnival would start its rounds as soon as the roads were passable for some of the large heavy wagons that didn't go by train. The owners owned train cars for many of their animals and performers, which shortened their passage and eased some of the heavy work. Nevy's wagon was considered a part of the entourage, which allowed him a place on one of the flatbed cars where he anchored his food wagon. Mary pulled the letter from her apron pocket and rifled through the pages until she found what she was looking for. "He writes that he has been married before, but she wanted him to give up the carnival life so they divorced. He has a daughter by that marriage, named Gladys. Isn't that something? I have a boy and he has a girl. He also has a brother named David and two sisters, an older one named Roxie and a younger one named Lizzie, living near

133

San Angelo." She went on to read that this year's itinerary showed the carnival arriving in Mineral Wells late in the summer on its way back to their winter quarters, and him to San Angelo.

"Well, now. That will give you time to make a few new dresses to wile his attention away from the carnival in his spare time," Arch teased.

"James Archie, when have you ever seen me *wile* a man for his attention?" she challenged. "Besides we are just friends and enjoy each others letters," she insisted.

Will joined in the tease, "Oh ho, did you hear that brother? Me thinks she doth protest too much."

Arch winked at Will and added, "Well, all I have to say, Sis, is if you set your cap for that man he won't stand a chance. I think he's already smitten by your charms. Why else would he still be writing all those letters? What does he have to say that makes those letters so fat?"

"Now just wouldn't you like to know!" she teased back. Picking her napkin from her lap she tossed it at Arch hitting him in the chest and down to his plate.

Looking down at the napkin sitting in the middle of his unfinished meal, then back at her through his eyebrows he tapped his fork at her. With a mock scolding "Here, here, sister dear, it's one thing to deprive me from the content of your letters, but when it comes to my dinner, that's a whole new can of worms you're stirring,"

The three adults burst into laughter at the same time startling Alva who had been told not to play at the table, now here they were breaking the rules.

No one heard a sound nor saw the shadow as it crept away from the kitchen window.

Chapter 25...Acey won't give up.

"Listen to me. I can do this. Just hear me out." Acey pleaded.

Checking to see if Edward was really sleeping, "All right, I'll listen, but keep your voice down," she whispered her warning.

"We've spent enough time and money checking on that pipsqueak detective's schedule. We know the route as well as we're going to. This time I'm going to do as I thought at first. I'm going to board the train from Rascal's back. When I leave the saddle he will head for that thicket because he knows there is water and feed there." Acey explained and hurried on before she could interrupt, "The trip is short enough that I won't have much time between stops to get everyone's money and get off. So I won't be that far away from the thicket that I can't walk to it, like I did that first day. This is how I will get them to place their stuff in the pillowcase." He held the pillowcase open, with one hand holding his pistol. "I can hold the case like this and still point my gun at them. When I get off at the next grade I'll do as you say and head opposite to where Rascal is and then turn back. I've gone over and over this in my mind and I know it will work, and you won't have to be involved. If one of us gets caught, there's someone left to take care of Edward. That was something we didn't take into consideration before. Remember how you felt about being sent to an orphanage when you ran away? Do you want that for him?" He had it all out. Now he waited for her argument.

"You are right about us being selfish when we omitted what would happen to Edward in our plans. We'll never do that again. Okay, Acey, I'll let you try this, but I don't know why you are so hell bent on using Rascal that way. It would be different if you had done this before, but you haven't," she stated.

"No, but it can't be that hard," he answered.

Lillie was standing in her normal stance with open hands on hips, thumbs forward and fingers back. She couldn't help but remind him, "Well, I certainly hope not. You stay behind those passengers and make them face forward. And keep the handkerchief over your face, and hat...."

"Lillie, I'll be careful. I can do this. I managed a few things before I met you, remember?" he asked.

She closed her mouth, but her eyes spoke volumes.

In his planning Acey decided that the best time to obtain the most from the passengers was in the early evening when they were headed into the city for an evening of dinner and perhaps the opera. He chose Saturday. He envisioned the fat wallets of the wealthy as he urged Rascal faster. It was a short trip from El Reno to Oklahoma City and he had to be precise in each of his movements. He touched his shirt to insure the pillowcase was still inside.

As his plan began to unfold, he reached the spot he had chosen to wait, but the train was already coming and he had to move faster and get close to the tracks.

The train began to pull the grade and slowed to a speed that Rascal was able to match. Acey pushed him a little harder to enable a good grasp of the handrail to the steps. He reached out, grasped the railing and slipped his boots out of the stirrups. As he pulled his weight free from Rascal's back, and the horse veered from beneath him, Acey realized he was in trouble.

He had not put all his weight on his hands for a long time. He was strong in all parts of his body and had never questioned his hands.

The pain he had experienced off and on for the past couple of years both in his back and hands, was nothing to the excruciating messages that shot from his hands to his brain and cried out to let go. The sight of the rocky rail bed below forced his hands to hold on. But the pain was severe and his weight became unbearable. His body began to slip down the handrail as he tried desperately to pull himself up. Then his feet began to bounce off the rocks and railroad ties below. He struggled to hang on but the pain ignored the danger signals from the brain and successfully demanded the hands to release.

Acey's body bounced and rolled across the rocks, rail bed and ground until it came to a stop a few yards from the tracks. The passengers, unaware of the man who would have robbed them, rode merrily toward their destinations, as he lay unconscious in the darkening night.

Pacing the floor and checking her pendant watch, Lillie knew something was terribly wrong. The horizon in the east was casting light that bounced off the clouds above, turning them almost scarlet. It would have been beautiful if she hadn't been so worried. "*Red skies at night sailor's delight, "Red skies in the morning, sailor take warning"* crossed her mind as she viewed the oncoming sunrise from the hotel window. *Where in tarnation is that man?* From her vantagepoint she could see the depot's platform a block away. Trains had come and gone and although she didn't expect to see him depart from one, she couldn't help but search the passengers as they left the train.

137

"Mollie, you stay with Edward. I have to go find Acey." She quietly spoke to the dog. A wagging thump of the dog's tail told Lillie that she understood and agreed.

Instinctively Lillie hitched Maudie to the wagon and headed out. She reined the mule in the direction she knew Acey had taken and began to drive parallel with the tracks. At the thicket she found Rascal leisurely grazing on the dew dampened grass along the small stream.

Fighting fear and desperation she tied the horse to the wagon. *Which way do I go? East? West? He had to have gotten on the train or Rascal wouldn't be here. Did he get caught? Is he in jail? Is he hurt somewhere?* Something told her to search along the tracks before going back to town. *Maybe he twisted an ankle and can't walk. Oh, I shouldn't have let him go by himself. If he would have just listened to me! Men and their stupid pride. What makes them feel that they have to take care of women as if we're helpless? Got to be the MAN of the house. So much hogwash!*

Maudie's ears came up and Lillie fought to see what grabbed her interest. *Something out of place, can't put my finger on it, but something's not right. It's ACEY! If there's a God in heaven, Please don't let him be dead.*

As Maudie came to a stop Lillie was off the wagon and at Acey's side. Where there wasn't blood there was dirt or both. She came to a running slide and fell to her knees. When she rolled him over he moaned and she cried out in relief. "ACEY, Acey, oh honey where does it hurt. Lie still. Let me check you over."

He moaned, "I knew you would come. I just had to wait. I knew you would be here. But it's my back. It won't let me get up. I can't move without a lot of pain. I tried to get to you, but it hurts too much to move."

"What can we do? You need a doctor, but what can we say happened? Did anyone see you? Did you get on the train? Did someone push you off the train? How can I get you in the wagon? I don't know what to do." She rambled as she gently moved her hands up and down each side of his body, checking for broken bones.

Acey groaned and shook his head. Looking at his hands before him he answered, "No. My hands wouldn't hold me, Lillie. They couldn't hold my weight. I was drug for awhile, but they hurt so much I had to let go."

He had abrasions and bruises and a scalp wound that had caused most of the blood. He tried to raise himself, but cried out.

She flinched with his painful cry and told him to lay still. "If you'd have listened to me this would never have happened, but no, you have to go out and try to prove something," she muttered.

"Not now Lillie, that is not going to help us one bit. You can scold me all you want to when we get out of this mess," he muttered back. "Where's Edward?"

"I left him asleep. Mollie is watching over him." She grunted as she moved to his other side.

Taking hold of one of his legs, and with one hand on the ankle and the other under the knee she slowly began to lift it. He didn't cry out. *That must be a good sign. At least I hope it is. I can't remember what Doctor Dan did with back injuries. Oh, yes, I think he used to help them to sit by first having them roll to their side, bending their legs and letting them swing the legs down as he lifted them up sideways, but that was while they were on an examining bed.*

139

"Just a minute Acey, I want to try something. Try rolling over to your side. Now bend your legs up. Can you do that without pain?" She asked.

"I think so. My legs don't seem to hurt much. My lower back hurts the most," he answered.

"Okay, now put your heels as close as you can to your butt. I'm going to get behind you and pull under your armpits to get you on your feet," she explained.

"I'll sure as hell try. We can't stay out here without eventually being seen," he said, trying to make light of their situation.

"Okay. Ready?" she asked.

"Ready," he answered.

"One, two, and thrrreeee," she grunted as she strained every muscle in her body.

He pushed with his legs and came to an upright position, but wobbly and unsure. She braced herself under his left armpit and reached her right arm around his back and grabbed his belt on the right side. Together they shuffled slowly around to the back of the wagon. As long as he stood perfectly straight the pain was less severe, but he could not even drop his chin without feeling the muscles all the way to his tailbone explode in fire hot pain.

Once seated at the tail end of the wagon with his knees hanging over, she had him hold on and keep as straight as possible as she very slowly coaxed Maudie forward trying hard not to lurch.

The ride back to town was the worst pain Acey had ever known in his life, with each lean of the wagon and bump in the road he fought not to cry out, knowing the pain had to be tolerated in order to get to a doctor.

It was full daylight by the time they pulled up to the doctor's house. The shingle hanging above his porch claimed "Dr. Dennis Heard" lived there.

Hurrying to the door she knocked soundly and waited, looking back to see if Hasten was all right. It seemed to take forever before she heard footsteps and the door finally open.

"Oh thank heavens doctor. It's my husband. He took a bad fall from his horse. It's his back that he is complaining of. Will you help me get him out of the wagon? She blurted out as she headed back to Acey.

"Just a minute ma'am, I think we'll be better off if I get my gurney," said the doctor. "If it's serious we don't want to make it any worse."

Lillie waited at Acey's side as the man brought the gurney through the door and down the steps. It was made of canvas, stretched between two heavy poles and had been rolled up for storage.

"Can he lay back on his side so we can push one side as far under him as possible?" The doc asked.

"Yes, I think so, if I raise his legs maybe. Acey, can you help us a bit? Let me know if lifting your legs hurts too much." She spoke anxiously as she and the doc worked at getting the gurney in place. "There, that's good. You're doing great, honey, yes, that's good. Ok, now lets roll you over nice and easy."

Acey gave a stifled moan but forced himself to do whatever was needed. As they got him arranged on the canvas between the poles Lillie jumped into the wagon bed and grabbed the handles near his head.

Doctor Heard just silently shook his head at the determination that he had seen over the years that takes hold of a woman when it comes to her loved ones. He has seen women push themselves beyond

141

what even a man can endure and go on until the crisis is over before they take inventory of their own needs.

He backed up to the gurney and took hold of the handles near Acey's feet. "Are you ready ma'am?" he asked. "We have to make sure we don't jar him more than we have to, so take it slow getting down from the wagon. And keep him level as we go up my porch steps."

Lillie did as she was told and the doctor never felt the difference of her decline. Again he just shook his head and took the lead with no doubt in his mind that this man was in loving hands.

After she was sure that Acey was comfortable and the doc was beginning to examine him she said, "I'll be right back. I have to go get our son."

"You take your time, Mrs…I'm sorry I didn't get your name. I understand his name is Acey, but that's all I've heard," answered the doctor.

"Oh, I'm sorry. My name is Lillie…Lillie Lykens and of course he is Acey Lykens. I won't be long," she stated. Keeping her eyes on Acey she slowly backed out the front door.

Chapter 26...The Prowler

"Arch, have you seen anything particular going on around here lately?" asked Will.

"What do you mean by particular? Seems like life is going along pretty good," Arch answered.

"Well, I don't know if it's my imagination or what, but it seems to me there's been someone or something prowling around the property. Seems like most every day I either see bushes move when there's no wind and sounds where I can't find the source," Will explained.

"Being's you brought it up, I thought I heard someone in the tool shed the other day. I came in the house for the rifle in case it was a varmint, but there was nothing there. Nothing misplaced or anything. I just shrugged it off," Arch paused a second then added, "Think we should set a trap? It would be awful bad to catch a skunk. We wouldn't be able to go in that shed for quite a while."

"No, but I think we'd better start closing up the doors and securing the latch for awhile, just to make sure. Better tell Mary to do the same."

"Sure you want to give her something more to worry about, brother?" asked Arch.

"You may have a point, but we've both got to keep an eye open and if she has a heads up about our concern she'll be more apt to keep it in mind," said Will.

"What do you think it could be? A wild animal prowling around?" Mary questioned, "We don't have livestock to attract them, so why would they hang around here? You don't suppose it could be something that could hurt Alva do you?"

"That's the point, Sis, I haven't seen it, and not really positive that there *is* something out there. It's

143

more like a feeling of being watched and bushes moving and noises I can't explain," said Will.

"Maybe I shouldn't let Alva play outside for awhile," Mary said in a thoughtful voice.

"As long as he stays inside the yard I'm sure he'll be fine. Like I said it maybe nothing," Arch stated, trying to minimize her worries. He got Will aside and said, "I think it'd be a good idea if we left the rifle near the kitchen door for awhile, just to be safe."

"Good idea, little brother," answered Will.

Days went by without another incident and the subject was all but forgotten. The brothers left early one morning, Arch to fill the grocery list Mary had given him and Will to deliver a rocking chair he had finished for a customer.

When Mary looked out the front window to check on Alva, he wasn't in the yard where he was supposed to be. She left the window and went outside on the porch, "Alva, Alva where are you?" she called. No answer. ALVA you come here this instant! She hollered. Still no answer. She panicked and left the porch, circling the house constantly calling his name. *Oh dear God, where is he? What if Hasten has stolen him too? What if he went to the stream behind the shed? Where could he be?* She continued to call and wait for a sound, afraid to go one way in case he was in another. Finally she headed toward the stream out back. She rounded the corner of the house and saw that the shed's door was ajar. *That boy is going to get his come-upance if he's in there. He knows he's not supposed to play with his uncles' tools. Most of them are sharp and he could fall... oh Dear God, don't let that have happened!* She prayed as she ran.

At the threshold she peered into darkness. *Should I take time to light a lantern or wait for my eyes to adjust? What if he's lying there bleeding to death...Oh God in heaven let him be all right. I promise not to spank him if he'll just be all right.* She continued to pray.

As her eyes adjusted to the darkness, she saw a movement. Her eyes strained to see before she ran forward. What she saw brought a scream to her lips.

Before her stood George Snider, holding a kicking squirming Alva. One arm held the boy against the large man's hip, head forward and flailing legs behind. The other hand clamped over the boy's mouth.

"WHAT ARE YOU DOING? LET HIM GO YOU BIG BULLY. HE'S JUST A LITTLE BOY!" She shrieked.

"Oh, I'll let him go when I get what I come for. Something due me for years and there's no one here to stop me this time," he gloated. "You want this boy to live you'll do as I say."

She quickly searched for some kind of weapon. No rake, no pitchfork, not even a hammer within her reach. "IN THE NAME OF JESUS, GIVE HIM TO ME THIS MINUTE," she continued to scream.

He seemed to revel in her desperation. He had only wanted a dance that night, years ago, and she put up such a fuss that he had been disgraced as Mr. Tirrell's interference sent him away in shame. If that wasn't bad enough, the next day he had been accosted by Hasten on the road headed to town and was soundly beaten.

He remembered Hasten riding up to him on the road and before he could raise an arm in defense he saw Hasten swing and felt the blow of a very hard fist on his left cheek. The next thing he knew they were on the ground and Hasten was over him hitting with one blow after the other until all went black.

After he awoke later and rode home, all he would tell people was that he had been thrown from his horse.

"There's no one to protect you now, little lady. You'll do as I say or I'll snap your boy's neck like a twig," he growled.

Scared now looking at Alva and how vulnerable he was made her plead, "What do you want? Why don't you leave us alone? I never did anything to make you follow Satan's path," she hoped the fear of God would persuade him to let Alva go.

"Don't you worry about what path I'm treading. You're so high and mighty you think you're sitting in the palm of God's hand," he accused.

Seeing that she had made him at least think of their heavenly Father she pressed, "But we all ARE, Mr. Snider. We are ALL in God's hand. He loves each of us and only wants us to follow the right path," she spoke quickly to keep his mind occupied. "Don't you see?"

"I see that this one is going to see Jesus right quick if you don't shut up and do as I say! Now get over here and show me how much you want this kid to live," he threatened.

When she hesitated, he swung Alva around to his chest and removing his hand from his mouth he placed it around the boys skull. "I'm warning you I'll snap his neck!"

George did not realize Alva's length nor the proximity of the boy's feet to his groin until it was too late.

Alva brought his right leg up high in front of him and swung it back with as much force as he could muster. The blow landed in the man's most vulnerable spot, sending him to his knees, gasping for air. Both hands left the boy and clutched the stricken area.

146

When Alva hit the ground he jumped up and ran to the safety of his mother's arms. While George was still on his knees, forehead on the ground she seized the opportunity and backed out the door. Still clutching Alva she raced to the house and locked the door behind her. It was then that she noticed the rifle beside the doorway. Setting Alva down she told him to hide in the broom closet. She realized that she knew nothing about shooting a gun. *Oh why didn't I let the boys teach me, or at least I could have paid closer attention when they tried to show me.*

After seeing that Alva had obeyed, she went to the bedroom window that faced the shed and back yard. The gun shook in her hands as she held it across her body and watched the door of the shed. *Where is he? Is he still in there or did he already come out and leave as I ran to the house? No, I don't think he had time. He's still in there.*

Then the door opened. Slowly at first, then she saw him standing in the doorway, holding on the frame for support. He started toward the house, slow but with purpose.

She yelled at him, "YOU BETTER LEAVE AND NEVER COME BACK. I'VE GOT A GUN AND I'M NOT AFRAID TO USE IT," she bluffed.

He hesitated. She set the gun down, unlocked and raised the bottom window, then stuck the barrel of the rifle out between the curtains so he could see it.

That did it. He raised himself as tall as his aching groin would allow and backed away with his hands in the air until he was around the corner of the shed, out of sight.

Fear kept her diligently pacing from window to window, checking for any movement. She finally allowed Alva to leave his sanctuary. They snuggled in the rocking chair, with the rifle across her lap, until they heard Will and Arch call out to open the door.

"What in blazes possessed you to lock the door?" Will asked

To their bewilderment she answered, "I'll tell you everything as soon as you show me how to shoot this thing."

Chapter 27...The Wheelchair

Lillie had searched Dr. Dan's medical books, one after the other trying to find some cure to ease the pain that Acey was forced to endure. She found what she thought was the main problem but could find no remedy.

Acey couldn't walk. His standing was minimal and then only with crutches. Lillie was near panic as she thought ahead of their future. *How can I help ease his pain? What work can he do until we find a cure? How long will it take? I can do laundry and such, but we are going to have to settle someplace where he can give his back the time it needs to heal.*

Every town they came to, Lillie sought doctor's advice but always heard the same diagnosis, "The body would either heal itself or not, there was no cure for spinal injuries." In disbelief they followed every possible lead, one of which was a small town to the southwest called Sulphur. It was rumored that for many centuries Indians of the Oklahoma Territory had taken their sick to the springs for cures. Being's this was so like the history of Mineral Wells they decided it was worth a try. They traveled south along part of the old Chisholm Trail to the town of Duncan where they turned and traveled east until locating their destination.

During this last journey Acey brought down what little game he could from his seat in the wagon. With arthritis slowly disfiguring his hands he taught Edward the skills of hunting, skinning and cleaning the game.

Lillie cooked over the open campfire near the wagon. She did what she could to ease Acey's pain and single-handed obtained expenses the best way she knew how. With each man left in an alley she was unsure if the tap on the head might have been a little too hard, or not hard enough, but her luck held and she was able to provide food for the family and medicine for Acey.

Edward got his bike before his birthday and as hard as he tried he had found it difficult to ride the trail very long without his legs getting tired. It got so the bike was in the wagon more than on the trail and he became despondent that he did not have streets instead of the ruts and obstacles that blocked his way. After they reached Sulphur, he rode it to school and was very proud that he was among the few that owned one.

It seemed at first that the baths at the springs were easing Acey's pain, which stirred their hopes, but his weight loss exposed a serious threat to his recovery.

Lillie again set up her laundry business and worked extra hard to meet expenses. After splurging and eating in a small café one night Acey brought up a whole new idea.

"I've been thinking about a change that would be good for us. You're a good cook, and I could help in many ways, and Edward too..."

"Get to the point, Acey, what are you thinking 'would be good for us'? She interrupted. "And what has my cooking got to do with it?"

"Well, you're wearing yourself out with the extra load you've taken on, and I think if we owned a restaurant your work would be easier," Acey said.

"Easier? What do you know about restaurant business that I don't?" she quipped.

"Nothing yet, but I'm sure if we bought one the owners would show us the ropes and teach us what we need to know," he offered.

He thought he saw an opening as she turned and gave him a doubtful look. "Come on Lillie. How much harder could it be than what you've been doing?"

"I repeat, I know nothing about restaurant business and neither do you. What is the *real* reason you want this change?" she asked,

"Like I said it would be easier work. You wouldn't have to lift those heavy baskets of wet clothes or bend over those tubs all day long," he said.

"No, I don't think that's the reason. You think that doing other people's laundry puts me in a lower class than a restaurant owner, don't you," she prodded.

"Well, you have to admit that at least they don't have aching backs and shriveled up hands, and they are looked up to by the customers, " he said.

Immediately she looked down at her hands. Then turned away before he saw how much his statement hurt her.

"These shriveled up hands have taken care of me for many a year and if it weren't for my aching back we wouldn't have food on the table," she snapped. She was sorry as soon as the words poured out, but he had hurt her deep and she had lashed out in retaliation.

"Don't you think it hurts me to sit in this wheel chair unable to hold down a job? Let alone having to have you or Edward push me when my hands hurt too much to turn the wheels myself?" he demanded "I just thought it would be a chance to get ahead for a change."

"Yes, Acey, I see the agony on your face when Edward struggles to push you when I'm unable to. Let's look into the background of the business and we'll go from there," she spoke soothingly to ease his pride. "We'll have to just wait and see."

The opportunity presented itself, and it was no time before they owned a small café and Lillie was starring in a whole new role.

She soon realized how much *more* work this business was than what she was used to, but kept her silence.

Their house was just behind the restaurant and Edward had built a wooden walkway linking the two, to accommodate Acey's wheelchair. On his good days Acey could wheel himself but usually it was up to Lillie or Edward.

Acey seemed to be happier and when his hands were not hurting as much, he helped with tasks after closing. With a dishpan in his lap he wheeled himself from table to table clearing and cleaning each one and then replaced the soiled tablecloths. He was also proud of Edward's helping in the kitchen; peeling potatoes while other kids were out playing. The boy never complained, but it seemed that lately he would disappear for hours, leaving more work for his parents to finish.

One evening, as a couple was preparing to leave, Acey overheard the man say to his wife," I just saw the owner back there and he's in a wheelchair. You don't suppose what ever he has is contagious do you?" The woman glanced over his shoulder and saw Acey was within hearing distance. The look on his face told her that he had heard the man's statement. Embarrassed, she shushed the man and they left the restaurant quickly.

Acey sat stunned. He knew he had lost a lot of weight but he had thought that it was his burden to bear. *I guess I can't blame the guy. How would anyone know by just looking at me that I don't have a contagious disease.*

As he sought out Lillie he found her in the pantry with her back to him, seemingly studying the shelves of groceries. She was in her habitual stance with fingers kneading the small of her back. Something was not quite right. He stopped what he was doing and watched her closely. *Something about her movements. She's crying! I've never known her to cry. It must be because Edward has not been helping enough. I'll get that straightened out as soon as we get home!* He quietly backed the wheelchair away from the door and called out to her, "Lillie? Where are you?"

She quickly retrieved her hanky and dabbed at her eyes. "I'm in the pantry, dear. I'll be right out"

This gave her the time to dry her eyes, smooth her hair and take a deep breath before returning to the kitchen.

He pretended not to notice the redness of her eyes and explained to her that he had overheard the customer's fears. "I guess it does look pretty bad doesn't it? I'm losing weight…and my hands…"

Seeing a way out of the work she had quickly grown to dislike, but bent on soothing his fears, she interrupted, "Don't let those idiots get to you. They don't know, and what they don't know, they fear. I've never seen you through other people's eyes, so I had no idea that anyone would think such a thing. Perhaps this isn't the best business we should be in."

"Does look that way, doesn't it? Maybe if I just stayed away…" He muttered

"I won't hear of you letting this bother you so much. As a matter of fact I don't like the restaurant business but didn't know how to tell you," she admitted.

"I guess it's time to rethink our future, and see what happens next" he offered.

After closing the café for the night and arriving home, they found that Edward was not there.

"That boy is going to get a whooping for leaving and not finishing his chores today," Acey declared.

Lillie sighed as she sat down on their sofa. "Oh don't be so hard on the boy. He works hard and he goes to school and he's been shuffled from pillar to post. It's a wonder he can even get good grades as many times as we've moved. He helps out a good deal and if he goes off somewhere to be alone, then he deserves it. Lord knows I'd like to do the same sometimes."

The door opened and Edward walked in with a big grin and said, "I've got a surprise for you, Dad."

"Well, I've got a surprise for you too. Where have you been these past few days, running off and staying away for hours at a time? You leave Lillie to pick up the slack and you know that I can't be as much help to her as I want. You ought to be ashamed of yourself. You're lucky I don't get the strap and give you a good whooping," Acey snapped.

Edward hung his head, "I'm sorry. I've been working on something that I think will help you," he responded quietly.

"You can help us by tending to your chores and responsibilities, young man," Acey shot back.

When Edward turned and walked back to the door Acey raised his voice, "Where do you think you're going now? You are staying home and in your room for the rest of the night!"

"Acey, Please, give him some slack. I'm too tired to listen to all this bickering. I just want some peace and quiet," Lillie pleaded.

Edward opened the door and stepped just out of sight for a moment. Then came backing into the room pulling something behind him. It was a three-wheeled bicycle of some strange design.

"Is this what you have been wasting your time on? Some of those parts are from the bicycle we bought you. What ever possessed you to make such a thing out of that fine bike?" questioned Acey.

"Dad, it's a wheelchair for you. I got the idea and asked Mr. Wheeler, the blacksmith, if I could use some of his tools. He liked my idea and said he thought it would work, he explained a few things but I did all the work myself. I felt you needed a better wheelchair more than I needed a bike," explained Edward.

The astonished parents silently moved forward. Acey looked again at the bike as Edward explained to them how it worked. "I came up with this because it hurts your hands too much to turn your wheels. This is chain driven, with a single lever mounted to advance you forward by engaging a pin between the chain sprockets and pushing forward. That's how Mr. Wheeler told me to explain it. Then when you lift and pull back, between your legs, it disengages the pin from the chain and is reset when you push down and forward again. The same lever turns the front wheel. You just have to push and pull to make it move forward and backward, and turn it in the direction you want to go, like this," Edward climbed upon the seat to demonstrate. "I found the chair out in the alley behind the bank in town. The people were throwing it away because a leg was broken." He was excited seeing their acceptance. Talking fast he continued, "But I asked first though, just to make sure and they said I could have it. See, the seat swivels and it has arms on it. Lillie can make pillows for it to make it more comfortable, couldn't you Lillie?"

Acey raised himself up and swung his body over to the seat of his new wheel chair. He followed Edward's instructions and found them to work very well, with no pain to his hands. "Well, would you look at this Lillie? Our son is quite the inventor! Buster this is really something special, I hope you know that. I'm so sorry that I scolded you for not getting your work done. This is the best present anyone has ever given me."

Edward was confused to see tears in his father's eyes, for he always thought that men didn't cry. As he moved forward to show how the lever steered the front wheel Acey put his arms around him and pulled him onto his lap and hugged him hard. The boy was so surprised that at first his body stiffened, but when he realized that his father was pleased he melted up against him and he threw his arms around his neck and they rocked back and forth in silence.

Chapter 28...Mary gains confidence.

"It was awful. I was so scared," Mary told her brothers, "But you know, I feel better about myself. And Alva was so brave. He fought like a little man and took care of that big bully." Then looking at Alva she continued, "I'm so proud of my little man."

He was standing beside her chair and accepting all the praise he could absorb. He too felt he had done a great thing.

Taking him upon her lap she hugged him and said, "Tonight I'm going to read you the story of David and Goliath. David was small too but he slew the mighty giant Goliath."

"Read it to me now, Momma," Alva pleaded.

"Not now, honey, wait til bedtime. Momma has many chores to finish, but I promise I will tonight."

"Why don't you report this to the sheriff? Maybe he could arrest Snider and put him in jail," asked Arch.

"All they would do is go out and have a talk with him and what good is that? I doubt if there's a law about just threatening someone. I just want him to leave us alone and never come back," she replied.

"I wish I was as big as he is, so I could pound the daylights out of him!" muttered Arch.

"Well, maybe after today he will think twice before coming around again. I know one thing, I'm going to make a rack for the rifle next to the door so it will always be handy," stated Will.

"And we're going to teach you and Alva to shoot as soon as he's old enough to hold it to his shoulder," added Arch.

"I can hold it Uncle Arch. I'm big enough!" boasted Alva.

"Not yet, little man, but in year or two," answered Arch.

"And we'll have you shooting like Daniel Boone!" chimed in Will.

"Now let's not get too hasty boys. He's a bit young to be shouldering a rifle that size," Mary protested.

"Well maybe we could get him a smaller one. Maybe a .22 to start with. He could target practice with one of those to get prepared," offered Arch.

"I don't want him playing with guns. 'Lessen the opportunity, lessens the accidents.' I heard that somewhere and it makes sense," she claimed.

"I don't want to alarm you, sister dear, but I feel that we won't be clear of that man until he's cold in his grave," argued Arch.

"We'll just have to be more attentive and try not to leave you alone again. One of us boys will be near you at all times," stated Will.

"That's not what I want. I want us all to be free to live our lives normally, without the threat of someone lurking behind the shed every time you boys leave for town. I feel much better about myself now. Alva and I were able to protect ourselves against that monster and I doubt if he'll be coming around this way any time soon," Mary argued.

"Do you think we should get a dog that could perhaps give us fair warning when intruders are about?" asked Arch.

"Can we? Can we? I know Grandpa would let me have one of Daisy's puppies," pleaded Alva.

"A puppy would take too long to grow into a true guard dog. Maybe we could find a stray that would bond if given a good home," said Mary, not wanting to be beholden to the Tirrells for any reason.

Knowing the reason for her answer Arch replied, "Well, a pup grows mighty fast and the bond would be more secure. We can certainly all keep our eyes, *as well as our minds* open to the first opportunity." He accentuated the words that would send a message to Mary that he understood, but for her to be reasonable.

"Yeaaa, were' getting a dog!" cheered Alva.

Chapter 29... Big Springs, TX.

"I don't know why I thought it would be any different owning a convenient store than the restaurant business. Why does everyone think that just because I'm in a wheelchair that I have some contagious disease?" Acey spewed his frustration toward Lillie.

She had heard the whispers too and hoped that Acey would be spared. "It's their ignorance that's all. I know it's a disappointment dear, but I think we'd better find a business that does not have food as a primary factor," she responded. "There will always be fear of the unknown and boorish people to express it."

"What do I have to do? Wear a sign around my neck saying, 'I'm not contagious'?" he asked.

"Of course not, but we have to think back to how long we've known arthritis centers around injuries like yours. Not until your accident did either of us know how crippling it could be," she explained.

Looking down at his hands and flexing them slowly, Acey said "My hands had it long before my spine, and I didn't injure them. What we've heard, from every doctor we've been to, there's' no cure. So what good am I?" he asked.

Lillie knelt at his feet and took one of his swollen hands. "I refuse to believe there is no cure. And I don't want you giving up either. We just have to keep looking. Time or circumstances will guide us. We just have to wait. The answer is out there. Just remember...*Tomorrow is tomorrow, not to be worried about today.*"

"You always say that, but look at our lives. We have nothing but a few measly belongings. I wanted to make your life easier, not harder. We're worse off now than we were before. Me and my stupid ideas of being a rich restaurant or store owner," Acey moaned.

"Well, it's not going to do any good brooding about what we have no power to change. As soon as Edward gets home from school we will decide what to do," she said.

When dinner was over and the family had their free time Lillie broke the news to Edward, "Son, it looks like we have met with another problem with choosing our business. People are still in fear that your father has some contagious disease. We have to find something else. Since this affects you too, we decided to ask you to join in choosing what we should do next."

"You mean were moving again?" asked Edward.

"Looks like it. Unless we can find a business that has nothing to do with food," answered Acey.

"Lillie, I know you've got those books that help you understand different ailments. Haven't you found anything that would help Dad?" He asked.

"I've searched the books, but they are getting old and out dated. I keep thinking that there will be a breakthrough in research and a cure could be found. It only says that most patients find warmer climates more manageable as far as the pain is concerned," Lillie answered.

"Well then, why don't we head farther south until we find a place that dad will find relief?" he asked.

"You never cease to amaze me how grown up you are at such a young age. Doesn't it bother you about all the schools and friends you leave behind every time we move?" Lillie asked.

Thinking back to the trouble he had in Clinton, Oklahoma he answered, "Not really. I just look forward to the next place and what friends I'll find there. It makes no difference to me," he stated.

So the family packed and turned their faces south in search of the sun and its healing powers. They followed the Chisholm Trail, skirting the larger towns and using the smaller towns to replenish their staples. Meals were meager and usually consisted of fried potatoes, whatever meat either Acey or Edward could bring down, and biscuits and gravy. But it was enough and no one went hungry.

Day after day and week after week found them facing south. Reaching the outskirts of Fort Worth, they veered west.

Lillie watched Acey's body language change, as Mineral Wells became closer and closer. Fearing that he missed his family, or that he had changed his mind and wanted Mary back, preyed on her mind. They had never discussed the situation but now she wanted desperately to know what was bothering him.

One evening when he seemed especially anxious, and after making sure that Edward was asleep she positioned herself across the campfire so she could read his expression. "Do you want to swing by and see your family?"

His brow furrowed as his eyes sought hers, "Are you out of your mind? Good grief woman, I left nothing back there that I want to go back for. Why? Do you?"

"No, of course not. But you've been so antsy these past few days, and being so close, I wondered if you may have changed your mind and wanted Mary back..."

"Well, stop your wondering. I've been worried sick that *you* may have changed *your* mind and wanted to go back to Samuel. I wouldn't blame you. You deserve a whole man, not someone all crippled in a wheelchair."

Relief flooded through her soul and she quickly went to his side, "Well, put that out of your mind, Mr. Lykens. I'm right where I've wanted to be for more years than I desire to count. My life is with you and Edward. I don't need anyone else."

He smiled as he reached for her hand and pulled her down onto his lap. "That goes both ways, little lady. I don't know how I deserve someone as loving and giving as you, but I sure am grateful."

With both their worries answered, they passed within a few miles of Mineral Wells, in search of an unknown destination, both reinforced in the knowing that their love was stronger than ever.

While camped on the outskirts of Big Springs, a group of people approached their campsite and introduced themselves.

They were mostly ladies, all dressed in fancy clothes and riding in a large two seated carriage. They wore bonnets to match their dresses and each gloved hand held a parasol to ward off the sun's rays.

One lady in particular retrieved a set of spectacles from her purse and placed them on the end of her nose. Without leaving the carriage, she raised her chin and looking down her nose through the lens, she spoke with a stiff lower jaw, "We are from the Big Springs Ladies Society. Your condition, sir, has been brought to our attention. We would like very much to know if you are carrying a contagious disease. If not perhaps we could help you by having our town doctor examine the problem and see if there is anything that can be done to cure your affliction."

Lillie was furious. She instantly recalled the woman and banker that tried to put her in an orphanage many years ago, 'for your own good' they had told her. They had forced her from the only home she knew and set her on the run at the age of nine.

But this was not about her. It was all up to Acey now. *He will have to decide for himself if he wanted or needed these ladies help.*

"Ladies, I assure you that it is not contagious and thank you very much for the offer, but I've had several doctors both in Texas and Oklahoma tell me that it is a permanent injury," Acey spoke kindly to the women.

"But have you been to specialists? They have them in the larger cities. Doctors that have decided to make one ailment their career and centered all their schooling on just the one they chose," asked a voice from the group.

This caught Acey and Lillie's attention. "You say there are doctors that center their education on one specific ailment?" She asked.

Astonished that this destitute woman could speak such proper English, the lady answered, " Why yes, yes that's true. Have you not seen one?"

"We've been to many doctors in many towns, but none that claimed to be a *specialist*," claimed Acey. And we've no more funds to hear the same answer.

"Please, follow us into town and we will see what we can do to help you," pleaded the stiff jawed woman." It will cost you nothing. We have funds set aside for...such purposes."

Wishing to show these women that she was of higher education than they assumed, and forgetting that she had just left it up to Acey, she stated quite clearly, "We are disinclined to accept charity, ladies, but appreciate your concern. Please accept our appreciation and our best regards." With that said she stood tall with hands on hips, sweeping the group with a defensive glare.

Knowing what was about to be exhorted from Lillie's lips, Acey spoke up, "We surely do thank you ladies, and if it would make you all feel better, I would be glad to take you up on your offer and have the examination by your doctor." And giving a warning look to Lillie he added, "One never knows where or when a cure may be found."

The Big Spring doctor gave them hope, and with that hope the Ladies Society sprang into action and booked train passage for Lillie and Acey to the Mayo Brothers Clinic in Minnesota. Edward was to stay with the mayor's family until their return.

The trip was long and tedious, pain was Acey's constant companion. He rationed the laudanum sparingly for fear of depleting his supply. The sway of the train and the 'clickity-clack' of wheels passing over jointed track helped lull them to sleep each night.

Acey and Lillie marveled at the sights that they knew they would have never seen if not for this ride. The rails wove a path across the country, through mountain passes, followed rivers and passed small farms and big cities along the way. They pointed out interesting sights in order to share each new scene as it unfolded in the panoramic view from their seats.

The train's scheduled stops made it possible for passengers to disembark either to stretch their legs, revive the blood circulation to their cramped muscles or to just feel a solid foundation again. At one of these stops in Hutchinson, Kansas, people were encouraged to visit a restaurant that accommodated the railroad passengers. It was called "The Bisonte" and was one of the "Harvey House" chains of eating-houses, constructed right on a town's train platform.

Acey used his crutches during the trip and was helped from the train by porters and conductors. At one of the stops one of the "Harvey Girls" explained to

Lillie that the need for Acey to go through all the trouble was unnecessary. Service to passengers unable to disembark was available upon request. "The next time the train stops for you to eat, ask a porter to fetch one of us 'Harvey Girls' and we will take your order and serve you in your seat."

"Well thank you dear, that is great to know. It is hard for my husband to manipulate his crutches along the narrow aisle and he has to be helped down the steps each time," Lillie said.

"As long as there is a Harvey House on the train platform, you have access to Harvey Girls," the young woman proudly stated, "Here is a brochure that tells the history of how Harvey Houses were started. It really is quite interesting."

Lillie read the brochure as they continued their travels north to Minnesota. She found it interesting and tried to share the facts with Acey. But he didn't care to listen to the success of some influential entrepreneur when he couldn't even provide for his family.

So Lillie read to herself about the founder who had come from England at the age of 15 and started in the restaurant business. Later changing his vocation to the more profitable railroad, just to change yet again and combine the two to build restaurants along the tracks for the convenience of not only the passengers, but the railroad personnel as well. She thought of how wonderful it would be to never have to wonder where, when or how your next meal would be provided. She looked over to find Acey fast asleep with his head rocking to and fro keeping with the motion of the train on the tracks.

As they were being ushered to a waiting room, before the examination, a guide told Acey and Lillie a little about the men who founded the clinic.

He reassured them that if the doctors at the clinic found a patient incurable, the Mayo Brothers sent that patient to Christian Science practitioners in the area. Then he showed them an article where Dr. William Mayo was quoted as saying, "I have sent people to Christian Scientists and they have got relief."

Acey and Lillie were not surprised to hear the doctor's report that his condition was incurable and permanent. And as the usher had said, the clinic doctor gave him a couple of options.

There was a group that evaluated the incurable patient's physical abilities and offered suggestions as to what vocation they were best capable of. Acey's diagnosis was wide open if he were highly educated. The wheelchair would not stop him from practicing law or teaching school, but these buildings usually had many stairs, which made access impossible.

"There is always the arts." one nurse offered.

"What kind of art?" asked Acey.

"Oh the possibilities are unlimited. You could paint, sculpt, basket weave...."

"Basket weave?" he interrupted. "Are you serious? I'm not crazy, I just can't walk. Besides, have you taken a close look at my hands?" He brought his hands from his lap and extended them toward her.

"Basket weaving is a true art and a lot more therapeutic than one might think," the lady defended. "As far as your hands go, let me show you something."

With Lillie close behind, the nurse steered Acey's chair into a room where people were so intent in their activities that they did not notice the intrusion.

Each table held a person, some in wheelchairs and some not. But looking closer Acey and Lillie could see that these people were all handicapped in one

167

way or another. Some were leg or arm amputees while others appeared to be blind. Those who could see were painting pictures on canvas set on easels at their level. A young woman had just finished a necklace of stringed beads and held it up for her fellow artisans to admire. Those with two hands applauded, while others verbally cheered her efforts.

A man with a metal hook for his right hand was learning to move his shoulder muscles to open and close the apparatus to make it grasp a spoon from his table. A blind man's clay covered hands sculpted a lifelike horse head, all by feel, with the image he retrieved from memory.

Lillie and Acey stood in awe. Looking from table to table they witnessed the beautiful art these handicapped people were capable of. One in particular caught Acey's eye and without thought his swollen hands went to the wheels of his chair and guided it toward a man, much like himself, working diligently over his task. He was striking, what looked like a metal spike, with a mallet.

As Acey rolled closer he realized it was a strip of leather under the tool the man was pounding, and with each strike a pattern was imbedded into it. The man looked up as Acey's shadow crossed his work and he smiled. Acey returned the smile and the man saw a look of appreciation for his talent in Acey's eyes and nodded his thanks. "You like my work!" The crippled man stated.

"Yes, very much. It's a belt isn't it." Acey exclaimed with admiration as he looked from the work in progress to the finished products at the end of the table. "It certainly is going to be a nice one."

"Thank you. It isn't hard to do, once you have all the tools. All you need is a good eye to make sure

168

you hit the tool and not the hand that's holding it," he laughed.

The man introduced himself as Claude Fisher and offered a gnarled arthritic hand to shake. Acey accepted with his swollen one and they each gave a gentle squeeze. When their eyes met they both knew they had found a new and understanding friend.

All but forgetting Lillie and the nurse, Acey moved closer and Claude began to explain and show him the tools he was using. One was a "handle" that snapped on to any number of "stamps" which held a pattern that would be transferred to the leather with a good rap of the mallet. There were books of different patterns and directions for cutting the leather and making purses with roses or wallets with acorn and oak leaves as well as silhouettes of different animals.

As Claude rambled on, Acey could see that this "vocation" could get rather expensive with all the different tools needed for the trade, but silently wondered if he could maybe manage with just a few.

A gleam of hope came into Acey's eyes. *I could do this and sell the products to help support the family.* He asked Claude how long it would take to learn the craft and was met with a chuckle.

"All you have to do is sit here beside me for an afternoon or two and you'll know all there is to know," came his answer."

He did not notice that Lillie and the nurse had long slipped away and left him in the Claude's capable, although arthritic hands.

"I didn't realize what all a person can do without the use of their legs or arms or even their sight," exclaimed Lillie.

The nurse smiled and shook her head "You saw only a small inkling of the achievements that these people, whom some want to call cripples, are capable of. Being crippled is more of a mental attitude than it is a physical one. Oh I know there is the paralysis and the loss of limb, but if a person's will to overcome their loss is strong enough, they will find a limitless world of ways to prove they are not disabled; merely inconvenienced."

"Well, it sure put a light in Acey's eyes that I haven't seen in a long time," Lillie offered.

Nodding she added, "Now you only have to step back and let him prove to himself and the world what we already know."

"Step back?" Lillie frowned.

"Yes," the nurse explained, "Spouses tend to protect their mates by making decisions for them or setting limitations, no matter how loving, that shouldn't be set by anyone except the afflicted. Don't coddle the man. Let him have his pride. Encourage new goals and praise the ones that he achieves."

Lillie nodded, then thought, *By the looks of it, I'll be buying a set of those leather tools.*

It was one thing for Acey to retain his pride and look forward to a new occupation, but along with that the doctors wanted him to have a new interest in life itself. That's why they still urged him to seek the Christian Scientist practitioners near by.

He was tested with different herbs and teas and physical therapies to determine which would ease the constant pain. A program using a combination of the three was prescribed and found promising. The therapists then urged him to continue the routine as Lillie was instructed on the how and why of each.

They presented a Bible to both Acey and Lillie while they ran their own tests and spoke often of the many blessings that the couple should be thankful for. "Open your eyes to all that is good around you and

170

use your affliction toward the good of the Lord," they encouraged him.

At first Acey rebelled and questioned them as to "What good can I find about my paralysis?" and "How can a cripple help the Lord?" But with each question, he was given positive answers as well as reinforced scriptures about why he should thank God for each and every day.

He wasn't sure of the exact moment or phrase that turned his mind, nor whether it was scripture or deed. It just happened over the course of his stay with these giving people, that he seemed to just *know* he wanted, no…*needed,* to turn his life over to God.

In all honesty he prayed for forgiveness and as the words were uttered, peace and relief began to fill his soul. His legs were still crippled, and always would be. The disease would get steadily worse, but he never felt better in his life. The contentment and warmth, the unburdened feeling of unseen weight now lifted from his shoulders, could only come from one source, a loving God! He found Jesus. He found God. He found his calling!

Lillie accepted his revelation as she had his other decisions, good or bad, with unconditional love and the silent feeling of, *Tomorrow is tomorrow, Not to be worried about today."*

During the stay with the mayor's family, Edward was given a thorough examination and found to be in good health, free of ticks and lice, then turned over to the mayor's servants with an order to "Bathe the boy and make him presentable."

Edward thought, *Boy are they lucky that Lillie didn't see or hear that. She'd have their hide!*

Later he was in his glory as he was taken to town with the family. He did not even mind that he had to ride on the outside box on the back of the car, inhaling the exhaust as it puffed up in front of him. *Wow, wait until I tell Dad and Lillie about this. I bet they haven't even rode in a car before!*

Upon their return to Big Springs, they found that the townspeople had sold their hack, Maudie, Rascal, and their .22 rifle "to offset the price of train fare". The small amount left over had been used toward Edward and Mollie's board and room.

Lillie was devastated and protested outwardly, demanding to know where their animals went. When told a family moving far to the east purchased them, she collapsed into tears.

Although he felt the loss of Rascal heavily, he spoke quietly to Lillie. "They had our best interest in mind when they sent us to the clinic. I loved Rascal as much as you loved Maudie, but we have to forgive and go on. You know they were both getting old and had only a few more years left. Let us pray that they were sold to God fearing, good hearted, animal loving people that will give them as good a home as we did."

Speaking through clenched teeth and fists to match, she glared at him. "YOU forgive them. I can't. They told us they had funds for their charity work. They gave us no clue that we would lose the animals we love. I suppose you would forgive them if they gave Edward away too! This *calling*, you say came over you, does not apply to me. It's YOURS not mine. I will remain your faithful wife and stay by your side no matter what, because I love you, but don't try to shove your God down my throat. Too many times in my life I've been forced to make my own way. I don't recall getting any help from Him when it came to the beatings I got from my father, my brother running away, my mother's death, my working for every piece of bread put in my mouth. I will be "the preacher's wife" for you, but don't expect me to sit in the congregation and yell Hallelujah or Praise the Lord. I'll take in laundry and help pay our bills, and I'll help you where you need to be helped physically, but don't ask more of me than that!"

It all came out in a torrent that left her breathless and shaky. She collapsed into the nearest chair in tears for the loss of her precious Maudie. She hadn't been just a work animal, she had been a friend.

Acey was so taken aback that he had to gather his thoughts before he replied. "I'm sorry, Lillie. I'm sorry that the Lord has not let Himself be known to you as He has to me. The feeling is so overwhelming that I thought that you could feel it too."

Dryly she stated, "Sorry dear, but this is your game, not mine. You can play it out whichever way you see fit. I've explained my feelings and I repeat, I'll stand beside you in all other ways…"

"It's not a game Lillie. It's what I know I've been searching for all my life. Remember I told you about my Uncle Elijah wanting so badly to preach that he would jump up on tree trunks and preach to the cows in our field. Well, I know how he felt now. He wasn't crazy after all. He was just so full of the Holy Spirit he had to share it to any ears that would listen."

"He was probably full of something," she muttered.

He heard her statement but chose to ignore it, to give her time to see God's work unfold. He prayed each night that God would light the path they now needed to follow.

Chapter 30... Pistol practices

Although Will nor Arch were skillful with firearms, they decided for Mary's peace of mind they would all learn how to be more efficient at shooting both their rifle and the pistol Arch purchased shortly after Mary's last encounter with George Snider.

Arch made a target out of one of the boards that had warped making it useless for his craft. He drew a large man on one side. They did not aim to kill their target, but to render it unable to pursue, so they aimed for the legs.

They went through two boxes of shells before they were confident that they each could at least stop the advancement of any predator.

The noise set Alva's nerves on edge, which sent his hands to his ears and his body cringing with every shot. But he loved the excitement that ensued as each adult became more proficient and laughter followed every bullet that contacted its target. He wanted to shoot too but was told it was a "no-no" and he mustn't dare to even touch the guns.

Mary turned to see Alva's expression, the furrowed brow and pouty lips told her that he was being left out of what he thought was a game. She knelt down and asked him, " Would you like to help Momma and your Uncles?"

His nod and widening smile was her answer.

She picked up one of the shell casings and showed it to him. "Would you find something to put all these pretty shells in? We'll find out if Uncle Will wants to do anything with them later, but we can't have them scattered all over now can we?"

He shook his head and ran for the house to find a container. It was fun collecting the shells, but he wanted to shoot the gun. As he placed the last casing in the jar another shot rang out and another casing hit the ground. He ran for it and was surprised to find that it was hot! By the time his mind told his hand to release the shell his fingertips were burned. It wasn't a bad burn, it startled him more than burned, but the yelp he let out made the adults all turn in unison.

Mary scooped Alva up into her arms, "Oh, Alvie, baby, I'm sorry. Momma forgot to tell you that you had to let them cool before picking them up. Does it hurt much?" She gathered him to her lap and examined his pudgy little fingers.

Pulling his hand away, he raised them to her lips. "Kiss and make it better Momma. Kiss and make it better," he whined.

She took the hand and covered it with kisses. Alva giggled and again pulled away. This time he encircled her neck with both arms and gave her a big hug.

This brought an end to the lesson and the guns were taken into the house to be cleaned before putting away. Alva was told that the Mason jar filled with shells were his to keep and he placed them on the nightstand by his bed.

After dinner each of the adults were tending to different chores when they heard Alva's voice break the stillness. "Hands Up, Uncle Will!"

Three pair of eyes turned to see the small boy pointing the pistol directly at Will. One small pudgy hand held the handle and the other rested under the trigger guard with two fingers on the trigger itself. Many thoughts ran through their minds.

Will:... *Did we empty the gun before coming indoors? Why was it left where he could reach it?*

Arch:... *Oh Lord, I forgot to put them out of his reach. Is he strong enough to pull the trigger?*

Mary:... *Dear Lord, don't let him shoot. He doesn't know what he's doing.*

Everyone froze. Somehow knowing that a sudden move could cause Alva to flinch and pull the trigger, Mary forced a smile and spoke with a quietness she did not feel. "Alvie, baby, give momma the gun. It's not time to play now. It's almost bedtime."

"No. I'm the Sheriff an Uncle Will is the bad guy and I'm taking him to jail," Alva answered.

"Ya got me dead to rights sheriff," Will played along, "no need for guns. I'll go peaceably."

Taking the cue from Will, Arch added. "Ya need any help there partner? I can be your deputy."

The boy had played the game with his cousins many times during his visits at the Tirrell ranch. And sometimes Uncle Lewis and his aunts Mattie and Sarah had joined in.

Now with these older uncles playing, he was in his glory. He shook his head and as he did the heavy pistol wavered back and forth in a figure eight pattern. "Nope, I got him, but you can be my deputy," he answered, and without taking his eyes off Will he growled, "I said reach for the sky."

"Well, sheriff, why don't I hold the gun so you can tie his hands behind his back," Arch suggested.

"No, YOU tie his hands, Deputy Uncle Arch, " came from Alva.

"I can't do that. Only the sheriff can tie the hands. That's the rules," Arch bluffed.

Alva eyes narrowed as he fought to remember the rules. He couldn't recollect this one, but if Uncle Arch says it is, then it must be so. Keeping a steady gaze on Will he walked slowly over to Arch.

"Alright, Deputy Uncle Arch," he agreed, "But watch him close so he don't try to get away."

"I'll keep him covered sheriff, you just make sure you tie him up tight," warned Arch.

With the gun safely in Arch's possession the adults all but collapsed with relief. But they continued to play out the scene so as not to alarm the boy.

The gun was found to be empty, but it was never again left where little hands could be tempted.

"I don't care what you say, Mary," Arch commented, "that boy is getting a play gun for Christmas this year, so he won't be hunting for this one when he wants to play."

"Alright Arch," she resigned, "As much as I hate the thought, I can see your point."

Another Christmas came and went, leaving Mary in no mood to celebrate. Her brothers put up a tree and tried to get her involved for Alva's sake, but she would have none of it. They tried to spark some life into her by showing the gifts they were making for the boy, but it didn't work. She did no more than what was expected of her, providing the family with a "holiday dinner" but is was by no means festive.

Remembering past Christmases, she could not help but miss Lillie too. Mary thought it strange that she did not hate her long time friend, but was somehow relieved that she was there to make sure that Edward was safe. She knew that Lillie loved both the boys very much since she had been with them since their births. They all had been so close, and her friend's deception only slightly altered the heavy loss she felt.

Another year had gone by with still no word of Hasten, Edward, or Lillie, so that Christmas was just chalked up as one she would just as soon forget, but was reminded almost daily.

Like the day there was a knock on the door and it was a census taker. "Hello. I'm from the federal government and I'm here to record the 1920 Palo

Pinto County, Mineral Wells population census. May I speak to the head of household?"

She remembered the last time one of these people had come to the door. It was just a month or so before her marriage to Hasten and her mother had been "Head of household."

The past ten years came flooding over her in snapshot increments. Her marriage, the Tirrells, the Briles, the birth of her boys, her mother's passing, Pa and Ma Tirrell's interference, Hasten taking Edward, His running off with Lillie....

"Ma'am?" a voice brought her out of her reverie. 'Ma'am, I'm from the federal.....' he began again.

"Oh, I'm sorry, just a minute. Will, Will it's for you. When he answered her call she added, "You must be the head of household now."

With his attention directed to the census taker, he didn't notice as Mary backed away, then turned and ran to her room and fell across her bed crying, *Dear God, Where is Edward? What census page will my little boy's name be recorded on?*

Chapter 31... One more time.

Lillie was scrubbing clothes once again, but this time she could not accept the situation. The more she washed the 'uppity ladies' laundry, the more she fumed until finally she couldn't stay quiet. Acey was reading his Bible in the corner. Edward was playing outside when she lashed out. "How are we going to get by now? You don't have a pulpit, or a church, let alone a congregation to fill it. You think people are going to leave the church they already belong to, to listen to you preach on some tree trunk out in the field?" Lillie asked. "You think they are just going to throw money at you? We have NO MONEY Acey. We have no way of getting out of this hellhole. I barely make enough to pay for groceries and rent. We need to get back to our old ways of getting by, and you can take up with your Lord later."

"Lillie, Lillie dear, it doesn't work that way. Once you've found the Lord you want to do what's right and just..." he tried to explain.

"JUST get me out of here! I hate it here. All these *hoi-de toi-de* old hags with their noses in the air. I swear, if it rained they'd drown! They've looked down those turned up noses at you, Edward and me ever since they "helped" us with that train ride and sold our belongings to pay for it! AND I suppose you forgive them for treating Edward the way they did while we were gone. You think THAT was right?" she spewed.

"Yes, I've forgiven them and no I don't think it was right, but we have no choice right now but to stay until I can earn enough for our fare out of here," he answered calmly.

"Well, YOU earn money your way, and I'll earn money my way. AND in the meantime I will do what I have to do in order for us to get out of here. I'm telling you now that I've reached my breaking point. I'm going "out" this evening.

"What do you mean "out"? You can't pull it off by yourself, it's too risky. We have to trust in God and put our lives in His hands now," he tried to explain.

"For how long, Acey? For how long? I am not waiting. Doesn't it say in that book 'The Lord helps them that help themselves' or something like that?" she countered.

"Now don't go twisting the words of the bible to fit your needs, Lillie. It doesn't mean it that way."

"Oh? Then you explain it to me, Mr. High and Mighty, holier than thou. I've spent my last days in this place and I'm leaving. If you want to come with me, so be it. If not I will mourn the loss but I'll get over it."

There was a tone in her voice that Acey had never heard before, and he knew she meant it. He also knew that he couldn't stop her from what she was about to do, and he regretted having to choose between her and this new revelation, but she had been right in most counts. They WERE being treated as lower class and they were not making enough money to see any change in the near future. *Maybe if we just got by this one more time, we could follow the right way to God from then on. Just one more time…*

"Alright, Lillie, we'll do it one more time and THEN will you pursue the way of the Lord?" he asked.

"WHEN we get to a place where we are no longer treated like second class citizens, I will repent my worldly ways the day that the money from the congregation plate is enough to support us three." She pledged mockingly with eyes rolling and hands waving overhead.

After making sure that Edward was fast asleep, she dressed in her finest, applied a bit of rouge and with the tip of her little finger she smoothed the

180

lipstick, then dabbed her face with peach colored face powder with the puff that came in the compact.

Acey watched in resignation, knowing there was no way of stopping her, and realizing he was experiencing an old familiar feeling of excitement. On one shoulder he had his conscience, the Holy Ghost, and on the other his desire, the devil himself arguing as to what should be done. All the time he was excusing his actions with *"just one more time."*

The original plan had to be altered because of Acey's condition, he would have to rely on his crutches. It would be a strain on his standing for any length of time, so time was of the essence.

She had chosen the restaurant and alley as she made her rounds returning laundry. It had a short bench against one of the buildings where Acey could sit until he saw her and her escort.

Lillie enjoyed first choosing the man and then the discreet flirting. This night she turned her attention to a slight of a man with thinning hair. He was quite finicky in the placement of his napkin and his etiquette and appearance were impeccable.

Finding her "mark" she glanced in his direction until she caught him looking at her, she quickly dipped her chin and glanced away, only to have her eyes drawn back in his direction. She smiled demurely as he boldly tried to lock eyes with her. Again she glanced away and ate a few bites before risking another glance. Without taking his eyes from her he tried to eat his meal, and she knew she had him hooked when his fork came up empty.

She finished her meal to coincide with his and went into action with the empty purse and appropriate apologies, keeping her voice embarrassingly soft, but loud enough to be within reach of his hearing.

He took the bait and came forward reaching into his vest pocket for his wallet. She played her part to perfection with precision timing of her expected embarrassment and then gracious acceptance, all along insisting the gentleman follow her to the hotel where she can repay his kindness.

The cold night had seeped into Acey's bones and he was growing restless. His conscience was still giving him trouble as he waited on the bench, wanting in the worst way to do right, now that he had found his calling, but being crippled gave him reason to justify his actions. *If I weren't crippled I could work and support my family. If I weren't crippled I would not be forced to do ill to my fellow man. If I...*

Feminine laughter reached his ears. It was the signal from Lillie. He knew it was too late to turn back now and part of him was glad. He quickly checked the street for bystanders and used his crutches for balance as he rose to his feet. He positioned them in his armpits and swung his legs forward bringing his body into the shadows of the alleyway. He leaned against the wall, balanced by the crutches and waited.

Everything went as in slow motion as the couple came even with the alley. She side-stepped and jerked the small man off his feet and into the shadows. Pulling her .32 special and placing it against his ribs she whispered, "Give me your wallet and you won't get hurt."

As her eyes started to become accustomed to the dark she knew that her escorts would too. "Turn around and face the wall! Hurry or I'll have to use this," pressing the barrel harder into his scrawny side.

"How can you mistreat someone that is only trying to help you? I was trying to do you a favor and this is the thanks I get," he whined.

"Shut up. We both know what you were thinking you would get after helping me. What would your little Mrs. think now?" she threatened.

"You were blatantly flirting with me and you know it! You are a Jezebel ma'am, nothing but a harlot!" The little man tried to defend his actions as he threw insults at her.

"Think of me what you want, but I told you to shut up and I mean it. One more word and I swear I'll shoot you where you stand," she hissed.

"Wait, wait. You can have it. You can have it all, just don't kill me," he pleaded.

Lillie widened the space between them, giving him room to reach into his vest pocket where she saw him replace his wallet. As she did he made a quick move to dart past her and back into the street. His body came to a sudden stop as his forehead came into solid contact with Acey's crutch. As he began to fall stiff legged backwards, Lillie automatically reached out and broke the man's fall. In one fluid movement she eased him to the ground and retrieved his wallet, giving it to Acey who slid it inside his tucked in shirt.

The darkness had dilated their pupils, allowing their night vision to easily see their way, back out of the alley and on to the sidewalk. As fast as Acey could swing his body between the crutches they headed back to their small motel room.

Mollie wagged her greeting as Lillie opened the door. After checking Edward she turned the oil lamp up just a hair so they could count the nights work. All was good, and now they had enough money to get out of this God-forsaken place.

Chapter 32...Trip to San Angelo.

Letters from Nevy and Ginny brought softness to Mary that Will and Arch found unsettling. They were glad to see her happy, but with each letter they could feel her desire to follow her instincts to get out of Mineral Wells, growing stronger.

They feared for her and Alva's safety on such a long trip and knew that they could not afford to make the journey with her. They would surely miss her and Alva, so kept their feelings hidden.

She had no idea that they knew she wanted to go. She too felt guilt. *Who would take care of the womanly tasks, or nurse them if they fell ill? Alva would miss them terribly. They are both like fathers to him instead of uncles*, and she too remained silent.

Making small talk one evening, Arch stated, "I guess that Private Detective Sarah hired has sent her a letter telling her that he gave up the search and is staying in Oklahoma where he has a job on the railroad as a security guard. No telling where Hasten and Edward are now. Sarah was smart in giving him half the money up front and the other if he found them."

The expression on Mary's face said more than any words could, and Will's frowning glare told him he had not considered their sister's feelings before speaking.

Mary gathered her sewing and placed it in the sewing box that Will had made her for Christmas years ago. It too brought back a flood of memories of happier times. "I guess it's best that everyone give up the search, but I was so hoping for different results. I think I shall turn in now and I'll see you boys in the morning."

As she shut her bedroom door Will turned and whispered hoarsely "Arch! Why did you have to go

184

and bring that up? Couldn't you see she was in a melancholy mood anyway?"

"That's why, brother dear," Arch replied. "She is trying to find reasons to stay here with us and she is wasting her life away. I think it's time you and I put our heads together and gave her a good reason to leave without a guilty conscience about how you and I could survive without her."

"But it WILL be hard if she goes. I feel better having her here where we can protect her and Alva," Will protested.

"Perhaps if she were away from here she may not need all the protection. Plus if she goes to see Jenny, she's more likely to run into Nevy. He's the only one that's been able to put a spark in her eyes," Arch argued, "Are you thinking of yourself or of her? She deserves more, brother, more than what you nor I can give her."

Dropping his chin to his chest, the older brother had to admit that he *had* been thinking more for himself than for her. "You're right. I'm just being selfish, but I will hate to see her and Alva go. What do you want me to do?"

Watching the closed door Arch murmured quietly, "I don't know yet. Let's keep our eyes and ears open and think some more on it, we'll come up with something."

Two letters came in the mail that made it unnecessary for the brothers to seek solutions, one from Ginny and the other from Nevy.

"Ginny says she wants me and Alva to come down to San Angelo for a visit. I think *this time* I will! She says she would like to see Alva," Mary spoke to herself as much as the boys. Folding the letter and putting it back in the envelope she looked out the window and added, "She may never see my little

Edward. But for sure she will see Alva." Looking up at the boys, she added, "Even after all these years I've never been able to shake the fear of Hasten coming back and snatching Alva too. I will at least be able to relax knowing that he does not know where we are."

Will realized that he had been holding his breath and he let it out in a long sigh. "Well, I guess that's it then. Arch and I have been setting a few dollars aside just for this purpose. We too, have held the same fears, but didn't want to alarm you."

With a sidelong glance and a smile she looked up at these two wonderful brothers and added, " I don't think that will be necessary because you see Nevy has sent round trip train tickets for both Alva and me!" she burst out exuberantly, fanning the tickets for them to see. "Can you believe it? They both wrote for us to come for a visit! That is such a coincidence, don't you think?"

"No, I think it's more like a sign from a higher power, don't you brother Will?" commented Arch.

"I have to agree, and it's one that should be followed immediately," Will answered. "So pack your bags girl, you are heading south."

Chapter 33...In search of a cure.

With money from their latest 'mark', and the overpowering desire to get away, Lillie and Acey decided it was time to start anew and began by purchasing their first automobile. They found a used four-door touring car and with the help of a gentleman that was headed in the direction they wished to go, the family found themselves being chauffeured southward by a kindly man named, Jack Grossland.

Again they were following a lead that would cure Acey's legs. This time it was the Hot Springs of New Mexico. "I've heard tell of many crippled folks who had tried other hot springs with no help, but after bathing in those of New Mexico were able to get up and walk again." Came from one resident in the Big Springs, Texas community. "Those seem to have magical powers and are known quite well for their successes," stated another.

So hope was renewed and they set off in their 'new' car. Grossland had Lillie sit up front beside him, so he could teach her to drive. He explained what he was doing as he was doing it and why, and Lillie was able to master the techniques within days.

Mollie sat between Acey and Edward, who also watched and listened intently to Mr. Grossland. He knew there would come a time when he would be doing the driving and he wanted to be ready for it.

They parted ways with Mr. Grossland somewhere in New Mexico after he was sure that both Lillie and the boy could drive the large car.

Edward was able to drive the car at the age of nine. He would either stand or sit on the very edge of the seat in order to reach the gas, clutch and brake pedals. His vision was above the steering wheel when standing, but through it while sitting. And as long as he drove they never had an accident. Not so for Lillie.

One day as she rounded a curve on a New Mexico road, an oncoming car was "taking his half down the middle" and the two cars collided left headlight to left headlight. The collision threw Lillie out of the car and onto the dusty dirt road.

Although unhurt physically, her pride took a terrible blow and she was madder than a wet hen. She was covered in dust from head to toe when she sat up and began brushing herself off. She looked up to find a man with his hands on his hips and smiling down at her. The humor on the man's face was all she needed to blow, "IF I WERE A MAN I WOULD GET UP AND KNOCK YOU OUT COLD!" She yelled at him.

Chuckling to himself he extended his right hand in an offer to help her up. "Well, Madame YOU might be able to, but there isn't a man alive that can." Mollie was between the man and her mistress and growled her defiance. Lillie hushed her with calming words and the hound backed away.

Lillie accepted his offered hand and he pulled her to her feet. Still holding her hand he bowed slightly and introduced himself. "My name is Jack Dempsey, Heavy Weight Boxing Champion of the World."

Unimpressed, Lillie spewed, "Well, WHO ever or WHAT ever you are gives you no right to drive the way you do and cause injury to people and damage to cars!"

"I am truly sorry ma'am. I accept full responsibility for my driver's mistake. *Are* you injured? Are any passengers in your automobile injured? As for the vehicle, if it is driveable we will follow you into the next town and make sure it gets repaired. At my expense of course, " he added quickly, still holding her hand and wearing a wide smile.

Lillie realized that she hadn't thought of Acey or Edward until he asked and looked back to find them free of injury. She also realized that he still held her hand, which she quickly withdrew. She took a stance with one hand on hip and the other to straighten her hair and brush the dust from her clothes. "Well, that's mighty white of you, sir, and I'm just going to take you up on that."

After examining the cars and seeing that they were both driveable, Mr. Dempsey had his driver follow them into the next town where he purchased a new headlight for each car and asked the station manager to do the repairs. He then took them for a bite to eat at a local restaurant where many people came to him for an autograph. Over the course of the time spent together, he explained he had been visiting family back to his hometown in Manassa, Colorado, and was heading to his next fight in New Jersey with a Frenchman named Georges Carpentier.

They parted as good friends and the Lykens family began to follow his career by listening to his fights that were broadcast over national radio stations.

There were many Hot Springs in New Mexico and the small Lykens family spent years trying one after the other in search of THE one that would bring them the miracle they sought. Each pool would bring relief to Acey's back and legs, but not a cure, and they would hear of another, better one, "just down the road a piece."

When they stopped for any length of time Edward was enrolled in school, Acey preached his sermons to any who would listen and Lillie set to her business of laundry. The small spas that were erected near some of these therapeutic pools were always happy to have them and supply them a cabin to live.

Mollie shadowed Edward on school days, hanging around in the shade and joined him and his schoolmates in play. One afternoon the boys were tussling around and Mollie seemed agitated, whining and growling and pushing against them. Finally she took a stance and broke into a growling bark with hackles from nose to tip of tail. The kids knew that this was not like her so they stopped to see what was bothering her. Her eyes were locked onto something at the edge of the grass.

When it became apparent that it was the movement of a snake the girls all screamed and ran toward the schoolhouse. One of the older boys planned to taunt the others by picking it up to chase them with it. At he approached the snake it suddenly coiled...it was a diamond back!

The boy froze and everything became very quiet. Fear ran rampant through the witnesses as they saw the snake raise its spade head and rattle its tail in warning. Slowly it leaned back and prepared to strike.

Everything became a blur of motion as Mollie sprang into action and rushed the snake, distracting it from the boy. There was a yelp from Mollie, which gave life to the older boy's legs, setting him in motion to join the girls on the schoolhouse steps.

All eyes were on the snake and dog as she barked and jumped sideways, eluding the strike and lunging and biting the snake as it retreated and recoiled for its next strike. Mollie kept herself between the snake and the children.

Another blur came when the teacher rushed through the children and began to hit the snake with her broom. Mollie and the teacher fought the snake, until it escaped back into the tall yellow grass surrounding the schoolyard.

Edward called Mollie to him as the students moved to surround them both. Everyone was praising the hound and petting her and patting her all over. It was when Edward hugged her neck that she whined and cringed a bit. The teacher had Edward stand as she examined and found the bloody area that was already beginning to swell. She had taken a strike on her right shoulder.

"She's been bit Edward. Take her home and see if your parents will take her to a veterinarian." Seeing his expression turn from disbelief to terror, she added, "Don't worry honey, dogs have lived from snake bites before. The animal doctor will know what to do."

"It's a long way home. She can't walk that far. What am I going to do?" The boy argued.

The older boy stepped forward, "Ya kin take my horse if'n ya want, Edward. That dog saved my life and I owes her somethin'. I'll double up with one of the others and follow ya. She needs looked after right away."

Edward climbed into the saddle and the boy and the teacher helped lift Mollie up. She was not at all happy with the situation, but trusted her master and became still under his loving hands and soft voice.

Lillie knew there was something wrong for she heard Edward's anxious voice calling her out of the house. "LILLIE, Mollie's been bit by a diamond back! We need to get her to a doctor right away. Dr. Krebs will make her all better, I know he will." He knew that Mollie was really Lillie's dog, but had attached himself to Edward since the boy's birth. Whenever his parents visited Lillie and Samuel, Mollie shadowed Edward's every step.

Upon seeing Lillie from her position across the saddle, Mollie tried to gather her hind legs up under her to jump to the ground. "No Mollie. You stay!" Lillie ordered her dear friend, as thought's raced through her mind, *The vet's office is about a mile away, she's too large for me to carry, and would exert herself too much trying to get there on foot.*

At her instructions, Edward reined up close to the porch and she mounted behind him, "Get a good hold on her and don't let her jump down." Then told the other boys to ride fast and warn the vet to ready himself with the snake antidote. She took the reins and nudged the horse into a soft lope, covering the distance as fast as circumstance allowed.

The boys helped Edward lower Mollie into Lillie's open arms. Staggering under the hound's weight she made it up the steps and through the door of the vet's office.

Dr. Krebs was waiting and motioned Lillie through the swinging doors and on to a clean white table. She stayed and assisted, seeming to know his next move and what he needed. *She's done this before. A little rusty, but the basics are there*

The shot of anti venom was first, followed by the anesthetic. Then he shaved the area around the two red fang marks, lanced and pressed around the wound to push the poison out through the incision.

Krebs and Lillie did everything they could, but all was in vain. Mollie died a hero, but when she left she took the hearts of her two most precious friends. Her mistress and young master would never know the unconditional and boundless love nor the loyal companionship of another friend as they had cherished in Mollie.

Chapter 34...Reunited.

Hearing that Mary and Alva had arrived at Ginny's, Nevy lost no time in courting his pen pal of the past few years.

As he pulled the surrey up to Ginny's door, Nevy thought, *Any wrong movement or statement could send this little woman flying back to the safety of her brothers, but I have to make a move before she heads in that direction.*

Removing his hat as the door opened he found himself facing the woman who infiltrated his thoughts by day and dreams by night.

At the sight of her he was at a loss for words. "Hello Mary," he said. *Oh that was a brilliant statement, Nevy. Couldn't you come up with something a little more unique than that?* He thought.
"You look very pretty today. Not that you don't look pretty every day, but today you seem even more so," he stammered. *I wish I were writing this. I'm better if she's not so close.*

As she stepped outside he reached for her hand and led her over to a porch swing. His heart was pounding and he couldn't take his eyes off of her. *She's more beautiful than I remembered.*

They had grown close with their letters, but now she seemed shy in person. Knowing the cause, he was understanding and cautious.

"Thank you, Nevy. It's nice to finally see you again. I'd almost given up... I mean I thought perhaps we may never see each other again," she mumbled. *Oh goodness, I must watch my words or he may think I'm awfully forward. Like that time in Mineral Wells with Hasten. I tried to sound confident and wound up not seeing him for weeks. Oh WHY do I think of Hasten at the strangest moments. Think before you speak!*

"You can't get rid of me that easily, little lady." he smiled, "I've been waiting for you to come for so long. Where's Alva? You brought him with you didn't you? I want to spend time with him too."

"Yes, of course I brought him. He's napping at the moment, but he'll be up and around and then we won't have a moment, uh, moment's peace and quiet. He's a rambunctious boy and is into everything left unattended." *Good, I don't think he heard what I almost said.*

But he had, and it boosted his confidence so he continued with trivial matters. "Yes, I suppose he is. Many boys his age are a handful, but if I remember correctly he also minded his mother quite well. "

Mary smiled and nodded. "Yes, he still minds me pretty good. He minded his uncles far more though and they said his unruliness was my fault because I am too lenient with him. I guess I over compensate at times."

"I think we are all guilty of that in one way or another, especially when it comes to children," he agreed.

They spoke of the weather and of her brothers back in Mineral Wells, and how they had all felt an unusual closeness for the short time they shared.

Do I dare bring up her other son? Will it make her melancholy and wish to be left alone? If I don't will she see me as cold hearted and uncaring? I'm just not sure what to say or do when I'm around her. He decided he would get it over with. Taking a deep breath he began, "Have you heard any more about your other son, or your husband, uh, I mean your ex husband?"

"No, the private detective Sarah hired has given up, so my only hope is for some miracle of someone seeing them somewhere. But he isn't my husband and I don't even like calling him my 'ex'. If you must speak of him at all, just call him Hasten," she stated matter-of-factly, putting Nevy more at ease.

"Yes, you're right. He's not worth bringing up, except as the father of your children, so we will drop it," Nevy agreed. "How was your trip coming down? Was it terribly weary, especially with the boy and all?"

"I'm certainly not looking forward to going back right away, " Mary said with a sigh.

"You don't have to. Not for awhile yet anyway. I hope..." *NOT YET. Don't rush her. Wait for at least a day or two before you scare her right back on that train.* "I mean you have plenty of time to relax and enjoy visiting with your sister."

"Oh, yes. She wants us to stay for a few days and perhaps I'll help her make a batch or two of pickles and different kinds of fruits and vegetables to preserve. She's very good at that sort of thing. Maybe I should pay close attention and learn to do it myself."

"If it's okay with you I'd like to take you and Alva down to the carnival winter camp. Some of the other circus's camp in Florida, but this one always holds up here for the winter. Makes it fine by me. Florida is a long way off. Do you think Alva would enjoy seeing what goes on behind the scenes?" He asked.

"Oh, that would be lovely, Nevy. He would enjoy that very much, as would I. Yes, Florida is a long way from here." Her eyes sparkled in anticipation of something new and exciting.

The first night he showed up with Mary on his arm and Alva by the hand. He proudly introduced them to his Carney friends as if to say, "see what I've got and you haven't?"

And so it went that the days were filled with her visiting with Nevy during the day and Ginny at night.

He tried hard to show her all the sights and make the day as long as possible. He hated when he had to take her and Alva back to Ginny's. It meant that his time with her was over for the day and he did not want to be apart from her. So he coaxed her to sit in the porch swing for just a few minutes before he had to let her go.

He knew that the time was drawing near for her return trip home, and feared that she did not share his feelings. The sun was beginning to set as they faced the west and the sky was in shades of pink clouds and blue sky. *I can't let her go back. I want her to stay in the worst way, but I can't find the perfect words. I want to tell her that I want her to be my wife and for her, Alva and me to be a family... What if she doesn't love me as much as I love her? What if...."*

"A penny for your thoughts," she whispered, bringing him back to the here and now.

"Well, Okay, but you only have yourself to blame. I was thinking that I wish you wouldn't use the return part of your train ticket," he blurted out, then seeing her puzzled look he hurried on in fear of her answer. "You don't have to go back. You can stay here. I mean... not *here*, but with me. I mean... you and Alva, can stay here, with me. I mean... as a family. I mean... Would you marry me?"

Mary's heart leaped into her throat and choked off any chance of a verbal answer. Tears came into her eyes as she tried to catch her breath.

Nevy misunderstood and rose to leave. "I'm sorry, I had no right to ask you that. I know you can do a whole lot better than me. You can have your pick of any man on earth."

196

As she fought to regain composure she reached out and took his hand.

He turned in time to see her other hand go to her throat as she shook her head.

"That's okay Mary. I understand. But if we could just remain friends, that would be fine with me. I don't want to lose your friendship," he stammered.

The words finally came, "No Nevy, You've got it all wrong. I'm not saying "no" to your proposal. I've grown quite fond of you since we met, through our letters, and spending these last few days with you. Please, wait."

Daring to hope, he faced her. Still holding her hand, he covered it with the other and pulled her up and toward him. Looking deep into her eyes he saw a spark, and then, as wind stirs spark to flame, he saw her answer. Tenderly he pulled her into his arms and knew that God was in his kingdom and had given him the greatest gift of all... the love of this woman.

Mary wrote Will and Arch the news of the intended early spring wedding and asked if they would pack, and bring, the rest of her and Alva's belongings.

The crates were loaded on the same train they rode to join Alva and Ginny in witnessing the couple exchange their vows in a simple ceremony.

The newlyweds moved into a small house, near Ginny, with a fenced in yard and a chicken coop out back. They purchased a half dozen layers and planned on purchasing more with money from their eggs.

The carnival's schedule was hectic and the young couple worked happily side by side in the food wagon, but were very happy to see the last performance of the year, meaning they were homeward bound.

It was there in San Angelo that Mary and Nevy's first baby arrived. Mary Lee was born on Thursday, January 19th 1922 and the couple couldn't be happier. With the birth falling during the winter break Nevy was there for the arrival and doted on them both.

Alva watched from the outside looking in, wanting to be loved as much as his new baby sister, But he could not find favor from Nevy. Everything he did was wrong or not good enough. At the age of six he found himself shut out and rebelled because of it.

I'll get attention one way or another. If I can do nothing right, then I won't even try. He can't boss me around. He's not my father. But my father didn't want me either. What's wrong with me? Why don't I count? Why did he only take my brother and not me? Momma didn't tell me. I heard it from my cousins at Grandpa and Grandma Tirrell's. Betty and Fannie told me that their momma told them all about it.

Chapter 35...Years later.

Always in search of a cure for the paralysis that Acey and Lillie refused to accept, each "cure" and destination for that cure pushed them onward.

Acey felt that if he could get closer to God in his self-studies, and perhaps convince his family to follow, that God would accept his repentance and restore his legs. Mile after mile and state after state rolled beneath the tires of the Model T Ford they now drove. The newer car was less cumbersome, not as open to the elements and easier for both Lillie and Edward to manage.

Edward was forced to listen to his father's sermons time after time, and became more and more confused. *How can he expect me to believe that he speaks for God when I've been told that God punishes those who break his commandments? Doesn't his legs prove that God is punishing him? What about what he and Lillie did to Uncle Will and Sam that night years ago? I've never told them that I was watching, but I believe they killed them both and God won't take kindly to that. How can he sit in that chair and tell others to "Follow the right path to a loving and forgiving God", when he has been so bad? I'll believe that God has forgiven Dad the day he gets up from that chair and walks again. I know one thing, I may have to obey Dad now but as soon as I'm old enough I won't ever be forced to attend church again.*

Lillie had already expressed her feelings about his revelation and Acey knew better than to even try to coerce her into anything she was not compelled to do. *The woman will just not be dominated. She knows that the Bible says she is to obey her husband, but it's like talking to a brick wall. Commanding her to do anything has only proved futile, and the look she gives me is down right scary.*

199

If she would just repent and let God take hold of our lives we could rejoice in His bountiful gifts. She is so bullheaded and opinionated that I know the only thing I can do is turn it over to God and wait. I have to set the example and by living it might bring her around. Then if Lillie sees the way, Edward will follow. He takes so many of his leads from her, I don't know why.

The Great Depression was just beginning and people from all walks of life were brought to the same level, most in search for employment to support their families. The year 1923 found the Lykens' family in Bisbee, Arizona, where their persistent quest for Acey's relief had led them to the nearby Sulpher Springs Valley and the desert heat.

They pulled into a very large barren field along the highway where people had created a "tent city" and lived basically out of their cars.

Individual campfires burned close to many campers and larger ones were being used to heat large tubs of water for washing clothes, taking baths, or sterilizing for drinking. Restrooms were made away from camp by digging deep pits and using rough board and/or blanket walls for privacy.

Children ran loose, stirring up dust in their wake. Some women did their washing while others gathered together in groups small enough to fit in the patches of shade created by using blankets propped up by tall sticks on one corner and fastened in the top of closed car doors on the other. Suitcases and wooden boxes were used for chairs and tables.

Men gathered at the larger campfires aiding the washerwomen with lifting the large tubs. They willingly shared their tobacco for smoke or chew, and like the women gave encouragement or sympathy where needed. It was a humbling time for everyone and there was no room for superiority of any kind.

Twelve year old Edward was shirtless under his patched bib overalls. After helping Lillie with the chores that Acey couldn't, he enjoyed running barefoot in the hot summer days and relished getting dirty and grimy. He knew he would pay the price if Lillie found he had neglected his ears or the wrinkles of his neck during his turn in the galvanized tub, but that was far from his mind as he joined his peers.

Games of Tag, Red Rover, Mother May I, Simon Says and Hide and Seek, were played by choosing sides with "one potato, two potato", or "enie, meanie, miney, mo." There were other boys on their knees shooting marbles and girls stirring up more dust as they jumped rope to a rhythmic chant.

The constant travel had curtailed his play with other children and he was thoroughly enjoying his dusty romp around the tents and campfires.

Parents scolded and chased children away from the cooking fires and the wet laundry draped over make shift clothes lines stretched between anything strong enough to hold them. Some used knotted ropes caught behind closed car doors much the same as their "awnings" for shade.

As Edward ran to his favorite hiding spot his eyes were drawn to what he thought was an angelic vision. The sun was behind the image casting all but the top in shadow. It appeared to have a halo around its head. He stopped short and stared, completely in awe of this apparition. Only his eyes moved. They followed it as it moved into the shade of one of the automobiles. To his relief he saw it to be just a child, half his age, but the most beautiful girl he had ever seen. Her white hair reminded him of the many cotton fields his family had passed and he realized the reflected sunlight had created the elusion of the halo. He couldn't help but venture closer for a better look. When she looked up and their eyes made contact he was looking into the bluest eyes he'd ever seen.

His body's self preservation took over, filling his lungs with air, bringing him the realization that he had forgotten to breathe. But the lungs had no sooner filled when a well-placed blow between his shoulders emptied them again. "YOU'RE IT", reached his ears as his hands and knees simultaneously hit the ground. He had totally forgotten the game he was playing. When he recovered his breath, and footing, he looked back to find the girl was gone.

The next day, a truck from across the Mexican border, stopped at the camp on their circuit to the markets in Bisbee, Warren and Douglas in hopes of selling some of their load of watermelons. The children begged their destitute parents. Seeing the plight of the penniless crowd the driver had his helper climb the side of the truck and hand down ten of the load's largest plump, ripe melons.

The campers expressed their heartfelt thanks to their benefactors and Acey volunteered to say grace before they all shared in a watermelon picnic, all due to the generosity of that sympathetic driver.

Edward again searched the crowd for the blonde hair, blue eyed girl, but she was no where to be found.

Chapter 36...An exchange of words.

"I'm not sure about this Mary. The tour will be too rigorous for you and the children. Alva needs his schooling and the baby...." Nevy protested.

"Alva is doing quite well with my teaching, and Mary Lee is over a year old." Mary cut in, "Besides, 'whether thou goest, there I shall go also'." Mary argued.

"Don't go quoting the Bible to serve your own purpose, my lady, besides I thought it said somewhere in that book that the wife is suppose to obey her husband," he laughed.

"Well, there are many different ways to understand and interpret His word." She sparred.

He shook his head, "I just don't think it's any place for children. It was hard enough last year. I've seen too many marriages fail because of the strain that the constant traveling does to a couple."

She straightened to her full height, "Well, I traveled with Hasten from one ranch to another while he repaired their broken tack and *that* was with two children. I think I know what I'm talking about. And we didn't have a "kitchen" with us."

"And where is that marriage now?" He blurted out before thinking. He saw the hurt in her eyes before they turned defiant and she shot back.

"It wasn't the traveling as much as the interference of his parents that ended that marriage, and the things that I found out that I could not accept. If you don't want us with you, then so be it." She turned with head up and chin out, and gathering handfuls of her full skirt she marched into the house.

He dropped chin to chest, *Oh what a fool you are Mack Neville Lacey. What in the world possessed you to imply anything about that marriage? But she brought the subject up, not I.*

treat any old way you want. He's MY son and I will not have him treated...."

This time it was Nevy's turn to interrupt, "That's it exactly. He's YOUR son and you want to make sure that I don't forget it. All I can say is that I will have no respect for him until he can carry his own weight in this family and prove to me he isn't a 'momma's boy'."

"Why did you treat him so nicely before we got married? You seemed to be very fond of him then. What has changed or was it all an act?" she asked.

"I thought that once we were married that I could change the boy into a man and not the spoiled child ..."

She couldn't believe her ears and interrupted again, "SPOILED? How can you say such a thing? He was LOVED. There *is* a difference. My brothers and I were all he had. I too, thought that after we were married *you* would be a good influence on him. I guess we were both wrong!"

"Momma, Mary Lee is crying." Came from the kitchen doorway. Turning they both saw Alva standing there.

"What's the matter with you, boy? Can't you see your mother and I are talking? Have you no manners that you just interrupt your elders?" Nevy growled.

Mary was furious, "Don't you speak to him in that tone of voice. He was telling us what he thought was important, or don't you think your daughter is important enough to be interrupted? Or are you angry because he just showed you that he is responsible enough to care for her?"

Realizing there was no way that he was going to get through to her, he decided to give her time to cool down and turned to leave the kitchen. Not knowing what else to say or do, he grabbed his hat and coat and walked out.

Walking down the road his mind was whirling with the events of this first significant fight with Mary. He knew that couples fought. He saw it many times in the marriages in the carnival troupe. But he thought that if there was true love that it wouldn't happen. *I know that I love Mary. And I believe she loves me too, so… what exactly happened? How did things get so blown out of proportion? How can I make her understand that I do love Alva. I just want him to be more responsible. Am I being selfish wanting to go on the road by myself? I've been alone so long, and now I have a family that I am responsible for and it scares me to death. Mary doesn't understand how dangerous carnivals are. Whether they are setting up or taking down there are animals of all kinds working or being loaded on to wagons to go to the railroad cars. The men can't be watching every time they take a step that a child isn't underfoot. There are dangerous animals too. Ohhh I just don't know what to say or do to make Mary understand that I am not like her first husband.*

Mary was tending to Mary Lee with Alva by her side. "Oh, I'm sorry Alva that you heard any of that. I'm sure that Nevy didn't mean the things he said. I'm proud of you for coming to get me. Mary Lee has a wet diaper and she doesn't like that one bit, does she?"

"No. She's pretty fussy about wet or messy ones," he agreed.

Forcing a laugh Mary said," And we can't blame her for that, right? I wouldn't want to sit in a messy diaper, would you?"

Wrinkling his nose and pulling his eyebrows together Alva shook his head. "Ewww, that would be awful, Momma."

"Well, I remember not too long ago when you had messy diapers, and you didn't like it either. You were quick to train to underwear," she offered.

After changing the baby and washing her hands, Mary went back to fixing dinner as if nothing had interrupted her earlier. But it was still on her mind and she too wondered about the argument. *If he knows about Hasten and me then why would he want to go off for months at a time without his family? How could he accuse me of being unfaithful? Maybe I have blown everything out of proportion. Maybe I have to learn to trust all over again. Maybe I've been judging him and comparing him to Hasten. Maybe I've got to trust more and not accuse him. Oh there are so many "maybes" I don't know what to say or do anymore or how to make him understand that I'm trying to put my past behind me and live a normal life.*

They were not alone in turning inward to their thoughts. Alva was a pretty mixed up boy. *When they were arguing I felt a familiar fear inside…of someone else fighting and another boy holding me and we were crying together. He always protected me and tried to take me away so I couldn't hear. He made me feel safe. I remember one night when Grandpa Tirrell was yelling and my Aunt Sarah carried me to the door in time to see him shoot his big gun at my dad. The noise was really loud and it smelled awful. I was really scared. But then I got to ride a horse with Uncle Will to his house where Momma was. She was crying so hard and hugged me up so tight. I don't know what that was all about. Maybe one day I'll ask.*

Later that night when Mary had cleared the dinner table, Nevy came back and quietly hung his coat and hat by the door.

Mary was unsure of what to say, and at a quick glance it seemed that he didn't either. Their glances at one another were timed so there was no contact, making the first to speak even more awkward. The lateness of the hour told him that it was past Alva's bedtime. She kept her head down, he walked to the kitchen and made himself a sandwich. He decided to sit at the table in the dimly lit kitchen. She kept to her rocking chair intent on her mending.

After he had finished his meal and had nothing else to keep him from joining her or going to bed, he cleared the table and headed toward the living room.

Listening to his little noises Mary pictured his movements and timed it so that she was still darning the sock long after it was finished. The silence was deafening. Again without making eye contact, he sat down and picked up the newspaper. He sat in his chair and pretended to read it, holding it in such a way as to block the view of each other.

Mary glanced up to see the newspaper and thought, *If that is the way he's going to act, then so be it. Two can play as well as one.*

An hour passed with nothing said between them. The pages on the newspaper were very slow to turn and Mary's mending had long since been finished. She decided to not wait any longer and got up from her chair and put her sewing box and the mending away. Still without a word she left the room and retired to the bedroom. *He's so stubborn. He'll never talk first. Well I've been through this before and I'm not going to be the one to apologize. He's the one that needs to apologize.*

Hearing the rustle of her clothing and the closing of the sewing box he pictured her every movement from memory. As the door of the bedroom closed he folded his paper and set it beside the fireplace to start fires with later. *She's so stubborn. She'll never talk first. Well I've seen this before with my first wife, and I'm not going to be the one to apologize. She's the one that needs to apologize.*

He entered the bedroom to find her already in bed and her oil lamp out. He went to his side of the bed, undressed, blew his lamp out and slid into bed, being very careful not to touch her in fear of her thinking he was giving in.

She hung close to her side of the mattress in fear that he would think she had weakened. A struggle with the bedding followed but was short lived as they each gave in. It was a long night with little sleep for either of them, trying desperately not to touch the other, in such a small bed.

When the rooster's crow awoke the couple they found they were snuggled comfortably in each other's arms. Neither of them wanted to be the first to pull away which brought a soft sigh of contentment from them both. As they simultaneously apologized they looked into each other's eyes and laughed.

"I think that old rooster can crow a few more times before we have to get up...don't you?" Nevy whispered in her ear.

"I don't know, he can crow pretty fast," she responded.

"Well, we better not waste any more time then, should we?" he murmured as he pulled her closer.

Nevy went alone this time, and as it turned out for the best, for Mary found a few months later that their "making up" had left her with a living memory of that morning after.

At the close of the season he barely made it through the door when he spilled forth with his news. "I've been offered a permanent job up near Ft. Worth, as a cook in a real restaurant!" he almost shouted. Then went on to explain, "I thought it was strange when a gentleman dressed in a suit and tie ordered item after item from my menu and then followed the carnival to the next town, and picked up where he had left off. He ate every item on the menu and then handed me his business card. He owns a fine restaurant up near Ft. Worth and he wants me to be the cook! He says my food is the best he's tasted in a long time and he's been traveling all over, trying out restaurants in search of a new cook. What do you say Mary? He said I could start as soon as I can get there."

Mary sat stunned, "Well, I knew your cooking is good, but a fine restaurant? That's quite a compliment Nevy. I'm proud of you."

"How soon can we get ready to move? Should I go first and find a place and send for you? Or should we go together and you can search for a place while I'm working?" He was so excited he didn't even wait for answers as he paced back and forth. "We can enroll Alva in school there, and ..."

"How much money is he willing to pay you?" Mary asked.

Nevy froze, then with a guilty smile he answered, "Uh, I don't know. I was so overwhelmed by the offer...my own restaurant Mary. Just think of it. Well, maybe not *mine*, but I would be cooking in a *real* restaurant!" he exclaimed, taking a breath he added, "Just think I'll work all year long and I won't have to follow the carnival and leave you and the kids home any more. We will all be together."

"I think it's important that you find out what amount he's willing to pay before we jump into this with both feet," Mary suggested. "And speaking of both feet, have you not noticed anything about me?"

"Oh I will, I'll…no *you'll* write him a letter and ask all the questions you want and I'll pretend it is from me. You're better at writing than I am," he added. "Here's his card. Write him…now…so he will get it and answer everything. Then we can pack. Oh this is so great, I have to tell you I'm more than anxious about this opportunity."

"Well that is obvious, dear," she smiled. "Let's just be a wee bit cautious and I'll write him tonight. It will go out in tomorrow's mail. Is that soon enough? If he's honest about the offer the job is already yours, right? Maybe we should wait until after the baby is born."

"That's what the man said. I guess if I have to wait…baby? Oh, yes, where is Mary Lee?" he asked.

She shook her head. In his excitement he had not noticed that she was now five months pregnant. "Remember the old saying, 'When something sounds too good to be true, it usually is?'" she asked.

"Yes, and I've also heard 'Don't look a gift horse in the mouth'. Go, go write the letter now. I can't wait," he said impatiently.

"Do you not see anything different about me Nevy?" she repeated, speaking each word separately.

He stopped his pacing and looked into her eyes. "What? What did you mean? What's different?" Then his eyes swept over her and he saw the fullness of her wasteline. His eyes left it and came back to hers, back to the waistline. Then she saw the look of understanding spread across his face and he came to her with open arms. "Oh, I'm sorry, honey. I was so full of myself that I didn't see. How long?"

"Well, it seems as though our making up just before you left, gave us something to remember it by." She patted her stomach. It should make an appearance sometime in January."

"Another January baby. I hope it's a boy this time...to continue the Lacey bloodline," he hurriedly explained.

And so it was that the offer was real and the family moved to a small town just south of Ft. Worth called Kennedale, Texas.

Nevy was in his glory and his cooking brought more and more customers, mostly by word of mouth.

The couple learned to call the food "cuisine", and his occupation elevated from cook to "chef".

"I've read the recipes left by other cooks and altered them here and there to enhance the flavor and the owner seems to be pleased," he stated proudly to his family. "I'll show you some of them if you want."

Mary wasn't as interested as Alva appeared to be and it was the first time the two males seemed to enjoy each other's company, and almost bonded.

Their second daughter, Myrle Neville Lacey came into the world on a cold Wednesday morning, January 30th 1924, in that tiny town of Kennedale, Texas.

"Are you too disappointed that she isn't a boy?" Mary asked.

"No, my love. As long as you and the baby are healthy is all I care about. There's still time for that boy," he reassured her.

"Well, I hope it isn't too soon. I have my hands full enough with the ones we have," she exclaimed as she touched the cheek of her newborn at her breast.

Chapter 37...They Put Down Roots.

Both Acey and Lillie felt "at home" in Bisbee. His arthritis was less painful, and Lillie immediately got back to her laundry business. It was the people that made the difference. With so many destitute families in the same boat, or as Acey called it the same Ark, there was no pecking order to have to abide with.

Acey was recognized as an outstanding preacher and gave sermons every Sunday, both morning and night. The only empty room big enough to hold a congregation of any size was in a large brick building sitting on a corner up "Brewery Gulch". The avenue was highly known for it's many bars and brothels and Acey had his work cut out for him. Those who heard him preach said that he sent many men home, with hat in hand, from the bar below and the brothel above. His voice was loud and he made it louder to awaken and strengthen the Holy Spirit of each man and woman that was frolicking in sin.

This did not fare well with the proprietors and caused them to unite and try to have him removed from the premises.

He would not budge, for he claimed with fist held high and voice like thunder that "God has led me here to cleanse the filth that runs rampant and threatens the souls of decent God fearing townsfolk."
Acey had lost a lot of weight and was quite frail by this time but it was still a struggle for Lillie and Edward each Sunday, because to gain entrance to the "church" there were many steep steps to climb.

Edward and Lillie struggled with the wheelchair, up each step, with one pulling from the back and the other pushing from the front. After watching their plight a couple of strong male members of the congregation took it upon themselves to meet them at

214

the bottom and carry Acey, in his wheelchair, up the stairs and into the building.

The self-proclaimed minister did not let a minute, or a man he saw as sinful, get by him. He would shout at them to "Go home to your wives and turn away from this den of inequity, or your soul shall surely be doomed to the depths and the fires of hell", as he was being carried up the stairs.

Brothel residents were known to lean out their windows and invite him to "Come on up to my room preacher, and I'll show you what heaven's all about," while bartenders yelled at him to "Shut the hell up".

"We have no choice Acey," explained Lillie.

"There has to be another way. We already said 'one last time' and I felt awful about that for weeks afterward," he argued.

"Well it got us where we are today and that is closer to your goal of being able to stay put in one place. I've been thinking. What if we had our own 'camp out'? I mean we could use this as our home base and go out to other towns to get what we need."

"What we'll need is forgiveness all over again, don't you see Lillie? He has provided us a place to start with a clean slate. I know there isn't much money coming in but the Lord will provide, He surely will. Have faith," he pleaded.

"I've got faith...in myself. And how I've gotten by since I met you. The camp outs provided amply for three families. Good solid cash gives me faith that I will be able to pay for my rent and put food on the table." She saw he was thinking and pushed in another direction, "Don't you see? If we hit it big we could build a church and us a small house where there would be no more rent payments. With a bigger church there would be a bigger congregation and

215

bigger tithes. But until that church is built there are a lot of people trying to find your God and no good place for them to gather for you to lead them. You would be able to save so many more sinners with a real church and not that room down on Brewery Gulch with a bar below and a cathouse above. Good decent folks don't want to attend a church where they have to wade through the drunks and nasty remarks from harlots to hear your words of inspiration."

Acey sighed deeply. "It sounds like you've been thinking on this for awhile. Have you made any plans?"

"As a matter of fact I've been mulling it over for awhile. If we watch for special events coming to towns near us, such as rodeos, carnivals, something passing through, we could go and watch for a big spender and set him up. The town's people would automatically believe that it was one of those event workers that done the deed. We could explain to the folks around here that you are answering a calling to be an evangelistic minister, and will be called out of town on various occasions... what?"

His eyes narrowed as they made contact with hers. Leaning back in his chair he shook his head, "I thought you said "ONE last time? It sounds like you are planning many "one last times." I understand the need for traveling to other towns where there is a shortage of preachers, but only to share God's Word, not to do the work of Satan. I'm sorry Lillie, but I can't do what you ask again. I just can't."

Her shoulders sagged as she realized that she almost had him convinced but in her pushing she had divulged too much and he had closed his mind. *I best drop the subject for now. Wait a while and when the opportunity comes again, I'll be ready. I'll go ahead with my plans and if worse comes to worse, I'll do it myself. I just have to wait; and I know that I am very good at waiting, after all, how long did I wait for him?*

Acey's pride led him to believe that he had talked her out of it and he immediately pushed it out of his mind, grateful that the Holy Spirit had won over Satan to keep him on the narrow path.

Lillie became silent. Allowing him to believe that it was all behind her, she would venture forth with plans to carry them out solo.

Bisbee was close to the Mexican border, and towns, with any size, were few and far between. She mailed letters to sheriff's offices under the ploy of seeking a need for a traveling minister in their vicinities, and offered Acey's service. At the end of each letter she asked, as though it were an afterthought, if there were to be any large event coming to their area that would benefit by his presence. She first sent to Tombstone and Sierra Vista to the northwest and Douglas lying almost on the Mexican border to the southeast. They each answered her query in the affirmative. If there was a preacher already established, it was given him the duty to write back to Lillie that they would not only welcome a traveling minister by sharing the pulpit but put them up for the night as well.

She pushed farther and sent letters as far as Flagstaff, and the smaller towns along the way. But she hadn't heard from them yet and she was getting anxious for a little excitement in her life. She decided she would try one of the nearby towns.

Tombstone was a much quieter town since the Earps and the Clantons had their OK Corral shootout, but as in any town, the folks were always ready to hear a new minister preach. It would supply them a new topic of conversations for days afterward.

Men gathered near the barbershop, some whittled on a current project, while others loaded a pipe or rolled-his-own smoke. They debated the topic of the sermon and gave their opinions on how well it was presented.

Women bent to their task as they circled the large loom holding taut their latest quilted creation. They, on the other hand, discussed the manner of dress, the quality of voice and the composure of both the preacher and his wife.

These groups compared each minister and wife to those who had previously shared their understanding of the word of God. At times discussion grew adamant with some of the congregation agreeing while others did not. These upstanding citizens preferred to use the term 'compared' instead of 'judged' as they all agreed, "Judge not, lest ye be judged," was made very clear.

Lillie had witnessed these people in action and chose not to sit through the sermons. Driving Acey to the towns and locating the churches were no problem. She was known to even designate strong men to deliver him to the pulpit, but she didn't stay. She refused to sit and have the public scrutinize her from head to toe, feigning a headache or "the vapors" she would retire discreetly back to the car and find a more suitable spot to kill the time. Usually beside a creek or meadow when weather permitted, or browsing in local stores when it did not.

After picking him up after one of these sermons he expressed his resentment. "Lillie, you must stay in church when we get there. People ask about you every time in every place. I'm tired of making excuses for your absence,"

"We've gone over this before. I will not be dragged into another argument with you about it now, so save your breath," she quickly responded.

Changing the subject, Acey began, "I've been thinking. I'd like to get my license and be a certified minister. I'll have to find out what all is required, whether I'd have to take classes, or what. I want to be able to perform marriages and baptisms and funerals."

"Sounds like that is going to require money and that's one thing we don't have any extra of. When you go to these traveling performances the church has been taking most of the tithes, at least that's what you've said. It hardly pays for our gas to get here, let alone our meals on the road. You come up with a way we can afford to get you certified and I'll be happy as a lark," she offered.

"You don't have to be sarcastic about it. And I told you the truth about the tithes. The church usually takes at least half if not more. The Lord will provide me a way to get the money I need. We will just have to wait and see how."

Lillie grew impatient. "We've got a lot of waiting time ahead and behind us. It will be interesting to find out how *your* God will present you with extra money that we don't need to survive on. Edward, bless his heart, takes work wherever it is offered, and my laundry has slowed down because I'm driving you around to these *side shows*."

"Lillie, you can mock me, but please don't test the Lord's patience. One day He is going to get pretty tired of your mouth and lock your jaw," he warned.

"Now why would He do that, since I'm helping to 'spread the good word'? Just by driving you to these…meetings…should account for something,

…like a few good Christian deeds such as one of those good Samaritans, in your Good Book."

"Why are you in such an argumentative mood? What happened to set you off like this?" he asked.

"Argumentative? My, aren't we using big words these days…that's a new one for you isn't it?"

"I'm through talking. It's impossible to carry on a conversation with you. What ever has your nose out of joint is beyond my comprehension. And before you say anything about *that* word, I've used it more than a few times in my life." He opened the blanket on his lap and wrapped it the around his shoulders, then used his Bible as a pillow against his side window.

Lillie wasn't sure what really did bring on her bad mood. Thinking back she concluded that it was the utter boredom of her life lately. She did not fit into the mold of a preacher's wife, or would not, but all the same it was part of Acey's life that she chose not to share. Perhaps that is part of the reason, but with the long road home she had time to reflect and as the miles rolled by she began to question herself.

Why are you upset? I don't know. Think. Think. Something had to have happened, but what? Start at the beginning. We were up at dawn…nothing. Then ate breakfast…no. Got Edward off to school… no. Drove to that jerk-water town back there…Now. What made you say 'jerk-water town'? Something about the town? Just horribly boring was all. I had a bite to eat at a little café… food was good. There was a store next door to it. I went in and browsed the aisles killing time… I remember seeing…what was it? Something caught my attention…Oh yes. Now I remember. It was a cameo brooch…much like the one I gave Mary for Christmas. I wonder how and where she is? Still in Mineral Wells perhaps. I've had Edward now as long as she had him. I now know what pain I've instilled in

220

my dear friend. I would grieve myself to death if anything ever happened to him. I've never let myself feel the guilt that God knows I have. God…here we go again. Is there really a God who knows everything, about everyone, at all times, every minute of the day? So many people truly believe and live their life as if there is. If there is a God like that, where was He when mother needed him? When my brother Lucas needed him? When I needed him? I can't believe that a 'loving God' would let Father beat on us as he did. How can there be a 'loving' God and let people suffer like I saw in Doctor Dan's hospital. Little ones that were too young to have done anything that would warrant the pain they endured. He takes the loving, caring, beautiful people like my Dan, yet allows people who are mean and cruel like Father and Albert live a painless life. I've seen no 'sign' of a God that controls the universe and each and every life within it. I never did a bad thing in my life until I met Hasten. I can call him Hasten in my thoughts. And then I just hid the boys in my root cellar. Hurting Sam was an accident. I hope he's still alive. It looked awful bad when the cart's wheel rolled over his chest. And then when William tried to stop us at the lake…I couldn't let either of them stop us. I waited so many years to be with this man sitting beside me. It might not have had taken so long, except I never told him my feelings and he never told me his. So many wasted years. And now I have nothing better to do than to be mean and…yes argumentative. Some day I pledge with all my heart and soul that I will reunite Edward with Mary…but not now, not yet. I love him too much to have him hate me for what I did. As much as I want forgiveness for stealing Mary's family, I can't, and I won't, give them up. She has Alva and she's young and beautiful. She will find a new life and have more children. I will never know the pain of childbirth or the warmth of an infant at my breast.

So…what you're saying is, it isn't just one thing that has you in this horrible mood, but several. And they each have guilt written all over them. Yes, Lillie Mae, you are guilty of many things that cannot be undone, but you can make life a little easier for this man beside you. Even though he's the reason for everything you have to feel guilty about. That's right Lillie Mae, blame someone else…it makes living life so much easier.

Edward, Lillie and a few volunteers from the congregation built Acey's first church with money collected from tithes and donated by local merchants. It was away from Brewery Gulch and there were whispers that there just might have been a few sizable donations from the owners of the establishments above and below his sanctionary that had found their way into the collection plate.

The sign over the door of this church read, "Sunshine Mission" in large letters, and "In this house Jesus Rules" was written in smaller print below. It was erected on the road to Naco a few miles south of Bisbee.

The family then purchased a five-acre plot in the Sulpher Springs Valley where Edward and Lillie teamed up and built their first permanent home. It was a small two-bedroom house.

They agreed that it should be unique and made a rectangle "Mold" of 2x4s. Standing the boards on the two-inch sides they half filled it with cement, then embedded smooth flat rocks into the wet surface. When it dried they removed each rectangle from the form and set it aside. They then cemented the

222

rectangles to the outside walls, and declared it their "Rock House."

Acey was inspired by many things and announced that he would write his next sermon on Matthew 7:24 where it states, *"Therefore whosoever heareth these sayings of mine, and doeth them, I will liken him unto a wise man, which built his house upon a rock."* Then added, "You know that scripture means Jesus is the rock."

Lillie rolled her eyes, gave Edward a wink and whispered, "I guess this isn't the time to tell him that that scripture speaks of the rock as a foundation... not a decoration." They shared a quiet chuckle.

The next project for the two was to find water. Edward remembered one of his classmates spoke of a neighbor that was a "witcher", by the name of Karl Clark. So Lillie hunted him down and asked him his price.

His smile left little distance between his chin and nose and his tongue constantly polished the only tooth he had left.

He was a scrawny little man with worn out, dirty clothes. His hat showed signs of age and seemed to be his crown of unkempt appearance. It covered his nearly baldhead, and what little hair he had escaped the hat and tangled around his ears and collar. Faded red flannel underwear could be seen through the elbows of his plaid flannel shirt and the knees of the canvas pants.

Lillie had seen pants like these in the local country store. The miners liked them for their durability.

The wrinkles on his face and hands reminded Lillie of a dried up riverbed with cracks and crinkles going ever which way and his beady little eyes peered through half open eyelids. His boots were old ten years ago by the looks of them, and the tongues had long since been cut out to patch holes in the bottoms. He was quite hard of hearing and spoke loud enough to hear himself.

"WELL, BEINGS IT'S FOR THE PREACHER I RECKON I CAN DO IT FOR FREE, IT MIGHT EVEN EARN ME SOME FEATHERS IN MY WINGS, ONEST I GET TO HEAVEN."

He came early the next morning and brought with him a green willow branch. He had cut it above and below a fork and trimmed it into a Y shape. He removed the bark and held the two-fork end, with one in each hand, thumbs toward himself and elbows away from his sides, level with the branch. He began to pace off the property, holding the pointed end between waist and chest high. He first walked the perimeter, then began narrowing the field by circling toward the center. When he was about 30 feet from the house the "wand" began to twitch and dip. He held tight and moved left and right until the wand bent to the ground while he tried to hold the two ends level. "

"YOU'VE GOT WATER LADY. LOOKS LIKE A LONG WAY DOWN THOUGH. MARK THIS SPOT, LITTLE FELLER AND I'LL FINISH THE PROPERTY AND SEE IF I CAN FIND ANOTHER," he shouted. He continued in his spiral path until he came to the center. "WELL, I GUESS THAT THERE'UN IS THE BEST I CAN FIND FOR YA" he shouted.

Raising her voice Lillie asked, "We brought a canteen of water, would you like a drink?"

"WHAT DO I THINK? BOUT WHAT? He asked.

Edward tried, "No, Lillie asked if you want some water."

DO I HAVE A DAUGHTER? NAW. NAW, NEVER BEEN MARRIED.

Lillie shouted this time, "Are you thirsty?"

"THIRTY? SHUCKS NO, I'M WAY OLDER THAN THAT! DON'T RIGHTLY KNOW FOR SURE."

Edward gave up. He fetched the canteen from the shade and offered it to Mr. Clark.

"OH, WATER, THANKS. I WAS GETTING MIGHTY THIRSTY AND WAS WONDERING IF YOU WERE EVER GONNA OFFER." Mr. Clark took the canteen and drank his fill. With a smile he waved at them and headed back to his truck that was as old and decrepit as himself.

Lillie and Edward could not wait until he was out of sight before they started laughing. And then they realized that he couldn't have heard them anyway.

They started on the well at sunup and worked as much as they could between other chores. Drinking water had to be hauled to the new house, but according to Edward, not for long. He was determined to get this well dug so they could have water near by.

As they dug they transferred the dirt to the back of the property with a wheelbarrow. A corner of the property held a ravine formed from run-off water during the area's torrential rains, and they began to dump the dirt there. Some of the richer soil was scattered around an area Lillie had sectioned off for a garden and some of it was spread around the house for a nice cool lawn someday.

But the goal at the moment was water and they set their minds to having it sooner than later. They put all their spare time into it. As it deepened to where Edward could not climb out. It fell on Lillie to lower a rope to him, wrap it around her waist and brace herself so he could "walk " up the side and out.

225

When that became a struggle they decided to build the "well" box over it. The sides were made to surround the hole and then a roof was made with the supports also holding the spool and crank for the bucket. Lillie and Edward worked side by side with Acey giving directions and answers to their questions.

Edward was in his early teens and although still smaller than boys his age he had hardened his muscles with hard work and was not a featherweight.

He would put his foot in the bucket and balance himself while holding a coal oil lamp as Lillie lowered him to the bottom of the well. They had dug down twenty feet with no sign. Each day, they said, "This is the day, we will find the water." Each night they said "Tomorrow for sure." It went that way, day after day, foot after foot. In the morning Lillie would lower him into the ever-deepening hole and he would work there, digging and shoveling the rocks and loose dirt into the bucket.

Lillie would crank the bucket load of dirt and rocks to the top, swing the bucket over to the edge of the stand, lift it, empty it into the wheelbarrow and lower the bucket back down to Edward. While he filled it again she pushed the wheelbarrow back to the ravine, emptied it, and brought it back to do it all over again. For his noon meal Edward would come up, or choose to stay down and eat a sandwich that she had lowered down to him in the bucket. They reached thirty, forty, fifty feet and still no water. But the witcher had said it was here and they all saw the rod bend. It HAS to be here.

Edward started smoking at a young age and he had his cigarettes with him in the hole. One day, after filling the bucket and Lillie was pulling the heavy load up, he decided to have a cigarette break. He stood and stretched and flexed his muscles, then straightened his back. and leaned against the side of the well. He just got the cigarette lit and leaned his head back against the dirt wall when he heard a scream. He looked up to see the bucket load of dirt and rocks fall inches past his face and body, hitting the bottom with such force that it broke the oaken bucket and spilled the contents. The rocks flew in all directions, missing him but breaking the oil lamp's chimney and extinguished the flame.

The well by now was so deep that the only time the bottom could have been seen was when the sun was directly overhead, at high noon, But the well now had it's "roof" and was not awarded the noon days light.

"EDWARD, EDWARD", louder and louder she screamed, Not hearing his answering call that he was okay. She was hysterical by the time Acey wheeled his chair out to where she was.

Seeing the spool empty and the rope's end in her hand, he understood what had happened. Panic rose in his throat, "SON, SON, CAN YOU HEAR ME?" He pulled himself out of his wheelchair and peered down into the darkness.

"I'M ALL RIGHT. I'M ALL RIGHT, Edward kept shouting back, but they were now both yelling so much he couldn't be heard.

It was pitch black at the bottom so Edward struck a match. When Lillie saw the light she almost fainted with relief. She turned to Acey and yelled, "He's all right. He's all right. Oh Good Lord, thank you Heavenly Father and Mother of Jesus."

After striking another match he found the unbroken bowl of the lantern and lit the wick. It gave off little light, but enough to see the shattered bucket and large rocks that would have killed him instantly if he had bent back to his work instead of taking that

227

cigarette break. He realized how close he came to death and knew that he too had reason to send his thanks upward.

Lillie's voice came down to him. "I'm lowering the rope. Tie it around your chest and I'll twist this end around the spool and crank you up."

After she heard him shout back his agreement and that he was ready, she began to crank again and watched as the rope wound around and around the spool until she finally saw his dirty face. And what a beautiful face it was. When he climbed out onto solid ground she grabbed his face in her hands and showered kisses all over it.

He was so happy to be above ground that he did not fight back. Acey was at his side and clutching one of his hands. It was a pretty tearful reunion.

When Acey gave thanks that night for their meal and for watching over his son there came a "Amen" in three-part harmony.

The next morning they discussed whether the well should be continued or try somewhere else.

"We are down sixty feet. Let's give it ten more and if we don't hit, then we'll try somewhere else. This Arizona desert doesn't give up its water easily, but we're Lykens and we don't give up that easy either, do we?" came from Edward.

"I'm going to leave it up to you, Son. You're the one doing the digging and putting your life on the line each day," answered Acey.

"I'm ready to start cranking if you're willing to trust me to go back down there," was Lillie's answer.

"It's not a matter of trust, Lillie. It wasn't your fault the knot didn't hold. I tied the knots, so if anyone's to blame it's me," claimed Edward.

"Well, we'll just have to make sure those knots hold from now on. I will check them with every load," she promised.

After breakfast Edward was lowered down into the dark hole again. As he descended he thought, *Why is it the deeper I go the colder it is? If my science teacher is right and there is molten lava in the core of the earth, why doesn't it get hotter the deeper I go? And well water is far colder than water in the pond... I don't understand this at all. All I know for sure is that I hope I hit water today, because I sure don't want to hit molten lava.*

They took a lunch break, if standing at the bottom of a deep hole, eating a sandwich, qualifies for a break. So far things had gone well and the scare was behind them. The sun was dipping toward the west when Edward's pick and shovel started bringing up damp ground. Wet dirt became mud and then water began to rise up around his boots. He dug faster and yelled for Lillie to make sure that she had the rope and bucket ready. She too had seen the change in the dirt with each bucket load and was getting excited. She called to Acey for him to come and see.

When water began to rise around his ankles he grabbed the lantern and then to his knees he grabbed his tools, stepped into the bucket and hollered for Lillie. One last time she cranked him to the surface and they hugged each other and danced around Acey's chair.

The well came in at sixty-six feet deep and measured four and a half feet across. It was a proud feat with just a pick and shovel and determination.

Chapter 38... The Lacey's

Life was finally going good for Mary. She was content and seldom found reason to bicker and fight as in her previous marriage.

One day Nevy came home all excited, "Mary, Mr. Dawson has added some of my...cough, cough... recipes to his menu, can you believe it? He loves my hamburger sandwich and has decided to add 'Deep fry potatoes' and a new 'Sarasota chips" to the menu. The chips were invented just a few years ago, up in New York, and have been very popular...cough... He has decided to serve them with the sandwiches."

"Well, that's good. Maybe you can make some for dinner tonight," she slipped into the conversation.

He looked at her long and hard, then laughed, "Oh no you don't, little lady. I do my share of cooking at work and do not want to have to do more when I come home."

"I'm just interested in these new potatoes and want to see how they are prepared," she smiled.

"Uh huh, well, I can *tell* you so you can visualize it," he said, not taking the bait.

"But it would be so much better if you were to *show* me so I can do it myself sometime," she teased.

With his hands on his hips he cocked his head and looked at Alva, "What do you say boy? Think I should...cough...cough...*show* your old ma here?" he asked

"Watch, who you're calling *old*, Mister" she feigned anger.

He threw his hands up in the air, "Old? Did I say old? I meant Ohhh...so lovely," he laughed.

"Yeah, sure you did. That's not what came out," she bantered, then asked, "When did you come down with that cough?"

"Oh, probably just a cold or maybe the flu. I've felt kind of puny of late, but nothing to worry your pretty little head about," he answered.

Mary reached up and placed the back of her fingers to his brow, "Let me be the judge of that Mack Neville Lacey. Your head feels a little warm, how do you feel? You might have a slight temperature."

He took her hand and kissed it. "Now Mother Lacey, you worry about the young ones. I'll be fine."

But the cough was persistent. Not getting much worse, but always in the background. A sort of nuisance to everyone, especially Nevy. He soon decided that it must be the flu, for he began to have chills and night sweats.

Later he decided it was an allergy of some sort, and dismissed the fatigue with not sleeping well because of the coughing and loss of appetite because he was too busy to eat regularly. He ignored the chest pain believing his lungs were just congested, and it would go away when whatever he was allergic to passed its cycle of pollination.

He smiled and waved her away each time she approached the subject so as not to worry her, but she started watching him closer and when he began to lose weight, she challenged him again.

"Woman, I'm working my tail off in a hot kitchen every evening and don't have time to eat, and too tired to when I come home. It's no wonder that I'm losing a little weight." And with a wink he added, "Am I looking more manly with these tight muscles and small waist?"

"Now you stop that kidding around. I'm getting worried about you. I want you to go to the doctor and see what is wrong with you for sure," she pleaded.

He let out a long sigh and promised, "Alright. I'll go as soon as you can get me an appointment, if it will make you feel any better and you will stop hounding me about it." *It will probably be a long time before she can get me in to see the doctor and by then it will be cleared up and no need to go. We don't need an unnecessary bill to pay.*

Alva had reached his tenth birthday and was trying hard to please his stepfather but Nevy only enjoyed the boy's attention when they spoke of his cooking.

If his schoolwork was caught up and grades were satisfactory, on special days, Alva was allowed to accompany Nevy to the restaurant, and when it was a particularly slow day he was allowed to do little odd jobs in the kitchen. He paid close attention to how things were done and how they were put away. Everything was so clean and shinny. He was particularly impressed that the other employees, as well as the owner, Mr. Dawson, treated Nevy with respect. *If Mr. Dawson looks up to him, he must be mighty important. If I learn how to do all this, I might get a job someday where I'm important too.* He discovered that if he was real quiet and did as he was told, he could watch from the sidelines and learn.

Days melted into weeks and during one of the days when Alva was at the restaurant, he heard Mr. Dawson call Nevy into his office. Alva quietly followed and leaned against the wall just outside the partially open door.

"Nevy, I'm getting worried about your cough. It's hung on too long to be a cold, the flu or allergies unless you're allergic to everything under the sun. Did you have allergies in San Angelo? Have you seen a doctor?"

"Oh, it's nothing to worry about Mr. Dawson. I'm sure it has to be some sort of allergy. No, I guess

232

San Angelo didn't have the same vegetation that grows around here. I'm sure it will clear up soon. If it makes you feel any better…cough…cough…sorry, I'll go see a doc and get some cough syrup," Nevy said

"Well I appreciate the way you block your cough with your kerchief or sleeve, but customers don't see that. They only *hear* you and picture in their minds that you are coughing on their food. I've been expecting one of them to complain about it. Or worse, they might not say anything to me, but to others outside of the restaurant and that would be bad for business. I just can't afford to have a coughing chef. It will drive my customers to take their business elsewhere," Dawson stated.

"Well we can't have that, now can we? Nevy assured his boss with a nervous smile. "I'll see to it this week sir. I'm sure…cough…excuse me…he'll give me something to stifle it and maybe get rid of it completely."

"Maybe it would be best if you took some time off and wait until after you've seen the doc and he's cured you of whatever it is. You understand, don't you Nevy? It's nothing personal, just until you stop coughing, then you can come back to work," assured the proprietor.

"If I'm not working how am I going to pay the doctor? I have to work Mr. Dawson. I have a wife and three children," Nevy tried to explain. "I know it isn't anything serious. Just allergies."

"I'm sorry Nevy, I just can't afford losing customers. Like I said, it's just until you're cured. I have your check made out and I put a little extra in there to tide you over until you can come back." He handed Nevy the envelope as if to say the discussion was over.

Nevy hung his head and nodded, "I'll get this cured up right away and be back in no time. Thank you for the extra, sir."

Dawson patted him on the back and said "And your position will be waiting for you. No matter if I hire ten more chefs, there will always be a spot for you. Just get yourself well."

Chapter 39...Lillie warns the school.

Mrs. Stamper walked up and down the aisles between the student's desks in the classroom, patting her palm with the ruler she used as punishment to those she felt were either misbehaving or not paying attention to their assignments. Many students felt the sharp pain of that ruler when caught daydreaming or squirming in their seats.

Edward was very familiar with that ruler. He had received many whacks because his mind wandered to more pleasant activities. One day in particular he was caught in another daydream and knew the routine. He stood beside his desk and held his hands palms down, as she demanded. He knew it was going to hurt like the dickens because she used the edge of the ruler and not the flat side. As she brought the ruler down Edward jerked his hands back. The thrust of her swing caused her to almost lose her balance, which caused a stifled giggle out of some of the other students.

"Edward Lykens, you stick those hands out and keep them there. You know you are never going to amount to anything with that mind of yours wandering around who-knows-where," she snapped.

He obeyed, gritting his teeth and squinting his eyes, he took the hit across his knuckles not once but three times. "That will teach you and the rest of you to not pull away from the punishment you rightly deserve!" she stomped back to her desk.

Edward looked down to see red bloody lines form across the back of his shaking hands. He sat down and forced himself to pick up the lesson book.

That night at the dinner table Lillie noticed that he was holding his fork and knife gingerly. Then she noticed the broken skin and thin lines of dried blood, "What happened to your hands, Son?"

"Mrs. Stamper whacked them with her ruler." He answered.

"The ruler doesn't make marks like that," she said in disbelief.

"She uses the sharp edge, not the flat side," he defended himself.

She reached for one of his hands for a better look. "WHAT? What were you doing to justify that sort of treatment?"

"I wasn't thinking about my schoolwork, and when she took her first swing I drew my hands back and the other kids laughed," he explained.

"Is this the first time she's done this?"

"No. But this time it was worse cause she got mad. She yanks us kids by the hair to sit us up straight if we're slouching, even the girls."

"Oh, Well, I can't do anything about the other kids, but don't worry about that happening to you again. I'll have a nice talk with that teacher," she murmured half to herself.

"Now, Lillie, don't go getting yourself all riled up and cause such a stink that we have to move again," Acey warned.

"I'm not going to have someone punish Edward in such a way that he'll have permanent damage to his hands, Acey Lykens!" she demanded.

"Forget I said anything. I wouldn't be able to stop you if I tried. Just try not to shed blood, okay?" he had to laugh.

Edward was relieved that he didn't get into further trouble and thought no more about it until the day he decided to follow some other boys skipping the last half of their lessons. At noon they took their lunch sacks and hiked up to a cave and hid until school was out.

When school was over, the boys came strutting down the hill feeling mighty proud of them selves. Little did they know that the principal, Mr. Fuller, would be standing in the schoolyard waiting for them.

He marched them back into the schoolhouse with instructions to sit in a line outside his office. He called them in one by one. The boys sitting just outside that closed door heard Mr. Fuller tell each boy to bend over his desk. Those waiting their turn couldn't help but cringe with each blow they heard.

Once punishment was served, the spanked child was sent home through a side door. Edward had been placed at the end of the line and had to sit through all the other spankings, blow by blow.

When it was his turn to face the paddle he stood on wobbly knees. Not in any hurry to receive what he knew was going to be a sound spanking, he took a deep breath and stepped inside. The principal pointed to a chair and told Edward to sit, then stood before him with his arms crossed. The four o'clock sun caused the dreaded paddle to cast a long shadow across the room.

"You know that you deserve a sound thrashing don't you," he stated.

Edward could only nod his head. He could not look Mr. Fuller in the eye. A large lump had formed in his throat and closed off his words.

"Edward, if you can promise me that you will never do this again, I will let you go without a spanking. But you have to promise me that you will not tell the other boys or you WILL get one. Do you understand?" he threatened.

Again Edward nodded.

"Then you may go. And you tell your parents about what you've done. Maybe you aren't quite out of the woods yet, young man," he warned.

All the way home Edward could not believe his good luck. *What could have come over Mr. Fuller to not spank me like he did the other boys? I don't understand. Unless...*

When he arrived home he had to know. "Lillie, did you have a talk with Mrs. Stamper about her hitting me with the ruler?"

Lillie turned from her cooking and frowned, "Yes, did she hit you again?"

"No, I was just wondering," he answered.

Making sure, she stopped her stirring and came to him. "Let me see," she demanded, as she took his hands to examine them. Finding no evidence of abuse, she looked him square in the eyes and pressed again. "What made you bring that up? I want to know if that woman has laid a hand on you."

Knowing that sooner or later it would be out with so many boys getting punished at the same time he decided he had better be out with it. "No, nobody did nothing, but I did something I wasn't suppose to."

"First off, It's 'nobody did *anything*," she corrected, " What did you do?"

"A bunch of us boys took off at lunchtime and went up in the hills and hid in a cave until school was out," he confessed.

"You got caught I reckon, or you wouldn't be admitting it to me now. So what happened then?" she asked.

He told her in detail what had been done to the other boys and how he had only received a scolding.

Lillie threw back her head and laughed long and hard. When she could finally speak she told him how she had gone to the school and had the principal call Mrs. Stamper into his office one day during recess. "I told her right in front of him that if she ever smacked your hands again or pulled your hair, that I would be back and she would get a whooping from me that she would not forget. Then I told him that it goes for anyone and everyone who ever harms my boy. I spoke very calmly, but they got the idea when I put my fist next to her nose and backed her into a corner. You mark my words, that man knew he had better not lay a paddle across your backside or it might get used on him. Don't get me wrong, Son, you know you weren't suppose to cut school. I don't want you to do it again."

As she gathered him into her arms he laid his head on her shoulder and snuggled against her, secure in the warmth of knowing that he was unconditionally loved.

"Alright Lillie, I promise," he sighed into her neck as they simultaneously patted each other's back.

Chapter 40...Back to San Angelo.

"I'll have to go back on the carnival tour until I get over this cough. Then I can get my job back at the restaurant," Nevy explained to Mary.

"Well, if that's the case then I want to be back near Ginny. If we're lucky we can find a place closer to her so we can help each other. It will make the time pass faster when you are away," she answered.

"I know I will certainly miss all my girls," he smiled in the knowing that she wasn't putting up a fuss. "It is a fact that has to be accepted in order to support the family. I'm hoping that when we get back there that this will clear up. I know it just has to be something that I'm allergic to."

The statement about his missing "my girls" did not go unnoticed by Alva, but Mary seemed as though she hadn't heard. "I hope you're right, Nevy. I know I'll rest easier once it stops," she answered.

They packed to go by train, with the little extra that his boss gave him covering the fare. They had arrived at the station and were waiting inside the depot with Alva, Mary Lee and baby Myrle when Mary's face went white. Nevy followed her stare and watched as she almost in slow motion slid the baby onto the bench beside her. She then rose without taking her eyes off some object that had captured her complete attention.

He watched her take hesitant steps toward the platform outside. As he went to her side he spoke, "Alva, watch the girls for a minute. Don't leave them." He approached her and asked, "What is it? What's wrong? You look like you've seen a ghost."

That's when he noticed her trembling hands and ashen complexion. She continued on her path without acknowledging him. She was almost on tiptoe

240

as she approached the door leading to the crowded platform.

Still, as if in a trance, she stepped through the open doors and stepped out into the full sunlight. Her pupils instantly decreased to pinholes as she tried to maintain the vision she had locked onto. She had to wait a few seconds for her eyes to adjust and when they did she began to panic. *Where did they go? I know it was them. It was Lillie! And she had a young man with her. He had to have been Edward, I know it was. Oh Lord in Heaven, don't let them get away. I've got to find them. Yes, Edward would be around twelve or thirteen now. Oh, the years I've missed. But we can make it all up. We can fill in the gaps and become a whole family again.*

Nevy followed her and placed a protective arm around her waist and taking her elbow he tried to restrain her, "Mary, tell me. What is it?" He could feel the tension throughout her body.

As if he wasn't there she answered, "It's Lillie and Edward. I saw them. I saw my baby boy. They're out here, right here, somewhere." She pulled away and began to push people out of her path, "Edward, Edward," she mumbled, afraid to raise her voice in fear of giving Lillie a chance to take him away.

There, there they are. She caught another glimpse of the pair and lunged in that direction. More aggressive now, she pushed and shoved these tall people who stood between her and her first born. Unable to maintain constant eye contact, she began to knock them off-balance into other bystanders. She dared not take her eyes from where she had last seen the two before the crowd swallowed them up again.

"Hey, Lady, watch what you're doing," came from one.

"What's your problem, lady?" shouted another, directing the blame away from himself as he collided with others.

"ALL ABOARED," yelled the conductor. "ALL ABOARD. SOUTH BOUND FOR WACO, AUSTIN, SAN ANGELO AND ALL POINTS IN BETWEEN."

NO, No, not yet. They can't get away. Not this time. OH, where did they go? They were standing right about here. There. There they are, about to board the train. I can't let them. But wait. He said San Angelo. We'll be on the same train and she won't be able to get away. I have to make sure that they get aboard and then while its moving... yes, that's it. She watched as the tall woman and young man got on and she counted the cars. *They are the second one from the engine. Okay. Okay. Now... Oh, Nevy and the children! I forgot. We have to hurry so we don't miss this train and lose my boy again. So close. My little Edward.*

As she made her way back toward the depot she spotted Nevy looking for her. Without explanation she hurried into the terminal and picked up baby Myrle and told Alva to hold on to Mary Lee's hand. As she turned she almost stumbled over Nevy.

"Do you really think it is your son? The one you lost?" he asked.

"Yes, it's Lillie and Edward. We have to hurry and board the train. They are in the second car from the engine. Once we get underway I will confront her for she will have nowhere to run. Hurry, hurry Nevy, we can't let them get away."

As each car filled, the passengers moved down to the next. By the time they gathered the children and baggage the Lacey family was in the fourth car.

NOW, all I have to do is wait, she thought as her trembling legs allowed her ridged body to sit.

She took the sleeping Myrle and looked up into Nevy's worried eyes. "I'll hold her until we get under way. Then I want you to take her and keep the children here when I go to face her," she said.

"Where is your...Alva's father? What if he's there too and they try to do you bodily harm? You'd better remember how they left two people near dead when they ran away. I think we can leave the girls with Alva for a few minutes while I escort you."

She whispered so Alva couldn't hear, "Please lower your voice. I didn't see Hasten. Maybe he's waiting for them somewhere down the line, or I just didn't recognize him in the crowd. They won't hurt me, not after all these years. I'm sure it was the spur of the moment that caused so much anxiety all the way around. I don't believe they meant to harm anyone, at least not Lillie. She used to be a good friend."

"What are you going to say? Your brothers told me about the incident. You, of all people, should be careful," he warned.

The rocking motion of the train had lulled the children to sleep, and now Mary felt the time was right and handed Myrle to Nevy.

She had tried and tried to think of something to say, but nothing came to mind. *All will take care of itself the moment we come face to face, the words will be there.*

Down each aisle she went. Hand over hand touching the top of each seat she passed. The muscles began to tighten again, and she felt her insides flutter with anticipation. She couldn't help but smile, *At last I'll have my boy back. I wonder if he remembers me. We have so much to get caught up on. I'm anxious to hear every detail, no matter how small.* She opened the outside door and walked out onto the landing. The rails and wooden ties were

243

racing passed beneath the wheels so fast that as she looked down she became very unsteady.

The rocking motion of the train and the wind passing between the cars caused her to reach out for a solid handhold. She found the railing and gripped it tight for a moment to clear her senses. *Don't go falling off the train now you silly goose. Edward is waiting right up there another cars. I just have to get to him. One car down and one more to get through, then I will finally have my boy in my arms again.*

She ventured across the narrow walkway between the cars and gripped the next car's railing. Step by step she moved forward until she was at the back door of the next car. Repeating her steps through the next car brought her to the back door of the one she saw Lillie and Edward enter. She took a deep breath and adjusted a few stray strands of hair that had escaped her bun.

As she opened the door to the car she scanned the passengers until she found them. Lillie's hair was the same. Brown, short and wavy. Edward's was a little darker than she remembered but that happens to most tow-headed children. They had their backs to her and she began her seat by seat travel to where they were. When she was beside their seats she took a step forward, turned and blocked their path in case Lillie tried to run.

"Lillie…Edward," was all she could get out.

The two raised their heads and faced her, "Excuse me?" the lady responded politely.

Mary gasped and then froze. *This Isn't Lillie!* "I'm so sorry," she squeaked out, "I mistook you for someone else." *She has Lillie's hair and height and the way she carried herself…and the boy…he must be my Edwards age… But no, she wasn't Lillie, and he has no resemblance to my dear son. The couple*

244

had fine features, to say the least, but they were NOT Lillie and Edward.

Her head reeled as she felt her knees go weak. Shadows closed her vision to a spotlight in which she stared first at the woman and then the boy. Their faces came at her one after the other, growing larger as they almost enveloped her. Voices were just noises, their questions rang in her ears, "Are you alright, Ma'am? "Is there anything I can do for you?", "Would you like to sit down?"

Noises that entered on warm waves of incoherent sounds, which ran over, under and through each other, like different Victrolas cranked and started at separate intervals causing each to run on different speeds.

She felt heat rise from somewhere deep within as the spotlight narrowed to black.

Mary woke to find a crowd surrounding her and someone patting her face, "Are you okay ma'am? Are you ill?" continued the questions. Then she saw Nevy. He reached for her and pulled her to him.

"She's okay folks, just exhausted from a long trip and needs a bit of air. Please, go back to your seats and I'll take her back to ours," he explained.

"Yes, thank you for your concerns, I'm fine now, just very tired. Please, forgive me for upsetting you all. My husband will see to my needs now." She assured everyone.

As they found their way back to the fourth car and the children he explained his presence. "I couldn't wait. I had to make sure you would be safe. I woke Alva and told him to watch the girls and followed you."

"Well, for once I'm glad you did not listen to me," she said as she let him guide her back to their children.

245

Chapter 41...Back on the Circuit

"Mack Neville Lacey, you've done it again," Mary wrote. "It looks as though we are going to have another mouth to feed sometime in January. You seem to leave me with child each time you go back to the carnival. I hope you get your son this time.

"All else is well; the girls are quite a handful and keep me busy sewing clothes to fit their ever-growing bodies. Alva is a great help and even though he is only ten years old he has found work a few hours a day, at a near by logging camp, as a cook's helper. He really loves the work and he has you to thank for that. I wish you both could come to terms and get along. He needs a father to look up to. Ginny sends her regards, and I send my love, Mary."

Nevy couldn't believe it. Another baby to feed and business was not showing a large enough profit. *I don't know how we're going to make it with yet another hungry mouth to feed. The money is being spread too thin as it is, and the girls show it. I worry about them being so thin and frail. Mary is doing what she can, but with baby after baby, how are we going to keep them all fed? If I could only get rid of this cough I could go back to the restaurant, but it seems to be hanging on way too long to be any sort of allergy. I can't let her know how worried I am. She has enough to worry about back there at home. I've got to hit more events. More rodeos... more county fairs... I must double up where I can, when the carnival overlaps some of these attractions. And when it winters this year, I'll have to find other events that will keep me working through the winter.*

And so it was that Nevy began to push himself and ignore all the warning signs that should have set off bells and whistles that something was seriously wrong.

Margie Nell Lacey was born on Friday, January 14, 1927, at the Lacey home in San Angelo.

If Nevy was disappointed, he didn't show it. He sat beside Mary in the porch swing. One arm around her shoulders and the palm of his other hand cupping her face. "She's beautiful Mary. Another angel sent, cough, cough... to us as proof of our love."

"Are you sure you aren't disappointed, Nevy? I know you wanted a boy," she questioned.

"Not at all my dear...like I said before, as long as you and the baby are healthy is all that matters." Then turning he added, "Thank you, Ginny. Mary is such a trouper, but I know she...cough...is relieved that you were here. When Myrle was born, up in Kennedale, she was pretty nervous without you."

"That's what sisters are for...being there for each other. She was there for me when my Ethel and Fred came into this world. It's just what family does."

He nodded, "That reminds me, since you haven't told my family yet I think I'll head over there. I have to brag to my brothers and sisters that I have another beautiful girl, just like her momma."

"How many you got, Nevy?" Ginny asked.
"There's Riley, from when Maw was married to Helfer, then there's Louis Walter, Roxie Bell, Elizabeth and David Clayton," he answered.

Ginny nodded, "I met Roxie when she came after the girls to take them for the day." Well, skeedaddle out of here and let Mary and I gossip for awhile. I haven't been over for a few days and we have some catching up to do.

247

Chapter 42... Offer from Cottonwood.

During weekdays Edward or Lillie would take Acey to the Bisbee train depot. He had received permission from the depot manager to sit in a corner of the waiting area and sell the leather goods he had began as a hobby.

Tools and precut leather, as well as his finished pieces were displayed on the "table" before him. Belts and purses were hung from nails on the wall and wallets were displayed on a small fold-up table beside his work area. Some were adorned with acorn or oak leaf patterns, while some men's items held deer or horse heads, jumping fish, or branding irons. The purses displayed a single rose with a leaf edging and an empty scroll pattern ready for personalization. The customers watched his crippled hands as they struggled to guide the thin tool in one, while wielding the hammer with the other. His best seller was the luggage tags, which he personalized with names or initials of the customers while they waited and watched.

Edward created the working area "table" from a wide board that nestled around Acey's body and was attached to the front of the wheelchair.

A sign, outside the depot, invited travelers to own "Personalized Luggage Tags, Made while you wait," The sign succeeded in coaxing many travelers off the train to purchase his wares, giving him a feeling of satisfaction and self worth.

Acey knew that he could now perform marriages legally, and rejoiced in doing so. He had performed funerals without the need of certification, but he was proud to see Lillie had framed and hung his certificate on the wall.

He accepted invitations to preach or marry couples wherever and whenever offered. He was accepted by congregations in various towns, both in public meeting halls and homes large enough to house them. On those days it was usually planned as an overnight excursion with Lillie accompanying him. They relied on the generosity of church members to feed and house them overnight.

The tithes, and the little he found in the envelope from the bride's father, on these excursions added to the earnings from the sales of his leather goods, were his share in helping to keep food on the table.

Lillie scheduled her laundry business around Acey's preaching and Edward worked where he could, doing common labor and pooled his paycheck for their living expenses.

One evening after a sermon threatening hell fire and brimstone to all sinners within hearing, with a voice that could penetrate their very souls, a well-dressed gentleman approached him.

"Brother Lykens, our town received a letter from your wife in search of towns without ministers. A couple of weeks back I visited your congregation and was so moved by your sermon that I went back to my hometown and spoke to the elders of the church there. As of recent we have been without a preacher and I told them about you. They have given me permission to offer you that opening."

Acey looked up at him and forced a smile. *Now I wonder what she's up to? She certainly didn't tell me what she was doing. Has she finally seen the light? Or is she planning something?* "Well, I'm flattered by your offer, sir, but perhaps you would like to continue this conversation in a place more private."

"Of course, yes, that would be fine. But could we discuss the matter this evening? I am here on other business, which requires my immediate return. I hoped to take care of both on this visit...'two birds with one stone' so to speak," he persisted.

"Here comes my wife. Let us include her in this, as it will be as much her concern as mine. Lillie, this gentleman received a letter from you seeking towns needing a traveling evangelist. He would like to speak to us about a position in his town. Sir, would you like to accompany us to our home?" asked Acey, "You may find you will reconsider your offer." He watched her closely, *was that a twinge of guilt, or perhaps relief that someone answered?*

As they settled around the kitchen table, Lillie asked," Would you prefer coffee or tea?"

"Oh, don't go to any bother. Just a glass of water would be welcomed," he answered.

Filling her teapot she answered, "No bother on my point. We always have a cup of chamomile tea before bedtime, but if you prefer water..."

"A cup of tea would be fine," he nodded.

"First off, let me introduce my wife Lillie, and I'm Pastor Acey Lykens."

Removing his hat once again, the stranger spoke, "Oh, I'm sorry. In my rush to speak with you I forgot to introduce myself. My name is T.J. Boswell. I represent the town of Cottonwood. It lies up state, between Camp Verde and Sedona."

Receiving a blank stare from them both, he added, "It's south of Flagstaff, about forty miles."

Acey nodded but remained quiet. Lillie poured the tea and settled into the nearest chair.

Accepting their silence as positive, he ventured on, "Well, as I stated before, our town is without a preacher and after hearing you, well, we would be grateful to have you consider coming to Cottonwood."

"I was a 'lay preacher' for many years, certified in the Church of God as an 'Evangelist' back in Sept of '31, which enables me to perform all services. I am currently working toward a degree as 'Bishop'," explained Acey.

"Well, that certainly qualifies you to become the pastor of our church. We are of the 'Church of God' affiliation also."

Lillie's thoughts drifted to the application he had filled out to receive his Evangelist credentials. *He had to lie in order to receive them. He swore on that application that his first wife was dead and that I was a widow also. Who knows for sure? Did the wheel of the buggy do more damage to Samuel than I thought? Will Acey's God forgive him the lies, if he brings more sheep to the shepherd? Will he be allowed to enter those pearly gates he preaches about after denying a mother her child? He has broken many of those rules God gave to Moses. Where does this God draw the line that says, "You've left a gap too wide to step over? You have not honored your parents, You have stolen, and you have coveted another man's wife, unless it can be twisted into loving thy neighbor. Aren't most of his sermons hypocritical? How can he stand there and condemn others when he has done the same and never confessed and asked forgiveness? Or, is that what he prays about every time I see his head bowed over his Bible? Does he hide inside that Bible and the wheelchair as he did in my root cellar? No one would recognize him now from the man I ran away with. He certainly preaches a convincing sermon, the best I've heard, but is he doing so in order to fool others or himself? He answered that he had control of his family. He knows*

251

he has had little influence in controlling me as well as Edward. What would happen if Edward were to find out that his mother and brother are not dead? I know only one thing for certain, I still love him with all my heart and will not forbid him nor make him choose between me and his God. For one thing girl, you aren't certain, which he'd choose! She decided to jump into the conversation, "Does your church offer a salary and parsonage?"

Mr. Boswell nodded, "I have been given liberty to offer you a salary, a percent of the tithes and a parsonage. It is a fine God fearing church that only needs the leadership of a minister that has your undeniable Christian faith. I'm sure our assembly will accept you with open arms."

After hearing the monetary offer, Acey suggested "Perhaps it would be best to place this on a trial bases. If for say…one month…your people do not approve of me, or if my wife and I don't feel that it is the right calling…we have the right to follow where I believe God is leading."

Lillie liked the proposition, but held her tongue.

Mr. Boswell finished his tea, stood and shook hands with Acey, bowed slightly to Lillie as he replaced his hat. "I will give the good news to the deacons. When can we expect you for your first service?"

Acey dropped his eyes in thought, "I have a commitment here with Christmas coming… pageants with the little ones and all, and I wish to give them ample time to find another minister. Let's try for a new beginning with the New Year of 1933. How does the first Sunday in January sound?" Acey asked.

"That would be acceptable…a new beginning for all. We will be looking forward to your arrival. Have a good day, sister and brother Lykens."

After the man took his leave Acey turned to Lillie and making eye contact, he asked, "Okay, now you tell me why you sent letters to communities trying to find another church? Don't you like it here? I thought we had put down roots and you didn't want to move again. What is going on in that pretty little head of yours?"

Straightening her back and letting her head fall backward, she looked down her nose while still keeping eye contact, "Well, one never knows what opportunities may lay in waiting out there. My letter brought this man who has offered you more than you are getting here. Isn't that answer enough?"

He tried to look into her soul, but she dropped a shield behind her eyes and donned a Mona Lisa smile. Silently they sat there at the table, he trying to read her thoughts and she blocking the attempt.

I know she's up to something. And I also know that I will be completely powerless to stop her. All I can do is pray…and pray hard!

If he only knew…

Chapter 43...More to bear.

April 8th of 1930, found a San Angelo census taker knocking on the door of the Lacey home. When he walked away he had recorded many of the names misspelled such as Neveal for Neville, Alva L instead of Alva H, Mural for Myrle and Marcie for Margie. Some of the census takers were either of an arrogant nature for not asking for spelling of names and using what they saw fit. Some were unable to understand the family member giving the answers or the family member was illiterate and unable to spell his own name forcing the census taker to spell it as it was pronounced to them. Either way, many names are wrongly recorded in every ten-year census. Also unable to find a category for Nevy's carnival wagon he recorded the occupation as "cafeteria".

A year later another name was added to their family list. This time it was Nevy's pride and joy. Mary gave birth to William Clayton Lacey on April 28th 1931. Nevy was one proud man. He and Alva then lost what little bond they had as Nevy turned his attention to the boy of his blood, and his cough eliminated the chance of returning to the restaurant in Kennedale.

The girls were playing with the neighborhood children, running in and out of the house, squealing and screeching as they ducked behind furniture and dodged sideways just out of reach of "IT" trying to tag one of the players.

"MARY LEE, MYRLE, TAKE YOUR GAME OUTSIDE. I CAN'T EVEN HEAR MYSELF THINK!" exclaimed Mary.

The girls stopped dead in their tracks. Mother had never yelled at them like that. Myrle sided up to Mary Lee who automatically put a protective arm around her. They stood there staring at their mother.

She shooed at them with a raised hand and a brushing motion. "GO. Go outside and play."

Seeing their mother calming down they ventured, "We're bored. We don't know what to play."

"Go play Red Rover," Mary suggested.

"No one will hold onto Myrle's hand. It's always sweaty." And sensing what was coming next she added, "I don't want to either."

"Well she can't help it. Besides, can't you put her on the end where she has no one on that side?" Mary asked.

As if her mother was the wisest person in the world she looked at Myrle and said, "Come on Myrle, let's tell the other kids. You can play again!"

Nevy waited until things had died down a bit then he softly asked, "What's wrong? I've never heard you speak so sharply to the girls."

"Well, YOU try putting up with it day after day, with no end in sight," she demanded.

"Mary. Calm down and tell me what is wrong. I understand you better than you think I do."

"Well, why don't you save some of that *understanding* for Alva? She spoke between her teeth to keep her voice down.

"So here we go again......" he started.

"Alva's run away again," Mary cried.

"Don't lay the blame at my door," Nevy defended, "He will not listen…cough…cough…when anyone tries to tell him anything. He thinks he knows it all."

Mary tried to explain again, for the umpteenth time, "It's not *what* you say but *how* you say it, Nevy. He is a lot like his father when it comes to being ordered around. He's proud and defiant and your way of "telling" him something is by shouting or scolding.

255

He is very sensitive and wears his heart on his sleeve. You *demand* instead of ask."

"I shouldn't...cough, cough...cough.. have to *ask* him to do anything. The boy is lazy. He knows his chores and he neglects them, or he's late getting around to doing them," countered Nevy.

"He's NOT lazy!" She defended angrily, "When you are with the carnival he works tirelessly. He never stops until the work is done and tools put away. You have never let him get close. I've seen him try and you either ignore him or speak harshly when he tries to ask you something. You needn't argue about it, I've seen it with my own eyes!"

Nevy saw the fire in her eyes as she stood tall and straight, with chin out and hands on hips. *I can't remember when I've seen her so angry. I know she's right, but I just can't make the boy toe the line. But, its time for you to keep your mouth shut Nevy old boy, and try to get on her good side.* "I'll go looking for him... cough...cough."

"Don't bother. I'm pretty sure I know where he is and if he doesn't come home in a day or two I'll call the sheriff and he will bring him home... again," came the cool remark as she turned her back and walked away.

Mary was inconsolable when Nevy was finally diagnosed with Tuberculosis. The doctor was unsure of the disease, making it hard to answer the many questions Mary and Nevy flooded him with. "No, there is no known cure at this point in time, but I read there is a vaccine being used in France that has been successful... BUT has not been accepted in the United States yet. Each patient is different and there is no given time for either the cure or length of time each has left. Yes, it is a fatal disease if not caught in

256

a timely manner. I'm sorry that I have no better answers for you. It's a wait and see game. You can enter a sanatorium where you will get round the clock care, or you can go home IF you quarantine yourself away from other people. Yes, that means your children too. Do you have adequate living quarters to meet the State Board of Health's recommendations? Mrs. Lacey, if you are going to care for him at home you must be on guard for your own health. If you show signs of ANY symptoms you are to report to me and I shall decide on what action to take. That goes for your children as well. We cannot afford to let this become an epidemic."

Mary's mind was in turmoil. *Tuberculosis, Incurable, fatal, quarantine, wait and see game, adequate living recommendations, sanatorium, watch the children, What are we going to do? How are we going to get by? Five children and a husband too sick to work...contagious. Must be careful. If I get sick what would happen to my babies? Must be strong, don't let Nevy see you worry. Why God? Why Nevy? I know you will provide, but how? A wait and see game? No, this certainly isn't a game.*

On hot summer days, in an effort to give Nevy the healing powers of sunshine and the children an outing, Mary packed a picnic and took the family to the North Concho River. While the young ones played in the water Nevy built a campfire where she set the precooked pot of beans. The heavy cast iron pot had legs and was set directly over the low flames. As the beans regained their boil, she poured cornbread batter on the turned up lid and they feasted on their usual diet, but being outdoors it seemed more flavorful and enjoyable. The children played games and gathered pecans from the trees growing wild along the river bank and shelled them later at home.

Chapter 44 ... Bishop Certification.

Acey flourished in the new church and the congregation accepted the Lykens family with open arms. He was completely absorbed in his sermons and his studies kept him vigilant in researching the Bible to make each sermon more powerful than the last. He brought many people to the altar to proclaim their desire in following in the footsteps of Jesus. He felt if he could show the Lord that he was truly repentant and he brought more and more followers on the right path, that his legs would be restored their strength. Week after week, he felt stronger both spiritually and physically, at times even fooling himself into thinking that he would someday walk again. In his all-engulfing efforts to prove himself worthy to the Lord, he was unaware of Lillie's comings and goings except when he needed her to get him from one place or another.

Lillie gave the impression she was accepting her position as "Minister's Wife," but it stuck in her craw. Again and again she feigned headaches, enabling her to excuse herself from the sermons and the wagging tongues of the ladies in the congregation. She was aware of the whispers and quick glances as well as the conversations ending abruptly as she entered a room. While this was happening, time and again she caught their husbands giving her admiring glances. She just didn't seem to care about fitting in.

"They just want you to wear drab old dresses and look like someone's old grandma. They are just jealous that you look prettier than all of them," Edward declared one day.

Surprised to find him somehow reading her mind, Lillie fixed their lunch while Acey remained at the church a while longer. "Well, thank you, Buster. That's mighty sweet of you, but tell me, when are you around those old battle-axes enough to know what they think? You don't like being in church anymore than I do."

"Oh, I've heard some of them when they don't know I'm close enough to hear. Have you noticed that none of them ever smile or seem happy at all? Church is not a fun place to be. And I'm not sold on the whole thing anyway," he offered.

Lillie stood and took her usual stance but then started walking back and forth in front of his place at the lunch table. "Now see here you heathen, you will be damned straight to hell with all those evil thoughts running through your head." She shook her potholder over head, as if it were the Good Book.

Edward laughed out loud at her imitation of Acey behind the pulpit. She continued her charade by shaking the potholder and slamming it down on the table. "To hell you are going young man, mark my words…if you don't have a changing of the ways and confess your sins and beg forgiveness!"

Edward fell into character of one of the parishioners, jumping to his feet and throwing both hands over his head and bowed before her, "I confess preacher, I confess. Please cleanse my soul and set me on the path of redemption."

Lillie dipped her hand in the dishwater and flicked it on his head saying, "Rise my Son, you are saved. Go forth and sin no more!" Then they both broke into laughter so hard that Lillie had to grab a chair and Edward sprawled across the floor holding his sides.

When he was able to regain his breath, Edward stood and shook his finger at Lillie, "You know we are both lucky that Dad didn't hear us. He would be either very angry or very hurt."

"Either way he would be praying for our souls even more than he is now," Lillie answered as she got up and finished putting the lunch dishes in the sink. "I just don't fit in here, Son, but your father is happy and I don't want to spoil that. He doesn't see their hypocrisy, and if he did he would just blame me."

"Like I said Lillie, they're just jealous. Don't let it bother you none. I'm not the perfect preacher's son either. I can't sit in those meetings and listen to explanations that creates even more doubts. How can one preacher stand up there and tell his congregation that his interpretations of the scriptures are the only way to understand them? And they are all different in their beliefs. Who is to say who is right?"

"Oh, I know, Honey," Lillie sighed, "I've wondered the same thing. Such as how Acey's God can be a loving Father, yet allow bad things to happen to good people, or for that matter sweet innocent children that have never had a chance at life, let alone sin against Him. But I guess your father knows about where we stand, and perhaps some day he might be able to convince both of us."

"Maybe. But like you, I have a whole lot of questions that I don't believe anyone can answer. Well, I'd better get back to work. I'm glad I found the opening at the garage. I like working on cars; sure beats horses," Edward said as he hugged her gently.

Lillie laughed at she hugged back, "But they don't have the heart of a good mule."

Lillie tucked the blanket around Acey's legs and turned to leave the podium.

He grabbed her hand, "Since I've received my Bishop rank can't you stay and show a little enthusiasm for my sermon? Or is it my sermons that give you these headaches?" Acey whispered.

Turning back and kneeling at his side she answered, "Let's just say I don't feel the calling you do, nor the challenge of keeping my mouth shut around all the hypocrites that fill those pews. I'm sure you would not like what I would have to say if I felt threatened by one of them," she whispered back.

"Is it them you feel threatened by, or the truth in the words of this Good Book? Or do you feel that I too am a hypocrite?" he asked.

So he DOES think of those lies he wrote. He must wonder where he stands with the Almighty. His insecurities don't show when he's up here and looking out over the pew filled church. Is it all an act? Is he just playing a role to elude the law and family? I know for a fact that he does not pretend to be a cripple, because he is too proud to not walk tall if he could.

He glanced around to see if they were still out of hearing distance, "How can I believe in myself, or make others believe in me, as a shepherd of his flock, if I cannot control my own wife? I'm sure many in the congregation do not believe in your headaches. Where do you go after you leave here? "

Lillie leaned forward, "Don't push me Acey, you wouldn't like the answers. I'm here for you. I've backed you as to where and when we go our whole lives together. I've denied you nothing except becoming something that I am not. I've tried and possibly convinced some of those people that I am faithful to your God, but in all honesty I am only faithful to you and Edward, those I can see and touch. And I know where I stand with you both. You know my background and why I believe in what I believe, so let's leave it at that and stay clear of this subject."

"We'll talk about this later, when we're at home," he pressed as she straightened, turned and walked away shaking her head.

261

Chapter 45…The Gang Brainstorms.

The gang no longer held boys. The youngest was Lewis and he was in his mid twenties when they all knew it would be the last camp out.

Samuel Briles, was the eldest and although the campouts were exciting and brought out his lost youth, he knew he was ready to end it too.

The others were all married now with families of their own. The split would be a much larger one, with each member's need to provide for his own family as well as their parents.

Prohibition had come and gone, actually helping the Tirrell family. With Pa's moonshine still running night and day, they supplied all the locals and made a hefty profit. The government finally decided that trying to eliminate liquor became more bother than it was worth. The loss of lives on both sides of the law was costly and gained nothing. The moonshiners made and distributed their wears right under the revenuer's noses throughout the ten years the ban was in place. After realizing this, the ban was lifted with nothing accomplished except making a few backwoodsmen a little richer.

October of 1929 began The Great Depression. Without warning the banks had closed their doors, leaving wealthy people destitute. Some were the very bankers that had turned a deaf ear to the farmer who had pleaded for help. Newspapers were filled with stories of influential men jumping from the high-rise buildings overlooking Wall Street. Those who had never known poverty couldn't face being poor or had no will to start over. No family was left unscathed in one form or another. It was those that never had the wealth in the first place that survived the best.

The Drought followed close on the heels of the financial catastrophe, adding to the misery of farmers and ranchers alike. The lack of rain during that period caused the crops to fail and the plants to wither and die. The lakes and rivers dried up, leaving farm animals and ranch stock to paw the dried, cracked earth in search of water. Their bony carcasses could be found by the circling buzzards above them. But those buzzards found little left to feast on.

Next came the winds that blew away the rich topsoil until there was nothing but dust blowing across the once fertile plains which became a barren wasteland.

The gang had survived the drought and the dust bowl that followed. They heard of hundreds of families moving west, leaving the farms that were handed down from generation to generation only to fall into the hands of the banks that held their mortgages. It was a sad time seeing the defeated expressions on those passing by clinging to their meager belongings.

The camp out meetings were slow to solidify, with each member offering suggestions and listening to others. Each of the ideas were accepted, rejected after a lengthy discussion, or given more thought until the next meeting. The town had to be a place that was least affected by the hard times.

Jake suggested, "Ya know, we might be better off finding another business other than the Feed and Grain Stores because they were hit hard too and no one is buying seed nor harvesting any. And there are more people than ever trying to deal on credit at the Mercantiles."

"That's good thinking Jake. And you're right. Do you have any other businesses in mind? I,for one, am not willing to go for a bank. I think now days they are being guarded more than ever," answered Sam.

"Well, that leaves the bars, restaurants, five and dime stores like a Ben Franklin or Woolworth they got in some bigger towns. Then there's the livery and now some gasoline stations for those that have automobiles," offered Lewis.

Samuel spoke up, "Now boys don't forget, we still have the trains like the James Gang. They may be a mite laxadaisy, being's they've had no problems in quite a while. I'm sure them Pinkertons are bored out of their minds; might not even have them on board anymore. Most people traveling by train might have a bit more in their pockets."

"What about hitting one of them big hotels that have restaurants connected to them? They probably have a lot of cash in their safes." asked Nate.

Sam shook his head, "I don't know. I hate to change now. We've had a good thing going by not having a large audience, besides, once those Pinkertons get on a trail they are mighty hard to shake. I've read dime novels about them and that's one bunch I don't want to mess with."

"If we hit a saloon we could be facing more guns than we came in with. Those men would not go down quietly that's for sure and we'd be asking for bad trouble," Lewis added. "Them picture shows wouldn't have much money, I don't suppose. Besides that gal is locked in that cubby hole and no way to get to her if she faints away or something."

"No, it's got to be something big," Jake said. "Let's just think on it a bit more, and maybe something will come to us. Check out the advertisements in different newspapers and listen when people are talking; that might give us a clue for this last campout. We have to make it worth our while."

"That is truly worth ponderin," stated Nate.

Chapter 46...Letters from Mineral Wells.

"Looks like you rang the bell and won the prize," Nevy said as he handed Mary the mail.

"Oh, letters! Who are they from?" she asked.

He smiled as he saw the excitement in her eyes. "Well now Missy, they are...cough...sitting in your hand and all you have to do is either open them or read the return address."

The cough had become so much a part of their lives that they both seemed unaware of it.

"I recognize Will's handwriting on this one, but this one says it's from Sarah Trout. Sarah Tirrell married a man named Fulfer, not Trout. I wonder who this is?"

He turned to hang up his coat and hat on the peg by the door. "Well, you're not going to know until you open it and find out. How did she find you? Why would that family be writing to you? Do you think they've found him and have your boy back?"

"Wait until I open it. Sarah, Mattie and I are still friends. It wasn't their fault that he ran off with Edward and Lillie. They were just as heartbroken as I was. That family was so close, I can only imagine what that did to Mrs. Tirrell."

He moved toward the kitchen to give her privacy when he realized she already had it. She was totally engrossed in the letter as she made her way to her rocker purely from memory of its whereabouts. He smiled and continued into the kitchen in search of a cup of coffee that was kept warm on the back of the wood cook stove.

Either by instinct or peripheral vision she knew he was back in the room and was quietly sitting on the sofa. "Sarah's letter is full of family news. She said she got my address from Will. He knew I wouldn't mind. And that they are all married and have children, except for Mattie. She found out that she is barren, much like Lillie, I suppose.

"But listen to this, those Tirrell parents wouldn't leave Sarah's husband alone and he ran off. She had to move back in with them. She says here that being's he didn't come back and she didn't know where he was she had to get a divorce like me. Then she found a new man named Irby Trout and ran off with him and got married in Roby, Texas. That's why her name is Trout now…but she left her kids and has decided to start over, and has not let her parents know that she is in Oklahoma. She has two children by this second marriage. A girl and a boy so far… I can't believe it! How can a woman leave her precious babies? She says here that she sneaks back to Mattie's house and Mattie goes and gets the kids for the day and takes them to her house so Sarah can see them, to let them know that she still loves them. She takes them pretty clothes and toys that they have to leave at Matties so Pa and Ma don't find out. Oh those meddling… anyway, she promises to keep in touch and I will write her a big long letter and let her know our family news. It's so nice of her to include me as a friend. I've always liked the Tirrell children… the girls especially.

"Do you know that Mr. Tirrell made the girls wear long sleeve dresses and long black stockings, and they were not allowed to cut their hair?"

Nevy smiled, "Well, my dear, that *is* the style of his generation, and it seems that you are in that mode of dress more often than not."

She looked down to find she was wearing a long sleeve dress and dark stockings. In self-defense she stated, "Well, at least this is by choice, not because I'm made to."

"I know dear, just thought I'd tease you. What else does your friend have to say?"

266

"She says that Sam married a girl named Sarah Elkins but he calls her Sadie. He doesn't live in Mineral Wells either. In one of Mattie's letters to her, she said that Sam and Pa had a big fight because the Tirrell's did not approve of Sadie, and Pa tried to tell him not to see her anymore. Sam was probably afraid that old man would bust up his marriage too…She says that he and Lewis are trying to out do the other in having babies. Last count Sam had eight, but the last two died as infants. Lewis and his wife Mary Belle Stone had ten but the first three were stillborn…Those poor mothers. My goodness I'm so thrilled that she has written and gotten me caught up on the families. She wrote that Lewis was in the army and when he was writing home he told his wife that the child that they were expecting was to be named "Texas", because he missed Texas so much. So his wife did. Luckily it was a boy. Can you imagine a family get-together with all of them under one roof? The Tirrell house is big, but not *that* big. I wonder if all the women still have to eat separate from the men? They must all have to bring their own tableware, and take turns eating. It would be a lot of joy having all those children running around, playing"

Nevy sat and smiled as Mary bubbled on about the large families. "Add Sarah's six and all the wives and husbands, how on earth would they hear each other above the children?"

He shook his head, "No, you just read that Sarah doesn't go to those get-togethers, besides they probably just make the children play outside"

"Oh, yes, you're right. But even without her last three, there's still Betty, Fannie and Oliver there. Poor Mattie being barren, I'll bet she certainly feels terrible."

"Or blessed. She doesn't have to worry about losing them to her parents. No children, no problem keeping them," he said.

Ignoring his comment Mary thought out loud, "Not being able to have children must be such a blow to a woman. It must make them feel slighted by God. Look what it made Lillie do. She was so desperate to have children that she stole Edward."

"I heard it was Hasten that stole the boy. Lillie might have decided to go with him in order to make sure the boy was safe and got a decent up bringing."

"That *boy* has a name...Edward," she snapped, "and I'm not sure why she ran off with them, but one day I will. God won't let me pass through this life without finding out if my sweet baby is still alive, or had a descent upbringing. I have a lot of questions for those two."

As she folded the letter and replaced it in the envelope she picked up the one from Will. She was unaware that Nevy had wisely taken his leave.

Chapter 47...The Camp Out Plans.

The men had gathered in Samuel Briles home, where they knew there would be no interruptions.

Sam scratched his chin and looked down at the map. "Well, Lewis, it certainly is a gutsy idea. It makes me nervous just thinking about it, but you're right, it's a new one, at least none that I've heard."

"I remember some of the other guys in my outfit during the war talked about the horse racing all the time and how there was lots of money to be won if you knew your blood lines. And I figured if there was a lot of money to be won, there must be a lot of money to be taken. They told me people came from all over to gamble and at one of the races the loser lost his horse. So he really had to 'put his money where his mouth is', so to speak."

"We've used the crowds to mix among them before and this has got to be one of the biggest crowds we'll be in. Think of the amount waiting for us if we can pull it off," agreed Nate.

" What da ya think Samuel?" asked Lewis.

"I'm running it around in my brain and thinking of all the possibles," Samuel answered, "I know that I've been to big towns before and have been surprised by running smack dab into a neighbor. It's always a possibility that we could be seen by those around here, and if we don't get away clean, they could have some of the best marshall's dogging our trail. AND they could be driving those automobiles that are a mite faster than our horses."

"Maybe we could keep to the old deer trails that criss cross the whole area between here and there, coming and going. We will have to stay off the main roads, that's for sure," Jake spoke up.

"What about not even taking the horses. What if we rode the train in and out? The streets and trains will be full, and we could easily carry a change of clothes in our saddlebags," suggested Nate.

"Why would we have our saddlebags if we didn't have our horses?" asked Samuel.

"Guess I didn't think that one through did I?" Nate added embarrassed.

"Well, don't give up on that entirely. The only kink was the saddlebags. What if we wore one set of clothes over another? We could wear ones that are pretty worn out and we don't care about, and throw them away during the escape. Question is, where do we find a place to change?" asked Samuel.

That's easy. Any outhouse could be used and we could dispose of the clothes down the hole. Remember when Lillie...uh...I'm sorry Samuel, I didn't think," sputtered Jake.

Waving his hand as though erasing the words hanging in the air, Samuel shook his head, "No problem, Jake, let's just concentrate on this for now. That is a good idea. But we can't get rid of our hats. I just got this one broke in good, a few years ago."

The boys laughed and what could have been a sticky situation was diverted.

Samuel offered an idea, "We know this is going to be bold, so we are going to have to be just as bold. What if a couple of us used that woman's stuff to dye our hair? Maybe have one of us black hair, one red hair...."

"Well, it's easy for you to say," Sam laughed, "You ain't got no hair to dye. What could we tell our families when we get home? I haven't told Sadie anything about this part of the camp out and I don't intend to. We learned that much from Hasten. We about lost it all that night." As soon as it left his mouth he closed his eyes, kicking himself for being the second to bring up old memories of the night Hasten took Edward and ran off with Lillie.

The silence that followed was broken by a forgiving pat on the shoulder from Samuel, "Don't beat yourself up Sam. I've dealt with it and it doesn't hurt so much any more. It's been slow in healing, but it's getting there. Go on, what were you saying."

"About that hair dye, I've seen Mattie use it a time or two. She says it can be washed out in a few washes, getting your own hair color back. Maybe we could stay out long enough to get it all washed out before we get home," said Lewis.

"You couldn't stay away from Mary Belle that long little brother. You'd have to join the army again cause it'd be pretty hard to explain. She's pretty jealous and I'll bet she could be a spit fire when it comes to explaining how your hair got red," teased Sam.

"I know. We could say it was all a friendly practical joke that was pulled on the sleeping victims. Let's face it Lewis, your hair is the lightest so you will be the red head. Or would you rather be a blonde?" Samuel asked, "Now who's going to go black?"

"Wait a minute," Lewis asked, "When are we going to do this dying of hair? Before? After? If it's before it would have victims giving wrong descriptions to the police, but it won't wash out fast enough if we get spotted. If it's after, who's to say we won't run into one of those we rob a few years from now?"

"Good point, little brother," said Sam

"BUT…what if we take some with us and find a creek on the way home and dye your hair back to its original color?" suggested Jake.

"That could work!" exclaimed Lewis. "And that way our wives won't know the difference. And if they notice anything we can always fall back on a brother's prank. I'm sure Mattie will help us out. "

"Now what about a train ride or the horses?" asked Nate.

"Why we even thought about the train is crazy. How can we have a campout and not bring back the winter meat….unless…" Samuel's eyes glazed over in thought.

"Unless what?" asked Nate.

"Unless we do both," answered Samuel.

"Huh?" came from Jake

"What? How?' came from Lewis.

"What if…Samuel began slowly, …we ride out on our horses as usual, find a place where we can do the changing, and buy tickets at the next train depot, leave our horses and hats at that towns livery, and do the opposite on our return. We could even squeeze in a weeks hunting to bring home some game afterwards. But…I think…we probably should not all be seen together, until we are a hunting party."

" Yeah, I don't want that dye stuff rubbing off on my hat. That could be a give-away too, if they caught up to us. After we find the place to change we could break up into teams and travel separately. Even if we ride the same train, we act like we don't know each other," added Sam, "like we've done before."

Nodding, Samuel said, "I think we've got something here. We are going to have to plan this down to a cat's whisker because this is the big one and we still have a lot more planning after we get there and check it all out."

"Dallas, Texas State Fair, are you in for a surprise!" chirped Lewis. Then placing an arm on Nate's shoulder he asked, "Wanna go talk to Mattie?"

Chapter 48... Angel next door.

"Lillie, have you met the new neighbors yet?" asked Edward.

Looking out her kitchen window and up the embankment to the neighbor's house, she answered, "Yes dear, and you won't believe where we've met them before."

He came up beside her and followed her eyes, "Where? I don't remember them. Looks like those boys are sure helpful in carrying in the boxes. They seem friendly enough. I think I'll go introduce myself and give them a hand."

She smiled and tussled his hair, pride swelled up in her as she looked at her boy growing so tall and nearly up to her shoulders already, "Well, now that would be neighborly of you. Have you seen the girl?"

"What girl?" He asked.

"That one, there," she said pointing. "She's coming out of the house now."

He froze. His eyesight began to darken on the outward edges that grew inward until it was as if he were looking though a long dark tunnel or sitting in a theater and all the lights were out except one spotlight shining on someone on stage... *It's HER. It's that angel I saw at Tent City that day. I thought they had moved on and I plumb forgot about her. But no, she's right there...even prettier than before...and she is going- to- be- living- right- next -door!*

"Edward...Edward. What is the matter with you, boy?"

"Look at the way the sun shines off her hair," he said in a low whisper. "It makes it look like she has a halo. You can see her eyes are blue clear from here, Lillie." He leaned against the drain board and lifted his body higher and his face closer to the window. "She's about the prettiest girl I've ever seen."

273

Lillie laughed, "Why, Buster Lykens, it appears to me that you have been smitten by that blonde haired girl. You just remember that you are a mite older than she is. Better stick to girls your own age."

"I suppose you mean Ima Gray? How many times do I have to tell you? That is something you, Dad and Mr. and Mrs. Ferr cooked up. Ima Gray doesn't want me any more than I do her. We've already discussed it and decided to go our own way and find someone else. I know she can't wait to get married and rid herself of that horrible name. Do you know she is teased every day 'Here comes Ima Gray Ferr...coat', she's miserable with that name. What was her parents thinking anyway?

"Besides, I wasn't planning on marrying this girl. Just think she's mighty pretty. She's a "Yellow Rose of Texas" that's for sure! I think I'll go over and see if I can help," he muttered to himself.

"You already said that. Go on, get. Introduce yourself and I'll cook something for them as a good neighborly gesture," she laughed as he checked the mirror, spit on his palms and tried to stick his cowlick down.

Edward decided to approach one of the boys first, "Hi. Can I give you a hand carrying in some of those boxes? I'm your next door neighbor."

"Sure, just grab whatever you find loose and follow me. My name's Sherman, this here is Sherwood," he said, as they passed a boy Edward guessed to be around six or seven years old.

"And over there is Jim." He motioned his head toward the only dark haired one in the bunch.

"Glad to meet you all, my name is Edward and I live next door," he spoke loud enough for them all to hear.

He followed Sherman single file into the house and asked where he should set the box.

"Open it and see if it's bedroom, kitchen or whatever," came from a voice behind him.

He sat the box down and turned to find himself looking down at the golden haired girl. His eyes were blue, but hers were the bluest he had ever seen. Her hair was done in finger waves, much like some of the women in the motion pictures.

He tried to swallow, he couldn't. He tried to speak, he couldn't. When he raised his hand to introduce himself he found it wet and clammy. He wiped the palm down the front of his bib overalls and offered it to her, "I...I'm...I'm Edward Lykens. I live next door."

She smiled and said, "I know. I saw you over there earlier. Thank you for helping. We have quite a lot to get in and put away."

"Oh, I'm sorry. Of course, I'll go get another box. Maybe it would be best if we did the heavy stuff and let you and your mother do the lighter ones," he suggested.

She laughed. "I'll bet I can lift more, and stay at it, longer than you. You seem mighty frail for a boy. My brothers and I can plant, chop and pick cotton all day long. I know, cause we've done it many times. But if you wish you can bring in the boxes and I'll decide which room to put them in."

"Yes. That's what I meant. Didn't mean to hurt your feelings. You just look so...so..."

"Hey, you gonna help or not?" Sherman yelled.

"I'm coming. Uh, I'm just going to go out and help the boys carry the boxes in," he stuttered.

"Good, then it will get done that much faster. Momma says that as soon as we get unloaded we can have some lemonade. Would you like some?" she asked.

"That would be great. I surely would like some lemonade. Yes, that would be nice. Thank you," he stumbled backward and nearly fell as he tripped on the threshold.

"That's my sister, Nellie," Sherman said, as he lifted a box of dishes. Maybe I'd better let you take this one. I'll carry that box of books."

"No, that's ok. I can handle the books just fine," Edward protested.

"You sure? It's mighty heavy. Besides these dishes have to go to the kitchen, so Nellie can put them away."

Edward spit in both palms again and reached down to lift the box. It did not budge. He tried a different angle. Nope. *I can't let this little kid out lift me. He can't be older than eight or nine, but he won't be able to lift it either, so I'll suggest that we both carry it.*

"How about we both carry it, Sherman?"

"That's ok. I'm used to carrying heavy stuff. We are hard working Fellers, for sure," said Sherman.

"Don't forget Nellie. She's hard working too, right?" asked Edward.

"That's right. She's a hard working Fellers too."

"Don't you mean she's a hard working *girl*?"

"She's both. Our last name is Fellers," Sherman said with a grin.

They both laughed and Edward reached down and picked up the box of dishes and stood back and watched Sherman lift the box of books with ease.

1. *Where in the world did these people come from? He's got the strength of a man half again his age. Well, dear Edward YOU are*

half again his age... or more. How does THAT make you feel?

Seeing the look of disbelief on his new neighbor's face, Sherman laughed. "It's leverage. My daddy taught all of us how to lift and carry so we don't hurt our backs. You use your leg muscles, not your back. You were bent over the box and tried to lift it with your back. You have to get beside it, squat down and lift with your leg muscles. I've toted more than my own weight, I reckon."

"Hey, thanks. I'll remember that next time. Like the teachers say, "Learn something new every day..." Edward began.

"And you'll die a wise man," finished Sherman.

They laughed out loud as once again Edward followed the boy single file back into the house.

When the old truck was unloaded and the last box set near its destination, they all sat in the shade drinking the promised lemonade.

Edward was brought up to date on his new neighbors, and couldn't wait to get back to Lillie to share the news. Stories were usually shared at the dinner table or afterwards, and he knew that she would be waiting to hear what he had found out.

It was Nellie that had offered their family history. She spoke of her father losing his ranching job because of the depression and drought, and that one of his brothers had written him from Flagstaff, Arizona, telling him of work there. They had packed what they could carry and headed north, when their truck broke down and they ran out of money.

Pointing to Sherman she began, "He's named after our father. His name was Sherman too, Sherman G. Fellers. He came from a very large family of eleven brothers and sisters. Mother's name is Mary Nora Frances Dabbs. She has twelve brothers and sisters, so we have lots and lots of relatives," she explained. "Dad got a job at the Copper Queen Mine and tried to save enough to get back on the road, but he and mama decided that this was as good a place as any to settle down. He said, 'One job in the hand is worth a better one in the bush.' I was ten when he died of 'Black Lung" from being down in that stupid old mine breathing that coal dust all day. I remember, it was September 27th, 1927, and ..."

"Nellie Frances. As soon as you get through visiting with the neighbor, can you help me by tending to Valerie?" Came a harsh voice from the doorway.

"Okay Mama. I'll be right there," shouted Nellie.

"Your middle name is Frances?" Edward asked.

"Yes and she only uses it when she's lost patience with me, " Nellie answered.

"That's my middle name too," offered Edward.

"How did we ever get so lucky?" Nellie groaned.

"I don't like mine either," said Edward. "I sometimes go by Frank. Dad and Lillie are all I have. My mother and brother died back in Mineral Wells, Texas, so dad says were orphans. 'Just us is all there is', he says. "I can't remember my mother and brother much, but Lillie has always been in my life and I couldn't ask for a better mother," said Edward.

"I go by Sherwood but my first name's Leonard." Sherwood offered.

"My middle name is Lawrence, piped up Sherman. "That's sure sad about your mother and brother. Was it some kind of sickness that took 'em both?"

With a thoughtful frown Edward answered, "I'm not real sure. We don't talk about it. It upsets my dad and I don't want to put him through any more than he has already. He has rheumatoid arthritis in his hands, back and legs. I built him a wheel chair that he can use without hurting his hands. He's a preacher, you know? And Lillie takes in laundry now and again. She don't charge much, but everyone says she's real good."

"NELLIE FRANCES...Get yourself in here and help with Valerie," again came from the doorway.

Nellie jumped up and headed for the house, "Gotta go...she's hopping mad now. I swear when I get married I ain't *ever* having any kids!"

Getting up and dusting off his pants, Edward said, "Guess I'd better get back home too. Supper should be about ready," said Edward.

"Thanks for your help neighbor. I'll see ya later maybe. We sit out after dinner most nights, wherever we live, so probably tonight won't be any different."

"Okay, Maybe I'll see ya then." Edward added over his shoulder.

Chapter 49...Why God?

Mary gathered her children behind her, "You can't take my children away. I won't let you! They are not sick. I'm taking good care of my family and we will not be separated. I'm their mother and I know what's best for them."

A nurse dressed all in white, with a matching starched hat spoke with a soft caring voice, "I'm sorry Mrs. Lacey, but the girls names on this paper have shown signs of the disease at school. I'm the county nurse and I'm just doing my job. We realize that your husband has been diagnosed with the disease and remains on the property, incapacitated. The law has a right to remove children from homes and be placed in an environment that will benefit both the child and the public."

"But my husband has not had contact with the children for quite some time. He has made himself a room out of his carnival wagon and stays out there for the safety of the children and me." she explained.

"Mrs. Lacey, try to understand, the Department of Health was notified when Mr. Lacey was diagnosed. They've tested all the children and these two girls tested positive. Think of your other children. And the residents that you come in contact with regularly. The girls will get the best of care and will be returned to you as soon as the Department finds them in good health."

"Tell me what to do and I'll do it here. Hang a 'Quarantine' sign on the door. I'll keep them home, in another room so the other children don't go near them. Please, you must understand. They are my babies," she pleaded.

Again, calmly and softly the nurse explained, "Mrs. Lacey, the disease is spread not just by touching, but through the air we breathe. When a person that is contagious coughs the germs are spread, contaminating everything around in a very large area. This includes bedding, pillows, clothing, which all have to be sterilized. If you take a dinner plate out to your husband and bring it back into your house to be washed, the germs come with it. If you don't have a sterile environment the germs multiply and last for weeks on any surface it comes in contact with. The girl's tests show positive they are carrying the disease. We want to catch it quickly before it has a chance to take their lives. Besides, you have your other children to consider."

"Patients benefit from these Tuberculosis sanatoriums because the staff is taught and pay scrupulous attention to sanitary measures and these procedures place the patients at an advantage. I assure you that the staff there takes every precaution to prevent the introduction and/or spread of it, or any other contagious disease, from spreading among the patients and themselves."

"Children, that are old enough to write, are encouraged to do so each Friday. The letters are then sanitized and posted directly afterward. You will have contact with them every week."

Thinking of how many times she had the girls help with the dishes and the laundry she realized her lack of knowledge about the disease had put them all in jeopardy. "How long? How long will you keep them from me?" Mary asked in resignation.

"Most patients are held for a period of nine months while being treated," answered the nurse.

"What about their schooling? What about their Bible studies?" she asked.

"There are teachers there for both academics and the Bible. And the girls will stay in the same room to make it easier on them."

"I'll pack their clothes," Mary muttered, fighting tears, she did not want the children to see, trying to make it easier on the girls. "Margie, Myrle, come with me and help get some things together."

"Momma, you're not going to let them take us are you?" cried Mary Lee.

"Mary Lee, you have to be strong for Myrle now. You must promise to watch after her. You are going to have to be her mama until you can come home again." She turned unable to face the fear and betrayal she saw in her daughter's eyes. The knot, wedged in her throat, made it unable to speak further.

The packing was easy for they owned very little. When Nevy was unable to work she again hired out as a laundress and seamstress, and used the scraps from the ladies dresses to make her family's clothes. Church members, at times, brought her used clothing. What didn't fit any of the kids she either altered so it would, or if it had enough yardage, it was torn apart and used to make something new.

After the clothes were packed Mary returned to the living room. She took first Mary Lee into her arms and held her tight for a few seconds, turned and hugged Myrle, then straightened and locked eyes with the nurse. In a husky, strained voice said, "I'd better hear from them every week and if you're a God fearing woman you'll make sure they come back to me as soon as they're able." She turned back to the girls and took each one by a hand and walked between them out to the waiting automobile. With a forced smile she said, "Look girls, you get to ride in a nice car."

"No, Momma. Don't make us go. We want to stay here with you and daddy. PLEASE Momma, we don't want to go," cried Myrle.

"Hush now, Myrle. Mama has no choice. We will do everything we're told so we can come home sooner. You'll see. It might even be fun," choked Mary Lee as she put a protective arm around her sister's shoulders.

Mary's heart felt like it was being ripped from her chest but she was proud to see her eldest daughter taking charge and seeing the problem for what it was. She grabbed each one again and hugged them hard, then turned her back and slowly walked into the house and shut the door.

She stood there, back against the door until she heard the car drive away, then she let go and crumpled to the floor. "Why God, Why? They are so young and precious. Please, please Mother of God take care of them for me." With handfuls of dress pressed against her face she sobbed uncontrollably.

Chapter 50...Unwelcome Guest.

They were relaxing around the campfire after a hearty meal of beans and cornbread. Mattie had followed Samuel to the packhorse and watched as he packed the jars so they wouldn't get broken. He smiled at her motherly attention. *It's such a shame that a loving lady as she couldn't have children of her own,* he thought.

"How many of you did any research on this here camp out?" quizzed Sam.

Jake reached for his back pocket as Samuel pulled a paper from his vest. As the pieces were unfolded their eyes went to each other and down to the one in their hands. Laughter broke out as they presented identical posters.

"Well, it looks like you two think alike anyhow. Let me see what you've come up with," said Sam. "Well, little brother, looks like what we came up with makes it unanimous, Lewis and I spotted the same poster in town and talked about it some. Makes it pretty much settled as to what part of the fair is going to get our undivided attention. Now we have to come up with a plan. I want all of your input," said Sam.

"We all know a good horse when we see it, so what if we pose as buyers? We can get in close and ask needed questions and check out the betting without raising a lot of suspicion," Samuel offered.

"I don't know. We ain't got no fancy duds to pass as rich men," Lewis stated.

Samuel nodded. "That's the point Lewis, *real* rich people don't dress so fancy. It's the want-a-be's that get all dressed up and strut around. The richer the man the less he has to prove to the world and he dresses for comfort. I've known senators that wore bib overalls and a red hanky sticking out of their back pocket."

"Are we supposed to go as a group? Or each one of us from different parts of the country?" asked Nate.

"What if we go in as teams, from separate ranches and appear to be competing against each other?" offered Jake.

"Or...we stay separate, each of us choose a jockey and become friends with him any way we can. That will get us into the paddock..."

"The what?" Nate interrupted.

"The stables...race barn... where the jockeys, trainers, groomsmen, vets and such all congregate and talk to each other." If we play it right, we will know more about which race is going to bring in the biggest purse." That's the one we want to concentrate on."

Frowning, Nate questioned, "PURSE? You think we should steal some rich lady's purse?"

Samuel sighed, "No Nate. The money that is bet on a race is taken and held by a cashier and the total to be won is called "The purse."

He looked across the campfire at four blank faces. "Never mind. Let's just call it the *cash*".

"Well, why didn't you say so in the first place? Who ever heard of a man holding a purse?" scoffed Nate.

"So what other information will we be trying to learn?" asked Lewis.

"We have to know all the exits. Where they lead, how many security staff they have on hand, what we are going to use as a distraction, places to change our clothes and dispose of the others (this could be in different places so we have room enough to do it as fast as possible) and where we are going to meet afterwards so that we know we are all safe. That could be anywhere and we wouldn't have to acknowledge that we know each other," offered Sam.

"Plans will have to be flexible so we can change without getting too confused."

Jake yawned, "It's been a long time since I've been in the saddle as long as we were today and I'm plumb tuckered out. Besides, it won't be settled tonight that's for sure so we best just get some shut eye and talk more tomorrow."

Everyone agreed and went for their bedrolls. They placed them, close in, around the campfire for its warmth and protection from wild animals.

Just as they were beginning to nod off Lewis broke the silence with, "Ya know? We probably should have some sort of code so that if there is a problem and we need a change of plans we can all meet and discuss it. And a place to meet if one of us uses that code."

"Hold that thought Lewis, and we'll bring it up in the morning. It is a good one though," praised Sam.

Lewis smiled proudly to himself as he pulled his blanket up around his neck.

The next morning everyone started stirring as the sun's rays split the gray dawn's eastern horizon, all except Samuel. He still lay on his back with his hat over his eyes. Each man sought privacy for his morning constitutional, glancing at the friend, as he made no move to rise. He appeared to be awake and was usually the first one up and either stirring the coals or building a new fire.

Sam went to the creek and returned with a coffeepot full of water, poured in loose coffee grounds and set it on rocks just inside the growing fire.

"Rise and shine, old man. It's daylight in the swamps," challenged Nate.

They all watched for his reaction and were confused to see his right hand slide out slowly from beneath the blanket and start to write something in the dirt beside him.

Sam knew there was something wrong. He held a palm up to the others as he carefully walked where he could read what was written.

S N A K E was scrawled in the dirt. Sam waved the men back and softly read the word aloud.

"Where is it? Up his pant leg? Between his legs?" whispered Lewis.

"Get a stick and flip his hat off so you can see his eyes and maybe make some sense of this, but be careful," warned Nate.

Sam found a long stick and caught the edge of Samuel's hat and gave it a fling. It revealed a very pale face and wide eyes.

"What should we do?" asked Jake.

Samuel's hand turned up and his fingers flared out as if to say he didn't have a clue.

"Where is it?" repeated Lewis.

The hand turned and pointed to his midsection.

"Is it inside your clothes?" asked Nate

The hand went palm down and moved slowly back and forth.

"That must mean no," offered Nate.

"Should we flip the blanket off of you real fast so you can grab it and throw it?" asked Lewis

The hand gave a definite "NO".

"I know what to do. Nate, get your shaving mirror out of your saddle bag," whispered Jake.

When Nate handed him the mirror Jake tiptoed close to Samuel and held the glass so that it would reflect the morning sun down on the mound where Samuel had pointed. "What I'm hoping for might take a while, but if you can hang in there a mite longer, I think he'll head for someplace a little cooler."

So there they stood, shifting their weight from one foot to another, afraid to make any noise that may startle the snake and make it strike.

Samuel's perspiration was evident along his forehead and the guys knew he was miserable. How long had he lain there, knowing the snake had been attracted to his body heat during the cool night?

"How much heat can that snake take? That mirror is about to set that blanket on fire," whispered Sam. "I don't know if I could lay that still for that long."

Just then the mound on Samuel's stomach began to stir. Everyone became very still and Samuel was hardly breathing. It moved again and began to seek an exit from the heat that had become uncomfortable.

The spade head of the sidewinder came out from under the blanket with tongue seeking cooler ground. Everyone froze as it uncoiled and slithered out from under the blanket, unaware of where it had spent the night. As soon as those rattles disappeared beneath the closest bush, Samuel was up and jumping around trying to get blood back into his limbs and shake the fear from his body. The boys agreed that it had to have measured a good six-foot long and sported a set of rattles near five inches.

Laughter followed as it does many times when a person faces death and escapes unharmed. It is a release of emotion that eventually calms the soul.

Chapter 51...The Neighbors.

Edward had cleaned up and changed his shirt before going back in the neighbor's yard. All the boys were stretched out in the cool grass, facing Nellie as she sat rocking a toddler on the porch.

"Why don't you bring that rocker down here so we don't have to shout when we talk?" asked Sherwood.

Nellie nodded then spoke softly, "Well, find a level place down there. It would help get her to sleep faster without us having to raise our voices."

"What's the girl's name?" asked Edward.

"Valerie," answered Sherwood as Sherman joined him on the porch to help carry the rocker down the steps.

"Valerie Mae", added Sherman, "She's our half sister. She and the twins are from the old man."

"Oh, yes, I've seen them briefly but they stay indoors mostly don't they," Edward said.

"Mama went into labor while we were visiting his family in Lalanda, New Mexico. That's where the twins were born on September 18, 1931. Even as warm as it was outside, they were so tiny that Mama made them beds out of shoeboxes and set them between the wall and the wood stove to keep them warm enough. Martha Sue was the first born and Margaret Lillie was close behind her. Your Mom...I mean...Lillie...found out later that Mama named Margaret after her. She remembered her from the tent city and liked the name," Nellie explained.

Changing the subject, Edward asked, "Are you really not going to have any children when you get married?"

"Not if I can help it," she whispered.

"She has always been more of a mama to us than our real mama," offered Sherman.

"Nellie has always had to take care of us boys," chimed in Sherwood. "She protects us against the old man."

"What old man?" asked Edward.

"Our step father. He is always hollering at us and threatening to whoop us if we don't do what he says. And mama abides by his say, so Nellie fights back and he knows not to mess with her. We do what Nellie tells us, not him."

Nellie spoke softly, "Like I was telling you, before mama yelled for me, my real father died a few years ago and mama didn't let no grass grow under her feet until she hooked up with that old man. I hate him with a passion. All he does is hire us kids out to one place after another to do whatever chore needs doin'. We've planted, chopped and picked cotton all over these parts while he sits in the house they supply for us. *Migrant workers* is what the owners call us.

We've even herded sheep. Counting them out in the mornings and back in at night. We had to make sure that we didn't have one missing sheep. Anyway I've been working every day since daddy died. Either in the fields or with the next baby mama cranks out. I swear all they do while we're out working the fields is staying in and making more babies. I've had to pick cotton and drag Jim when he was a baby on the top of my cotton sack. Trying to keep him shaded, fed and diaper changed...."

"Those cotton sacks are heavy enough without adding the weight of a baby to drag along," chimed in Sherman. "Have you ever picked cotton?"

Edward shook his head, "Nope, can't say that I have. It sure doesn't look like a fun job. I've seen people's hands all bandaged up from picking it."

"You don't have to tell us. The cotton grows down inside of a bunch of thorns that is shaped like a bowl," Sherwood demonstrated with his hands, "Ya gotta reach down inside to get the cotton from a narrow opening at the top. Can't help but get pricked good by one or more of them nasty thorns when you do. Then someone's always yellin at ya to 'pick faster' and when you do it gets a whole lot worse."

"And those cotton sacks are some eight to fifteen feet long," Sherman added, "You wouldn't think that cotton would be heavy, just holding one little tuff of it, but you get a sack near full and it is one heavy load to drag down the row. Tell him about when we was hired out to chop that first guys cotton, Nellie."

She smiled, "Oh, that was funny. The old man hired us kids out telling the owner that we knew all there was to know about growing cotton when we didn't know one thing about it. We were a might younger then. Anyway, they gave us hoes and told us to start chopping. Well, I'm thinking to myself, 'Why on earth do these people plant this stuff just to turn around and chop it all down?'

The old man went back to the cabin where mama was. So I go to chopping all them plants out of the ground, and the boys always follow my lead, so there we were about seven or eight foot down each of our rows when the farmer came a runnin and yelling at us, "Stop, stop what yer doin!' Then he says to me, 'I thought he said you kids knew about chopping cotton!'

"Well, I said to him, 'He lied to you. We've never chopped cotton before in our lives.' Then that farmer looked at the cabin and then to us kids and he became real understanding. He had us gather around and he showed how to use the hoe as a measure and leave a hoe blade width of the plants and chop out a hoe blade width. He explained to us, "Thinning the row this way, gives the plants remaining a better chance at survival and produces bigger crops." Once we understood that, then we were up and at it. I don't know if the farmer ever did say anything to the old man, but us kids sure know what it means when some body says, 'It's a long old row to hoe,' cause sometimes you can't even see the end of the row you're working on."

Edward frowned, "Don't your hands and backs get tired? How long do you have to work in a day?"

"All day. We get up with the sun and go down with the sun, all cotton season long. We can take a break to go to the outhouse and for water, and then for lunch," said Sherwood.

Sherman offered his hands, palm up. "Feel our hands. We have heavy calluses that most kids our age don't."

"What about school? Do you go to school?" asked Edward.

Nellie looked down at the sleeping girl, "Yes, unless the old man gets a notion to move on to other places or to follow the season. Like I said, planting, chopping, and picking. The old man don't take much stock in school book learning. He says 'The best way to learn is by doing, and you can't do that inside a school house.'"

"Tell him about when the old man got Sherman that job sheep herding," said Sherwood.

They were lounging around on the grass as the evening light was fading. "Maybe we should save that one for another night." protested Nellie.

"Come on, Sis, it won't take that long," Sherman smiled knowing the story was about him.

"Well, like Sherwood said, the old man had agreed with this rancher that Sherman was a qualified sheep herder, and him not knowing anything about sheep at all.

"One day a big thunderstorm came blowing in and momma sent me out to fetch Sherman out of the weather. Well, I got to the field and found the sheep all huddled around the gate to the corral, actually wanting IN and Sherman no where to be seen. So I let them in and tried to count them like we were told, but they bunched together and pushed and shoved their way though the open gate to a point that I lost count. Anyway, I went looking for Sherman and it started to pour down rain, with lightening and thunder loud enough to shake the ground. I hollered and hollered until he called back. About when I got to him it started to hail. Big old hailstones came beating down on us and here he was stretched out over the top of the big old ram that had went down and couldn't get up."

"I had to yell at him with my arms over my head and face trying to protect myself from the hailstones. 'Get up and come on! We have to get out of this storm!' I'm yelling at him.

"He's yelling back, 'I can't leave him, he'll die out here.'

"The hailstones were pounding him on the back and bouncing off his head. He wasn't protecting himself, he was protecting that stupid old ram. I tried to pull him off and make him come with me, all the time him yelling about that old ram. I'm yelling, 'If he doesn't have sense enough to get out of this hailstorm, then he SHOULD die. And if he can't get up there is nothing we can do for him anyway!'

"Sherman finally decided he didn't like getting pelted by those big hailstones and allowed me to drag him away from that dumb animal. What was surprising was the rancher didn't hold it against him, but Sherman wouldn't go back because of that old ram so I had to take over his duties and finish the season."

"Yeah, and when it come to payday she got all the money," muttered Sherman.

"Oh, sure little brother, like *any* of us *ever* gets to keep any money we make," scoffed Nellie.

"Well, the rancher made sure that he put the money in *your* hand," argued Sherman.

"Yeah, and the old man let me hold it until we were out of his sight. Then he took it away from me and bought food and..." wrinkling her nose she added, "himself some snuff. That stuff is plumb nasty,"

"Tell him about that big old cottonmouth," prodded Sherman.

She gathered the child in her arms up close and stood, "Now that one WILL have to wait until another time. It's late, the mosquitoes are out and they will eat Valerie up."

Chapter 52... The Fair.

As they arrived at the fair grounds it was quite obvious that they had terribly underestimated the size of the crowd. There were so many people pushing and shoving that it was hard to stay together without holding on to one another. First off, they couldn't find a racetrack.

Confusion was not expected and new to the gang. They needed time and quiet to sort things out. Their noses led them to a large tent that was a makeshift café. They sat down at a round table, now unconcerned about being seen together.

When the waitress came and handed them each a menu, Lewis asked, "Say, little lady, where could us good old boys find this famous racetrack we've heard mentioned?"

"Oh, that. They tore that out awhile back and built the football stadium. It's called the "Cotton Bowl" and it brings in more people than the racetrack did. You boys Texas or Oklahoma fans? Their teams play against each other every year come fair time." she answered.

"Well, I guess you'd have to say we're Texas fans. Not to say that Oklahoma isn't a nice state too, but were pure Texans," bragged Lewis.

"Okay, Red, now that we got that settled, what can I get ya'll to eat and drink?" she laughed.

The boys looked at each other across the round table, realizing the hair dye was working. Nate broke the silence, "Well, maybe we better have a couple of more minutes to decide, if you don't mind coming back."

"You just go right on and decide while I tend to this other group over here." She started to leave then came back and lowered her voice just above a whisper, "None of you boys pictures on any 'Wanted' posters is there?" she smiled as she nudged Samuel's shoulder with her elbow.

After a quick glance around at each other Samuel answered, "Don't rightly think so, but you know that last party we had did get kinda rowdy, now didn't it boys!"

She threw back her head and laughed out loud. Slapping Samuel on the back and bending down she whispered, "That there table is full of police officers in regular clothes. They think they will fit in and fool everybody. Don't fool me none. Known most of 'em all their lives, little whipper-snappers."

Samuel leaned in and whispered back, "Now that's a mighty handy piece of information to know. We'll have to keep our partying down to a dull roar next time."

She laughed and turned her attention to the other table giving the boys time to check over the menu. Little did she know how helpful she had been.

Speaking low, Jake ventured, "Well guys, looks like plans have changed. Got any more ideas Lewis?"

"Hey, it ain't Lewis' fault it was tore down," defended Sam.

"There anything else around here worth…our interest?" asked Nate, lowering his voice even more.

"We're going to attract more attention sitting here whispering to each other. Start a conversation that we could all speak in normal tones about," said Samuel.

Speaking up, Sam said, "Well, I don't know about you boys but this here steak and eggs looks mighty tasty to me. My stomach thinks my throat's been slit."

Nate followed suit; "My ribs are playing 'Chopsticks' on my backbone."

Not to be out done, Lewis added," My stomach has crawled up inside my mouth and started picking my teeth."

They all laughed and a glance in the direction of the plain-clothes officers found a smile adorning one or two faces.

The gang dawdled around long enough to outlast the officers. When they were gone and the waitress had cleared their table Samuel decided they needed a bit more privacy and suggested," I think we should get a room in a boarding house so we can make new plans."

Jake agreed, "Just one room?"

"Yes for now. I'll get the room and then come back and give you the key and room number. I'll distract him while you each join Jake. I'll join you when I know you've all gone up."

Samuel asked for a corner room on the top floor, overlooking the fair, "So I can look out at all the sights," he told the desk clerk.

The clerk shot a judgmental glance at his clothing and gave an understanding nod. "Yes sir. I do have one available. I'm sure it will be to your liking, BUT it will be $5.00 in advance."

Knowing that rooms like these brought in no more than $1.00 a night, Samuel raised an eyebrow. "For that price my good man, it had BETTER be to my liking. If I weren't a business man meeting reputable and influential parties here, I would take my business elsewhere."

Trying not to show his embarrassment for his rudeness, the clerk mumbled, " Well, er, uh, what with the on going State Fair taking most of the available rooms, one should consider themselves lucky to find one at all."

"With the State Fair taking most of the available rooms is exactly why I've been forced to make my accommodations at this establishment," countered Samuel.

Seeing a vein running across the clerks temple swell and begin to throb, Samuel knew he had struck a nerve.

With jaw clenched the clerk raised his chin so as to look down his nose as he took a key from the wall behind him and stepped out from behind the desk. "Right this way sir. Will you be needing help with your luggage?"

"I have it elsewhere and it will be brought later. And IF I decide the room is to my liking, I'm perfectly capable of handling it myself," was Samuel's icy response.

Samuel silently cursed himself for allowing the man to engage him in the hostile exchange, but he had a low tolerance of people who judged another by the clothes they wore or their manner of speech.

He felt confident that he had put the man in his place, but at what cost? He had brought unwanted attention to himself.

The confrontation proved to have been for the best after all. Samuel followed the clerk back to the desk and signed in with a fictitious name. Wishing to distance himself from further embarrassment, the clerk busied himself with errands that left the desk unmanned long enough for Samuel to pass the key to Jake who then crossed the lobby to the staircase, and for each of the boys to follow, unnoticed.

Earlier the boys had paired off and mingled with the crowd and made mental notes of the comings and goings of spectators and workers alike. In so doing they had spotted the plain clothes officers and where they were stationed. It seemed the most highly guarded area was the ticket booths at each entrance. It became obvious that the carnival booths, inside the grounds and the men tending the games and concession stands were ignored by the officers.

A young man tending one of the game booths caught Lewis' attention because he seemed quite sorry that a child had played his game and went away without a prize. The young man was friendly to the customers, not pushy or aggressive like the others, so Lewis struck up a conversation with him, pretending to be interested in joining the carnival.

"Hi. I was just wondering about joining up with the carnival. Sure would be better than farming I reckon. How do you guys get paid?" Lewis asked.

"Boy mister your hair is the reddist I've ever seen. We have a girl back where I came from and she has red hair and freckles, and her momma has red hair too, but it ain't near as red as yer's. You must be Irish. That's where her family says their grandpa was from. I never saw him, just her and her momma."

"Oh, yeah, well I reckon that's where my family hail from too. Somewhere over in Ireland for sure. But what about you working here. Do ya get paid much?"

"Well, not much that's for sure. Mostly it comes from what I take in. That's why some guys are so loud and pushy. The more they get people to lose, the more money they get for the carnival and the more money they get paid."

"That seems reasonable," Lewis baited him.

"Yeah, I guess, but I hate to see the little ones lose all their money and go away empty handed," said the softhearted young man.

"What if you just gave one of them a toy and *say* they won?" asked Lewis.

"There's bosses walking around all the time watching us. They're afraid that we will do that or maybe steal some of the money we bring in."

"Surely they have no way of telling how many people have paid at your booth or had tickets bought from over there," Lewis pointed to a ticket booth.

"They sure seem to. One guy one year tried to tell them that he didn't have very much business and they took him out behind the carney wagons and stripped him down and found money in his clothes. They beat him something awful," answered the youth.

"What's a 'Carney'? asked Lewis.

"That's what all us workers are called, 'Carneys', short for Carnival I suppose."

"What if you're innocent and they blame you anyway?"

"We have our own court system, as well as our rules and heaven help us if we break them. Usually you have a buddy and he's supposed to be either across from you or beside your booth and you all keep an eye on each other. That buddy can stand up for you and they will mostly take his word."

"What if it's an outsider. Ya know, someone that robs you while your buddy isn't watching or is busy with a customer? How can you make them understand what happened?"

"Oh, that. Well, we just holler as loud as we can, 'HEY, RUBE' and all the carnys know to come a running cause something bad has happened. It could be a fire, or an animal loose, or a tent about to collapse. But if it's somebody trying to steal from us, they usually catch the guy and there isn't much left of him to hand over to the local police," he explained proudly.

"Wow, that's really something. Sounds like you all look out for one another then."

"Like I said, unless you mess up big time. But I sure ain't making it as good as I thought I would when I ran away from home and joined this here carnival," sighed the lad.

"Where's home?" asked Lewis.

"Back in Ohio. I lived with my folks on a nice farm back there and thought it would be so much more fun to be out here making lots of money and getting to see the country. Sure isn't what I thought it would be."

"Why don't you just go on back home?"

"I'm afraid my mom and dad won't want me back. Being's I ran away. They probably don't care and might be better off without me. I left eight sisters and brothers, as well as my folks. They probably don't miss me no how," he said sadly.

"Gee, I'll bet they would be plumb tickled to death to see you coming down the road to home. I know my parents have sorely missed my brothers and sister that have gone off and left to make a life for themselves. Next time this carnival swings by your hometown, you just hop outta that booth and take off for home. I'll bet you would be welcomed with loving hugs from your momma." Lewis was surprised how quickly he cared for this young man. "I hope you do just that. I truly hope you do."

"You know, I might just do that. We're due to pass through there in a few months. I didn't know I missed them so much until I started talking to you. Thanks. I wish I could give you a toy, but I'm being watched all the time. I might even get into trouble with you just standing and not playing, but I don't care. They'll get over it. Thanks again. And if you ask my advice, I guess you got your answer. It isn't what I thought it was going to be when I left home and I'm terrible home sick." The youth mustered up a smile as

Lewis waved and walked away with a plan forming in his head that he wanted to mull over with the rest of his 'buddies'.

At the hotel he explained what he had learned to the others and laid out his idea. "What if, someone with a very loud voice were to yell 'HEY, RUBE' back behind the wagons away from all the game and ticket booths? The carnies manning the game booths have their money in aprons and will be taking it with them, but If they all leave their stations on the run like that kid said, well, we could mosey up to a ticket booth and clean them out."

'Little brother, did you also notice that those ticket booths are evidently locked inside and have a very small window, with bars, to keep people out?" asked Sam.

"Yes, but I also noticed what happens when the men come to make collections. They knock on the back door and say 'collection' loud enough for the teller to hear. IF the timing is just right, and someone hollers 'HEY RUBE' at collection time...and the collectors are busy elsewhere, we might just get the money handed to us with no one being the wiser.

"I like that. If we want to make it a big take we can wait until the night collection," answered Nate.

"What about hitting two at once, like we did the towns?" asked Jake.

"Okay, Okay, now let's slow down a bit. I'm all for the plan, don't get me wrong, but didn't you say if those carnys catch a guy there isn't much left of him to hand over to the police?" asked Samuel.

"Yes, that's what the boy said" answered Lewis. "Look over there, in that booth down on the left. See the one with the red pointed tent top? He's the one that told me all about it."

The boys went to the hotel window and looked down, searching for the booth.

"You're not saying that he is going to help us are you?" asked Nate.

"No. I think the boy is as honest as the summer day is long and is trying to survive on his own. I think I've talked him into going back home. He seemed pretty home sick that's for sure. But no, he won't help us, and I wouldn't want to put him in jeopardy with the thugs they have working there," said Lewis

Now they were in sync, and suggestions were flowing as fast as the ideas were born.

"So what does the guy do that yells "Hey, Rube?" asked Nate. "He's gonna have to either outrun those thugs or out think 'em. By the looks of the ones I saw, It'd be easier ta out think 'em."

"Well, we've always been good at that, haven't we boys?" asked Samuel.

"Sure have. And I've been thinking of using the other trick we used. Start a fire somewhere far enough away from people, but putting their business in danger, one of their wagons, or tents, maybe. It sounds like the local police care little about the carnival's possessions or security, only that of the local citizens. So they would be on their own to fight the blaze while we do the deed and head for home."

"Do you think we should take off that same night or hang around a day or so and see what happens?" asked Jake.

"You boys will head for home. I'll hang around for a day or so and make sure there are no loose ends," said Samuel.

"Okay. Now we have a plan. How soon do we put it into action?" asked Nate.

"We'll wait for tomorrow night. They will have a lot more money on a Saturday night than they will any other," offered Sam. "We'll split up tomorrow and determine each of our own escape routes. We will find a place to meet afterwards, change clothes, wash our hair, and find something or someplace to stash the money. Remember we won't have our horses or saddlebags."

"We should have our train tickets purchased ahead of time..." started Lewis.

"And time the hold up with it's departure," interrupted Nate.

"IF we can," added Jake. "If we can have time to get to the train without making a beeline for it, they won't suspect anyone would take a slow train for a get-away."

"If we are going to split up and hit two, then we can all four take the train. We can pretend that we got away from our wives and are really living it up," added Jake. "Wait a minute. Where are we going to wash our hair? And will we get enough of the dye out?"

It's going to be at night, so who's going to see what color hair we have anyhow? Lewis has that God awful red that stands out like a sore thumb, and he's been talkin to that kid down there."

"So what?" asked Sam, "He's established that he was thinking about joining the carnival."

"Because someone might put two and two together and realize that he pumped that kid for the information we used against them."

"Wait a minute and keep your voices down," whispered Samuel, "Take a deep breath and relax. Now, Lets go over this a little slower. And take one step at a time. Brain storming is good, but we have to take a breath and think things through."

Everyone became silent and began to think.

Nate broke the silence. "The way I see it, We let the crowd see us in our 'going home clothes'. We four are having a good time. We'll *act* like we're drinking more than we should, maybe pour a little whiskey on our shirts and swirl some in our mouth so people can smell it on our breath and clothes. Flirt with some of the girls like drunk men, away from their wives would. We have to pretend to keep each other standing at times. We won't be so loud and obnoxious that people get angry, just enough so the witnesses will swear that we couldn't have been capable of holding up ourselves let alone the carnival."

They were all nodding. Samuel picked it up from there. "I've established that I am meeting some important clients and that I have luggage elsewhere. One of us will have to purchase a well-worn suitcase and hopefully a traveling trunk of some sort and each of us will purchase a couple bottles of one brand of liquor as we can, and a couple of blankets to cover the cash bag.

I will be a liquor distributor, traveling with samples of my wares to offer the local bar owners. You will have found my wares and helped yourselves, causing me much anxiety. I will call the sheriff to have you arrested."

"I don't like the sounds of that. We don't want the law anywhere near us," said Nate.

"Oh, but that's the beauty of it. We will keep them confused with my complaint of missing liquor, that you will each blatantly display but will also have receipts for your purchases in your pockets! They will only have my complaint, and see a half empty traveling trunk and will want to be rid of all of us as soon as possible so they can concentrate on the larger issue...the carnival theft."

He knew that some had grasped the idea while others were still not seeing the big picture. But he also knew he still had time to explain it better.

Chapter 53...A letter from Will..

A horn honked outside and Mary Lee ran out to see who it was. She brought a letter in and gave it to Mary on her way out to play, "It was Aunt Ginny in her new car, she brought our mail."

Mary Lee and Myrle had been returned from the sanatorium after a stay of eight and one-half long months. And Mary was content that it was the end of it. They never had the disease and were not contagious, which she had known all along but couldn't get anyone to listen. A mother knows her children and she knew her girls were healthy when they were taken away.

Pleased to see a letter from Will, Mary settled in her rocker to enjoy it. He didn't like to write and it was always a blessing to hear from him. But she was not prepared for its contents. He wrote very few words, scribbled by a grieving hand, informing her that her sweet, precious brother James Archie, was dead! She sat, stunned, looking at the words but not accepting what they meant. *How could Arch be gone?* Will wrote that he had died on the 14th of January.*1934...That was Margie's seventh birthday. I made her a cake that day. Clayton and I sang 'Happy Birthday' to her. No, not Arch, not dead.*

"Read it to me, Momma. Read it to me," begged Margie. "Do you want me to get Mary Lee or Myrle to read it, Momma?"

"No child, but I need for you to go tell your sisters to come in for a minute. I have something to tell all of you."

Once the girls were standing around her chair she began to tell them. "This is from your Uncle Will and he has written that...choke... sob... your Uncle Arch has gone..." no more words could escape the hard lump in her throat.

"Gone where, Momma?" came from Mary Lee.

"Where did Uncle Arch go?" came from Myrle.

"Is he coming here to visit?" asked Margie.

"Can he stay with us? Why are you crying, Momma?" asked Mary Lee

"Hush for a minute dear. Let me talk. Uncle Arch has gone...to heaven," squeaked Mary.

Tears welled up in the girl's eyes. They had heard of death before, but could not comprehend its meaning. It was seeing their mother's tears and obvious pain that caused their sadness. As children, they felt helpless, not knowing what exactly was bothering their mother, but feeling the depression none the less.

"Why, Momma? Why did Uncle Arch go to heaven?" asked Myrle.

"Is he with Jesus now?" asked Margie.

"Isn't that a happy place?" asked Mary Lee.

Mary realized that she could not openly grieve in front of the children. She had taught them to love God and Jesus and live their lives to please Him so that He may accept them into His Kingdom someday. It was so easy to teach, but so hard to accept that Arch's 'someday' had come.

With tears streaming down her face, she reached down and picked up Clayton who had been sitting at her feet. "Yes, Mary Lee, it is a happy place and I'm sure that Uncle Arch is smiling down on us and not wanting us to grieve for him. My tears are because I am sad that I will not see him again until I too, am called. Now, would you be a dear and fix Clayton and the girls a sandwich?"

"Okay, Momma. I'll see to it. You can cry if you want to. I'm sorry that I won't see Uncle Arch too. Not until we all go to heaven," Exclaimed Mary Lee.

After Mary Lee took the others into the kitchen, Mary rose from her chair, clutching the tear stained letter she slowly walked out to Nevy's wagon. *He must be told. They were such good friends. Oh God, Why Arch? He was so sweet and gentle and loving. I'm not sure of the tests you want me to endure, or why, but it gets harder and harder with each loss.*

"I'm so sorry dear. So very sorry. Does Will say what caused his death?" Nevy asked.

"He has printed the word from Arch's death certificate. It is M-y-o-c-a-r-d-I-t-I-s. He said the doctor told him that it means an infection of his heart." She turned the page and continued, "He says, 'Arch had the symptoms of the flu or a bad cold. He had complained about fever, achy bones and being very tired.' Then Will says 'I had the doctor come in the day before, but that night Arch was real restless and when I went to check on him the next morning, he was gone. The doctor told me he probably felt a sharp stabbing pain in his chest and went quickly.'"

Nevy nodded, "Well, let's hope the pain wasn't too severe, and we know that he is in a better place now. We also know that I will be seeing him soon."

Mary's eyes came off the page and stared at Nevy. "Why would you want to go and say something like that when you know how bad I'm hurting right now? The doctors told us that there could be a cure found any day for this and you might out live us all."

"Mary, look at me. Really look at me! I have. I've seen the image looking back at me from my shaving mirror…cough…cough…It is not the image of a man that has long… a wheezing breath…to live. I'm skin and bone and my color is ashen to the point that I look like a walking corpse…another wheeze…if I *could* walk. All I do is lie here, day after day. I'm looking forward to the time that *I* am called and can be...cough... with our Heavenly Father."

"Don't talk like that, Nevy! He has taken so much from me that I feel He should be satisfied and not take any more. Don't give up, Nevy. I need you."

"For what? cough...cough...Need me to do what? What can I do to make our lives any easier, like a husband is...cough..cough...cough...supposed to do? I'm dying a little each day, and there's nothing left for us to do but accept it." he wheezed with each breath. "I can't even die in dignity. I can't support my family. Because of this disease we had two of our children taken from us and there was nothing I could do to prevent it. Is that a man? Is that a husband? A father? If I weren't afraid that I would go to hell, I would take my own life." Gasping for breath, he continued, "I can't play with my children and I don't want them seeing me this way, anyhow. You shouldn't even be spending this much time out here. I'm sure it is as bad as having leprosy. I should shout 'UNCLEAN, UNCLEAN' ...choke, gasp... to everyone that comes within hearing of me."

Mary could take no more. She whirled around and ran for the house crying, "I can take one of you on at a time, but I can't take both you AND God burdening me with all these infernal tests."

It was another full year of her burdens before Nevy succumbed to the slow killing tuberculosis on May 5, 1935. It had not only robbed him of his dignity in his last years, but also Mary of a loving husband and father to her children.

Will then came to San Angelo to live with Mary but found just a shell of the girl that once trusted in love and friendship only to find them unreliable. She found a seamstress job across town and walked both ways, unable to pay the five cents for the bus fare.

Chapter 54...Nellie Finds a Beau..

Pages of the calendar turned as Edward found that the nights spent listening to Nellie's stories were very special to him. He liked listening to her descriptions of places they had been and things they had done. She spoke of playing on the ruins of the Alamo at one time and passing by Billy the Kid's grave going to and from school at another. He liked to see her face soften as she spoke of her father. And the change it made when she spoke of "the old man."

She told how her mother met him at the mattress factory that he owned. She had applied for and got a job there, hand stitching mattresses. Nellie stood and boldly lifted her dress, exposing her right thigh. "See that scar? I got that when I walked up behind Mama while she was working there. She was using a very large crescent shaped needle that she pushed through the edge of the mattress then pulled it out beside and behind her. She didn't know I was standing there until she sunk that needle way into my leg." Sitting back down she shook her head and continued, "I don't know why he didn't keep that factory, but they were no sooner married and we were on the road like gypsies."

One night they were all visiting as usual when Sherman exchanged glances with Sherwood before speaking casually, "I guess Nellie done got herself a beau."

"Who?" asked Edward.

"A big tall fella that lives out in the Sulfur Springs valley. Name's John Key," shared Sherwood.

"I've seen him driving his fancy car around. He's pretty stuck on himself as far as I can see. I thought he's married, isn't he?" Edward asked hopefully.

"I guess he's divorced and he and his sister Bonnie like to party. I hear they're both wild," added Sherwood. "He looks like he's got some Indian blood."

Nellie had tried to ignore her brothers teasing, but she had heard quite enough, "What difference does that make Leonard Sherwood? After all Daddy's grandmother was a half breed. Her name was Eliza Hudson and she was born in Arkansas to a white man and an Indian woman on the Little Rock Indian Reservation, according to Aunt Georgia. I heard the adults talking one day when they didn't know I was close enough to hear."

"Well, we should all paint our faces up and run around with feathers in our hair," said Jim as he hopped to his feet and started a war dance, leaning forward then backward as he toe-heeled on each foot, around an imaginary bonfire.

"Sit down and quit your silliness. They don't do that stuff anymore," said Nellie.

"Maybe not out where white people can see 'em, but I'll bet they do when they get way out on those reservations," stated Sherman.

"Is it true, Nellie? Do you like that John Key?" asked Edward quietly.

'I think he's rather handsome and he always dresses so nice. He's asked me to go out with him and his sister Bonnie, so I don't see any harm. He's just more adult than the boys around here. Bonnie and I are good friends in school and she says he's kinda sweet on me, so I guess you could say that I'm interested."

Edward heard little of the conversation that continued as his mind raced on, *How can she like a guy that is so much older than her? But I'm older too. I'm probably as old as he is. But he's a no good that only thinks of himself. He wears fancy clothes even*

311

though he doesn't hold down a decent job. I know his kind, he'll break her heart for sure.

At home he sat at the kitchen table drinking a cup of coffee. Lillie could see something was bothering him but she was giving him time to decide if he wanted to talk about it. Finally he said, "I want to be called Ed from now on. It's more grown up."

"And what pray-tell has brought that on?"

"I've been thinking. I'm in my twenties and I'm still being called Edward, like a little boy. You don't hear grown men being called long names. They shorten them to make it easier...I want to be called Ed from now on."

"What about Sherwood and Sherman? Those are long names," asked Lillie.

"And they are still boys, a lot younger than me." he countered. "I want to be called Ed!"

"You already said that. Okay, for whatever your reason, I will call you Ed if that's what you want, Son," she agreed.

"What if I call you 'Buster'?" asked Acey.

"No. That's babyish too. I'm a man now and I want to be called by a man's name."

The parents exchanged a knowing glance and shared a smile. "Alright, from now on... *Ed* it is." Lillie patted his shoulder as she kissed the top of his head.

Chapter 55...The Gang Rides Again.

The plans were set in motion as Samuel found his way behind the carnival's traveling carts used as living quarters. These were parked near a large open barn that housed the animals used to pull them.

He clung to the shadows as one by one each gate latch and stall door was slightly opened and ropes were untied that secured animals in their stalls.

Samuel waited the designated time before he set a fire behind the barn. He then retreated far into the shadows and with as loud a voice as he could muster he bellowed, "HEY RUBE! HEY RUBE!" He was surprised at how quickly bodies came running, each repeating the code, "HEY RUBE! HEY RUBE."

He retraced his way through the shadows far enough that when he felt the time was right he came running, joining the main stream of the crowd.

As the fire climbed the wall of the barn and the smoke began to fill the nostrils of the animals, their panic added to the confusion. When they sought escape they found they were not secured and tried to put distance between them and the fire.

Horses, elephants and oxen fled the stalls and ran head long into the crowd that came to save them.

All the animals were hell bent on reaching safety and the carnies found that they were the only things between the crowd and the stampeding hoofs.

Samuel held his breath each time someone came close to being trampled. He saw men dive for lead ropes of horse halters, while others tried desperately to block the path of oxen. There was no way to stop the elephants, so their trainers ran before them yelling for people to clear their path.

Still others ran for the fire, gathering canvas gunnysacks and soaking them at the trough near the barn. Others bailed water from the trough and ran to the fire. Samuel decided to man the hand pump that filled the trough and tried to refill it for the workers. A line formed and a bucket brigade was set into action to get the water to the fire faster and more efficiently.

After Samuel's first yell the gang went into action. Each team waited until the crowd was either running to or from the call. A long thirty seconds went by before they stepped forward and knocked on the back doors of the ticket booths.

"Collections," Nate called. The back door opened a crack, then out came a large canvas bag, leather bound handles with matching hinge and lock secured at the top. The door closed as quickly as it had opened and the two men stood for a split second before making a beeline for the shadows. Becoming accustomed to the darkness, the boys were able to see their way fairly well.

"Can you believe that?" Lewis whispered. "I've never been so surprised in all my life. We done dyed our hair for nothing."

"Hush," came Nate's warning. "Later." was added as he slid a blanket over the bag and nudged Lewis back toward the hotel. People ran past them, unseeing, just a few feet beyond the shadows, in answer to the warning shout.

Jake and Sam reached their ticket booth precisely the time they heard Samuel's call. They too counted quietly to thirty.

Then Sam announced in a voice as confident as possible. "Collections." A stirring noise came from the other side of the door and the door opened a crack. "What's going on out there? What's the commotion?"

"I don't know yet. My job is to secure the money as fast as possible and I can't do that standing here answering your questions! You want to answer to the boss if anything happens to this collection?"

The canvas bag was shoved through the door barely wide enough to allow it. Neither man saw who had passed the money to Sam nor did they want to wait around to find out. They were in complete agreement as they also covered their bag with the blanket purchased earlier. They retreated back into the shadows and headed to their next destination.

Their planning days were well spent watching the collections the nights before, because they knew what size trunk to purchase and what back street held no street lights. The day of the hold up, each man had purchased two bottles of liquor, placing the receipts in their wallets. Samuel purchased hunting knives, blankets some clothes and five tickets on the train, whose departure best suited their plan, and placed them in the trunk. He then gave Sam a key to the trunk, checked out of his room and took the trunk to the depot, placing it near the back of the train station's platform, away from the lighted area.

Sam and Jake waited for Lewis and Nate in the alley off the dark street and behind the depot. When Lewis' signal whistle came, they waited ten seconds and answered it. Sam made his way along the back of the depot and found the trunk where Samuel had left it. The platform was about three feet off the ground from the back and Samuel had to reach up to insert the key into the lock. Without light his fingertips had to search for the keyhole and then insert the key. The lock clicked open, but the height of the trunk from the ground made it nearly impossible to lift the lid to any degree. Sam knew he couldn't manage the placement of the cash in the bottom of the trunk from his position, so he slowly, quietly pulled the trunk inch by inch close to the edge of the platform. Then he realized that he could not lift it down by himself. He edged his way back to the boys and whispered, "Jake, you're going to have to help me lift the trunk down to the ground so we can empty the money bags into it."

With a nod Jake followed him back to the trunk and eased it off the platform and into the shadows.

After Sam gave a muffled whistle, Nate and Lewis joined them with the bags. Quickly and quietly they removed the trunks contents which Samuel had purchased and placed inside, on top of the four-inch deep false bottom. Jake handed each man his train ticket, which they shoved inside their tucked in shirts.

Jake and Nate each took a canvas bag and cut them open with the hunting knives from the trunk. They each emptied the bags, handing the stacks of bills to Lewis and Sam who placed them evenly on the bottom. The top of the false bottom was replaced. The blankets and clothes were added along with the extra liquor after keeping out one bottle for each man. Then the tools were replaced in the trunks removable tray and the latch was locked.

The boys were ready to lift the trunk and replace it on the platform when they heard voices and footsteps approaching. They froze in the darkness, knowing that any movement could cause sound. It was two men, out for a breath of air and a 'smoke' as they waited for the next train. Their conversation drifted down to the boys as one man packed and lit his pipe. The flare of the wooden match illuminated four men standing like statues, just a few feet behind and below the men above. The flare subsided, leaving the smaller flame to light his pipe as well as his companion's tailor made cigarette. Luck still held, for the smokers were facing the disturbance from the carnival and were unaware of how close they stood to the Tirrell Gang.

It seemed like hours before the men finished their smokes and returned to the depot. The gang had not been able to move or take a deep breath as they waited in the shadows. As soon as the men were out of sight and hearing, they wasted no more time returning the trunk to the depot's platform.

Still silent but breathing easier, they retreated. Spotting a loose board near the depot's foundation Sam swung it open, slid in the moneybags and replaced the board. With a nod they made their way back to the alley. There they opened their bottles and doused some on their clothes, and swished a mouthful around before spitting it out.

Nate swallowed his and when he saw their accusing looks he said, "Hell boys, I can't let a fine liquor like this go to waste. We all know that it ain't as strong as Pa Tirrell's, and would take a lot more than a swallow to offset our thinking."

They laughed and followed suit, each taking a swig. Then nodding to each other and spacing their departures, they set off in different directions to establish their alibis of being too drunk to carry out such an elaborate plan as the holdup that had just taken place.

The commotion was dying down at the far end of the carnival. People were coming back after watching from their vantage points, all talking about the fire and how lucky no one was seriously injured. The buzz of the crowd stated that the fire was under control and safe to proceed with the festivities.

Nate staggered, between a couple on the sidewalk and slightly brushed against a dandy dressed man in a double-breasted suit. "Oh, shuuze me Misssir." Then swaying unsteadily he removed his hat and holding it over his heart, he added with a lopsided grin, "Howdy, purdy lady,"

"Be off with you, you drunken louse!" demanded the man.

"Oh, don't be so hard on him dear, I'm sure he means no harm," said the woman. "He's just enjoying the fair with a few too many."

The man gripped his own lapels, one with each hand, and straightened his jacket. Stiffening his spine he clicked his heels together and offered his arm to the lady. "Well, then, come my dear and let's be clear of the likes of him and his kind."

Nate bowed at the waist and scraped his hat on the sidewalk below, "Thank you purdy lady for seeing me as I really am...just happy go lucky me." As he straightened he gave her a little wink.

She blushed and smiled but turned and took her companion's arm and continued on their way.

Lewis was acting out a similar scenario with the carney boy he had met earlier, "Ya wanna sip from my bottle? I hate to drink alone."

The lad could smell the booze from behind the table front. Shaking his head, he answered, "Uh, no thanks. I'm on duty and it's against the rules."

"Hell, boy, I ain't gonna tell anyone. Who...whoose gonna know?" Lewis stammered.

Lowering his voice the lad said, "I told you before, there are bosses everywhere, keeping close eyes on us. Besides, I don't drink. Tried it once and got real bad sick. Couldn't justify the feeling of being drunk to the horrible morning after. Just don't balance toward the liquor."

"The trick is, is, is, uh, oh yeah," Lewis acted as if trying to remember the exact words. Then nodding as if agreeing with someone who had given him the answer he shook his finger "Ya gotta drink

318

more often and then ya don't have them hangovers."
Seeing the alibi was set, he continued, " Well, if I can't
get ya ta drink with me then I'll see if I can find
someone who will. You shtick to your guns boy and
shtay away from this shtuff. It truly doesn't balance."
With that said he made his unsteady way out of the
boy's sight to join the others.

Jake and Sam joined forces and walked side
by side, each gripping the other's closest shoulder,
allegedly for support. Their free hand clutched a bottle
to their chests as they staggered through the crowd.
They too, were barely brushing bystanders, so as not
to anger anyone. Creating their own alibis, they began
to sing, a little off key, but entertaining those nearby.

As they made their way through the crowd they
parted slightly and chose a young lady strolling with a
slightly built fellow. "Ain't she sweet. Just a walkin'
down the street. Now I ask ya very con-fi-denchalee,
ain't she sweet."

The girl smiled and dropped her chin to her
chest. The boy pushed her a little faster, past the
singers who then turned to another girl, removing their
hats to show the color of their hair, "Five foot two,
eyes of blue, but oh what those two eyes can do. Has
anybody seen my gaalll?" They tagged along beside
the girl and sang to her as she and her escort
continued on their way. Jake dashed ahead of them,
bending on one knee he held out his arms, one hand
clutching the bottle, "Schwanee how I love ya, how I
love ya, my dear old Schwanee, I'd give the world to
be… among the folks in D I X I E…."

"Out of the way you fool, before I call a
constable," warned her companion.

"Oh don't be silly Willard, the men are just
having fun. You could take a lesson from them and

loosen up a little yourself. Those around you would have a much better time," she scolded.

"Yeah Willard, loosen up. Wanna drink Willard? How about you little lady? Wanna ditch him and come along with us? We truly are good old boys and you would be purrrfectly safe," came from Sam.

"Miss, are these men offending you?" came from a gruff voice behind them. It was two of the plain dressed officers from the café.

She smiled and shook her head. "No, mister, but thank you for coming to my defense." Shooting an accusing look at her escort, "They are just enjoying the fair's party atmosphere, and will no doubt be very sorry in the morning," she gathered her skirts and turned back to her sheepish companion. He smiled stiffly and took her elbow, guiding her away and into the crowd.

"Well men, she may forgive your lack of respect, but I think you've had enough for tonight. You head back to your homes or hotel rooms and sleep it off," stated the bigger of the two officers.

With their alibis established, they made their unstable way to the train station, where the others were waiting.

Samuel was sitting on a bench close to the trunk seeming to read a local newspaper. Nate and Lewis were propped against the depot's wall, maintaining their drinking role, seeming to be telling each other jokes that caused a burst of laughter every few minutes. Jake and Sam came out of the darkness and made their way onto the platform, supporting each other, still carrying their nearly empty bottles.

"Well, I'll be a suck egg mule! Look who we got here; you boys lost?" burst from Lewis as he staggered to his feet, and approached them. Putting his arm around his brother's neck he slurred out,

"Looky here Willy, itch our neighburs, the Callaway boys! Wanna drink? Ahhh I sees ya got chur own. Y'all waitin' on the shame train as ush? Sure didn't want to go back sho shoon, but that big feller over there shaid it was time to go ho.home."

Samuel lowered his paper and glanced over the top of the page at the boys, shaking his head ever so slightly as if to tell Lewis not to be overacting.

The glance did not go unnoticed and Jake swayed his way over and took Lewis by the arm, "Come on little brother, let's sit on that there bench before you fall down. Howdy neighbors, come on over and join us. We've had some fun today, but I think Ned here had more than his share."

"Do…Don't look like you're too ffffar behind'em, Willy," stammered Nate.

"I think we'd better get both these boys off their feet fer a while. We've hit the bottle a wee bit mor'an we should've," came from Sam.

The boys quieted down a bit, knowing they had achieved their mission to this point. Everything relied on keeping control of the situation until they got aboard the train. They each thought if they could get away without further ado, it would certainly be a relief.

But it was not going to be that easy. The sounds of disturbance came from the carnival area, reaching the platform in a wave of shouting and cursing. Men and women armed with pitchforks, hammers, swords and sticks of firewood came as a mob.

"Where's the law around here?" bellowed the leader, brandishing a coiled whip overhead. "We demand to speak to the sheriff of this town! We've been robbed!"

The plain-clothes men were close on his heels and stood behind him with arms crossed. The crowd

321

behind them were shaking their fists and shouting in agreement with the leader about bringing the town's lawmen to investigate their loss.

The sheriff made his way through the townspeople, gathered out of curiosity, to face the furious carnival staff. The two groups approached each other and stopped with the two sets of train tracts between them, within hearing distance of the platform.

The carney ringleader and the sheriff stepped forward. "My deputy just now informed me that you want to speak to me. What's the commotion all about?"

"We've been robbed that's what it's all about!" the leader shouted. The mob began to shout, "WHATCHA GONNA DO ABOUT IT, SHERIFF?" "YOU GONNA GET OUR MONEY BACK?" "YEAH, WE WANT OUR MONEY BACK!"

The sheriff looked around for a vantage point and chose the platform. As he moved toward it he signaled them to follow. He positioned himself so everyone could hear and see him and raised his arms for quiet. "Nothing can be done by shouting and waving weapons around. Go back to your tents or trailers and let this gentleman and me get to the bottom of this!"

Seeing that the sheriff was duly concerned, The mob leader turned to his followers and agreed. "He's right, folks. Go back and make sure nothing else gets stolen while we are all up here."

The crowd muttered and mumbled their grievances but followed the man's orders, confident that he would get justice.

"How was this robbery achieved? What kind of weapon was involved?" asked the sheriff.

"Well, it all started when there was a fire at the back of the stables. One of the carnival personnel saw it and yelled for our attention. We managed to get the fire out without harm to people or animals, but while we were fighting the fire a man approached the ticket booths and asked for the money. My staff gave the money to him."

"Excuse me? You're telling me that your employees just handed over the money when the man asked for it? Without seeing a weapon? Without asking any questions?"

"Well, he seemed to know the routine of our couriers and pretended to be one of them, picking the money up at the right time...." stated the ringleader.

"What is this man's description?" interrupted the sheriff.

"Uh, er, well, the employees don't bother to look out at the couriers. They just hand it out the back door when the time comes," stuttered the leader.

"Well this doesn't constitute a robbery. A robbery is when someone takes your valuables using force or intimidation," explained the sheriff.

"I don't care what the definition is. That man took our money and we want it back. That is our families' and animals' livelihood," blurted the man.

Removing his hat with one hand the sheriff scratched his stubby chin, shook his head and took a deep breath. "I believe this falls under the section of theft. No, wait. That's not true either because 'theft', or 'stealing', is the illegal taking of another person's property without the person's freely-given consent. You said your employees handed over the money freely, without being threatened or intimidated. This is a new one on me sir, I'm not sure how I should file this."

323

Furious now the leader stiffened his back, lowered his chin and slapped the whip against his leg, then winced from the pain of his own action. "You have got to arrest all the people and not let anyone leave until you search everyone and their belongings! Certainly don't let anyone leave on the next train!"

With that said, Samuel proceeded with the back up plan. "Opening his trunk he began to shout, I've been robbed too! Sheriff, Sheriff, I've been robbed of my merchandise. My trunk was supposed to be safe here and someone has stolen most of my liquor! I agree, you can't allow anyone to leave on the next train until you have searched everyone. This is my living! I demand you investigate this immediately!"

"Now hold on everyone, one thing at a time." Pointing to the carny the sheriff began, "YOU say a man stole money from your ticket booths and YOU say someone has stolen your liquor?"

"Yes. I had a trunk full of liquor and now there is only a few bottles! Come, see for yourself. Wait a minute. What about those scally wags?" Pointing to four obviously drunken men." They probably got into my trunk and stole my fine whiskey."

Lewis pushed his body up from the bench and defended himself and Jake "Now jush a dog gone minute you...dandy. Me and my brother don't need ta steal nobody's whiskey. We done bought ourn up there in town at the saloon. See right cheer, I got me a ticket that says so. Shee here, Sheriff? I got me one of those tickets that says I bought my bottles fair and square."

The sheriff pulled his head back away from Lewis' hand and looked at the receipt. Then looking at Samuel he said, "The man's right. He's got a receipt for his purchase."

Sam wasted no time in staggering forward and shoving his receipt at the sheriff. "We all got proof positive that we done paid for thish here wishkey. You're gonna have ta look elshwhere for who done took yer goods, Mishter."

"Sheriff, SHERIFF! You have to find the man that rob…stole…TOOK our money," shouted the carnival leader.

"What time was this, uh, for lack of a better word… theft?" asked the sheriff.

"A few hours ago. The regular couriers were helping to fight the fire and didn't know about the pick up until we had everything under control and everyone was going back to their duties."

"HOURS ago?" asked the sheriff. "And you think that this person would just hang around here and wait for someone to catch him? He probably is miles away by now, in any direction you care to point."

Samuel stepped in, "What about my liquor? Who's going to replace my wares? I left my trunk on the platform in good faith that it would be guarded."

"Sir, what I said to him, goes the same for you. Was your trunk locked?" asked the sheriff.

"Well, of course it was! But they must have picked the lock or something," complained Samuel.

"Now you're going to tell me, with your trunk showing no damage, that someone stood out here on the platform, in broad daylight and picked the lock?"

The sheriff was getting exasperated, but took the lock that Samuel was demanding he examine. "This lock has not been tampered with. It's clean as a whistle. If anyone 'stole' your wares they had to have used a key or you left it open."

Samuel puffed out his chest and raised his chin, "WELL, I guess I'll get no justice here. I'll just have to take this up with my superiors when I get

325

back to the office. I guarantee this is not the end of this. My company WILL be filing a complaint."

The train was pulling into the station and the boys were staggering toward the loading area. Samuel re-locked the trunk and paid a porter to load it onto the train.

"You can't let anyone leave without frisking everyone! It could possibly be one of these men making their get-away!" commanded the carny.

Replacing his hat on the back of his head, the sheriff reached out and placed his hand on the man's shoulder, "Mister, you can't be serious about one of THESE men. They are so inebriated they can barely hold themselves upright, and which *pocket* would you suggest I search? You might just as well follow me to my office and fill out the paper work for this…theft. I'm sure sooner or later we'll get to the bottom of it."

The boys staggered to their seats, fumbling for their tickets as Samuel moved passed them, securing a seat a few rows behind. The exchange of amused glances were the only sign that they could breathe a little easier.

With all the excitement, none of them realized they had not eaten since breakfast until, without a signal, they each uncorked their bottle, tipped them up and felt the whiskey burn from their throat to their empty bellies.

Samuel smiled, eased further down into his seat and tipped his hat over his eyes. Stretching out his long legs and resting his laced fingers on his chest he settled down for a short nap. *Now, just tie up a few loose ends and head for home. I wonder it this truly will be our last campout. I wish Lillie would be waiting so I could share this with her. I know she'd be proud. I hope she's happy, wherever she is, I truly do.*

Chapter 56...A chain of events

Ed watched helplessly as John Key courted Nellie and absorbed most of her free time. He tried to warn her of the man's worldly ways, but it seemed that those were what drew her to him. The nights sitting around after dinner became fewer and fewer until one night she told her audience that John had proposed and she had accepted.

Keeping his feelings in tact until he was able to get away, Ed went to his best friend Johnny Anderson and confided in him his fears of Nellie's happiness with the womanizer he knew John Key to be.

"Ed, there's nothing you can do. You must have seen this coming, living next door to her and all. Why haven't you told her your feelings and let her decide between you?" encouraged Johnny.

Shaking his head, Ed explained, "I've been over there almost every night, visiting with her and the boys. If she was interested in me she would have given some sort of sign, wouldn't she?"

Johnny put his hand on Ed's shoulder, "Well, you're not going to find out unless you approach her and lay your heart on the line. That's how I found out that Lavada was just waiting for me to come to my senses."

"I don't have to ask. I can see, by the way she talks about him, that I don't have a chance. Thanks for listening, but I think I'll go talk to Lillie."

"Well, if anyone can give you a straight answer it'll be her. She really lays it all out and doesn't hold back if someone asks for her opinion," said Johnny.

Ed paid little attention to his surroundings and crossed his threshold with no memory of the walk home. "Where's Dad?"

"He's studying his next sermon in the bedroom." She answered. "What's up?"

327

He sat at the dining room table and poured out his soul to Lillie, as she prepared their evening meal.

She had finished peeling the potatoes and set them aside in a pot of water. "Ed dear, this is one problem I can't help you with. Love has never been my expertise. All I can tell you is that if you love that girl, and you feel she is making a mistake, you should tell her before she marries. If she chooses someone else there's nothing you can do but wait. I followed my heart when it came to your father and waited years until my chance came. I never interfered with his marriage to your mother, but I was there to step in when it was over.... when he needed me."

Not realizing her near slip up, Ed hung his head, "I have nothing to offer her. My job at the Lyric Theater cannot equal his parents owning that big ranch out in the valley. Even if he doesn't have a job he has more money to spend on her than I do. I know one thing for sure, I can't stay around here and watch her and him together. Lillie it would tear me in two."

"You are *managing* the Lyric, not just working there. What other choice do you have? Where would you go? We have no family or friends for you to turn to," Lillie stated.

"I saw a sign in the post office that the government has a program and is looking for volunteers to work in the Civilian Conservation Corp. They won't send me overseas like the military would, but maybe far enough away to get my mind off Nellie."

Lillie was sitting now with a bowl of fresh green beans on the table and an empty one in her lap. One by one she snapped the ends off and placed the centers in the clean bowl. "You know your father is completely paralyzed, from the waist down. He can barely get around on his crutches now. The arthritis has stiffened his legs in a sitting position and is

328

claiming more and more of his body. I'm not sure how much longer he has on this earth. I need you more now than ever before."

Ed unconsciously reached into the bowl and began to snap beans too, leaving his ends in a pile on the table. "You don't need me. If you need a helping hand now and then you can call one of the Fellers boys and they will gladly load him or unload him from the car."

Lillie was grasping at straws trying to find some reason why he could not leave her. She couldn't bare the idea of his not being close. "What about around the house? Who's going to help with him then?"

"He doesn't need help. He gets in and out of his chair for the privy and bed. It's time for me to get out on my own. Then maybe Nellie will see that I'm not a guy who's going to live with his parents the rest of his life. Do you think she may be thinking that?"

Lillie rose and tossed the ends in the garbage and added water to the pot of beans, then added bacon pieces she had fried earlier. She set the pot on the hottest area of the wood cook stove. "I have no way of knowing what Nellie is thinking. How could I? She doesn't confide in me but what I've gathered from Frances' visits, she feels you are a good friend."

"See? She thinks of me only as a friend, nothing more," Ed dropped his head and stared at his hands. "I'm going down and see if I'm qualified to join the CCC's and get more information."

"So you're going to just run away from your problems instead of facing them head on. Why won't you go ask her how she feels about you?"

He stood up and looked up into Lillie's eyes, "Because I don't want to know for sure what I already suspect. She loves someone else." He turned and left the house with a dejected but determined attitude."

Nellie married John Henry Key on the 18th of November 1934, with her mother Frances, and the preacher's wife as witnesses. Although they could have been married in Bisbee, as it was the Cochise County seat, they chose to drive to Lordsburg, New Mexico, three months before Nellie's seventeenth birthday.

One of John's stipulations to the marriage was that there would be no children, which was in total agreement with Nellie. He had two boys by a previous marriage and wanted no more. So when after a few months she found herself in the "family way" John was furious.

"Get rid of it!" he demanded. His eyes turned even darker and his stature grew to his full height. "I told you about this. I said no more children!"

"Well, I didn't want any either. What do you suggest I do?" She asked.

"Let me talk to my mother. I think she knows someone," he muttered.

The next day he came to Nellie with the plan. "It's all set. Mother knows a woman in Mexico that will do the job. We'll go over there this afternoon."

They rode in silence across the border, to an address scribbled on a piece of paper. After finding the shack they entered to find it dark a musty place.

The woman was all business and took the money Johnny offered and gave him an unmarked bottle, "Have her take this at bedtime, she will be sick, but the 'problem' will be over tomorrow. Be sure to put a pan by her bed because she will need it."

Back home that night Nellie looked deep into Johnny's eyes and asked, "How do we know this isn't going to kill me?"

He laughed and said, "Do you think I would try to poison you? Here, give it to me." He took the bottle and tipped it up and drank a little. "See? It's perfectly safe."

Nellie drank the concoction and went to bed, awakening later to horrible pains that doubled her over. She woke John with her groans.

He sat up and switched on a light. "Good. The stuff is working. She said you'd be sick."

Nellie was in so much pain she could hardly speak. "She didn't say it would hurt this much. I feel hot and sweaty. This hurts too much to be right. Please take me to the hospital."

He arose and lit a cigarette, not feeling too good himself. "Are you crazy? And let everyone find out that you aborted a baby intentionally? I'm not sure what the law says about that, but I'm not going to take any chances. Just bare with it and it will be over soon."

The sun rose and with each hour it climbed in unison to Nellie's temperature. John had to use the pan set for Nellie but was feeling better because of it. Nellie was not. She hadn't used the pan. The bed was damp from her sweating and she had gathered most of the bedding into a ball and had it pressed against her abdomen. He woke his mother with the problem and listened as she chastised him.

Out of earshot from Nellie she whispered, "I told you this could happen. I told you that it was not a sure thing. That stuff will either cure her or kill her. Isn't that what I told you?"

"I thought it was worth a chance. I didn't really think it would go this way. I drank a little of it and got sick, but she drank the whole thing and she's *real* sick, feverish and has awful pains. What should I do?"

"Take her to her parents house. *They* can take her to the hospital if she needs one."

Nellie could hear them whispering and strained to hear. When she couldn't she called out again. "John, take me to the hospital. It isn't getting better, it's worse."

"Well, get up then," he demanded, angry and frustrated. "This is all your fault. I told you I didn't want any more children."

She tried to move and the pain was too much, "I can't straighten up."

He approached the bed, gathered her into his arms and carried her to the car. His mother was holding the door and he placed her in the passenger's side. From there he drove straight to the West home, only to find no one there. Gathering her and the blankets again, he made his way to the sealed in front porch and deposited her on a cot there. Without a word he turned and left, not even bothering to tell the neighbors next door.

Frances came home from town with Valerie and the twins, Martha and Margaret. They found Nellie as he had left her, moaning incoherently and obviously near death.

With Lillie's help, Nellie was put in the car and taken to the Copper Queen Hospital. Trying to make sense of what had happened, Frances made out a few words, "poison, baby, John, dirty, Mexico."

Piecing the words together told the story and the doctor gave her an antidote for the local drug used to abort a child. Then turned to Frances, "It's really up to her and God now. The drug was taken too long ago for us to pump her stomach."

God decided that Nellie would live as well as the unwanted child. She received her uncontested divorce and moved back home.

Her stepfather, Sie West was not happy. He had no use for a woman that would abort a child and he felt she was not a good role model for *his* girls. He also held it against her that he now had to provide for his family as she was unable to do the hard labor in his place.

Nellie tried to ignore his sarcastic behavior and rude remarks aimed at her continually, usually out of earshot of Frances. Arguments led to screaming fights. One day Nellie was preparing supper when he and her brothers came home from working the fields.

As he opened the door and saw her, he spat out, "I see the tramp is finally earning her keep around here."

His quick reaction was all that saved him as the butcher knife she sailed through the air embedded itself in the door he was lucky enough to jump behind. The knife was still swinging back and forth as he peered around the door and saw that she was now unarmed. "That's the thanks I get for giving you a home and taking the likes of you in! You're nothing but a worthless trollop and you are no longer welcome here. Pack your bags and get out!"

"With pleasure you old fart. I've hated you from the first day mama married you. YOU are the worthless one. All you know how to do is make more babies and leave them for someone else to raise. You…You with a steel plate in your head. It left no room for brains! But you didn't have any to begin with, did you? IF anyone can believe the story of you showing off to your buddies and propping your crossed feet above the rim of a foxhole and getting a bullet through each heel, *then* being stupid enough to try to see where the bullets came from, and got the top of your head blown off. That all probably happened when you were, *DESERTING*, a lowdown coward, scared to death!"

"Get out. Get out, you whore!" Bellowed Sie. "I won't have back talk in my house. You will show me respect."

"I only respect those who deserve it, you murderer! You convict. You're nothing but an ex-con who was given the choice of prison or the army," she retaliated as she picked up a second knife. "It was partly my, and the boys', work that made the down payment on this house, so don't act high and mighty with me."

"Yeah, I did time for that killing, but it was just a nigger and there shouldn't be a law against them. I served my country and earned my freedom!" His arms were flailing around as he sidestepped behind Sherman. "Why are you standing around? Get out. Get the hell out!" His baldhead was turning crimson as his heart pounded the blood through his veins.

Nellie moved that night into the house her father had bought and paid for. It sat on the end of the same street and not near far enough away, but at least she didn't have to be under the same roof as the old man. Sherman and Sherwood moved in with her.

Ed had joined the Civilian Conservation Corp in near by Fort Huachuca where he would be close to home. But as luck would have it, there was a project needing men near Trinidad, Colorado, and many of the service men were sent there by train. Ed was one of them.

There he rose in rank to the equivalent of a sergeant in the armed forces. He and his 'boys' were put to work building a State Park. The work was hard, as they had to clear the terrain to ground level and replant to the engineer's specifications.

Moral was high among the 'troops' and a genuine camaraderie was shared. These were hard times, but with his room and board paid he was able to send money home and have a little left over. When time allowed some of the men huddled together for a game of poker or the roll of the dice, where Ed honed his skills at both. Many men found their pay diminish after an evening of cards with "Sgt. Ed" as these men affectionately tagged him.

These winnings allowed him to send even more money home, which unknown to him was sorely needed. Lillie never mentioned in her letters that Acey's paralysis was taking its toll and the pain from the arthritis had kept him from the pulpit more and more. On one of his few visits home, Ed asked Sherman to take a family picture of him, in his uniform, standing proudly between Lillie and Acey, whose head now barely came even to Ed's shoulder.

It was but a few short months after that photo was taken that Lillie was unable to get Acey from bed to chair and he told her that it was no use. He was too weak to help and they both knew the end was near. She went to the train depot and sent a telegram.

"The name is Edward F. Lykens, CCC Camp # 1809, Trinidad, Colorado. I want the message to read "Hurry home, father's dying.""

The commander gave Ed an emergency leave and he boarded the next train bound for Bisbee.

When Lillie returned home Acey called for her. He took her by the hand and made her sit beside him. Looking deep in her eyes he said, "I want you to promise me you will never tell Ed about his mother and Alva and the life we led back then."

"But Acey, he has a right to know. They may still be alive...," she tried.

Raising his head and gripping her hand tighter, he added, "Lillie I've trusted you the better part of my life and I want you now to do this last thing for me.

335

Promise me... that you will..." He had to lay back and get his breath. "Never tell him. You have to swear, Lillie. Swear to me that you will *never* tell him. I want him to remember me as one of God's couriers. I may not be worthy enough to be considered one of His apostles, but I have taken His word to the people and I've helped people open their hearts and lives to Him. Haven't I, Lillie? Haven't I been a good messenger for the Lord Almighty?"

"Yes, yes Acey. You have brought some of your God's flock to their Shepherd. I've seen it, and I know you did your best. Ed knows that too. He's also witnessed people's reaction to your words and saw them change before his eyes as they accepted Christ as their Savior."

"Then swear to me, Lillie. If he found out my other life he may not love me or accept me as one of God's chosen." Acey knew he had failed in bringing Lillie to God and feared facing God with his shortcomings. He felt he had persuaded Ed to at least believe in God and accept Jesus as his Savior, but had failed in bringing him to worship openly with others.

"Lillie, please, I'm asking you this one last time. If you love Ed, and me, you'll abide by my wishes." He closed his eyes, but when she still did not give her verbal promise he tried one last time. "I've got to hear you say it, Lillie. Promise me you will not tell him."

She sighed, "You have my word, Acey. I will never tell Ed about Mary, Alva or your family history. Now get some rest. Ed's on his way by train and he should be here sometime tomorrow. Rest so you can visit with him."

She had seen the signs many times before, at Dr. Dan's hospital in Stephenville. Too many patients passed away while she stood helplessly by. She

336

didn't agree when Acey's doctor said it was "up to God and Acey now". She felt it was up to Acey and how hard he wanted to fight to see his son one last time. She turned the light out and softly left the room.

Ed didn't make it in time. He was somewhere in between when Acey drew his last breath.

Lillie looked down at the pale, crippled, twisted, skeletal frame of the man before her and saw a young man just past the notch of her gun sight that night so long ago. She saw him the many times his head popped up from under the hidden door to the root cellar, always grinning with sparkling eyes.

She saw him laughing as he bumped into her and Mary leaving the grocery store. She smiled as tears rolled freely down her cheeks. She saw him leap across the wood stacked beside the fireplace, in the Tirrell house when everyone yelled "Happy Birthday" at his surprise party...his eyes wide with fear at the unexpected yell.

She saw him riding up the lane on Rascal, waving to her in greeting, She saw him coming to pick out his birthday hound, and leaving with two. She saw him coming to her with love in his eyes for another woman that nearly crushed her heart. She saw him with his arms around her as he swept her off her feet and twirled her around, when she gave him the wedding band, so he could propose. She saw his handsome face filled with pride on his wedding day.

She saw the determined man that came to her for help the night he left his wife and fought his father over his second son. She saw him bloody, from buckshot and how he trusted her to dig it out

She saw him dressed as a woman, when the bowler hat detective almost caught them.

She saw him riding Rascal, beside her wagon, as they traveled on the run for so many years. She saw how soft his gray eyes became when they made love.

She saw the relief on his face as she found him lying in the desert the night he tried to board the train from Rascal's back. She saw the handsomest man she had ever loved, back in his prime, as she took the sheet and slowly pulled it over his head.

"I've always loved, protected and honored you, my love. Forgive me now for what I'm about to do."

Lillie waited until she saw lights in the Fellers' kitchen, then she climbed the incline and knocked on their door. One look told them what brought her there so early. She asked if Sherman would go for the sheriff.

Sie was sitting at the table as Frances poured each of them a cup of coffee. As they waited she told them as much of the story as needed telling.

When she finished she sighed, "I want *you* to tell Ed everything I've told you. That way I will be keeping my word to Acey, while doing what I feel is the right thing, for Edward...and Mary."

In the Bisbee Daily Review of January 18th, 1935, Acey's obituary mentioned he had for the past several years been a minister of the church of God, had been a resident for twelve years and the survivors being wife Lillie and son Edward.

Edward arrived in time to help Lillie with the funeral arrangements, each trying to be strong for the other. He could hardly believe his eyes as he looked at the stranger in the coffin. This couldn't be his father. He was thin when he was home last, but this was half of what he saw then.

Acey was buried in the Evergreen Cemetery. After graveside services and the wake were over, Lillie and Ed found themselves alone in the house.

Son, I don't want to add to your burden, but there's one more thing we have to get through. Come, Sie and Frances are waiting."

Expecting they were invited for dinner, Ed tried to beg off. "I wouldn't make good company tonight Lillie. I'd rather not. Maybe in a day or two."

"Please, Son, I wouldn't ask if it weren't important. It won't take long," she promised.

He followed her across the lawn and into the neighbor's house. He was surprised to see all of them sitting quiet and sort of edgy.

Frances showed them to the kitchen and shooed the children outside. She poured them a cup of coffee and sat across the table from Lillie and Ed.

It was decided that Sie would tell the story and he reveled in it. He told it as Lillie had told him almost word for word, watching Ed's expression change with each added new bit of information.

To use the term "stunned" would be saying it mildly. Ed sat silently, sometimes looking at Lillie in need of proof of what he was hearing. The untouched coffee grew cold as he sat nearly motionless.

When Sie was finished Ed glanced from one to the other, then stood quietly, excused himself and told Lillie that he was going out for awhile but he would meet her back at home. He was much too quiet and reserved. He rubbed the top of his head, nodded to everyone and walked out the front door.

Sherman and Sherwood saw him coming up the street toward them and stood. As he approached they closed the gap, "Hey Ed, we're sure sorry about your dad, we know how it feels. Want a drink? We have some homemade hooch. A father of a friend of ours has his own still. It's good stuff."

Ed slowed and turned, "How old are you boys now?"

339

"Oh now don't be going adult on us. Hell, we're old enough I reckon. You know we don't live with the old man anymore? We're living here with Nellie. She's getting a divorce ya know. That is as soon as the baby is born. She went to the judge and he told her that if she divorced before the baby is born that it would be considered illegitimate and it would be printed on the birth certificate that way."

"What happened? Did she catch that womanizer out with one of the local girls?" Ed asked.

"No. He tried to poison her after she came up pregnant. You know he told her he didn't want no kids? Well, sure enough she got pregnant right off and he made her try to get rid of the baby by drinking some poison," spilled Sherwood.

"If I remember correctly she said she didn't want any children either. You sure it was just John's idea?" asked Ed.

"Well, for whatever reason she almost died and the baby is still in there kicking up a storm. She had a fight with the old man and he threw her out," added Sherman.

Ed was concerned, "How is she getting by?"

"We're living in the house our real father bought and paid for." Sherman said. "Mama never sold it like Sie wanted her to, so we're living here."

"What about groceries? How are you eating?"

"I sweep the grocery store up on Brewery Gulch and clean up messes the Bohunks leave after partying. The storeowners pay me a little for that," came from Sherwood.

Ed glanced at them both, "Be careful who hears you call them 'Bohunks'. That's a name they don't particularly like."

"What's it mean anyhow?" asked Sherman.

"It's their nationalities. Part Bohemian and part Hungarian. Some people decided to take the Bo from one and the Hung from the other and put them together. Only it comes out 'Bohunk'. Most nationalities when they first come to America seek out their own kind, like the Germans, Irish and the Italians. They feel more secure being with people that speak the same language," Ed explained.

Changing the subject, Sherman added, "I have a job at the mine. I clean the tools that miners bring up. I get them ready for the next shift. I don't have to go down in the mine and that suits me just fine."

"Nellie takes in sewing and tried to take in laundry, but the wet clothes are heavy and all the bending and stooping got to her back so she had to quit." Sherwood added, "Together we pool our money and so far we've been able to survive. Don't know what will happen when the baby comes, but we'll cross that bridge when we get to it."

"Yeah, what's that your mom says all the time? "Tomorrow is tomorrow, not to be worried about today." Sherman and Sherwood said in unison.

The boys were surprised when he quickly turned away and reminded them, "She's not my mother," as he headed for downtown.

Lillie waited for Ed to come to her. She gave him all the time he needed, knowing that he would sort it all out and when he was ready to talk she would answer all his questions honestly.

She nodded in silence when he came back home late that night and simply stated,"I don't want to talk about it yet. I hold no grudge toward anyone. I know that you love me and as far back as I can remember you have always been in my life. I don't want that to change. My love for you has not diminished. I just need time to think."

He drove over to Ft. Huachuca so he could explain his plight to his commander. They realized his need to take care of his "mother" and they put the wheels in motion for his discharge. He was saddened in a way, for leading the men had given him pride and he honestly liked those under his command. He affectionately called them "my boys" and shared photos of them and the camp with friends and Lillie.

He spent days mulling over what he was told and what he could and could not remember. What was true and what was a lie?

I adjusted to the fact that I was an orphan, like Dad told me...Now I find out he lied...I suddenly have a real mother and brother, both of which I cannot, for the life of me, remember...They're somewhere out there, if they're still alive.

In his solitude he had tried hard to remember. *Something about an Uncle Will...and a big man falling under the wheel of the cart...Were they the same man? No...not sure...something...about Dad and Lillie being bad...what's that all about? The more I try the more the memories slip away...not far, just out of reach...in and out, almost there, then gone.*

I believe Lillie when she says she honestly had no part in the break up. She had only been there when Dad came to her for help...so she can't answer my questions about what happened to cause the breakup...Maybe she's right when she says that perhaps this other mother can fill in the blanks for me.

When he finally approached her, he took her hands and looked deep into her eyes. "That's why you sided with me when I insisted in calling you 'Lillie' instead of 'Mother'".

342

She nodded, "I knew that you knew I was not your mother, and that this day would come."

Nodding thoughtfully Ed said, "It makes sense now why I could not accept Dad's preaching. It seemed all wrong to me, even when I knew he was truly dedicated. Somewhere in my memory, I knew that he was not living his words, and why I rebelled so much and would get into trouble as soon as you drove Dad on those evangelistic tours."

She smiled, "I had to bail you out of jail on more than one occasion. You always denied your participation in whatever it was, claiming it was "old lady Ferr" calling the law to get you in trouble, all in spite for you not marrying Ima Gray."

"Well, part of it was," he still claimed.

"Even the time you were arrested for having a party and everyone was drunk and dancing around the chicken coop naked?"

He looked at her and a grin pulled one side of his mouth, "Well, let's just say there was no harm done."

She reared back and laughed a hearty laugh. "Hell, Son, in my prime I might have joined you."

They shared a much-needed laugh as they tried to picture the sight. Neither of them noticed the endearment she had just used.

Lillie became serious, "I want you to know that I'm selling the church and house property. I'm giving you half and I'm taking half. You go on with your life. I'm going in search of Mary and Alva. Who knows, they may still be in Mineral Wells. Now, wouldn't that be something?"

Ed smiled, "You do what you think best, but the money is rightfully yours. You were Dad's wife by common law for eighteen years. You stuck through the "for better, for worse, in sickness and in health, until death separated you. He couldn't have asked for more. I haven't met my real mother yet, but I believe in my heart, that I could not have asked for a more loving or devoted mother than you've been to me, and I love you deeply for it."

Lillie's eyes filled with tears and the doubts that he may hate her for her part in the deception melted away. She knew then that she could face tomorrow with a clean slate. The only living person that meant anything to her had forgiven her. *"Praise Jesus!"* Then she stood perfectly still, moving only her eyes upward, startled at what she'd just thought. *WHOA, where did that come from?*

"Don't we have this turned around? Isn't the baby supposed to leave the nest?" Ed asked. "Why do you have to go back there? Can't you mail your letters from here?"

"If she's still in Mineral Wells I want to face her and get it over with. I owe her that much. I'm sure she will have a lot to say to me and it shouldn't be done through letters," she explained.

Lillie handed Ed the envelope of money. "It was hard to sell the house you and I built with our own hands. I know the church is in proper hands, can't say that about that little rock house that holds so many memories and love."

"Well, I'll try to keep an eye on it while you're gone and raise old Billy Ned if I see it being neglected. Besides, you're not going to be gone long are you? Just until you find her and then come back?"

"Who knows what lies around the bend? Our lives are a constant change and that's what makes it worth living. Besides, I've no place to live now." She smiled as she cupped the side of his face with her right hand and bent down to kiss his cheek.

He hugged her close and tried to speak through the lump forming in his throat. "You just hurry back, Lillie. You don't ever have to get a house of your own. You will always have a room in mine... always."

He saw her board the train to Mineral Wells. The times they'd been apart he could count on one hand and as much as he tried to maintain a 'man's' composure he began to see through tears and the first blink sent them coursing down his cheeks. He was glad no one had come with them, to see him cry.

When she arrived in Mineral Wells she rented a room at the old Octagon Hotel. It held many memories of a different time in her life. The grounds looked the same but the lobby had been remodeled. It was busier now, with people checking in and others sitting around having tea or quietly reading the newspaper. While she waited she picked up the phone book.

I hope that old man has allowed something modern on that ranch. He certainly was stuck in the old ways when we were here. The way he made those girls dress and wouldn't allow the women folk to eat at the dinner table. It's a good thing that I was only invited to parties where everyone ate from their laps. If he had told me that I had to eat on the porch or living room I would have given him something to think about for many years. Yet he would open his home to the community when a twister was coming. The girls said those who could get there in time all crowded into the basement until it was over. It's a wonder he let 'the womenfolk' down there. It twists my gizzard just thinking about that old Irishman.

As she feared there were no Tirrell's. She asked the desk clerk if there were someone she could hire to drive her around for an afternoon. "I don't want a taxi. I want someone I can pay a flat fee, and he'd have to be willing to wait for me if I lingered now and again."

"I'll see what I can do, Madame," he answered. Stepping back, he looked to his left, then raised his hand and snapped his fingers.

Lillie saw a Negro gentleman, with silver hair and slightly bent back approach, eyes downcast, searching for her luggage.

Her heart skipped a beat as she studied the old gentleman. *It can't be. Can it?* "Zeke? Zeke? Is that you?"

The servant raised his head and looked into the eyes of the lady calling his name. Nodding, he answered, "Yes ma'am. My name be Zeke."

"Zeke!" Lillie stepped forward and threw her arms around his neck in a full body hug.

Everyone had turned at hearing her excitement and was aghast at what they saw. A white woman was purposely hugging a Negro servant!

Lillie was the only one oblivious to her surroundings at the sight of her old friend.

Zeke stood with his arms at his sides, daring not to touch this white woman that seemed to know him. He knew his place in society and feared stepping out of its boundaries. He stepped backwards, dragging Lillie with him. His eyes beseeched help from the desk clerk.

"Ma'am?" The desk clerk interrupted. "Ma'am! You have to sign the register, please."

Turning she followed his darting eyes around the lobby and found statues where people had been, with eyes wide and mouths agape. She grew furious. "And just how do YOU people greet an old friend? This man made my life comfortable when I was going through a difficult time in my life and I value his friendship very much. I could care less that I have offended any of you FINE people, I'm only sorry that I may have embarrassed Zeke."

Throats cleared and newspapers rattled as the statues became animated again. Eyes dropped to the floor and cups made contact with their matching saucers.

The desk clerk broke the silence. "Zeke, will you escort Mrs. Lykens to her room?"

Zeke nodded and placed Lillie's luggage on a small dolly, "Yes sir, this way, ma'am." He dropped his eyes again and guided Lillie toward the elevator. As they moved in that direction the lobby began to buzz like mad bees protecting their hive.

Once the elevator shut, Zeke turned, displaying a wide set of brilliant white teeth. "MISS LILLIE! I *knew* it be you the minute you stood up and said your piece to them other guests. You always sho'd a high spirit, not 'fraid to tell people to mind their manners! It be good to see you! You have a differn't last name now? You gottsta tell me what's been happen' since…"

Lillie was laughing out loud now and patted his arm. "Take it easy, Zeke, I'll probably be here for awhile. I've got business in town; we'll have time to get caught up. Say, do you know how to drive a car?"

"Yes'm. I hadda bad time gettin the license, but the hotel, it helped. I needs to drive peoples to and from the train depot, at times."

"Well, you just got yourself a new job. I'm going to hire you to be my driver and we can take our time getting caught up with our lives. When you go back down you tell that desk clerk that I've asked for you personally," she nodded to herself, satisfied with the decision she made and how it was all just perfect.

347

When she began to get in the front seat Zeke cleared his throat. She glanced up and followed his eyes to the other hotel guests. He opened the back door and she realized his meaning.

She followed his lead and settled into the back seat as he closed the door, circled the car and slid under the steering wheel. "Don't let dem sees ya speakin ta me less it's for yer needs. We can see each other in the rear view mirror and do our talkin."

When he saw her start to protest he added, "It'd make my life easier, Miss Lillie. It be a white man's world, and they still hab a place for my people and we is to stay well inside it."

"Well, I'm white and I don't see separate *places* because of the skin color."

'I knows ya don't, and I 'preciate that, but I've got ta do whats I haf ta, ta survive. They still have lynchin's for a black boy that steps out of bounds."

"Good grief, Zeke, I didn't know I was putting you in jeopardy! Well, between you and me I will have to learn MY place. At least around these...idiots."

Her first stop was at the Mineral Wells Index to find out if there had been any deaths reported around the time of their leaving. Finding nothing she proceeded as if Samuel and Will were indeed still alive. Lillie told Zeke everything and they set out to the first place on her list. She went straight out to the Tirrell Ranch to find it owned by someone else.

The new owners had heard from neighbors that the wife had died shortly before they bought it and thought the youngest of the children might still be around. She thanked them and directed Zeke to the Hall residence, bypassing the ranch she and Samuel owned back then.

Later, I've got to work my courage up to face him. He must certainly hate me for how I treated him. It's hard to explain a love that is so deep that it overpowers one person to do inhumane things to others they love. I DID love Samuel, but it was a different kind of love, different than he wanted, and he knew it. He didn't know about my love for Hasten. He thought his rival was a dead man. And in some ways that was true too. I wouldn't have been open to Hasten if Dan had still been alive. My heart and soul was for 'Dr. Dan'. But they were separate entities, each coming into my life like some sort of plan that has decided my life's path. But, to what destination?

She snapped out of her thoughts to Zeke repeating, "Miss Lillie, Miss Lillie."

"Yes?"

"Is this be the place up here?" He pointed to a house with a picket fence.

Lillie nodded, "Yes. That's it. Someone has added another room or two and painted it recently, but that's the house. Thank you, Zeke."

A buxom woman was busy hanging clothes on a line stretched from the porch to the corner fence post. Lillie thought, *She's too large to be Mary.*

When Zeke opened the car door, she stepped out and approached the gate. Raising her voice she called out, "Excuse me."

The woman turned and looked at Lillie over a mouthful of clothespins. All but a loose strand of hair was covered with a triangle scarf tied at the nape of her neck. She took the time to hang the last garment before she set the left-over clothespins in the basket and lifted it to her right hip, "What can I do for you?"

"I was wondering if you could tell me where the previous owners have moved," responded Lillie.

349

Rubbing her hand across her wet apron and tucking the stray lock of hair behind one ear, she shook her head. "Sorry, lady. My husband did all the legals. If memory serves me right, the man lost his brother and then his sister lost her husband about the same time, and he moved closer to her. Never heard say exactly where though."

Lillie sighed, "Oh, that's ok. I was just taking a shot in the dark. Thank you for your time." She took Zeke's offered hand and stepped back into the car. "Onward and upward, Zeke. I've still got a few more places to visit."

He nodded, "Yes, Miss Lillie."

She held her breath as they turned up the drive that led to where she spent her last night as Mrs. Samuel Briles. She had no fear of physical harm, but knowing the emotional, if not physical, harm she had inflected upon this man that once shared her life, she was apprehensive of the harsh words he might spew, even though they were well deserved.

As the ranch came into sight her heart dropped. It was in shambles. Thick weeds surrounded the well and edges of the house, barn and fence. The yard was dead and dry leaves were piled high around the porch steps. The corral fence had loose boards hanging from rusty nails and there was no sign of livestock of any kind.

"You sure this be the same ranch you tol me about, Miss Lillie?" asked Zeke.

Frowning she said softy, "Yes. It's the ranch, but it's not the same. She stepped out of the car, not waiting for Zeke's help, and ventured up the steps and to the door. She swallowed hard and knocked.

The door opened a couple of inches and Lillie found herself staring down the two dark holes of a double barrel shotgun.

350

"WHAT YOU WANT?" came from inside.

Slowly taking a step back to show no aggression, and holding her palm toward Zeke to prevent him from approaching, she spoke evenly and straightforward, "Is this the Samuel Briles residence?"

"Not no more it ain't,"

"Could you tell me where I could find him?" she pressed.

"Might be livin' with his folks."

"Thank you very much for your time. Good day to you." She slowly turned and walked carefully back to Zeke already holding the car door open.

He wasted no time in getting her inside and himself back in the driver's seat. As they circled the yard and headed back down the drive he snorted, "Only *you,* Miss Lillie, could look down the barrel of a shotgun and tell whoseber on the other end 'good day to you!' I swear woman, don't you got no fear o' nothin'?"

After letting out a lung full of air she answered, "Let me put it to you this way, Zeke, first find me a bathroom and then a bottle of good whiskey!"

Chapter 57...Hearing from family

The season was early spring when Ma Tirrell took gravely ill. Since his leaving she had repeated to all who would listen, "I want to see my Hasey and the baby one more time before I go to the Lord." The years had not eased her mourning and their loss was something she held on to. The children that had chose to stay were sorely tired of hearing about the one that ran away.

Fear of hearing more of the same and the unpleasant smell from the open sores of her cancerous face, those in attendance did not venture into her room unless they were forced to. She had said her last words to each and had made sure her possessions were given to those she chose. As she lay breathing shallow she was hardly a bump under the thick quilts.

As the boys shuffled their feet, Mattie and some of the grandchildren sat on the edge of the bed, Ma slowly opened her eyes and looked upward.

A smile slowly spread across her face and she reached out to something she alone could see. In a calm, quiet voice she clearly stated, "You don't have to search for Hasey anymore. He's waiting for me." She took a few more breaths and was gone, wearing a soft, serene expression. There was no doubt in anyone's mind that she had seen Hasten and he was waiting for her with outstretched arms.

Martha Jane Lykins Tirrell (Ma) died on her seventieth birthday, March 16, 1935, two months to the day after Hasten's death.

There was a family reunion, of those that could attend, and as the day passed and Ma was buried, they gathered at the Tirrell Ranch. The men, down at the barn, where they could share the whiskey Pa was still making out back.

The ladies gathered in the kitchen and sat at the huge table that served them so well.

And as all reunions go the stories of past antics were shared. The younger ones enjoying hearing them for the first time and those taking a role in the story remembering the details and correcting the story teller as to *their* version of how it *really* happened.

"Hey, Sam, tell these young'uns how you and..." here he looked around for Pa's whereabouts and then whispered, "*Hasten* ran off that day."

"Ain't much to tell, me and Hasten had our fill of Pa and his ways and we took off. We headed for parts unknown and happy to be doing it. We would've gotten away too if that sheriff hadn't been so nosey. When he asked us why we weren't in school and did our parents know where we were, we just clamed up. Wouldn't tell him our names or nothing. Now he tried bribing us with food and threatened us with jail, but we just sat there, saying nary a word. Then here he comes and makes us stand up and he snaps a picture of us and puts it in the Mineral Wells Index, with writing that he needed to know if anyone knew who we were. Somehow Pa and Ma got wind of it and she called to claim us. That was the first time I got to ride in an automobile. The sheriff brought us back and dumped us off. Boy, Pa was ready with that razor strap but Ma stood up to him and she backed him clear out to the barn where he stayed for hours. She was a scrapper when she set her mind to it."

"Yeah, the clipping from the paper is floating around somewheres in the family. How's it feel to make front page news?" asked Lewis.

While in the house the ladies were doing the reminiscing as they cleared the wake's mess.

"I'm so glad that Ma got to see and hold Helen Frances," stated Betty Lee.

"Did anyone get a four generation picture? Ma loved children so much," stated Mary Belle.

"You don't have to tell us. I don't believe I will ever be able to trust another human being the rest of my life. After she and Pa run our father off, and Mom ran away, Fannie, Oliver and me were raised believing they had legally adopted us. It wasn't until my wedding day to Sam Makowsky that Ma pulled me off to the bedroom and informed me that when I signed my marriage certificate that I had to write Betty Lee Fulfer, because she and Pa had never adopted us! I felt betrayed and have carried that with me ever since."

"Oh, Betty, don't let whatever they did destroy your trust in people. I'm sure they meant well. You know they loved you, don't you?" asked Mattie.

Betty Lee scoffed, "It's easy for you to forgive them, Mattie. You never had any children for them to steal. They stole us first, then went after Edward and Alva. I'm proud of Hasten for standing up to Pa."

"And what did it get him? He only got Edward back by stealing him out of the yard and then a side full of buckshot for coming after Alva. I know. I was there and saw the whole thing. Hasten was bloody when he left here," countered Sarah. "I have to side with Ma for never truly forgiving Pa for that."

"Sam told me that it was one of the worst nights of his life. He still has nightmares sometimes, waking in a cold sweat and yelling something I can't understand," added Sadie. "He has missed that brother so much and wishes he knew what happened to him. He was so glad to take time from work and come down for their annual campout last year. I'll bet it was fun for all the guys to get together and go hunting like that. Us girls should do something like that. Get together, just us women and do something fun."

Mattie and Sarah exchanged meaningful glances and smiled. "Yes. They all talk fondly of those days. I guess us girls could have our own get-together and maybe do some canning or quilt making, perhaps during their next camp out," said Mattie. "But with everyone moved away as they are, and busy raising their children, it would make it pretty hard."

"Yes, I suppose you're right. I just thought how much fun it would be," answered Sadie. Changing the subject with, "I think Sam is in a race with Lewis as to how many children he is going to add to this family."

"Boy, ain't that the truth. Lewis keeps me barefoot and pregnant. I feared we would never have a child live, with the first three dying on the day they were born. I don't know what I'd have done if baby Richard had died too," added Mary Belle.

"That must be just awful, losing so many babies. Did the doctor ever determine the cause?" asked Sadie.

"No, just that Lewis is a big man and I'm not built to have large babies. And yes, Sadie, it was nearly unbearable, but what is a gal supposed to do when her man comes home all amorous after a night out with the boys?" asked Mary Belle. "I sure don't want to tell him no."

All the women laughed and took a sip from their glasses. Sarah and Mattie held just a tad of Pa's harvest in theirs. They inherited the Tirrell taste for good home cooked whiskey, and now with Ma gone, they could openly enjoy it without being preached to.

One of the neighbors asked, "What, if anything, have you heard from Mary? Has anyone found her?"

Sarah knew they were just prying into things that were none of their concern but she smiled and denied any contact. Mary certainly did not need these meddling old hens pecking at old wounds.

"Snookie, would you mind putting Richard Aaron down for his nap? The poor little fella is plumb tuckered out," asked Mary Belle.

Fourteen-year-old Naomi answered to her nickname and swung the toddler up to one hip. As she leaned to counter balance his weight she kept the swinging motion, pivoting on her tiptoes. Her auburn hair was long enough for the baby to grab handfuls and hold on. Trusting in the loving arms that held him, he giggled the baby laugh that comes from deep within. The sound was one that brought smiles to tired faces.

Back outside the men were still swapping tales and sharing the jug. It had made its rounds more than once when Nate smiled and said, "Hey, Jake, why don't you tell the guys what happened when you tried to give Lillie a bunch of wildflowers."

Exchanging glances with Lewis and Sam he knew if he tried denial, it would only make it worse. He carefully chose his words, "I just caught her off guard one day and snuck up behind her with a bouquet and slid them around her waist and up to her nose. Man, that lady came unglued! She first caught me with an elbow in the pit of my stomach, thankfully knocking all the wind out of me, cause I hit the floor before she came around with a left hook that would have flattened Max Baer! Then she stood over me as I lay flat on my back and proceeded to tell me how the cow ate the cabbage. She was a feisty one for sure."

Sam nodded in appreciation, Jake had told the story, but skipped over the where, when and how of it.

"Say, did Sarah ever hear anything from that detective she hired to find Hasten?" asked Nate.

Again the glances; this time, a warning one from Sam. Jake understood and spoke first. "Well, guys, I think it's time for Nate and me to give our condolences to the Tirrell ladies and head for home. Mom and Dad left right after the service, and they'll be waiting for us." With that said, he took Nate by the arm and headed him toward the house. Nate was in no mood to protest, for now his mind was turned to the ladies. He knew they were all married, but he loved to flirt and there was a prime lot to choose from in the house.

Sam looked at the neighbors' questioning faces and responded, "And to answer his question, No. He found neither hide nor hair of him and gave up after a few years. We've given up too. Now, where did that jug get to? Come on and pass it on around here." Finally all the neighbors had gathered their empty dishes and tired children and headed for home.

Mattie found Pa on the porch. "Pa, I'm going to write to friends and family unable to attend the funeral. Tell them where she is buried and such. Is there anything you want to say?" Mattie asked. "I think Ma would have wanted me to."

Slouched in his rocker and staring at nothing, Pa responded, "If they didn't care enough to come, they have no business knowing anything. Just leave it be Mattie. They have no right to know any of it."

"That's not fair to folks too far away, or those not able to afford the trip. I'll pay for the postage myself," she said as she turned to go back inside.

"Then why the hell did you bother me with it? Go on, do what you're going to do anyway, then go on back home and take that worthless husband along with you!"

She knew how mean he could get when he was drinking but she had had enough of his sarcasm,

"That's enough Pa! You have no call to be grieving me about J.W. He is a good husband and provider."

"I haven't seen any babies growing in your belly. What's he waiting for? It's been over ten years and he's still not man enough," Pa's words cut like a knife.

"Mattie, don't. We don't have to answer to anyone, and he's not going to run me off. He's old and mean and wants to hurt someone as bad as he's hurting right now. He won't admit how much Martha meant to him. It would be 'unmanly' in his eyes." J.W. stood holding Mattie in his arms just past the threshold of the open door. He knew his words reached many ears and waited for the rebuttal. It came when Francis slowly stood and turned toward the door.

J.W. slowly pulled Mattie behind him so there was nothing between the two men now standing face to face. It was so quiet the ticking of the grandfather clock in the living room could be heard.

They stood waiting. Then Francis turned and walked down the steps and out to the now empty barn.

Breaths were audibly expelled as the family members each released a lung full of air. Nervous smiles were exchanged, knowing what could have been an ugly moment had turned out for the best. Those not spending the night packed their belongings and left the ranch.

Chapter 58... Lillie faces Samuel.

As they approached the Briles ranch Lillie saw someone chopping wood between the two houses.

In comparison to the ranch she had just left this one was in good care. *The way I remember it. There's the cabin we built for Samuel and me. And the field where I accepted his proposal. He was so gentle, so kind. I wish I could have loved him the way he deserved. If Hasten had not came to me that night, I'd probably still be married to him. He was a good man.*

The car came to a stop and she asked if Zeke knew who the woodcutter was.

"Why tha's Mastah Thomas, ain't he growed into a fine figure of a man?" Zeke asked with a big smile.

"Of course. He would be a grown man now. How silly of me to think of him as still a boy, " she said as she took a second, closer look and found no sign of the little boy who stole her heart years ago.

Motioning to Zeke to remain seated, she took a deep breath and let it out, "Well, here goes nothing."

Thomas had stopped chopping and turned toward the car. Tilting his head to see better he spotted Zeke behind the wheel and came toward the car, still carrying the ax.

Lillie opened the back door and stepped out to face him. She was surprised to see that she had to look up to make eye contact. *He's grown so tall.*

He smiled as he waited for her to state the purpose of her visit.

"Thomas," Lillie said lovingly.

"Yes ma'am?" he answered, still waiting.

Taking another deep breath she let it out and stepped closer. "Thomas, do you still have a burn scar on your leg?"

He blinked and frowned, "How do you..."

"Thomas, it's me, Lillie," she offered.

She could see his mind trying to wrap around what was said and place the name. When she saw his features begin to change as recognition set in, she took another breath in fear of what his reaction would be. *Is he going to hate me? Cuss me out? Tell me to get off the property? I thought that I would only have to deal with Samuel and Mary. How many more hate me?*

"Lillie?" He almost whispered. "Lillie, is it really you?" Raising his voice back to normal, " Gosh, you're just as purty as you were years ago. Oh Lillie, it's so good to see you!" Then without hesitation he dropped the axe, reached out and grabbed her, swinging her off the ground in a big bear hug. "I've never forgot you Lillie. You were so nice to me and ...." Slowly he set her down, turned toward the house, then back to her. "Uncle Sam. He, he took it real hard... for awhile, but he's better now. Please, come in. Do you want me to go in first and tell him? Or just walk in?"

Her heart began to pound, "Well, I guess I'll just have to face the music and take what's coming. Lead the way sweet Thomas."

A familiar voice came from behind her, "Tommy, I thought I heard a car pull up. Who's your visitor?"

Lillie slowly turned to face Samuel. He froze. Then stood in silence just staring at her. Neither of them noticed that Thomas had backed away and gone to Zeke.

Long seconds went by as they stood there. Memories, thoughts and questions raced through his mind, forbidding his body to move. It was like a large, wide ribbon of electricity had entered his head and exited the soles of his feet, holding him in place.

Unable to stand the suspense any longer she broke the silence. "How have you been, Samuel?"

His body reacted first by expelling air that had begun to burn in his chest. He was surprised at his own reaction. "Fine, Lillie, and you?"

They locked eyes, as their souls united and communicated. Hers found he held no hostility, as his found hers in search of forgiveness.

Smiling slightly she nodded, "A lot better now. Would you like to take a walk?"

Knowing her intentions he answered, "Can't see no harm in that. Lead the way."

Thomas invited Zeke into the house for a glass of lemonade and they laughed remembering the times Thomas and Samuel were Lillie's guests at the hotel years ago and how she always ordered lemonade and cookies.

Thomas had been angry with her after she had hurt his uncle, but his memories were too full of love to tarnish with hate. He had tried, but memories that popped up now and again had always caused a smile before he remembered he was suppose to hate her.

The couple's conversation continued as they walked the familiar path along the fence line that surrounded the pasture. When they got back to the gate they stood facing each other, he leaning against a post as she stood in familiar stance, with hands on hips, thumbs forward.

Thomas stood talking to Zeke and watched the couple from the doorway, his mind wandered from their conversation to remembering the many times he'd witnessed this same scene. This time it was different. He knew somehow that she had no intention of returning, but was answering her tortured conscience's plea for peace.

"Is you okay, Miss Lillie?" Zeke asked from the front seat.

She looked up into the rearview mirror and answered, "Oh, yes, Zeke. These tears are happy ones. I'm so relieved that Samuel doesn't hate me."

"Yes, ma'am, That truly is a blessin. Praise Jesus for not hardenin his heart," he answered.

Drying her eyes she said, "Things keep going the way they are and I might have to start believing in Acey's God myself."

"Not sure I's understand, Miss Lillie. Who be this 'Acey's God'?"

"The one that my late husband believed in and preached about. I never got the calling to believe like he did."

"But, Missy, they be only one God. And He's fo eberbody. And He give his only begotten son to die fo our sins...."

"Yes, Zeke, I've heard all about him these past few years. But he's never let his presence be known to me." She was looking out the car window and watching the scenery go by. She started with her usual explanation, "I can't believe in a loving God that will allow harm to come to good people, and innocent children. Look at your life, Zeke. You still have to live in fear of being lynched because of the color of your skin. IF He is so loving and all-powerful why does He allow that? Why would He let people die that have eased the suffering and cured people...like doctors, or people that spread His word and brought 'His lost lambs' back to Him, as my Acey tried so hard to do?"

"I'm not sure 'bout all that, but I believes we'll all know in due time. But it hasta be in HIS time, when He decides. Just know in your heart that He's watchin' out for ya. He loves ya, Miss Lillie. He's guiding ya this very day in yer doing what is right to make your soul clean so you feel good about yo self. Don't ya feel it?"

Not wanting to continue the conversation Lillie smiled at him in the mirror and agreed, "Yes, I suppose so, Zeke, I suppose so."

Taking the hint he glanced up and asked, "Did Mr. Briles know where this lady is you be looking fo?"

"The last time he heard she had moved somewhere closer to her family, but that doesn't make sense because she was living with her mother and brothers when she lived here."

Zeke nodded, "Where to next?"

"I think I'll need some stationary. Let's find a five and dime store and I'll get enough to write a bunch of letters. I'll also need stamps, so we can swing by the post office after that. Oh, and I'll need a travel map of Texas. Then I guess we'll call it a day. I'm feeling very tired all of a sudden," she sighed.

In the mirror he saw her lean her head back on the seat and close her eyes. He silently prayed, "Good Lord in Heben I knows ya been lookin' after this fine lady, but please shine yo light so she can find the hebenly path in the darkness round her. She be cryin' out ta understand Lord Jesus, and she be searchin' for answers. Amen."

Lillie poured over the map and began her search by writing letters to the sheriff in each county surrounding Palo Pinto County. When she received negative or no response from those, she put an X inside them and extended the search to counties surrounding those and so forth, until one day the sheriff of Tom Green County answered. He knew of an Alva Terrell, spelled with an e instead of an i, now living in San Angelo, and did she want him to pursue with her query?

363

Lillie was exuberant as she responded in the affirmative and could think of little else as she waited.

The sheriff drove to the Lacey residence, with Lillie's letter in hand and knocked on the door.

Chapter 59... Families grow.

"Who do you think's been leavin' 'em?" asked Sherwood.

"I don't care as long as they keep coming," said Sherman.

"You both are so silly. It's gotta be Mama. She's probably sneaking them over when the old man goes to bed," Nellie said.

Nellie still held animosity toward Sie and felt smug that he couldn't hire out Jim who was only seven and Valerie two. She believed he was nothing without her and the boys, and finally went to his family and worked the cotton fields driving heavy machinery with the other West men.

Sherwood jumped in with, "OR, Maybe it's the old man sneaking them over, sorry for what he did but don't want no one to know. He wouldn't want to eat crow with an apology; he's too proud for that."

"MAYBE it's John Key and he wants to make up with Nellie," offered Sherman.

"Well, he can just want in one hand, cause it ain't gonna happen. The most enjoyment I had in my marriage is when Mr. Key asked me to work with him. John is too afraid it will mess his hairdo or dirty his clothes. I was the son Mr. Key never found in John. His brother, Orin, is okay I suppose, but Mr. Key preferred *me* when it came to a day's work driving the cattle from one pasture to another. He told me it was because he could count on me to stay with the herd."

"That's how you got your arm broke. Out there doing John's work. HE should have been riding that horse that got into the loco weed and took off with you that day."

"And if it weren't for their cattle dog you would have been killed. How do you suppose that dog knew to get between the horse and that cliff when it was hell bent to run right off the edge?"

"I don't know. But I'm sure glad he did. I couldn't control that loco horse, and when the dog ran straight at us was when the horse started to buck and threw me off in a rock pile."

"Yeah, you said you had a cut on your head and blood was running down your forehead and when you reached up to wipe it away only half your arm came up and you had to catch the other part with your other hand."

She nodded, knowing they had heard the story so many times they could tell it themselves word for word, but it was still fun in the telling. "Yes, it just hung there, limp." She remembered as she looked down at the left arm. "To this day I can't turn it over to accept change from someone. I have to make a cone shape out of my hand and they pour it in. The doc says the muscle laying across the top of my arm lay in the v of the broken bone while it healed and will remain permanently this way"

"It still should have been John's arm, not yours, and if it's him leaving the groceries, then it's your due." answered Sherman

"Well he can just forget that. He done let me know what he wanted and how he wanted it, HIS way or nothing. Besides, he could have prevented this baby just as much as me. Who says it's the woman's fault anyway? Now he and Bonnie can go running around to who-knows-where and have their good times on someone else's expense," she spat out.

"Now, Nellie," Sherman scolded, "How can you be jealous of his sister, Bonnie? You knew they were close when you married him. After all she was your best friend,"

"Yeah, well WAS is the word. One day she came over and borrowed one of my hats to wear to school and when John came home from work that night I found my hat in the back seat of his car!"

"So? What's that suppose to mean? Maybe he gave her a ride home from school or she asked him to bring it back to you."

"Don't you see? He probably didn't go to work at all. He picked her up at school and they rode around together all day, leaving me home alone to baby-sit his two little brothers! They could have let me join them. I would have liked to spend time with both of them. But he'd rather have his sister than me. I'm not sure why he even married me."

"Oh, Nellie, you don't know that for sure. Did you ask him? Did you ask her? You're just jumping to conclusions that may not be true," accused Sherman.

"Well, mister fancy pants, maybe you don't want to stay with me either. Maybe you'd like it better back with Mama and the old man," she half threatened him.

"Stop it both of you. You sound like when we were kids, for Christ's sake. We're grown ups now and I'd think that you both would want to act like one," scolded Sherwood.

"All I have to say is that if those groceries are from John Key he can just take them back. I want you to sit up tonight and find out if it is. I'll throw every bit in his face!" Nellie threatened.

The boys took turns sitting up that night, in the darkened living room with the curtains opened just enough so they had a clear view of the front porch.

It was well after midnight when Sherwood heard a car pull up outside. He went to the curtain and waited. He saw the form of a man get out and open the back door of his car, remove a box of groceries and deposit them on the porch, then turn and leave. Sherwood smiled in the knowing. *Of course, it made perfect sense now.*

The next morning he told his roommates and they all waited up the next night. As soon as the groceries were placed on the porch, Nellie opened the door and flipped on the porch light.

"Well, Mr. Lykens, how kind of you to stop by. You must come in for a cup of coffee. We've been waiting for hours. I have a lemon meringue pie to go with it. After all, *you* purchased the ingredients, so you might as well get some payment in return."

Ed dropped his chin and looked at her through his eyebrows. "I didn't do it for repayment. I wanted to help out some dear friends the only way I knew how."

"Well it *is* greatly appreciated..." Nellie started.

"And sorely needed." Sherman finished.

They all laughed and Ed came in and joined them for a cup of coffee and a piece of pie. *I wonder how she knows it's my favorite?* Then he smiled and took another bite.

The next day Ed took Nellie to the store and she was able to purchase her needs without having him guess. He invited her to the movies and the boys joined them. He wound up paying for all of their tickets. Everywhere they went her brothers stuck to them like glue.

One night he asked her if he could take her out without the chaperones. She smiled and said she thought she could arrange it.

The boys were not happy about being left out, but understood. They still got to go *some* of the time.

He made her feel like a queen. He opened doors for her and didn't heed the gossip when they were seen together at the Lyric Theater. She was large with another man's child and she was still married to him. Such a scandal!

She had never received as much attention as she was now enjoying from Ed. She knew he would be a good provider and after all, their families were close all these years as neighbors.

Ed lost no time in asking Nellie to marry. He knew she was unable to, as long as she was still married to John, and she couldn't divorce him until after the baby was born. He knew all of that and still wanted her *and* the baby.

One night as she and Ed were out with his best friend Johnny Anderson, and his date Lavada, Nellie told Lavada; "We used to be next door neighbors, with our bedrooms facing each other. He never pulled his shades so I know exactly what I'll be getting." The girls burst into laughter and giggled the rest of the evening, each time one would look at the other. The couples enjoyed double-dating often.

When Nellie's time came to bring a new life into the world she and the old man agreed to a truce. The local midwife was called and Frances assisted. Sie took it upon himself to tend to the kids. Ed was a basket case, waiting with the family, nervous as a father to be, smoking and pacing back and forth. They stayed down the street while Nellie gave birth to a beautiful baby girl.

Afterwards Sie came to the house and opened the bedroom door a crack and stepped in halfway. Quietly he asked Nellie, "John is outside. He wants to know if he can come in and see the baby."

Nellie clutched the baby to her breast and with a curled lip she said loud enough for not only Sie and John to hear but a few next door neighbors as well. "He will NEVER see this baby. NEVER!"

Sie nodded, "That's all I needed to hear," as he side stepped back out and closed the door.

There on Cochise Row, in Bisbee, Arizona, on September 10, 1935 found Ed and the Fellers/West family celebrating the birth of Joyce Yvonne Key.

After Nellie filed for divorce, she and Ed had to wait five long months before it was final and she was legally able to remarry. Nellie left Joyce with Frances as she and Ed drove to Lordsburg, New Mexico, on February 22nd 1936. Ed married Nellie, whom he lovingly called his "Yellow Rose of Texas". She knew she was marrying a man that loved her truly, unconditionally and permanently.

Chapter 60... Nightly Stories.

Joyce was precious. She seemed like an old soul locked in a tiny body. When she looked around it was as though she was analyzing each item she focused on. Movement and sound brought the few chirps of laughter she seemed to give out as tokens of appreciation. A person had to earn her smiles.

She saved most of them for her six year old Aunt Valerie. They seemed to bond instantly and Valerie would play with her for hours, dressing her in cute clothes Nellie made.

"It's like playing with a real live doll." Valerie told Nellie. Joyce was more content with Val than with anyone, outside of her "Daddy."

When one of the neighborhood kids came close, she would frown and study their features as if she needed to remember every detail for some reason known only to her.

Ed doted on her constantly. Holding and rocking her to sleep. Relinquishing her only when she needed Nellie's breast. Then he would watch as she suckled and made baby sounds. Between Ed and Val, Nellie had little time with her own daughter, except for feedings. She laughed when she thought that if Valerie could find a way to do that too, she'd lose Joyce entirely. One thing was certain, she knew Ed loved her and as young as Val was, Nellie never needed to worry about a sitter if she and Ed wanted to go to the movies or dancing.

Ed and Nellie shared their evenings with her brothers as before, in they yard, telling stories, only this time Nellie was rocking Joyce. And being's this baby was hers, she felt more love than she thought possible.

"Did you ever tell Ed about the cotton-mouth?" asked Sherman.

"No, I never got around to it," she answered, giving Ed a questioning look.

"Yes, I'd love to hear about 'the cotton-mouth', tell me." He loved the evening story times as much as a little kid because it was something he'd never had.

"Well, it wasn't much really. The old man and Mama had farmed us out on a cotton plantation, and we were bedding down for the night. It was hot and our water supply was from a faucet on a pipe sticking up out of the ground about three feet high.

"We were all bedded down when Mama ups and says, 'Nellie did you check that water spigot? Did you leave it on after drawing water for the dishes?'

"I said 'No', but she wouldn't listen.

"She says, 'I think you better go check; that foreman sees us wasting water he'll fire all of us.'

"Well, I muttered something like 'Whadda ya mean by WE when me and the boys are doin all the work?'

"The old man bellered at me 'get yor ass out there and do as yer told.'

"So out I went, barefoot and in my nightgown. It was a moonlit night, but clouds covered the moon. I knew about where it was, so I headed out in that direction. I saw something real white where the faucet was and I couldn't remember seeing a rag around it. Something made me stop and go back for a lantern. There he was a huge old cotton-mouth snake coiled around the pipe and situated so he could catch drips of water in his open mouth! If I had reached for that spigot he would've had me in a heartbeat!

"Well, don't you think that old man didn't get his sorry ass out of that bed and do his own checking after that. He killed that snake and it measured a good six feet."

Ed thought of all the travels his family made and were lucky enough to not encounter anything so dangerous.

"Tell him about the twister," said Sherwood.

Again she looked at Ed. He was smiling and nodded his desire to hear the story.

"Well, we were down where I was born in Uvalde, Texas, and that was when Daddy was still alive. We were about to sit down to eat with the table all set. I remember there was a red and white checkered tablecloth on the table and I was setting a bowl of mashed potatoes in the center, when everything got real quiet, except for Mama singing 'The great speckled bird'."

She dropped her voice almost to a whisper as she recalled the incident. "Dad hushed her and we listened. It was real quiet. I never heard quiet like that before or since. We went outside. No birds, no grasshoppers, no squeak of the windmill, nothing was making a sound. It was hot, without a breath of cool air and we had our doors and windows shut to keep the dust out. Well, the sky started to turn a funny orange color and it was scary. I looked at Dad. He was worried I know. He was frowning and searching for answers in the trees and the sky.

"When the sky turned even darker, everything changed. Our horses and milk cow became restless and was making noises. And the chickens all made a beeline for the coop.

"Dad seemed to jump out of his skin, 'Frances, get the kids in the house and up on one of the beds. Nellie, honey, wet a washrag for you and each of the boys. You kids lay flat and Mama is going to put a mattress on top of you. Hold the washrag over your mouth and nose and breathe through it. Frances, when the kids are ready and you've got the mattress on top of them, lie across them to hold them down. You kids stay put until Mama or I come get you. Go. NOW!'

"I heard him yelling at Mama to 'open all the windows and doors'. He went running to open both ends of the barn and let our animals go. They were about to tear down the stalls anyhow.

"Well, then it started to get noisy. It first sounded like a big old cotton truck coming real close, then it got louder and louder. Like when I was near the train tracks at the end of a cotton row.

"I peeked out to see where Mama and Daddy were, but I couldn't see them through the dust. Then I heard Daddy close by trying to yell above the noise. He kept yelling 'HOLD ON', 'HOLD ON.'

"It seemed like I was going to suffocate under Mama's weight and the mattress and the wet dishrag was hard to breathe through. The boys were squirming beside me and I knew they were about out of their mind with fear, cause I was.

"It was a long time before the noise started to let up. When Daddy finally removed the mattress, he carried each one of us outside and put us on the ground. I remember seeing the tablecloth sitting on the kitchen floor, every plate and spoon was still in place, and the bowl of mashed potatoes was in the middle of the tablecloth, just where I had put it. Everything was covered in dirt but not a plate was broken and everything was perfectly in place. I wish I could have seen how it did that.

"Anyway we stood holding on to one another, Mama, me and the boys. Dad went to sweeping the house and I thought he'd gone nuts. I kept thinking that we could do that later. Then all of a sudden this huge sidewinder came out from under the bed us kids had been on, and madder than the dickens. Daddy told us later that it came in seeking shelter from the twister and was coiled up in the corner. Dad only had a broom so he let the snake go. That one was at least eight feet long. Dad said so and he oughtta know. It was him that shooed it out of the house. That snake didn't even look in our direction. He just made a beeline for the desert."

Nellie looked over at Ed and smiled as he was sitting up and looking around in the grass nearby.

"Tell him about..." Sherman started.

"No, that's enough for tonight," Nellie interrupted. "We have many nights to share our family stories."

It was not long after their marriage, and close to dinnertime one night when Sherman came into the kitchen, "Ed there's someone out in the yard that wants to talk to you."

Seeing his brother-in-law's concern, Ed went outside to find a young woman waiting there.

Nellie watched from the kitchen window as he approached the girl. Although they stood close, facing each other she did not see them make contact. The conversation was quiet and it appeared that an agreement was made between them. The girl turned and left as Ed came back into the house.

"Who was that?" Nellie asked.

"Just a friend," he answered.

"What did she want?" Nellie pressed.

"She had a personal problem and needed to talk to someone about it."

"Why did she come to you with her personal problems?"

"We dated while you were married to John. She and I are friends."

"What was her personal problem?"

"Nellie...it's personal. That's all I'm saying about it. She is a friend. It was before *us*. Like your marriage to John Key was before *us*. Whatever happened before *us* has no bearing on *us* now. That's the end of it. Now let's have dinner."

Nellie was furious but how could she argue with the point made?

That night after dinner and the family gathered outside for their ritual story telling, Sherwood began, "Nellie, tell him about the hoop snake."

She was still fuming and retorted, "I'm not in any mood to tell stories tonight!"

"Well, maybe it's time I told one," Ed offered.

At their enthusiastic nods he began. "Well when I was a bit younger and a little more foolish, I got into a bit of trouble."

"Wha'd ya do?" asked Sherman.

"Not the preacher's son!" teased Sherwood.

"Yep. It was all because I got a BB gun for my birthday. There was this little girl who had one too and we decided..." Ed began.

"Might have known there would be a girl involved!" muttered Nellie.

Ed smiled slightly to himself. Now he knew she cared enough that she was jealous, and that did his heart good. "As I was saying..." He told the story of how he shot the insulators and got caught in a small town in Oklahoma. When he finished about how Lillie had hauled him back into that hotel room, probably saving his worthless hide, Nellie was ready to reclaim center stage.

"My Daddy was a lot of fun, and really lucky. His friends said he had a golden touch, whatever that means, and he played games with us.

"When it was time to rake the yard he wasn't like the old man. Daddy came out and helped us. He and I would team up against the boys and we'd try to rake up a pile of leaves faster than the boys could get them into a wheelbarrow, push it to the garden spot out in the back yard, empty it and get back. He'd be saying, 'Hurry Nellie, their catching up to us!' and we'd rake as fast as we could and the boys would be running and dumping, and running back as fast as *they* could."

Sherman couldn't help but jump in to tell some, "Sometimes the wheelbarrow would tip over..."

Sherwood followed with, "And we'd have to take the time to get them leaves all reloaded."

Nellie regained control and added, "It was lots of fun, not like with the old man."

Ed realized that their father had used psychology on them and achieved the same goal, as Sie would have, but by making the work a game, he got the chore done faster and made it seem easy because he had made it fun.

Nellie was happy when she told stories about her father and Ed encouraged it.

She began, "He was so lucky. One time a carnival came to town and Dad took us to it. They had all these prizes you could win for knocking these bottles off the barrel. Well, it was the first night and Dad was trying to win Mama this bronze clock with two horses rearing up on each side of the clock face." She was using her hands to describe it.

Ed nodded, "Yeah, I've seen them before. They're really nice."

"Well, Dad finally did it! He knocked them all clean off that barrel and waited for the clock. The man told Dad that he couldn't have it, that he really hadn't knocked them off. Dad argued with the man and then walked off. That carnival man thought he had given up, but not *my* Dad. He went straight to the sheriff and told him what happened. The sheriff followed Dad back to that booth and asked the man why he had not given Dad that clock.

"Well, the man says that Dad didn't really win it. 'His word against mine,' he says.

"Then that sheriff looks that carnival man right in the eye and says, 'Mister, I don't know of a more honest man than Mr. Fellers here, and I'll take his word over yours any day.

"Well, that carnival man drops his chin to his chest and mutters that it was the main attraction to bringing people to his booth.

"The sheriff says, 'Well, Sherman, would you be willing to let him keep the clock until closing time tonight? Then I'll come back with you and we'll make sure you get it.'

"Dad says that's okay with him, but what if someone else won it too? That made the sheriff think. He decided right then and there, that he wanted no more trouble out of that booth and he demanded the man give that clock to my Dad.

"When the man protested that no one would come to his booth, that sheriff said, 'Either close your booth or I'll close the carnival!' Dad got the clock!"

Ed laughed out loud. "Good for him; stood up for his rights and came out the winner!"

Enjoying an appreciative audience, Nellie continued, "A short time after that he bought a raffle ticket for something the Miner's Union was doing. The winner would get a brand new Star car. All the money Dad had to spare was the price of one ticket, so he figured, what the heck. He bought the ticket and low and behold he won that car!

"I was absolutely thrilled because none of our friends owned a car, paid for! Well, Dad drove it home, all legal and everything and he loaded up

Mama and us kids and we drove up one street and down the other of Bisbee, Lowell, and Douglas. People waved, because the word had spread that Daddy had won the car and there were people on the streets waving at us like we were real important. I felt like a princess in her chariot, in a parade just for us. When he had driven around everywhere he took us home and dropped us off. He told Mama that he would be back pretty soon. Well, he came back without the car! He had sold it outright and went straight to the bank with the money and paid off the mortgage to this house. I was absolutely furious.

"He saw me crying and asked, 'What's the matter, Nellie? Aren't you happy to have a house?'

"I told him, 'We already have the house. And I won't be able to feel important anymore.'

"He said, 'But now no one can sell the house out from under us and make us move. It's ours.'

"I was still mad because we couldn't take the house around, showing it off to everyone like we did the car, and I told him.

"He just scooped me up in his arms and said, 'I wasn't showing off today. I was showing people that good things can happen to good people if you take a chance once in awhile. Nellie, don't be afraid of taking a chance once in awhile. If you don't you'll never get any thing better than you already have. If you take a chance and lose, remember that other people are taking chances too and it was one of their turns to win.'

"Of course I didn't understand what he was talking about then, but it's stuck with me all these years," said Nellie

Looking at the boys sad expressions Ed knew that they still missed him very much, and nodding slightly he said, "Your father was a very wise man. I wish I would have had the chance to know him."

They all got real quiet and fidgety. Sherman had pulled up a dandelion and was plucking the tiny pedals off one by one, "He could do lot's of things, more than just that old coal mine. He hated going down in the dark pit and breathing that coal dust. It's a greasy dirt that Mama could hardly get out of his clothes, even washin' em twice."

Jim had joined them that night, and asked, "Do you remember Daddy having the bee boxes out back, out near the grape arbor that he planted? He loved that kind of dirt, the kind that would put food on the table. His garden was always the best. I think Lillie took a picture of him standing in front of those bee boxes."

Sherman ventured a question, "Ed, after your Daddy died, that night you come home from the CCC's, you said something about Lillie not being your Mama. But you told us before that she wasn't and that your mama and brother had died when you was little. Were you mad at her that night?"

"Not really, Sherman. I found out that night that my real mother and brother had not died like my Dad always told me. I've somehow always known that Lillie wasn't my real mother, but she loves me like she is, and I love her very much. She's gone now to try to find my real mother."

"What ya gonna do when ya meet your real Mama? What ya gonna say to her?" asked Jim.

"Don't rightly know, Jim. If she's still alive and Lillie finds her, I hope everything will be easy, and my brother too. He's about four years younger than me. I'm anxious to get to know him, IF they are still alive."

"Are you mad at your dad for not telling you the truth?" asked Sherwood.

"At first I was, but how can you stay mad at a loved one that has passed on? You're not still mad at your Dad for selling that car are you?" asked Ed.

Nellie sat there for a couple of seconds thinking. "I guess not. But it sure would have made all the other kids jealous."

"What do you care what the other kids think? They're no better than you. You probably know more about raising cotton than they ever will. And tending to sheep," Ed pointed to Sherman. "Look at how well you sew, Nellie. Can the other girls sew that good? You guys have a lot to be proud of, even if you have a stepfather you don't like."

"Well, one good thing I can say about the old man is, he taught me how to sew. He knew how because of the mattress factory. He would buy patterns and material and bring it home and I would sit at the machine with him standing behind me, watching. If I made a seam too wide or too narrow, he would make me rip it out and do it over again, and again, until I did it right. But that's the *only* good thing I can say about that man," she muttered.

Jim bounced on his heels, "Tell him about the hoop snake!"

"Yes, Nellie, what about this 'hoop snake'? I want to hear all about it," Ed encouraged

"All I'm going to say about the hoop snake is that some people claim that it is not real, but I'm here to tell you that I know for a fact they're real because I saw one and it chased me down a hill when I was a little girl. For some reason, when I got to the bottom, it just rolled right by me and I lost sight of it in the tall grass. End of story. I don't care that some people don't believe me. What I saw was a snake and it had its tail in its mouth and it was rolling down the hill right behind me." As she told the story she became almost angry for no reason. No one was arguing with her about it not being true, but she was afraid they might think she was making it up.

Ed decided to change the mood, "Do you boys want to hear about the night I saw a dead man sit up on a table?"

"REALLY? Where?" came from Sherwood.

"Is that for real?" asked Sherman.

"Cross my heart, hope to die..." Ed started.

"Stick a needle in your eye?" asked Jim.

"Stick a needle in my eye!" laughed Ed.

He saw that he had their full attention and glanced at Nellie. Her frown told him that she wasn't sure if she wanted to hear about it or not.

"I had this friend down at the Hubbard Mortuary that was a night watchman. Sometimes when I'd get bored, or he got lonely, he'd call me and I'd go there and we'd play cards. It was a hot day so we were down in the basement where they kept the bodies cool until their funerals. This friend was a black man and he was real nice. I'm telling you boys, if you have a black man for a friend you have a friend for life."

"Go on...about the dead guy," coaxed wide-eyed Sherwood.

"One night as I was dealing out a hand to each of us, this dead guy, laying on a slab and covered with a sheet, just sat up from his waist up, and goes, 'UAAHHH.'

"Well let me tell you, I was up and out of there in a shot and it took my friend a block and a half to catch me. There we stood, he's got a hold of my shirt and was trying to talk and catch his breath at the same time. He finally got enough wind to tell me that it was okay, that I was safe and to come back so he could explain. I wasn't too sure about it, but I trusted him so I went back.

"The body was lying back down, and he removed the sheet to show me that the man was truly dead. Then he explained that after death muscles can still contract for some reason and when this man's stomach muscles pulled him straight up like that, it pushed air trapped in the lungs out past the vocal chords, which made the sound.

"Well, like I said, I could see that he was dead, and I trusted my friend, so we turned back to play cards. That's when we found them scattered all over the room; my chair was tipped over and a trail of cards led to the door where I'd made my escape.

"It took us a better part of an hour to straighten everything and find them cards. I don't think he ever found the three of diamonds."

They all broke into laughter, and laughed so hard that the boys laid on their backs holding their stomachs and Nellie had to use her apron to wipe the tears from her eyes.

Chapter 61...Lillie Succeeds.

Mary wasted no time in answering the letter from Lillie with her address. Nothing passed between them except the exchange of information.

When Lillie was informed that Ed and Mary were reunited, if only by letters, she felt she had succeeded, at least part way in clearing her conscience. She now felt she could go on with her life and face Mary when the time presented itself.

In the summer of 1938, the West family was planning a trip.

"Sie, why don't we plan on swinging through San Angelo on our way home from visiting my family in San Antonio?" asked Frances.

"Now what's going on in that head of yours? You think you can just waltz in there and pave the way for Ed and his mother's reunion? Besides, you can't kid me, you want to be the first one to meet her and tell her everything before Ed even gets a chance to meet her," answered Sie

"Don't be silly, I just think it's not that far out of our way, and only right to stop by and pay our respects. After all, we're family now," she said. "It would be the neighborly thing to do."

"Yeah, IF we were her neighbors, and we're not. She might not take kindly to us just showing up and barging in on her." He tried to scold her out of the idea but he could see that her mind was already set and he wouldn't know a moment's peace if she didn't get her way.

"Alright, Frances, have it your way, but you had better not do anything to harm the relationship between this mother and son. From all I've heard it's going to be a sensitive reunion as it is," he warned.

"We'll just pop in for a minute to show our respects," she repeated.

As soon as introductions were made, Alva slipped away and came out with a packed suitcase. "If you don't mind I'm going to hitch a ride with you. I've found my brother and I'm not going to lose him again."

"Son, you can't impose on these people and their travels. You can go later," Mary argued.

"No, Momma. I'm going now, if the West's will allow. When I get there I'll get a job and a house so you and the kids can come."

"Alva, no one has said anything about us moving. We have no reason to impose on Edward's life. He may not even want us..." she tried.

"I'm going, if you want to stay, then so be it, but I'm going to be with my brother!" He demanded.

Sie spoke, "It's quite alright Mrs. Lacey. We've plenty of room and we'd be glad for the company. Come on young man, let's see where we can fit that bag of yours."

Mary spoke little during the visit. She listened intently when the West's spoke of her long lost son, but she had little to offer in the conversation except for one or two word answers.

So, with not getting a response that they could relish in retelling, the West's bid Mary goodbye with Alva already in the car.

As they were pulling into the outskirts of Bisbee, Sie spotted Ed driving a truck and flagged him down. "Alva, before I take you to your brother, I would like you to meet someone." Alva was impatient with the man, but remaining calm he stepped out when Sie brought the car to a stop.

Fearing a problem, Ed pulled over and jumped out of the truck, meeting Sie as he climbed out of the car. Beside him was a tall, dark stranger and Ed asked, "What's up, Sie?"

"Ed, I have a man here I want you to meet. Ed Lykens, this is Alva Terrell. Alva Terrell, this is Ed Lykens. As the two men shook hands, Sie laughed and stepped back. "You two are brothers!"

Realizing the familiarity of the names, the two men froze all but the handshake, which continued. When reality finally set in, they began with manly slaps on the back that led to an awkward embrace. Sie was quite pleased with himself, at their expense.

Finances postponed the mother and son reunion until just before Christmas of 1938 when Ed and Nellie made the trip with Joyce and their son, Edward Alvin, born on May 31, 1937.

"I thought Alva's name was Alvin. That's how Edward got his middle name," Ed explained.

During the hours of visiting, he had felt overwhelmed in the small house, as he met his new family, starting with each of his half-sisters and brother. Then later a woman came in and was introduced as "Aunt Ginny", Mary's half sister. Then her children trailed in, as his cousins. Conversation was a struggle as the room filled with relatives being introduced and curious about the long lost member.

Joyce was shy and stayed tucked under Nellie's arm, while Edward was in his element with so much attention. The room was warmed by a cast iron heater with a narrow hearth sticking out from the front of it. There was a small door just beyond the hearth with which to put in the wood or take out the ashes. As the family was visiting, little Edward backed up and was about to sit down on that hearth when one of the family members reached out and grabbed him in his downward motion. He was saved from being horribly burned by his rescuer's fast action and everyone drew a relieved breath to see that he was unharmed.

For the first time in his life, Ed experienced a wave of claustrophobia. Feeling the panic creeping in he knew he had to get out. "Excuse me, ladies I'm going to step outside for a minute. I need a cigarette."

He stood out in the cold and took several deep breaths before lighting his cigarette. Then flipping his collar up and tucking his empty hand in a pocket, he leaned up against the porch support. *All my life growing up it was just Dad, Lillie and me. That's all. 'Orphans' Dad had said, 'with no other family". Now they're coming out of the woodwork and I don't know what to say to any of them. It's nothing like I thought it would be. I'm not sure what I expected, but not this. I can't have a personal visit with my own mother; I have so many questions I've carried since the night I was told. I want to know WHY. I want to know her side of the story. I've heard Lillie's, now I want to hear hers.*

As if Nellie could read his thoughts she continued the conversation with his family. "I come from a family of seven kids, and each of my parents had close to a dozen brothers and sisters. When I met Ed and he said he was an orphan, I thought 'hallelujah'. I did most of the raising of my sisters and brothers and I sure as hell didn't want more! Joyce is a mistake from my first marriage. That son of a bitch left me as soon as he found out I was pregnant. Ed wants kids, so here's Edward, still in diapers, and I'm pregnant again, due about mid April. Now Ed has found all of you…so much for not having a big family! Do you have an ashtray?"

Not wanting to seem inhospitable, Mary rose from her chair to find something Nellie could use as an ashtray. She glanced at Ginny and saw that she too was shocked to hear a woman use the term 'pregnant'. Most people used the term "family way" or the "Lord's blessing." This woman seemed brash, cussed like a man, didn't seem at all thrilled with their moving to Bisbee, and she even smoked cigarettes!

Outside on the porch Ed stood deep in thought as a taxi slowed and came to a stop. The driver's door opened and a man stepped half way out, "Hey, are you Mary's boy from Arizona?"

Ed looked up in surprise, "Yes, I guess I am."

"Well, I just wanted to introduce myself, I'm one of your cousins!" The driver declared, standing with one foot still inside the cab.

Ed took the final puff of his cigarette while still looking at the cabby he dropped it and smashed it out with the sole of his shoe. Then he nodded, waved and returned inside. *That's it, I've had it. I can't deal with all of this.*

Upon reentering the tiny house, now wall to wall with people, he stated frankly, "Nellie, I think it's time for us to be on our way. We've got a long trip back," he said cautiously.

Looking up Nellie saw his nervousness and knowing the house was too small to accommodate their spending the night, she agreed. "Yes, We have to get back on the road and get as many miles behind us as we can. Thank you for everything. I'm so glad to have met you all."

They quickly gathered Edward's toys, diapers and bottles into a bag, and picked up Joyce. Nellie followed with "Little Edward" as the new family called him. The whole family trailed after them to the car.

Ed turned to his new mother, gave her a brief hug, and explained, "I've been helping Alva to get a job and house ready for you all. As soon as he has everything set we will get you moved up to Bisbee so we can all be together. Maybe then we can be more relaxed and have a private talk."

Mary had tears in her eyes as she cupped the left side of his face with her right palm. "Yes, dear. We will all be together soon. I'm a better listener than I am a talker but I'm looking forward to it. God be with you and keep you and your beautiful family safe."

He nodded, "Thank you, you too." Turning he nodded and waved to everyone and climbed behind the wheel. It had been a long trip down, and it will be a long trip home, but he felt he could not have stayed another minute. *Perhaps when we are all in Bisbee, with a lot less people, I can get some answers.*

For unexplained reasons, four years after their father's death, children's welfare found their way to Mary's door again. This time they took Mary's two youngest to the same sanatorium that Mary Lee and Myrle had visited years before.

Only this time there was a boy and a girl and they were not allowed to stay together. Clayton was taken to a boys dorm on the property while Margie stayed in with other girls.

Margie was called out of one of her classes one day. "Margie, come here child. I've a letter here from your mother stating that she has not heard from you since your arrival here," the hospital supervisor said. "We promised her that she would hear from you weekly and letters go out on Fridays. We have supplied you well with stationery and pencil. Why haven't you written your mother?"

Margie shifted her frail body from one foot to another and answered meekly, "I did."

Not believing, the woman continued, "Your mother wouldn't be writing me, worried out of her mind, if you had. I'm asking you again. Why haven't

389

you written to your mother? I know you can write because you do well in your classes. She needs to hear from you that all is well."

Margie repeated, "I did write the letters ma'am."

"If you wrote the letters, why hasn't your mother received them?" Insisted the woman.

"Because no one gave me any stamps and I don't have any money to buy them," was Margie's reply. The stamps were immediately provided.

Moving from the security of Will, now living with her, and Ginny close by, caused Mary grave distress. "Will, please, come with us. I would feel much better if you were there. You're not in the best of health and I can look after you. You've always been my protector and it's time I helped you."

Will's throat had been diagnosed with cancer of the esophagus, which caused him to speak in a raspy voice, "No, Sis, I'm too old and too tired to move again. I like it here. The weather is good for breathing and besides, you'll have Alva, and Edward there. They will take care of you. I'm too set in my ways, and to be honest, children tend to get on my nerves, not just yours, but everybody's. I'll stay here and do just fine."

"Who's going to look after you if you become ill? Or if you take a fall and are unable to get up?" she asked.

Will strained to talk, "Probably Fred. He likes to try to beat me at checkers, but I think deep down he knows he hasn't got a chance. There are no meals to cook, with soup, milk and raw eggs being all I can swallow. If I fall he'll make sure I get back on my feet. And if I die he'll let you know," then he winked and patted her arm.

Mary knew that Fred Taliaferro, Ginny's son, and Will had become close since Will's move to San Angelo and he would do the things Will said, but she wanted desperately to hang on to her last brother. It seemed every argument she made for his going he countered with one for staying. She finally gave up and resigned herself that she would be moving to Bisbee without him.

It was the fall of 1939 when Alva and Sherman arrived and loaded Mary, Mary Lee and Myrle, with all their possessions, and moved them to Bisbee.

"LOOK, MOMMA! The house has running water and a bathroom inside, and all you have to do is pull this string in every room and lights come on!" Myrle was running from room to room turning on lights and watching the water run. "Did you see it Momma? Did you see the bathroom indoors? No more outhouse or chamber pots! Isn't it wonderful? I'll bet this cost Alva a whole lot of money! He must be rich now."

"Yes, I see all those things, but you mustn't be wasteful, Myrle. Shut the water off and turn out those lights. Alva works hard to pay for these special things. Just because we have them doesn't mean we're going to waste them." Mary scolded.

Alva had secured employment at Phelps Dodge Mercantile Company, as a miner in the Copper Queen Mine. He worked hard to provide for those that depended on him. His payday came once a month, with credit extended at the 'company store'. Ed helped where he could, but he had his own family and the brunt of the bills fell to Alva. As the family's needs grew with his siblings attending school, there were times when Alva went for his check only to find that the line of credit had absorbed it entirely. He never complained.

Time and time again Ed pleaded with Mary to talk to him about the past but she refused. Each time he asked, she answered, "It's best you not know." She felt she was protecting him and he felt she was depriving him. Frustration faded to indifference then the lack of conversation dashed all hopes of a mother and son relationship. He finally gave up trying.

If only she would have trusted him, they may have bonded.

Mary was notified that Margie and Clayton were being released after a stay of only three months. She joined Sherman and Alva on the trip to bring her two babies back and make the family whole again.

The children found gifts waiting for them in the car. There was a toy truck for Clayton and two dolls for Margie; one of which was a Shirley Temple doll that she cherished for many years.

But about that time, when it looked as if Mary would finally have all her children in one place, Ed suddenly moved his family to Los Angles, where he was assured, by his friend Johnny Anderson, that he had not only a job, but a house waiting for them.

"What do you mean there's no job or house? My God, man, I have a family to support and I believed you!" Ed uttered in disbelief.

"It's the only way we could get you out of that desert hell-hole. We missed you guys! This is California, man, the land of opportunity and sunshine. Don't worry about it. We'll find those things, and until we do you can stay here," stated Johnny.

"Oh, come on, Nellie, it'll be fun with us four back together again," offered Lavada. "Our kids can grow up together. Little Johnny, and the twins Billy and Bobby and Joyce, Edward and...Let me see that baby. You say her name is Mary? Aren't both your mother's named Mary? And how old is she?

Nellie sighed and handed her the baby. "Her middle name is Lillie, so she's named after *all three* mothers. She was born April 20th, 1939. You have any more coffee in that pot?"

After a week of living in a tent, in the Anderson's back yard, with a very angry wife, two small children and a baby, Ed *did* find a good job and a nice home for his family, *and* remained friends with Johnny and Lavada Anderson.

Lillie was not in Bisbee when Mary moved there and after years had passed, she decided it was time to face the long awaited confrontation.

The meeting was arranged to take place at Mary's house and when she answered the door the women stood for seconds, searching each other's faces.

"Lillie," Mary said calmly, stepping aside and inviting her in.

"Mary," Lillie answered softly, as she accepted.

As Lillie entered, Mary turned and shooed the children out. The women spent the time in private and their conversation was never revealed.

The End...

What Happened to them afterward?

Lillie Mae Rodgers

The winds that blew Lillie in directions of her life's events found her uprooted. Hasten was gone, Ed married and reunited with Mary, and he now had a family of his own. She felt alone.

This time she let the winds guide her westward, once again in search of the unknown and the insatiable desire to experience each new day.

From her past she revived the excitement of skillfully choosing her victims and executing the skills she had perfected over the years.

She rode the trains, choosing destinations that offered an adequate amount of gentlemen just waiting to help a lady in distress. She timed each encounter to put herself safely on the westward train, well fed and eluding any would be authorities. Success in her endeavors brought her a substantial financial security.

One day she had reached her farthermost point west, Los Angles, California, where she walked the beaches and waded in the gentle waves of the Pacific Ocean.

During this time she married a man by the name of John J. Dunlop on November 10th 1937, there in Los Angles, and was divorced on December 17th that same year. One month and one week was all it took for the couple to find they were "incompatible". With a Mexican divorce, Lillie was on her own again.

Among the documents found in her belongings, was another marriage. This one was to a Joe Alec Brown on January 3rd 1939, in Ranger, Texas. No divorce papers were found of this union.

She chose not to share the incidents of these two marriages, so the only history is the documents that she saved.

An envelope, also found among her things, explained why she was not in Bisbee when Mary came to live there. She wrote the following:

"Left Ranger Sept. 13th 1944 for California. Arrived at Eds Sept 15th stayed there till Nov 25-44. Went to work for Buelah worked there until March-45 Short job in Long Beach also short one in Compton. Then went back to Eds stayed there till July 6 1945. Worked for Howards till Aug 1st 46 then went back to Eds stayed there till Oct 24 then went to work for Godfreys Oct 24 1946- Left Godfreys May 30th 1948- went to Eds Left Compton Calif with Ed Dec 3 for Washington arrived Dec. 6th I rented cabin Dec 19th at Mabton Wash. April 16 1949 I married Eddie Rixon and started out for a new life at Mabton Wash. Is this the end? Only God knows. 4 years 7 months and 3 days from beginning."

Her statement about God leads me to believe that sometime during her later years she found out that "Acey's God" was her God too.

Eddie Rixon was the only man my siblings and I ever saw her with and we shared giggles of how odd we thought the couple was at the time. He was a tiny, kind old gentleman, who had a Scottish accent and surprised us with his ability to knit. He told us kids, "I knits me own svetters and I knits me own soks!" One Christmas he proved it by presenting us with wool hats, scarves and socks. But the marriage didn't last.

All us children felt the unconditional love that radiated from Lillie and we returned it wholeheartedly. The devotion that began with Hasten, those many years ago, overflowed onto Ed, and then to Ed's children.

I was the 4th child of Ed and Nellie and spent more time with Lillie than my siblings. She and I shared a bedroom more than once over the years.

Lillie fell victim to a stroke, which caused a loss of mind to mouth speech. (She would try to say what she wanted, but couldn't, then get angry and spew out a string of curses that would surprise a logger.) Her manual dexterity loss left her unable to continue to write, tat and crochet. She regained her verbal skills, but as far as I know never did her manual ones.

She died on a stormy March 9th, 1967 at Hillcrest Nursing Home in Grandview, Washington. Ed was living in Redding, California, and the bad weather deprived him of attending her funeral.

She was buried in Sunnyside, Washington, with Nellie's mother, Frances, and one of her nursing home friends attending her funeral.

Her 85 years on this earth was a challenge from childhood to the grave and she met it head on and gave it everything she had. I think her spirit has been standing behind me, just to my right, with her hand on my shoulder and reading as I write. Sometimes I can almost hear her whisper the words that flow through my fingers and onto the keys. She's been here with me all along, and she just might have volunteered to be my guardian angel. I sure hope so.

Mary Melinda Dikes/Tirrell/Lacey

She lived out her final years in Bisbee, Arizona, passing away with Ed living in Los Angeles, Alva stationed in Mississippi, and her brother Will too ill to travel from San Angelo, Texas. Mary Lee was attending Bible college in Oakland, California, Myrle was married and Margie was living in Los Angeles.

She was hospitalized in the Cochise County Hospital for almost five months before she succumbed to 'cardio vascular disease' on March 14th, 1943, four days short of her 51st birthday.

Ironically, she is buried in the same cemetery, and within sight of, Hasten's grave in Evergreen Cemetery, Lowell, Arizona.

Alva Homer Terrell

He married Olive Mary Bickle on July 25, 1941. He was inducted into the army on April 11, 1942, and stationed at Camp Shelby in Mississippi. He served overseas in France and Africa and the beaches of Normandy. He was awarded the good conduct medal, the Purple Heart, Bronze Arrow, and Silver Star while in service and was mustered out at Ft. Bliss, Texas, on October 25, 1945.

He pursued the ministry and was ordained in Ft. Worth, Texas. He chose the First Baptist Church. After their move to Los Angeles, he and Aunt Ollie escorted us Lykens kids to church on many Sundays.

Unable to have children of their own, they adopted four year old Eddie, who has many happy memories of him and his dad working on different farms and ranches in southern Arizona, and the unconditional love that Ollie bestowed upon him.

No one knows what happened to Alva's mind in his later years, for he began to drink and forsake God, and his family for the bottle.

He died alone, still married to, but estranged from, his devoted wife "Ollie", on July 17, 1979, in Benson, Arizona, at the age of 64.

He is also buried in the same cemetery as his parents. Ollie was placed beside him when she died November 8, 1984.

Mary Lee Lacey Cole

She never followed her calling in the ministry. She married at age 39, to Floyd Cole. There were no children. She had a lovely singing voice and sang at my wedding in 1960. She had a whimsical personality and dressed as a clown to sing a telegram to Ed at his 80th Birthday Party.

She donated generously to her church and those she believed in. She died Sept. 1, 1997.

Myrle Neville Lacey Olson

She has been an invaluable source of information on Mary's life after Hasten, and shares my love of genealogy and family history, and has been very patient with my picking her brain with a deluge of questions. She is a retired secretary for Borden Co. and has volunteered to act as my editor.

Married and 'snow birding' between Kent, Washington, and Mesa, AZ, she and husband Harry Olson had five children. They share a close relationship with God.

Margie Nell Lacey Hayes

She has also been a great asset to my book by sharing her childhood memories. She was an invaluable aid to me, remembering things the rest of the family had forgotten. Her marriage to Vernon Hayes produced four children. She lives with her only daughter in Florida.

William Clayton Lacey

He retired from the Boeing Aircraft Company after almost thirty years in the Aerospace Division. One of his talents is singing and he belonged to SPEBSQSA, which meant "The Society for the Preservation and Encouragement of Barbershop Quartet Singing in America." The name has recently been changed to BHS, the Barbershop Harmony Society.

The name of his quartet was The Four-Do-Matics. Ford Company first sponsored them, although the spelling is different from the old Ford transmission, which was called a Fordomatic. (hence the name). The quartet served them well, performing in every state and throughout Canada, as well as a USO tour during the Viet Nam war, entertaining our troops. Sadly, only two of them remain today. Prior to that, he was a member of a group called The Rip-Chords, performing up and down the west coast and was with the Arthur Godfrey CBS radio and television for awhile in New York City.

He married Sharon Johnson. The couple have two children. He regrets that the age difference between him and his stepbrothers hindered a closer relationship.

Pa Tirrell

After Martha's death it was rumored that he sold the ranch and hooked up with an African-American woman and later married her. He died of Pyelonephritis (kidney infection) at the VA hospital in Temple, Texas, November 17, 1947, one month short of his 80th birthday. Verbal history also has him buried next to Martha in Pyron Cemetery, but there is no headstone found, and no record made.

Sarah Ann Tirrell

Her second marriage to Irby Vernon Trout produced three children. She died June 21, 1971, in Brownwood, Texas, and was buried at Greenleaf Cemetery.

I found her Fulfer children. Her daughter, Betty Lee's baby picture was in my father Ed's mementos but he had no idea who she was. My research found they were first cousins and I located her living no more than a hundred miles from him in Washington State. They both had been victims of their grandparent's interference. I introduced them and they visited shortly before his death in 1994. Betty and I met a couple of more times and we corresponded until her death in 2000. She was able to identify many of the photos that had been given me.

I found her sister Fannie Maude living in Texas, not far from their brother Oliver Francis, but time was too short for us to have a valuable conversation.

Oliver Francis allowed me to interview him in his home in Odessa, Texas. He had the family Bible that he also allowed me to photograph. The family record pages gave valuable information unknown to family members, at the time.

Samuel Tyler Tirrell

He and wife Sarah (Sadie) Elkins had eight children. They married in 1920 and the first four children came one year apart, all girls. 1921,22,23,24. They spaced them a bit better after that with two boys and then two more girls. 26,31,34, and 36.

He tried ranching, but lost it in the depression. They moved back to the Tirrell Ranch where Pa allowed them to live in the chicken coop for four months while Sam sharecropped and helped build the road between Post and Snyder. Texas, and Cobblestone Square where the Snyder County Courthouse sits today. He later purchased a railroad car and remodeled it for their first home. He died of ruptured appendix in 1944.

Their 6th child, Huburt Franklin married Mildred Jackson and had Randal Franklin who married Tina Sue Shirley who has been instrumental in sharing her research and aiding in my quest of digging-the-bones.

400

Mattie Lou Tirrell

She married twice. Once to Wheeler Gooch and next to Harvey Kemp whom I met and interviewed at his home in Brownwood, Texas. He was a rich resource for photos and verbal history and told me as soon as I got out of the car that I looked just like her. Mattie died childless on April 13, 1985, of heart failure at the age of 83, and is buried in Brownwood Cemetery. He took me there for photos.

Lewis Richard Tirrell

He was the baby of the family. Born August 16, 1906. He was the only sibling born in Texas, (near Mineral Wells). He married Mary Belle Stone who gave birth to twelve children. He was a veteran of WII where he served in the Army as a flame thrower operator. I interviewed her and she too gave me photos, verbal history, and took me to his gravesite. He died of a heart attack on February 16, 1979, at the age of 72.

(All of Hasten's siblings' spouses that I met and interviewed are sadly deceased, as well as all three of Sarah's Fulfer children.)

Edward Francis Tirrell/Lykens

During WWII Ed and Nellie had a boy named Jerry Lee, born August 12, 1942. He died January 24 1943, barely over five months old when pneumonia released his precious soul.

During this time Ed worked in the Los Angeles Shipyards, repairing the vessels and getting them back into the war as fast as possible. It was here that he felt the repercussions of having two last names. Being's it was a government job of high intelligence and wartime, he was told he had to clock in and receive his pay as Tirrell.

This led him to seek legal council who explained that he and all of his family were indeed legally Tirrells. And it would be far cheaper and less hassle to change his name to Lykens instead of changing all documents from marriage and birth certificates, to school records of his children, driver's licenses for both he and Nellie, etc.

The entire family had to appear in Los Angeles County Courthouse on April 3rd 1945, before a judge to change all names to Lykens. I remember looking down from that height and agreeing with my sister Mary that people on the streets below, were the size of ants. I was told I sat on the judge's lap during the proceedings, but have no memory of it.

Changing Joyce's name to Lykens during these procedures was impossible because that fell into an entirely separate category of adoption. So she was left with the Key name.

Polio was the dreaded disease of the times and by the late 1950's the third child on our dead-end block had been stricken. Ed and Nellie purchased a moving van, packed up and sold out, moving us children to safety, north to Washington State.

Sherwood was then living in a small apartment built on the end of a large cherry barn, in White Salmon, and welcomed our family of six to join his family of six. It happened to be the worst winter on the West Coast, freezing most lakes solid and the Columbia River passable on foot while a few adventurous people drove their vehicles across.

When funds passed escrow Ed bought his first service station, a Mobil with gravitation pumps, two miles above Lyle, Washington. He converted the moving van into a wrecker. The station came with a tiny one bedroom house and the family lived there for a couple of years until Ed once again sold out and purchased the Shell Station and rented a family sized home set on a cliff above the Klickitat River, in Lyle's downtown proper.

He sold again and ventured out with a partner to own and run the "L and M Logging Company," once again converting the wrecker, this time into a logging truck. The venture failed and he sold his half to his partner and found employment in construction on The Dalles Dam. Later he followed up with placing the power towers in eastern Oregon. An injury layoff gave him initiative to seek employment back in his chosen field of diesel mechanics.

He accepted a position in Eureka, California, and then Grants Pass, Oregon. Then on to Redding, California, where he remained for over eighteen years, with Emmett Baugh Logging Company as shop foreman.

He claimed he was the "Jack of all trades but the master of none", but it didn't show in his work. He was a perfectionist. He remodeled the tiny house they bought in Redding, into a comfortable home with separate guesthouse where we held many family reunions. He retired and made his last move, back to Washington. This time to the town of Bingen where he helped Nellie run her ceramic business.

He was a very loving father. I waited nightly for his return from work as a small child and met him at the door to ride his foot across the living room and check his lunch pail for a treat that he always saved. He instilled in me a love of photography and I spent hours with him in his dark room, developing photos.

He was never too tired to get down on the floor and play, with us kids, and tried his best to keep up with us whether it was in sports or board games.

His love for Nellie shone in his eyes and his patience when she got riled. He always introduced her as 'my bride'.

He took pride in teaching each new member of the family the art of poker and played it 'according to Hoyle'. Whether the newcomers were newly married into the family or a grandchild finally old enough to play they found that they did not sit to play if they weren't willing to lose. He never played for fun, and if you lost you did not get your money back. We learned our lessons well and when gathered for a friendly game at family reunions, his name and techniques are still often mentioned. I'm sure he hovers nearby, enjoying the family unity.

He died in Bingen, February 26th 1994, and is buried at Lyle-Balch Cemetery near Lyle, Washington. He had spent his last years as the caregiver to Nellie, "His Yellow Rose of Texas," who was a victim of Alzheimer's disease.

She held on to life, if only physically, for years in a nursing home in Yakima, Washington where my brother Edward had placed her, to have her closer to him. She died on March 3, 2001, in the nursing home and was buried next to Ed.

Joyce Yvonne Key (Cox, Osberg, Iman)

She married Babe Ronald Cox and had three children, losing the eldest in a car accident at the age of six. She was a hard worker, supporting two of her three husbands which all ended in divorce. She was a mother hen to her siblings and loved her family deeply, if not demonstratively. She was a loner, still doling out smiles only to those deserving.

Joyce won a battle with cancer, only to die by the hands of an incompetent hospital staff after a routine surgical procedure. She found contentment after retiring and moving in with me during her final years. She was a great inspiration to me and instrumental in my becoming a writer. Joyce passed away on June 30, 2006, at the age of 71, but I feel she still 'visits' now and then.

Edward Alvin Lykens
That diapered boy back in San Angelo, of the late 30's was first to graduate high school in the Lykens family. His sense of humor and love of family has been a blessing that has aided many members in their trials and tribulations of life. He served his country in the Navy and eventually followed in Hasten and Alva's footsteps, becoming an ordained minister. He married twice, the first ending in annulment and the second, Janeth Colleen Day, a loving woman that is the perfect minister's wife. He chose the Nazarene Church and accepted his assignments wherever he was sent, from his first mission in Yellowknife, Canada to where he ministers now in Murfreesboro, Tennessee. They have two sons, both in the ministry, making it four generations of serving the Lord.

Mary Lillie Lykens Sorensen
The baby named after all three grandmothers married her high school sweetheart, Larry D. Sorensen. They had two children that were supported in all their childhood interests, with Mary volunteering in social events as well as becoming a 4-H & Cub Scout Leader, and was an avid sports mom.

Family gatherings are her expertise. She has hosted reunions and birthdays for close to 50 years, and loves surrounding herself with family and friends.

When asked, she accepted Joyce's children into her home, keeping one for a year and another for three, and shares a loving bond with both.

She is now widowed and we are traveling companions, trading off riding shotgun on weekend trips with a local RV club, and many of my genealogy quests. We are now checking off our own 'bucket list'.

And there's me,

Mildred Elaine Lykens. (Wright)

I wasn't in the story although it has been a part of me since childhood as I listened intently to the stories and later interviewed many of those who are.

I married Leonard Dale Wright and had three children who gave me 10 grandchildren, (one angel only visited us for six weeks before returning to God) and those grandchildren have so far blessed me with four great-grandchildren and another "on the way".

I began writing at the age of 60. After divorcing my best friend and making a life-changing move, I began emailing "updates" of my new life to friends and family left behind. Many of these recipients expressed their desire for more, with one in particular encouraging me to become a writer. This inspired me to become a reporter, covering local events for four separate newspapers, with many subjects of these feature articles commending me on my accuracy and insight to their situations.

Back living in my "hometown" of Lyle, Washington, these life changes have also motivated me to volunteer for community services and strengthen my relationship with God.

Genealogy began with a strong desire to uncover the facts about this grandfather, which lead to writing the book. The research has led me to relatives, both dead and alive, who were previously unknown to the family, and taken me back and forth across the nation gathering the crumbs sprinkled along the Tirrell trail and uncover the Lykens legacy.

Continuing saga of The Tirrell Gang

Pa and Ma Tirrell had intruded into the marriage and removed the feuding couple's boys, instigating a final explosive conflict between Hasten and Mary. In his wrath he divulged too much, threating the security of three families. Defying his tyrant father, he kidnapped back his eldest son, Edward and turned to the one person he trusted most, Lillie.

Although married to another member of the gang, she had waited years for this moment and allowed nothing to stand in her way to be with him. In their escape they left two family members badly injured, if not dead.

With Hasten now split from the gang and wife Mary, everyone has to alter plans. Continuing their lawless ways, the 'camp outs' are now lead by Haston's brother Sam, while Mary seeks a new life.

Hasten and Lillie fight for survival by assuming new identities, and constantly running from not only the law, but a relentless detective the family has hired to find them. Circumstances once again alter their lives, which directs 'Acey' to add 'Reverend' to his new 'Lykens' name and Lillie to struggle with her conscience in setting things right., which, in all, creates.... The Lylens Legacy.

www.ingramcontent.com/pod-product-compliance
Lightning Source LLC
Chambersburg PA
CBHW020253030726
47499CB00001B/180